TEXAS-SIZED TROUBLE

BY
BARB HAN

First Published in Great Britain 2017
By Mills & Boon, an imprint of HarperCollins*Publishers*
1 London Bridge Street, London, SE1 9GF

© 2017 Barb Han

ISBN: 978-0-263-92859-4

46-0217

Our policy is to use papers that are natural, renewable and recyclable products and made from wood grown in sustainable forests. The logging and manufacturing processes conform to the legal environmental regulations of the country of origin.

Printed and bound in Spain
by CPI, Barcelona

USA TODAY bestselling author **Barb Han** lives in north Texas with her very own hero-worthy husband, three beautiful children, a spunky golden retriever/standard poodle mix and too many books in her to-read pile. In her downtime, she plays video games and spends much of her time on or around a basketball court. She loves interacting with readers and is grateful for their support. You can reach her at www.barbhan.com.

Many thanks to Allison Lyons and Jill Marsal, the best editor and agent I could hope to have the privilege with which to work.

Brandon and Tori, the two of you make everyday life a joyful adventure. I love you both!

Babe, you are forever the love of my life. Can you believe one of our babies turns eighteen this month?

Jacob, aka Jakey Bear, February used to be a cold, short month until you were born, filling our world with sunshine and warmth. Eighteen years have gone by in a flash, and our journey has been a lot like Texas weather: exciting, full of sunshine and *always* an adventure! College is close, a job will follow, and no matter how far away you venture, home will always be your soft place to land.
We love you!

Chapter One

There was a chill in the air, the promise of a cold front moving in on the last day of winter. Texas weather in early March was unpredictable. Ryder O'Brien walked toward his pickup and saw Faith McCabe leaning against his ride. He didn't do regret. So why, all of a sudden, was he filled with it as he walked toward her? Those long legs tucked into tan fringed ankle boots. Her white off-the-shoulder dress contrasted against the long chestnut waves cascading over her shoulders, and ended slightly above midthigh. He didn't want to notice those details about her. Ending their affair and walking away from her hadn't exactly been a choice. She'd burned him. Thinking about how easy it had been for her to break off their relationship made him frown and stirred residual anger.

"What are you doing here?" he ground out.

"I came to see you," she said, folding her arms like when she was secretly insecure but needed to cover.

"We have nothing to talk about." He clenched his teeth. He could acknowledge to himself that his words were angry. It had been only a few months since their affair ended. His feelings were still raw. She looked good, though, and that frustrated the hell out of him.

"I do," she hedged, flashing her eyes at him.

"What's wrong? None of your other boyfriends around?" Ryder stopped. There was no need to get close enough to see the gold flecks in her honey browns. "You're wasting your time."

"I need a favor." Her right shoulder dipped, another move that gave away her true insecurity at being there. She might be trying to stand tall and come off as confident, but Ryder could still read her despite the show she was putting on.

"Then you're wasting *my* time," he said. The last thing he needed was to trust that she was different from her family. He'd taken that bait once and been burned. "Let me save us both the energy. The answer is no."

Her cool facade broke. "Please, I'm desp—"

"It's a little late to play the innocent 'help me' card, don't you think?" he shot back, anger replacing any trace of regret. He looked her up and down, not holding back the annoyance in his glare. "You broke off our... whatever we were doing...with a Post-it note. Who even uses those anymore?"

Yeah, he was letting his anger get the best of him. He couldn't help it. His pride had taken a huge hit. When it came to Faith and the way she'd left things, he couldn't keep cool.

"I'm sorry about the method, but I only said what we both knew. Anything more than good sex between us would be asking too much," she said, and he knew she believed that. To say their families had deep-seated bad blood running between them was a lot like saying werewolves turned at a full moon.

"Whatever," he said as dismissively as he could, given the fact that his pulse pounded and his body seemed keenly aware of hers. Another detail he didn't want to overthink.

"I wouldn't be here if it wasn't important, Ryder." The sound of his name on her tongue made him feel things he didn't want to. But then everything about Faith stirred up unwanted emotions inside him. She might've been right about them not having a future, but they would never know now, not after the way she'd handled things. He could admit to being curious about what she thought he could help her with, though. *Hold on.* That was exactly the thinking that had gotten him in trouble in the first place.

Faith McCabe had always been off-limits to Ryder, and that was most likely the reason he couldn't resist sneaking around to spend time with her a few months ago and not because of a real connection. He'd always been a renegade at heart, always bucking the system and insisting on handling his life his own way. But when his and Faith's relationship had started getting serious and, in his view, interesting, she'd retreated and refused to see or speak to him again. He chalked his current feelings of betrayal up to a bruised ego.

When he'd stepped into the parking lot of the Dusty Trail Bar and Grill and saw her standing there, it was more than muscle memory that had him on edge. Faith still looked good, too good. Her skin was glowing and her hair shone under the lamplight. He couldn't help but go to that place in his head—the one where she lay in his arms until morning after a long night of making love. And that was about as productive as washing down a jalapeño with gasoline.

"What is it? You miss me?" he asked, trying to goad her into the fight they should've had months ago. Not being able to say his piece was probably the reason he'd held on to the hurt this long.

The pinched look she shot him next said she didn't appreciate the sarcasm.

Her gaze shifted until she was studying the toe of her boot a little too intently. Even now, he couldn't deny a draw toward Faith, or a need to protect her. But then instincts were as hardwired as attraction.

"I have a half brother who's gone missing," she started without looking up, a sign that her confidence had waned.

"And you're telling me this because?" Ryder asked, not giving an inch, maintaining the intensity of his glare. This was news to him, although with a father like Hollister McCabe anything was possible. The man and Ryder's father couldn't have been more opposite, and that was part of the reason they'd clashed when his father was alive. Ryder suppressed a sarcastic laugh. *Clashed* put their conflict lightly. When McCabe had tried to strong-arm Ryder's father for a piece of the family land years ago, they'd almost gone toe-to-toe and had been bitter enemies ever since.

"He's in danger, Ryder. I know he is. He lives two towns over with a mother who hustles drinks at a dive bar and leaves him alone days on end to fend for himself." She started to walk toward Ryder and then stopped, glancing up pensively.

He didn't need her moving any closer. Not with the way his pulse pounded already, reminding him of the strength of the attraction he'd once held. So much had changed in the past couple of months, including him. The sobering reality that came with learning his parents had been murdered had made Ryder a different man. After hearing the news, he'd taken leave from the successful transportation company he'd started and returned home to Bluff, Texas. Running tourists back and forth from the airport to various ski resorts in the Denver area was a big change from his life in Texas, and he was ready to take his rightful place alongside his brothers running the family cattle ranch and rifleman's club, nicknamed the Cattlemen Crime Club. The best perk of running his company had been that he'd spent many days pushing his own limits on the mountain. Coming home had been the right thing to do but didn't offer the adrenaline rushes he craved. Dating Faith on the side had most likely been an attempt to reclaim some of his renegade ways and blow off steam, he tried to convince himself again. The thought of real feelings developing between an O'Brien and a McCabe had the word *avalanche* written all over it. That's exactly what it would be—out of control and devastating to everything it touched.

Hence, the thrill, a little voice in his head reminded.

"Sounds like a bad situation all around," he said, not wanting to let anything she had to say twist his emotions. Faith had a way of getting under his skin, and he had no intention of giving her permission to use him again. "Call child welfare and report her."

"They'll just take him away, throw him in the system, and I'll lose track of him. At least now I can watch over him." She took a tentative step forward and then rubbed her arms like she was trying to stave off the chill. She needed a coat, but it wasn't Ryder's place to tell her.

"Whoa. Not so fast." He held up his hands to stop her from coming any closer in case she decided to play on his weakness for her again. It wouldn't work. Burn him once, shame on her. Burn him twice, and he deserved everything he got. Ryder knew better than to touch a hot stove twice, and he'd been taught both sayings as a kid. He'd be damned if she threw flames his way a second time. "Tell me why this concerns me, Faith."

"It doesn't. Not directly." She straightened her back and folded her arms across her chest. "He's a good kid, well, teenager, and he doesn't deserve the life he was given."

"Why come to me? Why not ask Trouble for help?" It was a low blow bringing up one of her exes, and Ryder felt the same sensation as a physical punch at thinking about her together with Trouble. Again, Ryder reminded himself that Faith couldn't be trusted. She'd proved that to him and everyone else in town when she'd shown up with Timmy "Trouble" Hague a week after cutting ties with Ryder and claiming the two were in a relationship. There was nothing worse to Ryder than having his nose rubbed in a breakup. She didn't stop with Trouble. She'd dated several others like him within a monthlong span. She hadn't needed to convince Ryder to walk away by parading a new man in front of him every week. The Post-it had done the trick.

"Hear me out, please," she pleaded, and he was having a difficult time ignoring the fact that her teeth were chattering. He didn't want to care.

"Step aside. I have plans tonight," Ryder said, unmoved. Or, at least that was the vibe he was trying to give off. Internally, he was at war. Those residual feelings had a stronghold and he couldn't afford to let them dig their heels in further, because they were tempting him to give in and agree to help her. He tried to convince himself that being a Texan would make him hardwired to help any woman in trouble and that the pull had nothing to do with the fact that it was Faith.

"Can we go somewhere we can talk?" she asked, her gaze darting around. Was she afraid to be seen with him?

Seriously? After running around with Trouble?

"Like your bedroom?" Ryder scoffed. "Sorry, sweet cheeks. That ship has sailed."

Her hurt look made him almost wish he hadn't said that. As far as he was concerned, she didn't have the right to look pained. It wasn't her heart that had been stomped all over.

Even so, guilt nipped at him for the low blow, and he half expected her to give up and walk away. He was making sticking around as hard on her as he could without being a complete jerk.

She didn't budge. She just stood there shivering.

"Spit it out. What do you want from me?" he demanded, not wanting to drag this conversation out more than necessary. He was tired and this was taking a toll. He had plans with a soft pillow. It was late, and work on the ranch started at 5:00 a.m. sharp.

"I need your help finding Nicholas." Her eyes pleaded.

"You need a coat," Ryder said.

"What?" She seemed surprised.

"You look cold." Ryder motioned toward her arms.

"Mine's in the car," she said. "And I'll get it as soon as you agree to help."

"Can't you microchip kids these days? Or, better yet, why not just call him and wait for him to get back to you like a normal person?" He put his hand up between them. "Oh, wait, I forgot. You're not a normal person. I should've known a McCabe wouldn't have time for common sense or following the rules."

Faith sucked in a burst of air. That comment scored a direct hit. Ryder should feel a sense of satisfaction. He didn't.

"He's somewhere hurt or he's been taken and I'm worried," she said, recovering. Her gaze locked onto his.

"Take out an ad or check his social media pages. Kids love to broadcast their locations for the world to see." Besides, Ryder had other, more pressing things to focus on, like bringing justice to the person who'd murdered his parents.

"He's not that kind of kid and I already checked—" her tone rose in panic before she seemed able to recover and reel it in "—or I wouldn't be here." She had that no-other-choice quality to her tone. Again, Ryder had to ask himself why she thought it was a good idea to come to him. He didn't figure she'd give an honest response. So, she was genuinely concerned about her half brother. Good for her. Maybe it proved she had half a heart in that chest of hers after all. That was about as far as Ryder was willing to go.

"I'm sorry about your family being messed up, but being in the perfect one isn't as easy as it looks. Everyone's got problems," Ryder snapped, needing to keep emotional distance between them. In truth, he loved his brothers. They were a close-knit bunch and about as perfect as a genuine family could be. Sure, they had issues from time to time, but they always managed to work out their differences. He and his twin brother, Joshua, were especially close. "And I'm done here."

"I have to find him and I'm not giving up. It will put me in danger if I go alone but I don't have a choice, Ryder. I have to do it," she said, standing her ground yet again. The sound of his name rolling off her tongue had always stirred his chest in a way he couldn't afford to allow. This time was no different. All his warning bells sounded.

"Sounds like you're making a big mistake." He shrugged. "Free country."

"Do you really hate me that much?" she asked, and the desperation in her tone struck a chord. "You'd allow an innocent kid to be hurt just to prove a point?"

Now it was his turn to take in a sharp breath.

"No. But I can't help you, either." Maybe he could take a second to talk her out of being stupid. "If you're really worried about this kid, call Tommy. The sheriff would be better at tracking down a missing teenager than me. Besides, you know the reality as much as I do. The kid's most likely having fun with his friends. He'll check in once he sobers up in a couple of days."

"Tommy is friends with your family, not mine. He won't help a McCabe and you know it," she said defensively.

The chilly air goose-bumped her arms and Ryder had to stop himself from offering his jacket. Chivalry was ingrained in him, and he had to fight against his own cowboy code so that she wouldn't think she was getting to him. Give her an inch and she'd stomp on him again with those fringed boots.

"Even so, he's the law and he'll help you," Ryder said. "He took an oath, and he takes it seriously."

"Braxton is a few counties over and out of his jurisdiction. That's where Nicholas lives," she said.

"Tommy can make a few calls, do a little digging. If it makes you feel better, I'll ask him myself." Ryder had no clue why he'd just volunteered himself like that. He'd have time to curse himself later. The sheriff in Braxton wasn't exactly known for being cooperative.

An anguished sound tore from her throat. "That's not good enough, and Tommy doesn't care about Nicholas. I need answers now and I'm afraid something very bad has happened to him. I can't afford to lose any more time, and someone follows me when I check on him."

Didn't that get all of Ryder's neck hairs to stand on end?

"What makes you think so?" he asked.

"I drove to Nicholas's house to check on him when he stopped responding to my texts three days ago and an SUV followed me to the county line."

"Could've been random," he said.

"I've been out there every night, and last night the SUV tapped my bumper," she said, rubbing her arms as if the memory gave her chills instead of the cold night air.

Ryder didn't like that. He'd take a minute to consider her position. He could concede that she'd had a point a few seconds ago. Tommy wasn't likely to go above and beyond the call of duty for a McCabe. He'd arrested her brothers, who were immediately bailed out by the family lawyer too many times to have sympathy for any of them, even Faith.

Her concern for her half brother seemed genuine. Ryder could tell based on the desperation in her honey browns. If the situation were reversed and one of his brothers had gone missing, he'd do whatever it took to find him. All five of his siblings were grown now, and good men, but they'd gotten themselves into a few tricky situations as teenagers. Ryder could buy the idea that a good kid could get into trouble. He had a harder time swallowing the idea that a McCabe offspring could be anything but trouble. Bad was in their blood. He'd believed Faith to be different from her family, and look how that had worked out for him.

"How do you know he's missing exactly?" he asked.

"We talk every day without fail. I was supposed to help him with geometry homework and he stood me up. He's never done that. Ever." Her wide eyes conveyed panic and worry. When he examined her features, he saw how tired and worried she looked.

"Have you spoken to his mother?" The teenager could have gotten himself in over his head or involved in drugs. Even so, none of this concerned Ryder, and Faith hadn't given him one solid reason he should get involved. With her family's money, she could hire an investigator.

"We're not exactly on good terms and I have nothing to say to the woman," Faith said, and her left shoulder shot up. He'd seen that move before. She was being indignant.

From his viewpoint, a quick phone call could most likely clear this whole thing up. If Faith was too stubborn to make that call she didn't need to be reaching out to him to do her dirty work.

"Then I can't help you. That was my only card. I'm folding. If you really believe he's missing, then you should talk to someone in law enforcement. His

mother might've reported his disappearance already."
He threw his hands up in surrender. As it was, he was
having a difficult time keeping a wall between them
and maintaining his neutral position. A woman in trouble wasn't something he could normally turn his back
on. He blamed his Texas upbringing and the fact that
he'd had amazing parents.

"I'll sweeten the pot," she said quickly.

"You don't have anything I want," Ryder said, pushing thoughts of how soft her skin had been when he
ran his finger along the curves of her stomach out of
his mind. Or how much the sound of her laughter had
temporarily suspended the pain of losing his parents.

"You want to know the real reason I walked away
from you, Ryder O'Brien?" Now she was the one who
was angry. He could see the fire in her eyes. Good.
She'd get mad, spit out a few hostile words meant to
offend him and then leave.

Problem solved.

"It doesn't matter." But his wounded pride said
something else entirely—he wanted to know.

"You sure about that?" she asked in her one-last-
chance tone.

"Have never been more certain of anything in my
life." If she wanted his help, making him angry was
the wrong way to go about it. He didn't like the idea of
her putting herself in danger if that was the case, and
he'd tried reasoning with her by telling her to bring
in the law. If she didn't have enough sense to stay out
of harm's way there wasn't much he could do about
it. "Why ask me to help in the first place? You had to
know that I would refuse. You're not exactly high on
my list of people I want to see again."

"You won't turn me down. I know you and there's something I've been keeping from you…" She paused long enough to put her hands on her belly. "Anything happens to me and your child goes with me. You're going to be a father, Ryder. And that's why I left you. If anyone found out this was your child, then my life, heck, *your life*, would be over."

"Good one, Faith." She wasn't afraid to pull out all the stops on…

Hold on a damn minute. The look on her face slapped him with a new reality. Was she serious?

"That's right, Ryder. I'm carrying your child." Her lip quivered even though her words rolled off her tongue steady as steel.

She wasn't lying?

He stood there for a long moment and stared at her, daring her to break the glaring contest and tell him she was joking. There was no way…

Was there?

A memory came back to him in a rush. He remembered one time when they'd been so lost and so into each other during their lovemaking neither had noticed that the condom he wore broke.

Okay, so it was *possible*. But that didn't mean…

Ryder took a step toward Faith to really look into her eyes.

"You're pregnant?" he asked, knowing full well that he'd be able to tell if she faltered. She'd never been able to look him in the eyes and flat-out lie. Or at least that's what he'd believed. How much did he get to know the real her in the few months they'd spent time together? She'd already shocked him once by walking out. And now she'd thrown him the last news he'd expected to hear from her.

"Yes," she said plain as day.

"And the child is mine?"

"Yes," she said with that same certainty.

She wasn't lying.

"If that's true—and I need a little time to come to terms with that fact—why are you telling me now?" he asked, trying to absorb that news. He couldn't begin to process the idea of becoming a father, and he wasn't immediately sure how he felt about it. All he knew was that his life was about to change forever. He'd seen firsthand the effects of the baby boom on the ranch with a few of his brothers.

"Like I said, I need your help and I'll do whatever it takes to get it," she said, her gaze a study in determination.

"Including lie about me fathering your child?" He'd thrown that question out to see if he could knock her off balance.

She stood her ground. "We both know I'm not."

"Then I expect you to take care of yourself. Running straight into a fire doesn't exactly fit that bill," he said, and he meant every word. Until they sorted this mess out and knew for sure that she was, in fact, pregnant and he was the father of her child, he expected her to treat herself like a princess.

A thought struck. Was there any chance she could be so desperate for help that she'd bluff to get him to agree to help her?

Ryder studied her expression. If she was lying, she was a pro. Then again, he hadn't seen their breakup coming, either. He'd need time to digest the possibility of being a father, especially considering all that he'd been through in the past few months. He forced his thoughts away from the fact that she'd been his sole comfort during the most difficult time of his life and their relationship had been about more than just the sex. It was saying a lot that they could be so into each other that a condom had broken and neither one realized until it was too late. Sex with Faith had been right up there with the best of his life. If he was being honest, it topped the list. Not something he cared to admit right now or dwell on too much. Even though the sex was great, there'd been so much more. He wasn't normally one for a lot of words but holding her in their afterglow and doing just that—talking—had been even better than the sex. And that was saying a helluva lot.

"You know this qualifies as blackmail," he said, his brain refusing to fully comprehend the news. He'd want a DNA test to be sure. And if the results proved his paternity, then he'd do what a man should—take care of his own.

"Does that mean you'll help me?"

"Get in. You're damn right we need to talk. Not here where everyone can see us," Ryder said, opening the passenger door of his pickup and then walking around to the driver's side without waiting for her to climb inside.

Faith almost backed out after seeing the hurt in his eyes after dropping the pregnancy bomb. She thought better of it. Yes, he was angry at her, but she'd realized that it was the only way to secure his help, and he was the only person she could trust right now.

All plans to find the perfect time to tell him about

the pregnancy and have a civil conversation had flown out the window with her desperation. What she'd said was true, though. Her life would be over if her father found out she was carrying an O'Brien child.

"Don't take me home or into town," Faith said as she positioned herself in the seat of his dual-cab pickup and then buckled in. She hadn't expected to play the pregnancy card with Ryder, but she was frantic. His shocked reaction braided her stomach lining.

Seeing him again had hurt like hell and she was still trying to regain her balance. He looked even better than she remembered with those sharp jet-black eyes and dark hair. He was six feet three inches of masculine muscle. And even angry, he was gorgeous. Walking away from him after finding out she was pregnant had nearly killed her, but she'd been his temporary shelter in a storm—a storm that was about to become a hurricane. Once the storm blew over and he regained his bearings he would've realized the same thing she had—a McCabe and an O'Brien didn't stand a chance.

"What? Afraid to be seen with me?" he bit out. His voice poured over her, netting a physical reaction she couldn't afford.

"Of course not." She did her best to shake off his bitter tone. It was a temporary reaction to having his world rocked. He needed a minute to cool off so he could start thinking rationally again. It was a good sign that he wanted to talk. Deep down, he was a good man.

Besides, Faith could relate to the emotions that had to be zipping through him right now. The pregnancy wasn't supposed to happen. The decisions she'd made after weren't supposed to be part of her plans. And all that was predicated on the fact that she wasn't supposed to fall for an O'Brien, let alone the renegade twin brother. And that was probably it. Her attraction was so strong because he was exciting and a breath of fresh air. Ryder had always been so alive, when she'd felt restricted for so many years living under her parents' roof with three older brothers watching her every move. The family's double standard that the boys could run buck wild and she had to practically be a nun had been suffocating.

Ryder represented danger and excitement, and her foolish heart had fallen hard for him when she'd seen him wandering around the lake, looking lost after news of his parents had made headlines. Everything about the O'Briens was news. Murder had been beyond scandal.

The next few months of their relationship had been insane and incredible. Secret rendezvous at his fishing cabin. Both of them escaping reality and getting lost in each other. Talking for hours into the night. She'd almost forgotten that he was an O'Brien and she was a McCabe until she'd overheard him on his cell phone with his brother, cursing her father, questioning whether he'd had anything to do with his parents' murders.

She could understand his distrust of her father. The man was a shrewd businessman and even she could admit that he pushed the legal boundaries beyond their limits. Worse to her, the man was a philanderer, and she'd watched her mother fade over the years as she accepted his behavior even though he could be quite charming when he wanted to be. But murder?

Her father might have loose morals and no conscience when it came to business, but he wasn't capable of killing anyone.

And then another blow had come when Ryder's brother asked where Ryder was and what he was doing all those times he'd been with her. He'd responded that he hadn't been doing anything special. He'd just been getting away for fresh air and spending time alone to sort out his thoughts.

Reality had been a hard slap. Spending time with her hadn't been as special to him as it had been to her. They'd been sneaking around like teenagers and she started to wonder if the reason was because he'd been embarrassed to be seen with her. He would always be an O'Brien and she would always be a McCabe. And he, like everyone in Bluff, would always see her in a different light because of it.

When she'd learned that she was pregnant, she panicked. A real life with Ryder was out of the question. Dating Trouble and the others had been her way of throwing everyone off the trail, including Ryder. He wouldn't want a McCabe baby any more than her parents would ever accept an O'Brien. It would be bad enough in her parents' eyes that she was pregnant without being married, but having an O'Brien in the family would be all-out war. Not only would her parents make her life miserable but they'd make her unborn child miserable, too.

And that wasn't even the worst of it. She feared that Ryder—who was just spending time with her, not getting serious—would want to man up and do the right thing by his child. His Texas upbringing would influence him, and he'd probably propose marriage. If hormones got the best of her—and they had made her crazy so far—she might actually accept. And then what?

Would they stay together for the sake of the child eighteen unhappy years until said kid went off to college and the two of them could finally separate? That's exactly what her parents had done. Her own mother had been forced to come back and had never been the same. Faith's father didn't curb his appetite for chasing pretty much anything in a skirt. Faith had known since she was old enough to figure out what was happening. And her mother was broken. Still broken. She seemed different lately. Worse, if that was even possible.

Faith's siblings seemed blind to it all. And they were another reason a relationship between her and Ryder could never work…if her father didn't kill him, her brothers would. The O'Briens and McCabes were worse than oil and water. They were gasoline and forest fire.

Even so, maybe it was good that her secret was out. Working side by side, she could convince Ryder the best course of action would be to keep the secret. Surely he would come to the same conclusion she had. Besides, she had a plan.

Break the news and each guy she'd gone out with would distance himself from any suspicion of being the father of her child. And then she could tell her parents that she wanted to bring up her baby alone. She didn't really care who the father was, even though her heart screamed at her that she did. Her father wouldn't interfere with her plans to leave town. Heck, he'd tell her to get out after embarrassing him. And then she and her baby could live in peace. That was the only real chance her child had of growing up normal.

Righteous or not, telling Ryder complicated her plans. Had she really believed that she could've left town without telling him about the baby? She'd initially feared that he'd put two and two together when news of her pregnancy broke. And that's exactly the reason she'd handled their breakup the way she had. The O'Briens were proud, honest men. And her actions had been the only way to ensure Ryder wouldn't do anything stupid, like propose marriage for the baby's sake and ruin both their lives. A fist tightened in her stomach. *Breathe.*

She'd take things one step at a time. For now, she'd secure Ryder's help. Finding Nicholas had to be her top priority even if it meant turning her life upside down.

"Getting out anytime soon or do you plan to sit in here all night?" Ryder asked, and he sounded concerned.

Faith hadn't realized the pickup had stopped.

"Yeah, sure." She blinked at him.

He sat there, staring at her, making everything harder than she expected. In her heart of hearts she'd known that she couldn't keep the pregnancy secret from him forever. Her obstetrician had said she could expect to start showing soon. This being the first pregnancy had bought her some extra time and she could easily cover what was going on so far.

Time was supposed to bring wisdom as to how she should handle sharing the news. It hadn't. She hadn't breathed a word to anyone. And keeping a secret like this had been more than difficult. It felt good to finally tell someone about the baby, but she needed to stay on track. None of her problems seemed as important or immediate as finding Nicholas.

The sky was pitch-black as she climbed out of the truck. The chilly air nipped at her through her dress. She wished she'd worn a coat as she shivered. Normally, the hot hormones had her wishing she could pack herself in ice. Not today.

A blanket of clouds covered the stars. It was too dark outside to see where he'd taken her, and she'd been in a daze for the ride over, not paying attention. As she gained her footing in the gravel it hit her. Ryder had taken her to the fishing cabin.

A wall of memories crashed around her. This was the place they'd met countless times, made love more than she cared to remember…and she'd lost her heart.

Doubts crept in as to whether or not she was doing the right thing being with Ryder at all with every step toward the cabin. He had the power to crush her with a few words.

"Maybe we should go somewhere else to talk." Panic squeezed her chest as she approached the basic log cabin. A reasonable voice overrode her emotions. Ryder was the only one she could tell about Nicholas and the only one who understood how much was at stake as she made the decision to locate him.

"No one will find us here. Isn't that what you want?" His deep voice, warm and soothing, was like pouring whiskey over crackling ice.

"Yes," she conceded, very aware of the masculine presence behind her, guiding her with his hand on the small of her back.

Chapter Two

Faith sat on the edge of the couch in the living room, ignoring the sensual shivers climbing up her arms. She wished she could block out memories as easily. The last time she and Ryder had been at the cabin, their naked bodies had been entwined until morning.

Tall, with the muscles of a well-honed athlete, Ryder had a physical appeal that hadn't dimmed in the least and her hormones had all of her senses heightened. His dark hair framed a squared jaw, and he had the most piercing jet-black eyes. Everything about the way he looked communicated strength, confidence and a little bit of danger. And after the news she'd broken, fierceness. All of which would be a good thing if she could harness it toward helping find Nicholas.

"Take me back to the beginning. How do you know the baby is mine?" Ryder's question was a bullet to the heart.

"You were the only option," she fired back, and her plan of using the other men to throw everyone off the trail seemed to dawn on him.

"Did you plan on telling me eventually?" he asked after another uneasy minute had passed.

"Yes, and we can discuss anything else you want

after we find Nicholas." She needed to direct the conversation back on task.

"Holding a pregnancy over my head is blackmail, Faith." His normally strong, all-male persona faded with the look of confusion in his dark eyes.

She hated that this was her fault. Well, not the pregnancy. It'd taken two to dance that tango. She took the blame for the way Ryder was finding out. Seeing the hurt in his eyes knifed her. But she needed to stay strong for Nicholas's sake and not let anything else derail her from her search. She knew in her heart that her brother was in trouble. "I'm sorry for how this has gone down, Ryder. I truly am. But I'm desperate to find Nicholas and you weren't going to help me any other way."

He seemed to take a minute to contemplate that thought while he assessed her, his attention on her belly.

"How much longer before the baby comes?" he asked.

"I'm almost five months along," she said, her hand instinctively coming up to her stomach.

"Boy or girl?" His voice was steel, giving nothing away of his emotions now.

"One of those," she said. Having her doctor tell her the sex of the baby made it that much more real. For that reason, she'd decided to wait. And then there was the fact that it seemed wrong to know without the father present.

"They don't know?"

"I asked my doctor not to tell me," she said.

Another few minutes of silence passed. Her need to press Ryder in order to get his agreement to help find

Nicholas warred with her better judgment. She'd played her hand with Ryder and there wasn't much more she could do to follow the trail without his help, not without the possibility of putting their baby at risk given that the SUV driver was becoming more aggressive.

Three days was a long time to be missing. Anything could be happening to her little brother right now...

Tears burst through just thinking about any harm coming to Nicholas.

"I'm sorry," she said, trying to pull it together, "it's just hormones giving me mood swings. They make it hard to think rationally."

Ryder studied her.

"How do you know your half brother didn't get fed up with his mother and run away?" he asked as she tried to force her gaze away from his lips—lips that made her body zing with awareness at the thought of how he'd once used the tip of his tongue to trail her curves. Faith admonished herself. That thought couldn't be more inappropriate under the circumstances. Her hormones didn't just make her emotional. They made her miss having sex even more.

"We had plans, and besides, he would've told me," she said.

"You sure about that? Even people you think you know can shock the hell out of you." Ryder's tense, aggressive posture would strike fear in any reasonable person. She knew him well enough to know that he would never do anything to hurt her.

Faith told herself nothing mattered more than getting his agreement to help find Nicholas. And she was making gains on that front; she could tell by how bunched his face muscles looked and the tic over his left eye—all positive signs she was making headway. He was in conflict with himself and that was a good thing for her. The very fact that he'd agreed to discuss the matter privately was her first real step in the right direction. She could put up with his intense scrutiny if it meant gaining his agreement to find her brother.

"As sure as I can be. We're close. I've been checking on him ever since I found out about him, so around kindergarten, and he doesn't have any other siblings. Well, none that he knows," she said. "My brothers would never acknowledge him if they knew, and he's so much better than they are anyway. I would do anything I could to keep them separate and make sure they had no influence over him."

This wasn't the time to recount all the shortcomings of McCabe men.

"Why do you know about him but your brothers don't?" he asked. It was a fair question.

"I spent summers working for my dad. I was being groomed for the family business and my job was learning the paperwork. I don't have to tell you how much running a ranch is about dealing with stacks of documents. Legal papers were on my dad's desk. I guess they got mixed up with a stack of bills. He was being sued for child support by Nicholas's mother. You can imagine how that turned out. My dad got himself out of paying. Actually his lawyers did. So I've been sneaking money to Nicholas for the past ten years."

"How do you know he's your blood relative?" he asked.

She retrieved her cell phone from her purse and then scrolled through pictures, stopping at a recent one of her and Nicholas together. She held out her phone to Ryder so he could see.

"There's no denying the resemblance," he said, studying the likeness.

"He looks like a mini, younger version of Jason, only he's nicer." Jason was the youngest of her three brothers and her senior by four years. He'd been the toughest, too, having spent his life proving to his two older brothers, Jesse and Jimmy, that he could hold his own.

"I've learned not to trust the actions of any McCabe," Ryder said flatly. He was obviously referring to her walking out and the pregnancy news.

She had that coming.

Glancing down at her stomach, she said, "I didn't do this alone."

Ryder made a face like he was about to say something hateful and seemed to think better of it, when he pressed his lips into a thin line instead.

"It's probably for the best if we stick to the reason we're here. *For now*," Ryder said. Those last two words came out as a warning she knew better than to disregard.

"Fine." She had no doubt the two of them would be doing a lot of talking about the future of their baby once the dust settled. A very large part of her had been dreading the inevitable conversation with him for months now and yet another side couldn't deny that she wanted to involve Ryder. The first trimester had been too much about trying to keep food down to worry about what she would say to him. Who knew morning sickness actually meant throwing up all day? Her queasiness had finally let up a couple of weeks ago and she'd been trying to plan out her words ever since. She'd tried to convince herself that it would be a good idea to leave town without ever telling Ryder. She knew in her heart that she could never do that to him. No matter how strong the arguments against it waged inside her head, he had a right to know.

Ryder pulled a chair from the kitchenette, turned it around backward and straddled it opposite the coffee table. "Tell me what really has you so worried."

"Nicholas might be a McCabe but he's nothing like the boys in my family, despite having a worthless mother. He's fifteen and plays on the school soccer team. His grades are good. He's always talking about a future, getting a scholarship, going to college," she said, probably more defensively than she'd intended. "He's a decent kid, Ryder."

"If that were completely true, we wouldn't be having this conversation." Ryder had a way of looking right through her. She worried he'd see her fear while she was trying to put up a brave front.

"That's why none of this makes sense. He wouldn't just disappear like that. He's not that kind of kid."

Ryder's look of disbelief struck a bad chord.

"I know you can't stand my family and you may never trust me again, but I know Nicholas wouldn't up and disappear without telling me," she said, hating the defensiveness in her tone. Ryder's not believing her hurt more than it should.

"What else do you know about his life besides what I could read on a college application? Have you met any of his friends?" Ryder asked.

"We kept our relationship secret. So, no," she said honestly.

"Seems you're full of deceptions," he shot back. "I'm guessing that's why I never heard about him before."

Her first instinct was to fight back. She let that zinger go for the sake of her little brother, even though it scored a direct hit. Common sense said that arguing with Ryder wouldn't get her what she needed. Besides, a little piece of her knew that Ryder had every right to be upset with her and he was still reacting to the bomb she'd dropped on him. She should've gone to him with the news or given him a better reason for the breakup, instead of chickening out while she was waiting for him so they could talk and deciding to scribble her exit on the only thing she had in her purse, a Post-it.

"My father went to great lengths to cover up his relationship with Nicholas's mother. I thought he might dish out repercussions against the two of them if he knew I was seeing my brother. That's the reason for the deception. I couldn't risk telling anyone. Not even you," she said.

"He would've been angry with you, too. Are you sure you weren't protecting yourself?" Ryder said in that unnerving steady tone.

"I don't care what happens to me," she retorted. "Or at least I didn't until now." She touched her belly.

"What about your mom?"

"I was fairly sure she had no idea about Nicholas. But she's been acting stranger than usual lately. Jumpy. But that could just be a change in her anxiety medication."

"Self-preservation seems to be a genetic survival trait in McCabe women," he said in a low enough voice that she could still hear it.

She chose not to respond.

"What are you really afraid Nicholas got himself into?" Ryder asked.

She shot him a grateful look for the change in subject. "He wouldn't stand me up without a good reason, and he always responds to my texts. I'm afraid for him, Ryder."

"Could he have a recreational drinking or drug habit?"

"No." Her shoulders slumped forward. "He has a good head on his shoulders. He's a decent person despite bad circumstances."

RYDER COULDN'T HELP but notice how many times Faith had mentioned that her little brother was a decent kid. Was she trying to convince him, or herself? As much as he doubted any McCabe son could be good, he would give Faith the benefit of the doubt. His trust was an entirely different story.

If he was going to help—and there was no refusing now that he knew she was possibly pregnant with his child and there was the slightest chance of foul play—he needed more information. Besides, the faster he could help her find Nicholas, the sooner he'd be able to focus on what he really wanted to know more about—the baby she was carrying.

"You haven't spoken to his mother. There could be an easy explanation for all this, Faith," he said, ignoring the tension sitting like a wall between them.

Faith shook her head. "I didn't want her to know about our relationship. It would only cause more tension between the two of them and I doubt she'd welcome a McCabe anyway, considering my father hasn't stepped up to help her in any way. She can't be happy that he refused support, and I'm not saying that he's right but neither is sleeping with a married man."

"She may be able to clear this up in five minutes. We have to talk to her," he said plainly.

"After the way my father treated her I doubt she'll want to see anyone from his side of the family again." Faith made a harrumph sound.

"That may well be true. Doesn't mean we skip a step," he said. If one uncomfortable conversation could clear this up, so be it. "Besides, she can't be all that bad if Nicholas has turned out as well as you say."

"Fine. But Nicholas isn't close to his mother and he wouldn't tell her if he was in trouble."

"She may have filed a missing persons report. If she hasn't, we'll need her help since she's his legal guardian. How long did you say he's been gone?" he asked. Cooperation from Nicholas's mother would go a long way with the law. In fact, she'd have to be the person to officially report him missing.

"It's been three days," she said with a voice so weak Ryder's heart squeezed. He couldn't afford to let his emotions overrule logic this time. They'd had him thinking that getting mixed up with her was a good idea in the first place.

"I've been on campouts without cell service longer than that," he said, trying to offer what little reassurance he could under the circumstances.

Faith shot him a look.

"If his mother filed a report, three days would be enough time for law enforcement to take her seriously," he said. What if the kid ran away? From what Faith said the boy came from an unstable home. "There are other logical possibilities. Maybe he got impatient. Or he and his mother could've gotten into a fight and he's staying away while they both cool off. She might've done something that he didn't want to tell you about since you don't like her in the first place."

"I have to think he would've called me like he always does. And he's never missed a tutoring session." If that was true she made a good point.

"Maybe he figures you'll try to talk him into going home and he's not ready."

"It's a thought," she said without much enthusiasm, and he could tell she was going along with him even though her heart wasn't in it.

"There's another more likely possibility," he offered.

"And that is?" She was clicking through the possibilities with him, and he could tell from her subdued expression that nothing was sparking.

"He might've met a girl." He held his hand up when she started to speak. "Hold on. Hear me out. Fifteen-year-old boys are hormones on legs. It's possible that he hit it off with someone and is staying at her house for a few days."

Faith held up her cell phone.

"Last thing a hormonal teenager wants is the voice of reason in his ear. Believe me, I speak from experience," Ryder said. "We had a lot of those in our house over the years between the six of us boys."

"I'll take your word for it," she said. "I remember you at that age. And the need for an adrenaline rush hasn't dimmed, has it, Ryder?"

"I like to think I'm more mature now."

"I'd like to think I'm a supermodel," she jabbed

back. That quick wit of hers still made him want to smile. This time, he resisted the urge.

He glanced at his watch. "It's late. I'll get coverage on the ranch tomorrow, so we can get started first thing in the morning. We'll start with his mother."

An emotion he couldn't put his finger on flashed in her eyes. Disappointment? Regret?

If Faith thought this was the beginning of the two of them bonding, working together as life partners, she was sorely mistaken.

THE HOUSE WAS SMALL, a two-bedroom bungalow with cars parked on the street and, in some cases, right on the front lawn. Those were on cinder blocks. There was a couch positioned on a porch or two instead of actual patio furniture. Chain-link fences surrounded mostly barren yards with patches of yellow grass. Ryder couldn't help but take note of the contrast to the McCabes' expansive ranch in Bluff.

Ryder parked in front of 622 Sycamore like Faith had instructed and cut the engine. They'd made small talk on the way over, mostly about the cold front that had blown through last night and the irony of this being the first day of spring when temps were barely hovering above freezing. In Texas, anything was possible when it came to the weather.

"What's her name?" Ryder nodded toward the house.

"Celeste Bowden," Faith supplied.

"Okay. Let's go talk to Celeste Bowden." He made a move for the door handle and stopped when a disgusted grunt sounded to his right.

"Fair warning, she's not going to be happy to see me," she said on a sigh.

"I already gathered that from our conversation last night." He shouldered the door of his cab open. "Does she love her son?"

"In her own way? Yes," Faith admitted.

He glanced around the neighborhood. "She may not take care of him in the way you'd like but she won't want anyone taking him from her. If she hasn't heard from him by now then she'll be worried. And that's the only shot we have at her talking to us, so keep a low profile and let me take the lead."

Ryder tried not to focus on the fact that he didn't sleep a wink last night, tossing and turning over the news that he might be a father. Two cups of black coffee first thing this morning had sharpened his mind.

Following closely behind Faith, he couldn't deny a new protectiveness he felt for her because of the child she was carrying. He still didn't know how to deal with the news other than to be stunned. Sleeping had been a nonissue. He kept waiting for the shock to wear off so he could figure out his next steps. He'd stayed at the fishing cabin last night, forcing down thoughts of the times he and Faith had spent there. Last night was the first time he'd been back to the place where too many memories could impact his judgment.

This morning, she'd left her car there and they'd decided to take his pickup, leaving long before sunrise. Conversation was a strain now, and he missed the easy way they used to talk to each other.

Ryder hopped the pair of concrete porch steps onto the small patio, and then opened the weathered screen door. It creaked and groaned. No way could anyone slip into this house quietly. And especially because a few dogs in neighboring yards fired off rapid barks. At this rate, the whole neighborhood would be up, trying to figure out what was going on. On second thought, he might need to talk to neighbors. Maybe it was good that they'd be up.

Ryder knocked on the wood part of the door. Most of the top half was glass. White paint chipped off the rest.

No answer.

This time, Ryder pounded on the door, rattling the glass in the window. The neighborhood dogs reacted again, going crazy barking as a figure moved toward the door. The woman came into view as she neared. Her hair wild, she wore jeans and a half-unbuttoned flannel shirt, no doubt the same clothes she had on last night. Worry lines and too much hard living shadowed what might have been an attractive face at one time.

"Who are you and what do you want?" she asked, cracking the door. Her gaze bounced from Ryder to Faith. Her eyes widened as she zeroed in on Faith, no doubt picking up on the fact that she was Hollister Mc-Cabe's daughter. "Never mind. You're not welcome here. Get off my porch."

Celeste tried to slam the door but Ryder stuck the toe of his boot inside to stop her. "I'm sorry to wake you, but we're here out of concern for your son. Is there any chance we can come inside?"

"No." Angry lines did nothing to improve the woman's hard features. On closer appraisal, she couldn't have been older than her midthirties.

"I know he hasn't been home. We just want to get some information so we can figure out where he is," Faith said.

"My son is none of your business." Celeste stared

at Faith before giving Ryder a disgusted look. "Now move so I can close the door."

Bringing Faith might've been a mistake. Ryder shifted to the right a little in order to block a direct line of sight between the two of them.

"No need to do anything you'll regret," Ryder said quickly, trying to bring the focus back to him. "We're here to ask a few questions and then we'll be on our way."

"You with the law?" Celeste asked, glancing at the pocket of his jacket, most likely looking for a badge.

Ryder shook his head.

"Then let go of my door and get the hell off my property," Celeste ground out.

"But—" Faith started.

"Last time I checked, trespassing was against the law. If you're not gone by the time I count to three, I'm calling the cops." Celeste's tone intensified with her rising anger. Her gaze was locked onto Faith and he could tell that she was struggling to get past coming face-to-face with a McCabe.

"Okay." Ryder held his hands up in surrender and shifted his boot, allowing her to shut them out.

The woman slammed the door so hard he thought the glass might break. She took a step back, folded her arms and stared them down.

"I hope you won't let anything happen to your son because you're not thrilled with us. We want to work together to find him and make sure he's okay. We all know he wouldn't disappear like this without answering his cell," he said through the thin glass.

An emotion crossed her features, briefly softening

her hard stare. She made a move for the door handle, but hesitated.

And then she shook her head.

Damn. He was so close to getting through to her.

"Did you eat breakfast this morning?" Ryder asked Faith. He spoke loud enough for Nicholas's mother to hear.

"What? No. Why?" Her brow knit in confusion.

"There's a diner in town." He turned and hopped off the porch.

"That's it?" Her voice outlined her shock as she stood rooted. "You're giving up just like that? And now you're hungry?"

"Get in the truck."

"But she might know something. I can't walk away without figuring out a way to make her talk to us."

"She won't. Not like this. She needs a minute to think it over. Besides, she's listening to us and watching every move we make." Ryder slowed but didn't turn; he kept right on walking.

"Then we should talk to the neighbors. Someone might've seen something. Don't tell me we drove all the way out here to eat breakfast." The desperation in her voice almost made him turn around. Almost.

"If you want her to help find Nicholas, get in the truck."

"Fine." Faith stomped so hard the earth should've cracked. The only thing that did was Ryder's face, in a grin. She still had that same fierce determination.

As soon as she took her seat and slammed the truck door closed, she whirled on him. "I hope this means you have a plan, because you just blew the only lead we have so far."

"I didn't but you almost did," he said, keeping that wry grin intact as he turned the key in the ignition. The engine fired up.

"Me?" She was so angry the word came out in a high-pitched croak. "You're joking, right?"

"Never been more serious." He navigated the pickup through the one-lane street. "And you should calm down. Getting upset can't be good for…*it*." He motioned toward her belly, not really sure what to call the baby yet.

"Well, then, you're going to have to explain everything to me as if I'm a two-year-old because I don't understand," she said, dodging his baby comment.

Chapter Three

Downtown Braxton, Texas, had a post office, a diner, a bank and a city hall. The diner was across the street from city hall and anchored an otherwise empty strip center. Ryder parked, fed the meter and then opened Faith's door for her.

"You still haven't told me what we're doing here," she said, taking his hand.

He ignored the frisson of heat where their fingers touched. Sexual chemistry wasn't the problem between them, never had been. Trust was, and it appeared to be an issue on both sides. As for him, there'd be no way to get around her deception and build any kind of bond. Yes, he was still angry at her, and that was why he didn't want to think about the attraction he felt or anything else that didn't directly impact finding Nicholas.

"She'll come and then she'll be ready to talk," he said. "She needs a minute to come to terms with the fact that you care."

"How do you know that?" Faith didn't bother to hide her frustration; angry lines creased her forehead.

"Curiosity will get the best of her. She loves him. I could see it in her eyes. She wants to find him as much as we do, and we planted the seed that we're concerned," he clarified.

"I hope you're right," she said.

"She's also proud. She might not take care of him the way you would but that doesn't mean she doesn't love him. He might be the only family she has and she won't let go easily," he clarified.

"Celeste didn't get what she wanted from my dad. I figured she was just using him, maybe even got pregnant on purpose hoping for a free ride. But she kept Nicholas and has been bringing him up ever since even though my dad was a jerk and refused to pay support," she said thoughtfully.

He didn't address the irony of that idea given their current situation, and she acknowledged that she was thinking the same thing with a quick flash of her eyes toward him. It was a good sign that she'd calmed down and could think through the situation clearly. Faith was smart.

"Oh, no." She suddenly stopped at the diner door, turned and ran toward the trash can.

"What is it?" he asked.

"This isn't good." She bent over and clutched her stomach. "I feel awful."

"Is it the baby?" Her expression made him worry that something might be truly wrong. A feeling of panic struck his chest faster than stray lightning and he was caught off guard by the jolt of fear that came with thinking something serious might be wrong.

"What can I do?" he asked as she emptied her stomach. He followed her and held her hair back from her face, helpless to offer any real comfort. He could see that her cheeks were flushed. The back of her neck was hot to the touch despite the frigid temps, so he swept her hair off her neck to cool her down, offering what little support he could.

"Sorry," she said before emptying another round into the trash can.

"Don't apologize for being sick. What do you need?" Watching her retch over a garbage bin made him wish he could do something to make it better. Anything besides just keep her neck cool. He'd never felt so useless in his life.

When she was finished, she glanced up at him looking embarrassed.

"Are you okay?" he asked.

"I should've skipped that cup of decaf I had this morning on an empty stomach." She leaned against a brick pillar next to the garbage can for support. "I'll be fine in a few minutes. It's probably just nerves."

She looked at him and must've seen the panic in his eyes.

"Promise. It'll pass. I went through worse than this in those first few months," she said.

"Hold on." He retrieved a bottle of water from the cab of his truck, unscrewed the lid and handed it to her. "Maybe this'll help."

She rinsed her mouth out before wetting a cloth and dabbing it on her face. "That's much better, actually. Thank you."

He shouldn't feel such a strong sense of satisfaction. He needed to be stockpiling reserves against that dam he'd built, tossing bags of sand against it for reinforcement, because seeing the way she looked a few moments ago had threatened to put a crack in a wall he couldn't afford to break.

An old two-door hatchback buzzed into the parking spot on the other side of Ryder's truck with Celeste behind the wheel.

"You're sure you're better?" he asked Faith, relieved that her color was returning.

"Yeah. Much. The cold weather is helping."

"Let's get inside before she sees us out here and takes off. We have a better chance of getting her to open up if she can't easily hop into her car if you say anything to frustrate her."

Faith shot him a severe look.

"Hey, I'm just making sure she doesn't slam the door in our face again," he said, taking her arm. Holding on to her was a bad idea, especially while she seemed so vulnerable. He ignored the hammering against the fault line of the dam wall and the way his pulse picked up as he guided her inside the diner, chalking his reaction up to residual sexual chemistry. Even through her coat he felt the sizzle between them. "Table for two."

The place had about twenty tables in a dining space to the left and a counter with bar stools for quick service on his right. There were plenty of windows at the front and only a few customers. Most of whom were spread around at tables in the back.

"Sit anywhere you like," a waitress said from behind the counter. She was filling an old-fashioned soda glass from a spout.

Ryder motioned toward a booth in front near the half wall of windows, farthest away from anyone else in the hopes that Celeste would feel more comfortable talking. As it was, she looked ready to turn tail and run, and he couldn't afford to lose his only lead. Faith was right earlier. They would circle back to talk to neighbors. He didn't expect to net much since no one had come outside to check on why the dogs were barking earlier. Even if someone had peeked from behind a curtain, they wouldn't talk. Celeste's was a neighborhood that minded its own business.

Faith took off her coat and laid it across the booth before taking a seat. Ryder didn't bother to remove his jacket.

The two of them had just sat down and gotten comfortable when Celeste walked inside. She made eye contact with Ryder almost immediately and he could see just how tentative her trust in either of them was. It didn't matter. She was there. And he'd dealt with enough injured and spooked animals over the years to know it was in his and Faith's best interest to tread lightly.

Celeste had thrown on a pair of yoga pants and a T-shirt underneath a long coat and furry boots. Her hair was piled on top of her head in a loose bun. She didn't look much older than his eldest brother, Dallas, now that she was cleaned up. Fifteen years ago, she would've been barely been twenty years old. Faith's father was a real jerk for taking advantage of someone so young and then leaving when she was in trouble. But then Hollister McCabe had never been known for his morals. His being a jerk was most likely for sport.

Ryder glanced at Faith's stomach as Celeste pulled a chair up to the booth, hoping the stress of the morning wasn't taking a toll. He also wanted to get some food inside her now that he knew she hadn't eaten breakfast. That couldn't be good for her or the baby.

The waitress popped over and asked for drink orders.

"Coffee for me." He looked at Celeste, who nodded.

"Make that two. Can we get some water and toast for my friend?"

A quick look at Faith showed she appreciated the gesture. Thankfully, she'd taken his earlier warning seriously and seemed to realize that it was best to leave the talking up to him.

"You need menus?" the waitress asked.

"Yes," Ryder said. "And can we get a rush on that toast?"

The waitress disappeared, returning a minute later with drinks, menus and toast. She set everything down and then said she'd give them a minute. Celeste shifted in her seat a few times, looking ready to bolt at a loud noise.

"I wasn't going to show but I figured you asked about the diner loud enough so I could hear it on purpose in case I changed my mind about talking," she said, staring at the fork rolled in a paper napkin. She seemed conflicted about being there. "You seem like you want to help. And I'm starting to get real worried about my boy."

Ryder nodded, letting her take the lead. He'd learned a long time ago that when someone was making an effort, it wasn't smart to get in their way.

"First off, I don't trust anyone with the last name McCabe." She glanced toward Faith, who was nibbling on her toast.

"I don't, either, if it makes you feel better," Ryder said, not bothering to mask his disdain for the McCabe family.

Celeste cocked her head sideways.

"I'm here to help find your son and I still haven't exactly figured out how I was talked into it," he said honestly. There was no reason to lie to the woman, and he figured they'd get further if he gained Celeste's trust.

"Since you showed up with a McCabe, I have to ask why you care about what happens to my boy."

"Faith and I have history. She's worried about Nicholas and couldn't go to her father. I'm not exactly thrilled to be here, but I couldn't walk away from someone asking for my help, either."

"Okay then." She must've picked up on the tension between him and Faith because she shot another contemptuous look toward Faith.

"We might not want it for the same reasons, but we all want the same thing. To find Nicholas and bring him home safely," Ryder said. "It doesn't matter why."

Celeste nodded. Her shoulders slumped forward and she looked completely wrung out. "I didn't sleep last night from worry. At first I thought he found a girl and ran off."

"He wouldn't do that," Faith said a little too intensely.

"How would you know?" Celeste said with disdain.

Faith suddenly became interested in the tabletop. "I know my brother."

A noise tore from Celeste's throat. "You don't know fifteen-year-old boys."

"Nicholas isn't like that," Faith said, her defenses rattled. Her reaction was putting Celeste on edge, and that wasn't going to get them what they wanted: her cooperation.

"I can remember a few times when I did stupid stuff at that age. Hormones and a still-developing brain don't exactly make the best combination," Ryder intervened with a warning look toward Faith.

Celeste angled her body toward him, effectively closing Faith out of the conversation. "My point exactly. He's a good boy but that don't mean nothing when it comes to teenage hormones. That's what I thought three days ago. Now, I don't know. It ain't like him not to call. He's never done that before."

"What about his actions in the days leading up to his…" He didn't want to say the word *disappearance*. "Had he been staying out later than usual?" Ryder hoped to cash in on her conspiratorial feelings.

"Not that I know of," she said with a tentative glance toward Faith. "I work nights but he's always there by the time I get home the next morning."

"What time is that usually?" Ryder asked, nodding his head. Celeste was holding something back. What?

"There's no set time," she said.

"Bar closes at two o'clock," Faith said, scorn in her tone. "Nicholas said she doesn't come home until the next morning and sometimes until lunch."

Ryder shot her one of his you're-not-helping looks and then refocused on Celeste.

"Was he hanging out with any new people or had his behavior at school changed recently?" Ryder pressed. "Any notes or calls from the counselor?"

"None. No new people, either. At least none that I know of, but then boys don't exactly tell their mothers every little detail," she said after a thoughtful pause and a long hard look at Faith.

"What about his cell phone?" he asked. "I'm sure you've tried calling. Texting? I'm guessing there's been no response."

"None. And I haven't seen or heard it since he left.

Figured he took it with him. That thing goes every-where with him, including the bathroom."

"Did you search his bedroom for it?" Faith asked, looking determined to get her two cents in. Ryder had never been able to control her, and maybe that was the point. Maybe she was showing him that she was the one who should be in charge. Or maybe it was genu-ine concern for her little brother, a brother who'd been abandoned by her side of the family and who needed her help. Either way, her talking wasn't a good thing. If he'd known her presence would cause this much of a stir with Celeste, he would've come alone.

He took a sip of his black coffee while Celeste shot Faith a sour look.

Celeste fished out her cell phone, entered a pass-word onto the screen and pulled up her message his-tory. "Look, he makes me text him every night to make sure I got in my car safe. No one's ever done that for me before. Plus, he hasn't tried to get a hold of me using anyone else's phone, either." She flashed her eyes at Faith. "I know my Nicholas is a good boy but even the nice ones get mixed up in the wrong crowd some-times. That's what I figured happened when he didn't respond to my text three nights ago. It's not like him to stay away this long, and that has me figuring he's done something he shouldn't. Something real ba—"

"He wouldn't—" Faith started to say, but Ryder shushed her.

"Let her finish," he said with a look that said this would all be over if she kept pressing her agenda. Nich-olas's mother was talking to them, and Faith needed to cool it.

Celeste pulled a piece of paper out of her purse and flattened it on the table.

"Look there. Doesn't seem like you know Nicholas as much as you claim to." She fired the accusation directly at Faith.

It was a note from Nicholas, saying that it was his mother's turn to wait up for him and wonder where he was for a change.

Faith's face went blank.

"Can I see that?" Faith asked.

Celeste didn't immediately move.

"Please. Just for a second," Faith said, softer this time.

The woman relented.

Faith took the paper and then studied the words as she traced her finger around the shapes.

"Nicholas didn't write that." She folded her arms with that indignant look on her face again. Before Ryder could remind her that she wasn't helping, she scooted back in her seat.

"Well, it has his name right there." Celeste pointed to his signature.

"I don't care what it says. I've done homework with him a thousand times and that's not his handwriting," Faith said matter-of-factly. The shaming quality to her tone wasn't going to help matters.

"When have you been here to help Nicholas with anything?" Celeste leaned back in her chair, got another sour look on her face like she'd just sucked on a pickle.

"All the time," Faith shot back, ignoring the warning look Ryder was giving her.

"That's it. I'm done here." Celeste pushed off the table and stood.

Ryder popped to his feet, too.

"Don't leave. I'm just worried about Nicholas," Faith defended.

That was all it took for Celeste to snatch her keys out of her purse and then head for the door.

The waitress appeared as Ryder took off after the distraught woman.

Faith made a move to follow.

"Don't you dare get up. Order food. I'll try to clean up your mess," he barked.

Celeste revved the engine, one hand gripping the steering wheel as she craned her neck to check for clearance. She was ready to gun it and get the heck out of there as Ryder jogged up to her window, hoping he could perform some major damage control.

"She doesn't mean to come off that way," he said, startling her.

"I don't need no one judging my life and especially one of Hollister's snot-nosed kids. She doesn't know what me and Nicholas have gone through because her SOB of a father wouldn't support us," Celeste said through a sneer.

"No, she doesn't. And you're one hundred percent right about Hollister McCabe. I can't stand that family personally," Ryder agreed. "There's no excuse for him abandoning you and Nicholas."

"Then what are you doing with one of 'em?" She put the car in Park but didn't take her foot off the brake.

"I was honest before. She came to me asking for my help," he said. "Before you think I'm some Good Samaritan, I turned her down."

"How come you showed up here anyway?"

"I believed her when she said Nicholas was a good boy. I won't try to convince you that she's better than her family, but I know you'll understand that because of who her father is she had nowhere else to turn but me."

Celeste stared out her windshield, didn't move. That was a good sign.

"She's been sneaking Nicholas money for years, even though getting caught would end her relationship with her father. Hollister McCabe doesn't care if someone's flesh and blood if they cross him, as I'm sure I don't have to tell you," he said.

"Now that she's turned up I figured it had to be her giving my Nicholas money all these years," she admitted.

"It's money out of her pocket. Her father doesn't know," he said. "And she needs to keep it that way."

"I don't give two hoots about her family problems," Celeste said, searching out a pack of cigarettes from the dashboard. She pulled out a smoke and lit it. "You want one?"

Ryder shook his head.

"I'm not saying she's perfect, believe me. She cares about Nicholas, though. And if he is in trouble, he can use all the help he can get no matter whose last name is attached. Don't you think?"

That seemed to strike a chord. She twisted the cigarette around her fingers.

"If you know anything that can help find your son, I'd appreciate you telling me. I understand why you don't like Faith and I won't argue against your points, but I'm not the enemy. I'm only here because Nicholas could be in trouble, and if that's the case we need to work together."

"You don't think he's with a girl? Now that I think about it, that Swanson chick was hanging around our place an awful lot before he took off," Celeste said, taking a long drag. A smoke cloud broke around her face as she blew twin plumes out of her nostrils.

"Maybe. If he's as good a kid as the two of you say he'd let you know where he is. Has he ever stayed away overnight?"

"No. Never. He worries too much about me. He won't even sleep over anyone's house because he wants to be home for me." Celeste took another drag off her smoke and stared out the windshield. A few tears trickled down her cheeks. She quickly wiped them away and took another pull. "I didn't come home the other night. I thought maybe that's why he took off. Then I found the letter. He's been threatening me with that one for years so I guess I had it coming."

"You haven't reported him missing?" Ryder asked, noting that if someone had kidnapped Nicholas they didn't want to raise suspicion right away. Another bad sign as far as Ryder was concerned. This must've been targeted and someone was buying time. Ryder wouldn't allow himself to go down the road that said they were already too late.

She shook her head.

"Then let me help you find him."

Celeste flicked her cigarette out the window, taking care to miss Ryder. He crushed the butt under the heel of his boot.

"I'll stop by the sheriff's office and see what he says," she relented.

"That's a good start. Ask him about an Amber Alert and see if he's willing to go there. What about friends?" Ryder pressed.

"He kept to himself mostly." She shrugged. "There was one boy who always came around. His name's Kyle. He's the Sangers' boy."

"You have his address?"

"No." She shook her head for emphasis. "I'm not too good with writing stuff like that down. Nicholas said he lives in the pink siding house two streets over."

"I'm sure we'll be able to find it," he offered, thinking there couldn't be too many houses with pink siding in the neighborhood.

"I never did catch your name," Celeste said.

"Ryder O'Brien."

Her eyes widened at hearing his last name. It was a common reaction and usually benefited Ryder.

"Nicholas is a good kid. Can you bring him home?" she asked.

"That's the goal."

"He ain't never been in trouble." A desperate sigh slipped out before Celeste could quash it and regain her composure. She looked like the kind of person who hadn't had many breaks in life. She obviously cared about her son, and Ryder couldn't help but feel sorry for the situation McCabe had put her in.

"I know she's going about it all wrong, but Faith cares a lot about Nicholas," Ryder said, testing the water. Maybe he could smooth things over a little between her and Faith. Convince Faith that it would be better for Nicholas if she made an effort with his mother. Besides, Faith seemed to have genuine feelings for her half brother, and she would need all the family she could rally around her when her parents learned that she was carrying his child. He'd almost like to be a fly on the wall of that conversation just to see Hollister McCabe's reaction. And even if Faith wasn't worried about losing the support of her father, Ryder knew her well enough to realize that she wouldn't want to alienate her mother. Faith had always felt protective of her mother, and especially since the woman had started depending on so many pills to get her through the day.

"My boy is none of her business." Celeste's lips turned into a sneer, a chilly response.

"Understood. I just wanted you to know she has just as many issues with her father as you and she's carrying a secret that will cause him to turn his back on her, too," Ryder added.

"That's impossible on both counts," Celeste said, her tone flat. "I want nothing to do with him or his family."

"He's no friend of mine, either," Ryder said. "I'm on your side."

"I appreciate your help but I don't have no money—"

"None's necessary," he cut her off. "This is for Nicholas. If something happened to him, we'll figure it out and bring him home."

Celeste wiped a stray tear.

"You have a pen? I want to give you my number in case he makes contact." Ryder pulled out the business card of his family's lawyer, wishing he'd thought to have some of his own printed.

Celeste searched around in her car and in the glove box. "Afraid not."

"Hold on. I'll grab one from inside," he said.

She nodded.

He jogged into the restaurant and to the counter.

He still had a long way to go to gain Celeste's trust but he'd made progress. "There a pen I can borrow?"

"Sure thing. Should be one right over there." The waitress motioned toward the register.

Ryder thanked her as he located the blue Bic pen. He scribbled his name and number on the back of the card before turning toward the all-glass door. He stopped and issued a frustrated grunt.

Celeste was gone.

Chapter Four

"I can't keep running interference between you and Nicholas's mother," Ryder said, taking his seat at the table. Anger stewed behind his dark eyes and he wore a disgusted expression. "Finish breakfast and I'll take you home."

"I'm sorry." Faith meant it, too.

Ryder's shoulders were bunched. The muscle in his jaw ticked. He was done.

She really hadn't intended to insult Nicholas's mother even though the woman needed a few stern lessons in parenting. Hormones were hell. "Meeting her had an unexpected effect on me and I promise not to let my emotions take over next time."

He gave her the glare that left no room for doubt that there wouldn't be a repeat because she was on her own.

"Ryder, please. I'm begging. I'll handle people however you tell me to if you'll give me another chance."

"Where was this attitude ten minutes ago when it would've made a difference?" he shot back, but the hard lines on his forehead were already softening.

"Not where it should've been. I admit." She'd gained a little ground, but he wasn't exactly happy with her yet.

He picked up his fork and stabbed it into his eggs. Another good sign.

"Well, keep it in check next time because we need her and you probably just pushed her away." The bite didn't make it into his mouth before he continued, "No. You know what. You asked me here and then made it next to impossible to gain her cooperation."

"That's not entirely true. I didn't ask you to bring me to her. I already told you that she can't help us. Or won't." As soon as the tart words left her mouth, she regretted them. She put her hands up in the surrender position. "I didn't mean that, either. I don't know what's wrong with me except that every single emotion I've ever had is at full tilt these past few months." She didn't even want to talk about the crazy changes going on inside her body, changes that weren't visible to others and yet she was keenly aware of her hips starting to expand and her belly having a little pooch. Then, there were the hormones.

"Take it easy." His tone was meant to calm her down. His look of pity made her feel even more frustrated at how fragile she must seem. That didn't go over well. Concern was one thing. Pity was something altogether different. Faith wasn't helpless.

"I want to reassure you that I can have an adult conversation without putting people off. That woman… Nicholas's mother…gets under my skin. I mean Nicholas had it tough enough without a father around and then she adds to his stress and…confusion by making him responsible for her. He's just a kid and he doesn't deserve any of this battle going on between people who are supposed to be grown adults."

Ryder caught her gaze and held it as he folded his hands and placed them against the edge of the table.

"You make a lot of good points about her situation and I can't help but see the similarities to ours," he said. "We're going to need to learn to work together so our differences don't affect our child."

Faith took in a breath.

"And you might not like what I have to say but you need to hear it anyway. As far as I can see, she's the only parent the boy has who loves him. Some kids don't even get that much and he's damn lucky to have someone in his life who cares about him. Which leads to my second point. Nicholas has two."

Faith knew Ryder well enough to know better than to argue his points, and especially because they stung. The hard truth had a way of doing that when someone was being too stubborn to see it. And Faith could admit to being at fault there.

Besides, Ryder would've seen the damage firsthand that neglected children deal with and could probably recite the statistics on what happened to them because of his and his mother's generous work with children's charities. He'd said that she'd been the inspiration for him and his brothers to become more involved in the community. Ryder might like to push the boundaries in his personal life, but he also was smart enough to appreciate the privileges he'd been given growing up an O'Brien and he was decent enough to want to help others.

"We might disagree about his mother but you're right about one thing. My brother will always have me," she defended. She stopped him from going down the neglected child road with Nicholas.

"It's not the same as a mother or father being present and you know it." His voice was a frustrating sea of calm.

"Why not? I probably should've petitioned the courts years ago. I'm old enough now and I have plenty of money to fight for him." Ryder was striking a chord of truth and it grated on her.

"Which your father would cut off the second he knew you were involved with his bastard son." The words were harsh and she knew that he'd used that term to shock her. It was exactly what her father would call Nicholas. And no matter how much it pained her to admit, her father would see this as black-and-white. She had to think that there was still decency in him, but that part of her was shrinking, especially since she had to confront the reality of the way she feared he'd treat her when he learned of her pregnancy.

"Let me put this to you another way," Ryder said.

"I'm listening," she said, doing her best to calm the tremors in her arms. Hormones made her body do crazy things, not the least of which was shaking when she got angry or nervous.

"Have you ever asked Nicholas if he wanted to leave his mother?" His voice was a study in calmness.

"I don't have to. I see how she treats him with my own eyes," she fired back, her defenses on high alert.

"You just made my point. You can't do what's best for a teenager without actually consulting with him to find out what he really wants. He may not think he needs what you're offering and you might end up pushing him further away with your good intentions," Ryder said, and he was making more sense than she wanted to admit.

Faith wouldn't share the fact that she'd been plotting and secretly saving money for years. Her father was watchful of her finances. She wasn't crazy enough to think that her father's good will would last forever. She had an overseas account—a safety net—that she'd been building for her and Nicholas. She might actually have to use it now in order to protect her own child. Her father would cut her off in every way possible and freeze her personal accounts the minute he heard the news about the baby. She had no job outside of working for the family, and so he could easily cut off her livelihood. Faith couldn't imagine that her mother would stand up to the man, not even on her behalf. Her mother wasn't strong like Faith and she had always issued her mother a free pass in that department. The pregnancy was starting to give Faith a new perspective. She could acknowledge that she felt even more protective of Nicholas. Ryder's words hit her full force. Was she being unrealistic in thinking that she could make better decisions for Nicholas than he could make on his own? Or worse, had she turned into her father?

The realization startled her because she knew firsthand how stifling it was to have other people make her decisions. What she was thinking was no different. What a slap in the face that thought was. Ryder was being logical while she was being fueled by sentiment.

"My hormones make me feel like every emotion I have is on steroids and I may have taken some of that out on his mother," she admitted. The truth left a bitter taste in her mouth. "I know you understand the need to take care of your own, Ryder. I've seen your relationship with your brothers, especially with Joshua, and how well you take care of family. Surely you can at least see where I'm coming from."

Ryder didn't immediately pick up his fork. He just sat there staring at the food, contemplating what she'd said, and that was the best that she could ask for.

"Under the circumstances, I can see where you'd feel overprotective of Nicholas," he finally said. "While I don't have a lot of experience with pregnant women, we've had a baby boom at the ranch and I can see how different my brothers are now. They're more defensive of everyone and everything around them. I'm sure it's primal. Nature's way of taking care of these helpless little creatures. But it's a fine line to becoming over-bearing and one you don't want to cross."

"Point taken." She paused a beat. "I heard about Dallas, Tyler and Joshua. I don't even know where to start. Congratulations to all of them." Three out of six O'Brien men were engaged and in settled relation-ships in various stages of wedding planning, or so she'd heard. Her direct line into that family had been sev-ered when she'd been forced to walk away from Ryder.

"The ranch has turned into a kid farm," he said with a laugh, his easy O'Brien charm returning—that same charm that caused a thousand butterflies to take flight in her stomach.

"Is that a bad thing?" She couldn't read him when it came to his feelings toward kids.

"No. Not for my brothers. They seem happier than they've ever been. Maybe that's why I'm feeling tender-hearted right now, so I'll let it slide that you basically ran off our only real connection to what might've hap-pened to Nicholas." He wasn't exactly offering forgive-ness, but she'd take what she could get from him under the circumstances and be grateful for the progress. Ryder was back on board and he was speaking to her.

"If you're being honest with yourself—" he held his hands up in the surrender position "—and I can tell you've been taking this seriously, then you have to consider the possibility that your father might be involved."

"I wondered how long it would take you to get to that accusation. For a minute, I didn't think you'd stoop that low." A bolt of anger shot lightning-quick down her spine as she remembered just how much Ryder disliked her family.

"It's worth considering," he defended.

"Not to me, it isn't," she said.

"What makes you so sure he's not involved?"

"First of all, my father might be a cheating jerk, which makes him a scumbag and bad husband, but he'd never hurt one of his own," she said, her pulse rising as she defended him. Granted, her father wasn't father-of-the-year material but she hated how easy it was for Ryder to sling that accusation. This situation was back to the McCabes being the bad guys.

"Unless he doesn't consider Nicholas part of the fold. In which case, he wouldn't give a hoot what happened to him, and I doubt Celeste would give us information about any recent exchanges she's had with him if there have been any," Ryder said calmly.

"Nicholas is as much of a McCabe as I am whether anyone wants to acknowledge him or not," she cried, voice rising.

"To you. Maybe. To your father…" He rolled his shoulders and his right brow shot up.

"He wouldn't do something like this," she repeated, and she had to believe it was true.

"While I'm digging around I plan to investigate every angle. And that's one." He set his fork down, signaling that he was done with breakfast.

"Where to next?" she asked stiffly. She should've seen this coming. It always came down to this, to the fact that the McCabes were horrible people. Granted, it didn't help that her father and brothers seemed eager to support that notion. She brought her hand to rest on her belly. Not all McCabes were horrible people.

Ryder motioned toward her plate. "We don't go anywhere until you finish eating."

RYDER PULLED IN front of the only house with pink siding in a three-block radius of Celeste's place in either direction. It was similar to hers, bungalow-style and in the same neighborhood a few streets over just as Celeste had said.

"Let me take the lead," he said to Faith, who'd been quiet on the ride over, and he hoped that she was seriously considering what he'd said. Without a doubt, Hollister McCabe could be involved and if not directly then indirectly. He knew that she couldn't exactly ask her father outright without giving away the fact that she'd been in touch with Nicholas all these years. None of which would matter to her if she truly believed that her father wasn't involved and/or would be willing to help.

"Okay. I won't say a word." She held up her hands trying to mimic the Scout's honor pledge. Her eyes tried so desperately to convey sincerity.

It shouldn't make him laugh. He recovered quickly.

"You better take this seriously," he warned.

She rolled her eyes at him. "Like I wouldn't. I was trying to show you that I'm not just a raging head case."

"Keep the hormones in check and we'll get answers faster. *Hormones in check.* That's your mantra," he said as flatly as he could. It wouldn't do either one of them any good to get too comfortable. Once this was over, they were going to have a sit-down about the pregnancy and Ryder's role in his child's life. Working together given their current state of mistrust wouldn't be easy, but he was seeing firsthand just how important it would be to get along for their child's sake and he was willing to make a few concessions to ensure that happened.

"Got it." The amusement left her brown eyes and he did his best not to let it affect him. She was only doing what he said, taking this seriously and showing that she wouldn't do anything to get in the way of their investigation.

Ryder ushered her to the door of 225 Oak Drive, which had a similar wood and glass door combination as Nicholas's house except this one had a shade so he couldn't see inside. There was no screen door at this address. He figured he had a better chance of a person answering if they saw a woman standing there rather than a grown man, so he put Faith front and center while he moved off to the side.

Three knocks went unanswered.

"We can come back," he said, realizing it was close to eight o'clock in the morning and probably too early for anyone in the house to be awake and moving.

"Wouldn't Kyle have to get up for school?" she asked.

"Good point. Maybe he already left. I have no idea when kids have to be at school," Ryder said as he heard movement coming from inside. "Hold on."

The door cracked open and a smiling teen with tousled hair blinked his eyes open. Disappointment caused him to frown when he opened the door wide enough to see Ryder. "My aunt's not here."

Ryder nudged Faith, trying to communicate the message that she should take the lead.

"Are you Kyle?" Faith asked.

"Yeah," he said, leaning against the door. And then a scared-doe look passed behind his eyes and he stiffened. "Are you truant officers or something? It's not even time for school yet."

"No, believe me, it's nothing like that. I'm trying to find Nicholas Bowden. Have you seen him around?" she asked.

Recognition dawned. "Oh, you know Nicholas? Yeah, he's a friend of mine. I haven't seen him in like… forever."

"Do you remember how many days it's been?" she asked. "Two? Three?"

"It was last weekend, so, like, what…three days."

"Are you two close?" she asked. "Is it normal for you to go that long without talking?"

"Is Nicholas in trouble or something?" Kyle asked. A worry line dented his forehead.

"No, nothing like that," Ryder interjected when Faith seemed to blank on an excuse. He put his arm around her waist, ignoring the fizz of energy that came with touching her. "We're related, well, she is. We're driving through town and his mom thought you might've seen Nicholas. He's not picking up his cell."

The teen's expression morphed as he tossed his head back. "Got it. No. I haven't seen Nicholas for three days, maybe more. Not since he and Hannah starting getting hot and heavy. He hasn't been returning my texts, either."

"Hannah?"

"Yeah, she's some chick we met, well, *he* met, while we were hanging out down at Wired." He glanced from Faith to Ryder like they should know what that meant. "It's a place where they host LAN parties."

They looked at each other blankly.

"Come on. You don't know what a LAN party is?" he whined, sounding every bit the teenager that he was.

"Afraid not," Faith said with a smile and a shrug.

"It's a gaming thing." He brought his hands up in the air and moved them like he was typing on a keyboard. "Computers."

"We'll take your word for it," Faith said with the same smile that had been right on target at melting Ryder's reservations about the two of them dating. He didn't want to admit just then how much that smile played a role in his attraction to her. Her bright eyes, intelligence and sense of humor had been a welcome surprise, considering all his preconceived notions about her. She'd been quiet in school and he could admit now that he'd believed she was stuck on herself, which couldn't have been more off base. His experience with McCabes came from knowing her brothers. Once he got to know her, he realized just how wrong he'd been. Faith and her brothers were polar opposites. Ryder had had a few run-ins with Jason, the youngest. That kid had been born ready to fight. O'Briens didn't start trouble. They didn't back away from it, either. If trouble was stupid enough to snare one of them, the response came in the form of six angry brothers. McCabes had never been good at math or anything else that required using the head put on their shoulders as far as Ryder could tell. So when he'd run into Faith near the fishing cabin and they started spending time together, he'd been most surprised at her intelligence and wit, which had only made her more beautiful. The fact that he'd felt lost and alone at the time, with darkness all around him, had drawn him to her light even more.

Kyle also seemed to notice her looks, because the kid was standing there beaming at her. It shouldn't grate on Ryder's nerves as much as it did.

"You know where the girl you mentioned lives?" Ryder interrupted.

"Sorry. Can't help you." The kid's eyes never left Faith.

"What about her cell number or social media?" Ryder asked.

"Sorry." Kyle shook his head. "This was the first time I'd seen her, and she went for my friend."

Ryder understood the logic. Kyle wouldn't try to connect with her after his friend got together with her, which didn't help their investigation in the least.

"How about you? You got a cell?" Ryder asked, and he was starting to get annoyed. He suppressed the urge to put his arm around Faith's shoulders and show the kid just how far she was out of his league. It was stupid and childish. Ryder knew that on some level. But primal urge had him needing to keep everyone from the male species away from her. He lied to himself and said it was because she was carrying his child. That he was protective of the baby, and not territorial about her.

"Uh, yeah. Sure. Hold on." The kid disappeared and then returned a minute later. He'd wet his hair and run a quick comb through it. Now that made Ryder crack a smile. *She's way out of your league, kid. And not even when you get hair on your chest will she give a second look.*

Being stunning had never been Faith's problem. All the good looks in the world couldn't replace honesty or the fact that her last name was McCabe—and everything that brought along with it. Not that Ryder had minded the second part once he got past the initial surprise that she was nothing like her family. Sure, there'd been a burst of adrenaline from being with someone he knew better than to want at first. But that had died the second he got to know her and started having real feelings for her. Real feelings? They'd sure felt like it based on the sting he felt when she walked away.

And she'd rewarded him by returning when she needed him for something. He hadn't pegged her for the manipulative type. Like his dad had always said, "When people show you who they really are, believe them."

He could be objective about Nicholas, whereas Faith couldn't. Knowing that her brother had met a girl changed his thoughts about what might be happening.

"Where was the LAN party?" Ryder asked.

"At Marcus's place on Lone Oak. It's called Wired and it's about ten to fifteen minutes from here," Kyle said.

"Can you describe Hannah?" Faith seemed to catch on.

"Wow, yeah, she's a knockout. Black hair, brown eyes and—" he glanced from Faith to Ryder "—you know, great bod."

"And she's fifteen?" Based on Faith's frown, Hannah didn't match the type she thought her brother would go for.

Kyle shrugged and shot a look like *why would she ask that question?*

"Will you let us know if you hear from him?" Ryder asked. This interview was a dead end. Ryder exchanged cell numbers with the kid and walked Faith back to the truck.

"That was a bust," Faith said as soon as Ryder took his seat.

"We're certain there's a girl involved now. We didn't know that before," he said. That information would change things for Ryder if it hadn't been for the forged note.

"His mother mentioned a girl but it must not be the same one since his friend has no idea who she is. Where does that leave us?" she asked on a frustrated sigh.

"Speaking of Celeste, I want to circle back and drop my cell number in her mailbox. She needs to have a way to contact us if she hears anything."

"Good idea," Faith said.

"We might find out more about the girl if we hang around Wired," he said.

"It's a waste of time pursuing her. Nicholas would've told me if he liked someone," she said on a sharp sigh.

"You sure about that?" Ryder had his doubts.

And his mind kept circling back to her family being involved in the disappearance. He just couldn't put his finger on why or how.

Yet.

Chapter Five

The business front of Wired was the enclosed front porch of a house on the outskirts of town. The lots were a good acre in size, so there was plenty of distance between neighbors. A pair of compact cars were parked on the side of the house in tandem. Ryder parked on the street to make sure he didn't get blocked in. Although he doubted there'd be a rush when it opened at noon. The place gave new meaning to the words *small business*. There was a closed sign hanging on the screen door but he could see activity inside.

"Act like we know what we're doing," Ryder said to Faith as she took in the place. Her wide honey-brown eyes told him she was learning something else new about her brother. That gnawing feeling returned, and Ryder kept circling back to her family.

He opened the screen door and instructed her to stay close behind him.

A sallow-cheeked guy who couldn't be a day older than twenty was parked behind a desk, his gaze fixed on the screen in front of him.

"Hold on," he said without looking up. His chair was balanced on the back legs as he swished a mouse back and forth on an oversize pad and made barely audible grunting noises.

There were a couple of kids hunkered over a keyboard in one corner. A few open computers were dotted around the small room. There wasn't much in the way of decor, a few folding tables with poker chairs tucked underneath. The walls were covered with gaming posters announcing the next big release.

Sallow Cheeks cursed before tossing the mouse to the side. "So close to winning that one. What can I—" The second his eyes connected with Ryder and Faith, he froze.

"We're not cops, if that's what you're worried about," Ryder said, assuming that most kids were going to confuse them with people in positions of authority. There was no question that they looked out of place at Wired.

Sallow Cheeks regained his composure. "Oh, no. Didn't think you were. Besides, I run a legit business." He waved his right arm toward a framed permit hanging on the wall behind him. Ryder couldn't fault the kid for making money.

"She's looking for a relative. We were told he comes in here sometimes," Ryder continued, forging ahead.

Faith fingered the screen on her cell phone and then held it out toward Sallow Cheeks.

"I'm Marcus, by the way," he said, pushing hair off his forehead as he squinted at the picture of Nicholas.

Ryder introduced both himself and Faith.

"Yeah, I've seen that kid before. He doesn't come around much. He has a friend. What's his name?" He tapped his knuckles on the desk.

"Is it Kyle?" Faith asked.

"Right. Kyle usually swings by on Friday nights. He's brought this dude before."

"Nicholas Bowden?" Ryder asked.

"I guess." Marcus shrugged. "The kid was kind of quiet, you know. Mostly hung in the background when Kyle showed up to play."

"Do you remember the last time he was in? Nicholas?" Faith asked.

"A week ago." Marcus glanced at his computer screen. "Maybe two?"

"Was he with a girl?" Faith continued.

Marcus rocked his head and his eyes went wide. "Hannah."

"Do you know her?" Faith asked.

"She just started coming in a few weeks ago. Never saw her before that," Marcus said.

"You don't have an address for her, do you?" Ryder asked, wondering what a knockout, as Kyle had described her, would be doing hanging around with tech geeks. And there was no other explanation for hanging out at a place like Wired other than being a bona fide computer nerd.

"Nah." Marcus leaned backward, balancing on the back two legs of his chair.

"No credit card record?" Ryder asked.

"I wouldn't be able to give that to you anyway, dude. But, no, a girl like that doesn't usually have to pay her own way if you know what I mean."

"Are girls like Hannah common around here?" Ryder asked, figuring he already knew the answer but needed to check anyway.

"Nah. It would be nice, though," Marcus said.

"When was the last time you saw her?" A look

crossed Faith's features that Ryder couldn't exactly pinpoint.

"Not since that kid was in. They paired up and left together. Haven't seen either one around since," he said. "But that's not really saying much. He wasn't a regular."

"This might sound like an odd question, but do you remember who was doing the picking up?" Ryder asked, and that netted a strange look from Faith.

Marcus nodded with a wink toward Ryder. "Definitely her. And that's probably why I remember it so clearly. I mean, she was hot and he was okay if you know what I mean." He shot an apologetic look toward Faith when she frowned.

"I hear you." A guy would notice something like that. "If you happen to see him, would you mind asking him to call his sister? He's probably caught up with this new girl and just forgot to check in with her, but she's worried."

Marcus nodded with a knowing look that said it wasn't the first time he'd received that kind of request. "I'll let him know if he shows up here."

"Thanks a lot." Ryder offered a handshake before escorting Faith outside.

Neither spoke until they reached the truck.

"I can't believe Nicholas has been there and never mentioned it," she finally said after buckling in.

Ryder could see where that detail might still be on her mind. However, he'd locked onto something else. "She targeted him."

"What do you mean?"

Ryder put the gearshift in Drive and rolled the wheel left with his palm, guiding his pickup onto the street.

He banked a U-turn at the next driveway. "She came on to Nicholas, not the other way around."

"He's a good-looking kid," she defended.

"Hear me out." Ryder located the highway and followed the GPS's instructions. "I get that Nicholas is nice-looking. He's also fifteen and full of hormones. He'd be attracted to any pretty girl who walked in front of him."

"Sounds pretty Neanderthal when you put it like that but, yes, I'm sure he is a normal, healthy fifteen-year-old boy," she said, her arms folded across her chest.

"So, let's think this through for a minute, because while Nicholas might still be young I don't get the impression this Hannah is his age and certainly not as innocent."

"What are you suggesting?"

"That there might be a reason a girl so out of his league became interested in him," he said, guiding them back onto Main Street.

It dawned on Faith. "She was some kind of decoy to get him alone so someone could snatch him."

"Once she isolated him, he could be kidnapped a helluva lot easier and everyone would think that he'd run off with a pretty girl," Ryder said. Between that and the note, someone was going to great lengths to buy time. "And the question should be why? Why would Nicholas be a target? What purpose would it serve? The first thing that comes to mind is money."

"Maybe someone figured out he's a McCabe and has contacted my father for ransom," Faith said, catching on to the theory. "That note wasn't his handwriting.

"It's not like I can ask my father outright. Hannah might be the key to finding Nicholas," she added.

"Where do we start looking? Marcus back there doesn't know who she is, and neither did Kyle."

Ryder one-handed the steering wheel. "Can you access your father's email or desk?"

"Ryder." The distress in her voice had him taking his eyes off the road long enough for a quick glance at her. She was bent forward, holding her stomach.

"What's wrong?" he asked. He was already looking for an exit.

She must've picked up on his worry because she added, "Sick." Her hand came over her mouth.

"Hold on the best you can until I can get off the road," he said.

"Gas station," she managed to get out with a dry heave.

Ryder navigated onto the service road, and got to a Valu-X gas station pronto.

He'd barely come to a stop when her door flew open and she hopped out, bolting toward the little patch of grass near the service road. Bent over, she heaved as he pulled her hair from her face and rubbed her back. He wasn't cut out for feeling helpless.

"What can I do?" he asked when she finally straightened up.

"Water would be nice. And maybe some crackers," she said, and he didn't like how small and vulnerable her voice had become. He was used to strong and fiery Faith. These changes must be part of the hormones she'd talked about earlier. If so, he had a lot to learn about pregnant women, because he intended to help her through this and the next four months until the baby was born.

"I'll see what they have," he said. "Will you be all right?"

"Yeah." Her face was sheet white.

"Is it normally this bad?" he asked.

"It's much better than it was. Any little thing upsets my stomach now. I guess the stress from the day isn't helping. Don't worry, I'll be fine in a minute," she said, her cheeks returning to a pale pink, which he liked a lot better than the ghost-white hue from a few minutes ago.

He stood there another couple of seconds, not wanting to leave her.

"It's already settling down," she said, urging him to go.

Ryder nodded, only because she looked steady on her feet and her lips were pink again.

Inside, he located a bottle of water and a package of saltines next to the dustiest can of Campbell's soup he'd ever seen. At least they had crackers. His mother used to give him 7Up to settle his stomach, so he grabbed a bottle of that, too. As for himself, a shot of black coffee was all he needed to keep his mind clear. He poured a large cup.

Ryder pulled a twenty out of his money clip as he heard what he thought sounded like a muffled scream coming from outside.

A quick glance out the window warned that something was dead wrong. There was an SUV angled toward his pickup, blocking Ryder's view.

He tossed the twenty on the counter and tore out of that store faster than the clerk could say that he forgot his items. Suddenly none of those mattered. Not while Faith might be in trouble.

FAITH TRIED TO scream again, but a hand clamped over her mouth. She'd thought the SUV that had pulled up beside Ryder's truck was there to use the air pump until a man had come around the side toward her. Then it had dawned on her that this was the same SUV that had followed her before.

The man's dark beady eyes that had been focused on her left no room for doubt about his intention—he was coming for her. The rest of his face was covered and she couldn't get a good look at him. She'd bolted. Her weak legs had threatened to give out, and that was the only reason the man caught up to her.

He'd hauled her off her feet and was carting her toward the familiar-looking SUV. She could see that there was another man at the wheel, but his features were hidden behind sunglasses and a bandanna. If the guy holding her managed to get her another twenty yards and inside that truck, there'd be nothing Ryder could do.

She twisted and turned but couldn't shake free from his viselike grip. She had to think fast or he'd stuff her inside the cab and they'd be gone.

Lifting up her right foot, she jabbed it backward with all the strength she could muster, scoring a direct hit with the heel of her boot to his groin.

He grunted and dropped to his knees, taking her down with him. She popped up on all fours, struggling to gain purchase in the gravel. If she could crawl, claw or scoot to Ryder's truck she could hop inside and lock the doors.

"Ryder," she managed to shout through heaves as she scrambled to her feet.

She succeeded in gaining a few steps of forward

progress before a hand closed around her ankle, the iron grip brought her down flat on her face. She hit the pavement hard; her hands smacking down first were the only things keeping her head from banging against the cracked surface.

Before she could get her bearings, she was being hauled upright again. The driver was there, too, gripping her around the midsection as Dark Eyes clutched her legs from behind. There was no fighting her way out of this one, but that didn't stop her from trying. She kicked, twisted and screamed. Her only prayer was that the baby wasn't being somehow hurt in the process.

She glanced up and screamed again in time to see that Ryder had heard her and he was already barreling toward her.

He was going to be too late, she thought as she was being tossed inside the cab of the SUV.

"That man coming toward us is Ryder O'Brien. You won't get away with…whatever it is you're planning to do to me. And if you do, that man will see to it that both of you rot in jail or don't live long enough to see another sunrise. So think very hard about your next move." Threatening was the last line of defense, and she could only pray it would work.

The driver shot a look toward Dark Eyes. "Hey, man. I didn't know an O'Brien was involved. That wasn't part of the deal."

"She never told me anything. I don't care who he is. *Go*, or we'll both end up in jail," Dark Eyes demanded.

"Who is *she*?" Faith asked. If the men were talking about being hired by a woman, then her father couldn't be involved. Could he?

Chapter Six

Ryder hopped inside his truck and jabbed his foot onto the gas pedal. The forest green late-model SUV was fifty yards ahead as he navigated onto the road. The license plate had been removed so there was no way to call this in and get Tommy's help. Since this was outside Tommy's area he couldn't do much except make a call to the local sheriff. Not unless the driver took her into Collier County where Tommy had jurisdiction.

Even so, Ryder would see it snow in the middle of a Texas summer before he'd allow these jerks to get away with Faith. They'd better not harm a hair on her head if they knew what was good for them. Or do anything that might hurt the baby growing inside her…

A solid wall of frustration and helplessness slammed into Ryder. He felt a knife cutting through his chest, ripping out his heart. And that sent all kinds of confusing emotions slashing through him.

He understood his feelings for Faith, no matter how complicated they'd become. Hell, they'd defied logic from day one. But a baby he hadn't even met yet? How could he be ready to trade his own life for a little carpet-crawler he hadn't even seen? Faith barely had a bump as far as he could tell. But that didn't matter to Ryder. All his protective instincts were jacked into high gear and the thought of losing anyone else bit through him, hard and sharp. Residual feelings from losing his parents?

He was making good progress toward the SUV when brake lights surprised him and the vehicle pulled to a complete stop in the middle of the road. Ryder followed the driver's lead, keeping a few yards of distance between them in case they opened fire. Adrenaline shot through the roof. He opened his door and eased out, making sure to keep metal in between him and the SUV in front in case someone started shooting. His pulse hammered and all he could think was how much the men would pay if they did anything to hurt Faith or his child.

He expected to see one of the men and was shocked when Faith stepped out instead. Her hands were high in the air as she turned toward him.

Were the men baiting Ryder? Did they have plans to hurt her? Right in front of his eyes?

He slid his right hand in the back floorboard until he felt his shotgun. If these guys decided to be stupid enough to hurt Faith in any way or send metal his direction, he planned to take them both down. Leave Faith unharmed and they could live. The thought of watching as Faith was shot hit him harder than a physical punch.

Faith started walking toward him. *One step at a time. That's right.* He had no idea what these guys were up to, but he planned to be ready for anything.

"Don't follow us and we won't hurt the lady, okay?" the driver shouted and there was too much tension in his voice.

Could it be that easy? Or was this a trap?

The man was staring at Ryder from behind the barrel of a rifle, and Ryder couldn't get a good description of him.

"You got it, man." Ryder's heart hammered harder against his rib cage. A few more feet and Faith would be home free. He didn't dare make a sudden move for fear the driver would react.

"We don't want trouble," the driver said. "You get her and we drive away. No police. No trouble. Got it?"

"No one's been hurt so no harm's been done," Ryder said. "That changes and we're talking a different story."

"You're cool with the terms?" The tension in the driver's voice had all the hairs on Ryder's neck pricked.

"As long as nothing happens to the lady, I have no reason to go after you," Ryder shouted back. A few more steps and she'd be close enough for him to make a move to save her if the driver fired. He'd throw himself in front of her to block the path if needed.

"Throw your keys into the field," the driver barked.

Ryder did.

Even so, this was too easy, and Ryder figured that as soon as she got to him the driver and whoever else was in the SUV would open fire. Then the driver surprised him a second time by sliding into the cab and pulling away.

Ryder bolted toward Faith, putting himself between her and the truck as it sped away.

"Are you hurt?" Ryder asked, taking her in his arms and pulling her around the door of his own cab to shield them both.

Her heart pounded against his chest and her body trembled.

"I'm fine," she said, clearly shaken, but her defiant chin shot up, strong. Or maybe she was just too stubborn to let herself show fear. Probably a little of both, having grown up with three older brothers who didn't exactly have a reputation for being soft on anyone.

"They were afraid of you," she said before burying her face in his chest. "That's the only reason they let me walk away."

"How do they know me?" He lifted her chin up so he could examine the scrapes on her face to make sure she didn't need emergency care.

"I told them your name. I said you'd hunt them down and throw them in jail yourself or kill them if they hurt me, and they started panicking," she said, gripping handfuls of his shirt as if holding on for dear life.

"That was smart. You did the right thing," he reassured her, surprising himself by kissing her on the forehead. He tried to convince himself that he'd done it for her and not himself. Her physical scrapes weren't as bad as he'd feared, but he had no idea what taking a fall like she had might do to a baby. Then there was the stress she'd been under. Worrying about Nicholas had been bad enough, but this? "How do you feel?"

"Like I could use a good cup of chamomile tea," she said on a half sob, half laugh. It was her nervous tic and a good sign.

Still, he wasn't ready to relax yet.

"Think you need to see a doctor?" he asked. "Just to make sure everything's okay."

"I think I'm fine, nothing more than a good scare, but you have a good point. It wouldn't hurt to be on the safe side," she conceded, and he was grateful that she didn't argue. His biggest fear was that she was in shock, and therefore, the pain hadn't kicked in yet. The thought of chasing after the men who did this to her crossed his mind. No way could he risk it with her in the truck. He'd have to let this one go. But he would find them. There was no question about that.

"They said something about a woman giving them this job," she said with emphasis on the word *woman*.

Was she trying to point out that her father couldn't be involved, or convince herself? It was possible that someone had discovered Nicholas was a McCabe, kidnapped him and tried to get a quick ransom out of the senior McCabe. Effort was being made to keep law enforcement out of the picture. A person could've set Nicholas up and tucked the note in the house while Celeste was at work, figuring McCabe would pay and the boy would be home before his mother realized what was going on.

"They can't mean Hannah. This is too complicated for a teenager to coordinate." He'd let ideas churn in the back of his mind while he found a hospital for Faith. This stress couldn't be good for the baby. Ryder helped her into the truck, retrieved his keys and then checked for the nearest ER using the GPS locator on his phone, pausing occasionally to scan the road in order to make sure the men didn't have a change of heart.

He plugged in an address and they arrived fifteen minutes later.

Being inside an ER brought back a flood of bad memories that Ryder wasn't prepared to face. Feelings about walking inside the hospital after learning that his parents had died resurfaced, and his chest tightened. The sound of boots clicking on the tile floors was another reminder. Everything had been drowned out but that sound, as his brothers filed into the room to learn the news, their somber expressions stamped in his thoughts. The news that their parents had been in a fatal car crash hit full force as if Ryder was hearing it again for the first time.

An image of Faith in the same situation rocked him.

Ryder forced his thoughts to the present. This was different. He was here with Faith and she was alive, he reminded himself as she was ushered into a small room. She held on to his arm, her grip a little too tight for him to relax.

"What's your name, honey?" the intake nurse asked after a few routine-sounding questions about what had brought her to the ER today.

A billing clerk stood at the doorway, clipboard in hand.

"Deborah Kerr," Faith said.

Ryder leaned against the wall staring at Faith, wondering why she'd just given them the name of her favorite classic movie star. Then it occurred to him that she'd need to give her insurance card. It took another second for him to realize that she wouldn't want to give out personal information to strangers for fear an ER bill would show up at her door later and alert her family to the fact that she was pregnant.

"I'm responsible for the bill. She lost her insurance when she was laid off from work a couple of months ago," he said, covering for her.

"My name's Kayla. Any unusual pains today, Deborah?" the nurse asked.

"Not right now. Not pain." Faith shot a furtive glance in his direction.

"How about bleeding?" Kayla continued, unaware of the signals being sent between them.

"No. Nothing. Just a little bit of cramping," Faith said. Didn't that kick Ryder's heart rate up.

"You mentioned that you'll be financially responsible?" the nurse asked Ryder.

"Yes," he agreed. "I'm the father of Ms. Kerr's child."

Faith's cheeks flamed bright red.

The nurse nodded, shooting him a look like she understood their situation was complicated. That was a great word to describe everything that had to do with Faith, Ryder thought. And especially covered all the emotions he had roaring through him right now—a mix of confusion and stress and overprotective instincts.

"The billing clerk will finish processing the paperwork at her station," the nurse said to Ryder. "Do you mind following her?"

"Not at all," he said, but that wasn't entirely true. He didn't want to leave Faith's side.

Another quick glance from her said it was okay to leave her alone. She wasn't exactly by herself. She had the nurse.

By the time he came back fifteen minutes later, Faith had on a hospital gown and had her eyes closed with her head resting against a pillow. He slipped inside the room, trying not to disturb her.

"Hi," she said, opening her eyes and glancing at the IV sticking out of her arm.

"Hey there," Ryder said, tamping down the stress at seeing her in a hospital bed.

"They want me to get started on IV fluids since I've been vomiting so much. I may have let myself get a little dehydrated," she said in a voice so soft that Ryder sat on the edge of the bed to get close enough to hear.

"I'm sure it's just nerves with Nicholas missing and everything that's happened since."

He nodded. This wasn't the time for the conversation he wanted to have about her letting him take the lead on finding Nicholas. She needed to strap herself in bed and stay there until the baby was born as far as Ryder was concerned.

"The nurse seemed a little too eager to get me out of the room earlier," he said.

Faith smiled. "You should've heard the questions she asked once you left."

"Like what?"

"She wanted to know if I was being abused." She laughed, but it wasn't funny to Ryder.

"That's nice of her," he said defensively.

"She was just doing her job. She didn't mean anything personally by it," she said. "The statistics are staggering. She rattled off a few when I had the same reaction as you. A woman is beaten every nine seconds in America."

Ryder clenched his hands, making tight fists.

"She obviously doesn't know your family or its reputation, or she wouldn't have had to ask," Faith said, clearly picking up on his disgust. A look passed behind her honey browns that he couldn't easily read, another sign things had changed since they'd been together.

"Abuse happens in wealthy families as often as it does in poor." *Every woman should be safe with the person she loved*, he thought bitterly. "I'm more concerned about you than my reputation right now. Feeling any better?"

"I'm probably going to have a few bruises on my face. I saw the red marks when I asked to go to the bathroom before the nurse put the IV in. That'll be fun to explain to my family."

He started to speak his mind, but thought better of it. Again, this wasn't the time to bring up her relationship with her family or why he thought she needed to come clean with them about the pregnancy and her relationship to him. The sooner they all knew that he planned to be part of the baby's life the faster they could all adjust to the fact that they were tied together by that little boy or girl she was carrying.

"It's more important for you to rest and take care of yourself right now," he said, thinking of how much more protective he'd be of a little one once he held the baby in his arms.

"I didn't plan on this." Her hand rested on her tummy. "Now that it's here I don't want to lose it even though that makes no sense. Is that crazy?"

"No." He shared the sentiment. It would take some time to get used to the idea that he was going to be a father. He had four months to adjust. Ryder wasn't sure if that was enough time or not since he'd never been in this situation before, not even a scare because he was always careful, but he'd do whatever it took. For now, he needed to make sure she was safe. "You didn't recognize those men."

She shook her head. "I still can't believe they let me go. I threatened them using your name and they said *she* didn't mention anything about an O'Brien being involved."

Maybe one of McCabe's exes thought she could get his attention by kidnapping his son. His mind circled back to greed being behind this.

The doctor came in, interrupting them. She was

younger than Ryder had expected, and part of him hoped she wasn't too green. He suppressed the urge to ask her age.

She introduced herself as Dr. Field and shook Ryder's outstretched hand. She moved to the bed beside Faith and asked a few routine-sounding questions. A bad feeling settled over Ryder. It could be Faith's revelation. Being in a hospital also brought back too many haunting memories of waiting on word of his parents.

"Have you had any bleeding since the fall?" Dr. Field asked Faith as Ryder, once again, stood helplessly by.

Faith said the same thing she'd told the nurse about the cramping.

He didn't figure there was any way he'd be able to talk Faith into seeing Dr. McConnell later given that the doctor knew everyone in town. He trusted McConnell, since she was a close friend of his mother's. He could see how Faith wouldn't feel as secure.

Ryder had to figure out a way to gently break the news to his brothers that Faith McCabe was having his child. This news would come out of the blue for them. He'd never once mentioned dating anyone, and they'd never suspect he'd see a McCabe. That one wasn't going to go over very well. They, just like her family, would have to get used to it. He knew that his would support him no matter what. But Faith's? Hers was dysfunctional. There were no indications of physical abuse, but mental abuse was just as bad and left no outward signs. He thought about abuse statistics and her mother. She'd been married to Hollister McCabe for a few decades. What would that do to a person?

Ryder would find a way to shield his child. This

situation wasn't going away, and since the thought of losing the baby left a weird pain in his chest, he didn't want it to. Not that he would've picked this timing to have a child. Clearly, he'd had no plans before this surprise. He needed to get his head around how his life was about to change.

Four months.

Ryder could figure anything out in sixteen weeks.

"I don't see any reason why you can't go home once that bag is empty," the doctor said, pointing to the pole by her bed. How old was she? Twenty-two? Her credibility wasn't helped by the fact that she wore adult braces.

Faith tensed on the word *home*.

"Thank you," she said.

"I'll send someone in to check you out in a few minutes," Dr. Field said.

Out of courtesy, Ryder thanked the doctor before she left. It sure wasn't because he thought she knew what she was doing.

"You should see a real doctor when we get back to Bluff," he said in a low voice once he was sure the door was closed.

"What was she, like, sixteen?" Faith asked, a smile breaking out over white teeth.

"I wanted to ask what her SAT scores were and what she planned to do after high school graduation," he quipped, grateful for the break in tension. A lighter mood was welcome at this point. It had been one hell of a day, and his normally cool emotions were all over the map, not to mention the chemistry between them hadn't dimmed despite their circumstances.

The rest of the time spent while waiting for the IV

bag to drain went by fast. Checkout was speedy and the two were back on the road soon after.

Ryder had a lot on his mind, and the deeper they dug into Nicholas's disappearance, the more questions mounted. The two men who'd tried to abduct Faith were obviously hired by someone. Who? And again, why? He had to wonder what these men, and Hannah, could want from a fifteen-year-old boy. Ransom was the only thing that made sense, and he doubted that Hollister McCabe would pay anything for an illegitimate child. But then whoever took him might not know that.

"Where do we go now?" Faith asked.

"You? Home." There was going to be no argument over that one.

"I can't. Nicholas is still missing."

"Did you get a good look at the kidnappers? Can you describe them?"

"We can't go to police," she insisted. "They might hurt him."

"They didn't seem like the most skilled criminals or even like they'd thought their plan completely through when they snatched you," he said, eyes on the road ahead. "I keep going back to the same question. What do they stand to gain from taking Nicholas, and my mind keeps cycling back to the same response…money."

"Me, too. I mean, those guys were scary as all getout and strong. But they hear your name and are willing to let me go. I'm grateful, believe me, but I can't figure what that's all about," she said.

"It makes more sense now that I know there's someone else pulling the strings," Ryder said. "Those guys were only willing to go so far."

"Maybe they were just trying to scare me in order to stop me from investigating Nicholas's disappearance," she offered.

"That's possible," he said. "So, whoever's doing this doesn't know you very well."

"Then they most likely planned to release me all along. So I wasn't in as much danger as I—"

"Hold it right there," Ryder interrupted. "I see exactly where you're going with this and there's no way I'm standing by and watching you—"

"That's why I came to you," she said.

"We need to involve the law. I understand that you want to put Nicholas first—"

"Because he's in danger. I would do the same thing for this baby. Besides, Celeste is going to the sheriff to report Nicholas missing." Ryder wouldn't get far as long as her defenses were up.

"I get it. I do," he soothed, figuring he needed to take another tack. "Today has been a long day. You've barely been able to keep food down and the only reason you're hydrated is because you just spent an hour on an IV. If you're not ready to go home you can rest at the cabin. I'll keep working on finding Nicholas. You don't have to do this alone now, and I won't stop until I have answers. You have my word on that."

"Okay," Faith said, and his chest swelled with pride that his word meant something to her. "Take me to the cabin. I can't go home right now."

FAITH WOKE WITH a start. She sat up and glanced around, trying to get her bearings. The last thing she remembered was curling up on the couch at the cabin.

The clock on the mantel read eight forty-five. It was

dark outside. Her mouth was dry. And she needed to go to the bathroom. Another great pregnancy side effect was an almost constant need to use the restroom.

Her stomach cramped as she pushed off the oversize tan suede sofa. That had happened a lot in her first trimester and she'd called her doctor to make sure everything was okay. Into her second trimester, it'd stopped and she gave in to a moment of fear that something was wrong with the baby.

She checked outside and Ryder's truck was gone. Only her car was still there.

Keeping a positive attitude had gotten her through many dark days, and so she chose to think positively now, too. And that lasted right up until she saw the blood. There wasn't much. But it was enough to get her heart racing and cause fear to threaten to swallow her.

She needed to call Ryder and find out where he was.

By the time Faith made it back to the couch, she'd calmed herself down. Spotting was completely normal, and the cramp was gone. That had to be a good sign.

Instead of involving Ryder, she phoned her doctor's private line.

He picked up on the second ring.

She explained what had happened and he reassured her, as he had so many times in the first trimester, that it was most likely nothing. If it worsened, she was to go directly to the hospital. She thanked the doctor, grateful for the reassurance.

Despite being stressed, she was hungry. She moved into the kitchen. There was a note on the fridge from Ryder. *Food's in the fridge. Help yourself. I'll be back later.*

She found a few of her favorite things, including

fresh red apples and Greek yogurt. There was a box of graham crackers on the counter and a container of decaf coffee.

Thinking about how many times he'd "fixed" her breakfast—which basically meant half-burned toast, yogurt and fruit with a good cup of coffee—had her heart doing things she couldn't afford. She would always be a McCabe. He would always be an O'Brien. And there wasn't a bridge long enough to cover that gap.

It was getting late. Spending so much time with Ryder today had taken a toll. Every time he was close, her body was aware of his all-male presence. And since her increased hormone levels amplified all her senses, she felt even more attracted to him.

The sexual chemistry pinging between them could almost drive her to distraction. And her stubborn heart tried to tell her that her feelings for him had grown. It was probably for the best that he wasn't at the cabin. She'd driven her car to meet Ryder at the cabin early this morning, so she didn't have to wait for him to get a ride. She needed to get home to check on her mother. There were other things she needed to investigate at home, too, like her father's private study.

Chapter Seven

Faith slipped inside the back door at the ranch and took the rear staircase up to her room, thinking her life would've been far less complicated if she'd moved to the city after college instead of coming home to learn the family business and look after her mother— a mother who had her increasingly worried lately.

She went straight to her en suite bathroom and stripped off her clothes. Stepping into the shower, she felt the warm water sluicing over her sore body. She took her time washing off, giving herself permission not to think about her missing brother for a few minutes. *Or Ryder*, a little voice added.

She looked down at her growing stomach as she toweled off. Her pants no longer fit, and it wouldn't be long before her belly would be too big to cover and she'd have no choice but to tell her parents. A clean oversize T-shirt and pajama pants hid her small bump. *Not for long, little bean.*

Thankfully, there hadn't been any more spotting since earlier in the evening.

A quick mirror check, a little face powder and her scrapes and bruises were concealed fairly well. She'd left the door between her bedroom and bathroom cracked open and she cradled her stomach with one hand as she walked into her bedroom.

Her mother sat on the edge of her bed in the dark. Faith jumped and let out a little yelp.

"Sorry, sweetheart. I didn't mean to scare you," her mother said, sounding distant. That wasn't a good sign.

Faith's blood pressure hit triple time. *Breathe.*

"Everything okay, Mom?" she asked, dropping her hand to her side and praying that her mother hadn't noticed. Faith needed to find Nicholas and put the next phase of her plan into action—a plan that was far more complicated now that Ryder knew the truth.

"You didn't come home. I was worried," Mom said, embracing her in a tight hug. Her hands were so cold.

"I was out with friends." It wasn't exactly a lie. Although her heart would argue that she and Ryder had been so much more.

Mom's shoulders deflated.

"Have you seen your father?" Her mother stared at the wall.

"Not today. Why?" Faith turned on the soft light on her nightstand and then moved closer to her mother, dropping down by her side.

Her eyes carried dark circles as she sat there wringing her hands together.

"He's not home. Didn't make it to supper, either," she said, and she sounded on the verge of tears. With her mother so involved in her own situation Faith figured she was too distraught to notice any physical changes in her and was grateful.

Faith rubbed her mother's back. "It's okay. He'll be home. He's probably out with a business partner. You know, making another deal."

"Or maybe he's with that woman again," her mother said, sounding a little hysterical.

Faith stopped herself from asking which one.

"I'm sure he's just tied up with work, as usual." Faith hated lying. "I'll be dealing with the paperwork from his deals until the end of summer."

Her mother just sat there, her gaze fixed on a spot on the opposite wall.

"Come on. Let's get you ready for bed," Faith said, urging her mother to her feet. She was probably off her medication again. Faith would get an anxiety pill and tuck her mother into bed.

Her mother mumbled a few words that Faith didn't quite catch as she helped her into her pajamas.

"Stay right here, okay?" Faith asked, helping her to the massive four-poster bed she shared with Faith's father. The bed looked so grand and so…empty. Sadness fell like a curtain as she thought about how lonely her mother's life must be. And here, Faith was about to make it worse. She could only hope that her mother would be okay. Guilt assaulted her again at the thought of leaving her mother alone in a mentally abusive relationship.

The woman still looked distraught, and Faith wasn't sure if she could trust her mother to stay put. In her heightened emotional state, the last thing she needed to do was wander the house by herself. Anything could happen. Faith had found her mother curled up in a ball in a corner of the dining room, shaking, with only a light gown on in the dead of winter once. Faith had just turned twelve. There were other times, too. Once her mother had taken too much medication and wandered into the backyard. She'd fallen into the pool and if Faith's golden retriever, Sparks, hadn't barked, her mother would've drowned. She'd been too out of it to realize she was about to die.

Her mother's emotions had been overwrought lately, and she was a walking ball of nerves.

Shaking off the bad memories, Faith retrieved the bottle of little white pills from her mother's medicine cabinet and a glass of water from the sink.

"Here you go. Take this and he'll be home before you open your eyes," Faith soothed. How many times had she gone through this routine with her mother in the past year? Things were escalating, and Faith could only pray her mother would take the step and get help someday. Guilt hit her again at the thought of leaving the woman behind.

"He's coming home?" her mother asked, calmer after the medicine starting kicking in.

"That's right. He's on his way. All you have to do is close your eyes and when you open them again he'll be right next to you," Faith said. She sat with her mother until she fell asleep, thinking about how vibrant she'd been when Faith was young.

The thought of walking away, leaving her permanently, didn't sit well with Faith, but she would have no choice. How much longer could she get away with no one noticing her bump? Or realizing that she hadn't worn a pair of jeans in weeks even though it was cold outside? She'd barely managed to get through those first few months of feeling like she wanted to barf all the time without raising any red flags.

Luckily, her father worked outside most of the day and spent most of his evenings with "business partners." He had a huge office in the barn. He'd said it was to be close to his men so he could keep an eye on his workers.

Inside the house, he maintained a private study, and that door was almost always locked.

Faith glanced down at her mother. Hollister Mc-Cabe's love was toxic. Her eyes were closed and her breathing had changed to a steady rhythm. Faith tiptoed out of the room. She could've stomped and her mother wouldn't know the difference. And that broke Faith's heart.

Instead of going to her own room, she checked out front for her father's Suburban. It was gone. Rather than head back upstairs, she hooked a right and walked to the back of the house, to her father's study. She picked up the spare key that had been tucked inside the vase in the hall bath and unlocked the door.

If she'd thought, she would've brought her phone with her and turned on the flashlight app. As it was, she'd have to rely on the dim light from the hallway in case her father returned. The ranch was huge, and she wouldn't be able to hear him pull in. The wood paneling made the room even darker. Doubt crept in.

This was crazy. She couldn't see anything. She heard a noise in the hallway and her heart skipped a beat.

Her father wasn't home, she reminded herself. Her mother was asleep. The hired workers at the McCabe ranch all slept in separate bunks in the barns. Women who worked inside shared adjoining rooms in the horse barn. There was a foreman and several hired hands who slept in the second barn. Her brothers were almost never home this early. There shouldn't be anyone in the house but Faith and her mother. Their interaction left Faith unsettled and that's the reason she was jumpy.

Time was running out and she needed to make her move soon. All she needed was to find Nicholas. Then she could disappear.

She made sure to keep all the lights off in case someone came home. She had three brothers who would be quick to bust her if they found her in their dad's private study.

Her father's desk had a couple of stacks of paperwork on top. She fanned through the first stack, determined not to upset the documents. Most of those were bills and a few others were contracts marked with a Post-it note for his signature. There was nothing earth-shattering there. Although she had no idea what she was looking for. Even though she'd denied Ryder's accusations that her father could somehow be behind Nicholas's disappearance, he'd planted a seed in her mind that had taken root and she needed to know that her father wasn't somehow involved.

The possibility that Celeste could be the female involved died quickly. Celeste had taken care of Nicholas on her own with little money for fifteen years. She wouldn't use him to get back at Faith's father.

A noise sounded in the hallway and Faith froze. She hadn't heard her father's Suburban. Was there any possibility that her mother could be walking around?

She stood for a quiet moment until she was sure the coast was clear. She touched her belly, thinking how she would never put her own child through any of this mess.

The built-in set of drawers on the right-hand side of his desk held tax documents and titles of ownership for various pieces of property and equipment. The large drawer on the left had a few boxes of keepsakes, one from her grandfather. The middle drawer was locked. Faith felt around for a key but didn't find one. No, her father wouldn't be careless enough to keep a key so close. *Especially not if he has something inside that drawer that he doesn't want people to find,* a voice in the back of her mind said. She dismissed it as letting Ryder influence her too much.

She pulled out a hairpin and played around with the lock, listening for the *snick* that said she'd hit the right spot to release the mechanism. Living with three brothers had taught her to be resourceful, especially when it came to getting inside their rooms when she needed something. All three boys locked their doors, and part of her had wondered why all the secrecy. So many secrets.

The sound she was waiting for came and with it a jolt of pride for still being able to get the job done as needed. The temporary feeling was replaced with guilt. Was she stooping to her father's level of distrust? Becoming just like him and the boys?

She shuddered at the thought.

Faith rejected the notion that she was anything like her father and the three McCabe brothers. She was like her half brother Nicholas, and she would go to any length to find him even if it meant violating her father's sacred space.

Faith took in a breath and opened the drawer. On top was a legal document. She scanned the page to figure out what it was. A lawsuit? She used her finger to guide her way down the middle of the page looking for the complaint.

There it was in bold letters. He was being sued for paternity, but it wasn't Celeste being named as the complainant. Faith didn't even recognize this woman's name, but apparently her father might have another son. The boy was three years old and the complaint was filed a year ago. Faith was certain that her father's lawyer would get him out of this one just as sure as he'd gotten out of paying Nicholas's mother.

A heavy feeling settled on Faith's chest. Did her mother know about any of these children? She must.

The complainant was a waitress in a café in Louisiana, according to the paperwork. He traveled all over the South and Southwest. Did he leave a string of children and desperate mothers behind? One desperate enough to come after one of his children for revenge?

Faith didn't want to acknowledge this side of her father, this smooth-talking jerk who used women. And yet the documents were staring her in the face, quashing those moments in her childhood when she'd looked up to him for being a smart businessman and a doting father.

She touched her stomach again as a few tears rolled down her cheeks. Her child would never know this kind of pain. The hormones had her ready to cry at a TV commercial if it pulled the right heartstrings, and something about this whole scenario had her missing Ryder. There was something about his presence that made her feel wanted, safe.

Shuffling through the folders inside the drawer mostly made her sad. Sad that this family wasn't enough for her father. Sad for the kids who would grow up without support, alone. Sad for the mothers who'd have to work extra hours. She wiped away the tears and refocused. Was there anything in here about Nicholas?

Rechecking the folders, she caught a piece of paper sticking out from in between two manila folders near the top of the small stack.

Her finger dragged across the name Nicholas Bowden. There it was in plain sight. A report about Nicholas. His whereabouts. His hangouts. There were photos, too.

Faith's heart dropped and her pulse raced. Because there were pictures of the two of them together.

"Find what you're looking for, Faith?" her father's voice boomed from the doorway.

There was no point in trying to lie her way out of this one.

"How many are there, Father?" She picked up the small stack of files. He'd know full well what she was talking about. "Half a dozen? More?"

"Nothing in my private study is of concern to you," her father said, flipping on the light.

"Everything about this family is just as much my business as it is yours." She held the stack toward him. She tried to use sheer willpower to stop her hands from shaking, but it was no use. "Why don't we wake up Mom and see if she shares your opinion?"

The fire in her father's eyes nearly knocked her back a step.

"You leave your mother out of this or I'll see to it that you never see her again," he fired back. The anger in his voice sent an icy chill down her spine. He meant every word of that threat. Little did he know she was about to disappear on her own.

She'd known her father was dishonest and that he

cheated on her mother, but she had no idea the extent of the damage. Part of her didn't want to know, either. Had she put her head in the sand in order to avoid the humiliation?

Yes. Guilt nipped at her.

"Where's Nicholas?" She stood her ground even though everything inside her was screaming to run, to get out of there or hide.

"Leave it alone, Faith."

"I can't. He's innocent and he's a good kid," she kept pushing.

"He's someone else's bastard and he'll never be a McCabe." His angry words were like hot pokers searing her. The little balloon of hope that her father was a better man than this popped, leaving pieces of her heart scattered on the floor.

"Well, then maybe he'll have a chance at a decent life if you have your goons let him go." She threw the accusation out there again to see if it would stick. Her father hadn't exactly denied knowing about Nicholas's disappearance.

"I already told you to stay out of this. What happens to that boy doesn't concern you," he said again, which wasn't a denial of his involvement.

"Is he hurt?" she was shouting now. She stomped across the room and got in her father's face. "What did you do to him?"

"Me?" His brows knit in confusion. "I didn't *do* anything to the boy, and I won't tolerate being blackmailed, either." Fiery darts shot from his glare.

"If you didn't do it, then who?" she managed to say through her blinding anger. The word *blackmail* registered somewhere in the back of her mind.

"I want nothing to do with that boy," he said bitterly. "And I don't have the first idea who's behind all this. I don't care, either. But know this—I don't give a hoot what they do to the child."

"There will be consequences to your actions," she said as she stomped past him. He caught her by the arm.

"Like what? Are you threatening me, little girl?" he said as he squeezed.

"I'm not your little girl," she said, trying to jerk free from his grasp and failing.

"You won't be if you keep messing with that bastard," he ground out. For a split second, she thought he was talking about Ryder. And then she remembered that her father had no problem calling his own son by the derogatory term.

"You're hurting me." She looked into her father's eyes, searching for something. Compassion…love… regret. Anything from the man she used to look up to as a child, used to love. His steel eyes were cold. There was nothing soft or kind left of the man who'd bounced her on his knee.

"No bastard children will ever be recognized as a McCabe." The words were like bullets being fired at her.

She jerked her arm free and pushed past her father. "Is that right? Well, know this. I'm going to find him and do whatever I can to help. And you better not get in my way."

"Leave it alone," he threatened, shouting after her. "Or you're the one who'll deal with consequences."

Her father shouted curses and threats as she made her way back to her room, threw on some clothing, grabbed her purse and keys and then shot out the door.

Tears flooded her eyes as she slid behind the driver's

seat and buckled up. She had no doubt that he'd deliver on his threats if she didn't walk away from Nicholas. And she'd never been more certain that he'd turn his back on her the second he found out about the baby she was carrying.

A few deep breaths calmed her enough to stop crying. One more gave her the boost she needed to start her car and drive away. She needed to get as far away from the ranch and her father as possible. Nicholas had been taken for ransom that her father had refused to pay. Fear gripped her. She couldn't allow herself to think that she was too late to save her brother.

The minute she found Nicholas—and she would find him—she needed to get him and her baby out of town and far away. All three of them could start fresh in the quaint house in Michigan that she'd purchased using a dummy company that she'd set up out of her Cayman bank account.

The paperwork to change her last name to her mother's maiden name was almost finalized. Faith had planned this new life for her and her baby, and now she would include Nicholas.

The first phase of her plan was in place.

At this point, she would welcome being kicked out of the family. *What family?* she asked herself through blinding tears. What kind of family treated each other like this? There was no love, just expectations and heartache.

The thought of leaving her mother alone to fend for herself ate at Faith. If she was going to be allowed to stay in contact with her mother, she could never allow the true paternity of her baby to be known. If she had to plead with Ryder to keep her secret, she would.

Faith still hadn't figured out how she was going to handle the situation with Ryder. Part of her, the part that had known she had to tell him all along, was relieved that her secret was out in the open with him. Ryder was a good man and he deserved to know. That fact had warred with the reality that she lived in. The one in which her father's realization would be harmful and toxic to everyone involved.

Could she tell Ryder about her Michigan plan? She wiped away a tear that rolled down her cheek. Maybe they could figure out a way for him to visit the baby without the entire town knowing their business. She held on to that hope as she pulled down the gravel lane.

The fishing cabin was blacked out. Her heart sank at the realization there was no sign of Ryder's truck. It was probably for the best since she didn't need another emotional complication, even if part of her brain argued that being with him was so much better than being without him. Faith parked near the front door. Her headlights would time out automatically in sixty seconds, so she made a mad dash for the cabin.

Exhaustion started wearing on her as she crossed the threshold, closing and locking the door behind her. Pregnancy exacerbated everything. Her need for Ryder felt a thousand times stronger because of her hormones.

And then there was the issue of not getting enough good-quality sleep lately. Her mind was spent, her bones tired. So she let herself think about Ryder and how amazing she'd felt in this very spot not so long ago with his arms curled around her, their legs in a tangle. And the feel of his warm breath against her neck as he feathered kisses there.

RYDER STARED AT the ceiling. It was two o'clock in the morning and he hadn't had any shut-eye. Activities at the ranch would pick up in a few short hours. All he could think about was Faith and if she was okay. She'd disappeared without leaving a note. He'd texted her and she responded with one word. *Home.*

And tonight, the thing that was on his mind the most as he lay in bed unable to sleep was how much he missed being with her, holding her, feeling like she belonged with him—*to him,* a rebellious part of his brain interjected.

Her soft skin, the way her body molded to his…

He threw off the covers and pulled on his jeans, needing to get out and clear his head.

Standing on his back porch, looking up at the open sky he loved so much, brought no peace tonight. The fact that Ryder was going to be a father hit hard, but not for the reasons he'd suspected. He'd thought there'd be regret—not normally something in his vocabulary—and was surprised when there wasn't a hint of it. He'd need to make a lot of adjustments in his life to be ready for a little one, but the idea itself was starting to take hold. The thing that bothered him was that he'd never have the chance to introduce his child to his parents.

Getting through the holidays without them had been brutal, even for a tough bunch like the O'Briens. Hitting a major milestone like this—becoming a father— and realizing they wouldn't be around for any of it had him gripping the wood railing overlooking his yard so hard his knuckles were white. Texas, this land, was a piece of his soul. And yet even the land he loved couldn't settle his anguish or lessen his pain.

Being here at the ranch without them was hard. Reminders of the two of them were everywhere, even on the porch his mother had insisted on helping decorate. Her touches could be seen in the Kyra Jenkins wildlife bronze sculpture behind his coffee-colored sofa and the matching hand towels in his guest bath. He should've reined her in on that last one, but she'd been beside herself when she'd brought them over. She'd done a good job and his house was cozy. Someday, all of those reminders of her might bring comfort. Now they just made him feel hollowed out.

There was a different feeling settling in his chest since Faith had returned. He was more at ease and yet he couldn't sort out the reason. Not much had changed. His parents' killer hadn't been brought to justice. And yet the hole in his chest was less cavernous. Did that have to do with learning he was going to be a father? Ryder had thought about telling his brothers about the baby Faith was carrying and decided against it. He wasn't ready to talk about it with them, not until he and the mother of his child sorted out important details like how they were going to handle the news with her family. Complicated didn't begin to cover the journey they were about to be on. Speaking of Faith, the thought of her being at the McCabe ranch sat like scalding coffee on his tongue.

It was the middle of the night. He should be tired. Instead, his mind raced. There was no way he was going to be able to go back to sleep now. He didn't want to be on the ranch tonight.

Within five minutes he was on the road, and twenty minutes after that he was pulling up at the fishing cabin.

Faith's car was parked out front and relief flooded

him. Ryder stomped the brake. He should turn around and go back home. It was late and his mind played tricks on him, tricks that had him thinking that he wanted to feel her in his arms again, to find that same comfort he'd found there after learning about his parents.

All the lights were out, so he figured she was asleep. He should give her the cabin.

On second thought, someone had tried to kidnap her earlier. It might have been a scare tactic, as she wanted to believe. She'd said the guys who'd taken her didn't want to get on the wrong side of the O'Brien family. So those guys wouldn't likely make a second attempt. Didn't exactly mean she was safe. Whoever sent them could've hired someone else to finish the job by now. Then there was the issue of her father. Ryder didn't trust Hollister McCabe. And he couldn't shake the feeling that the man was somehow involved in Nicholas's disappearance.

Instead of making a U-turn, Ryder pulled into the spot next to hers and parked.

Protecting his child was the reason Ryder told himself that he'd parked his truck and was heading inside. And not because he needed to see Faith.

Chapter Eight

Ryder closed the bedroom door and then made a pot of coffee using the light on the vent hood in order to see in the small kitchen. Knowing that Faith was sleeping in the next room played havoc with his pulse but was so much better than before when she'd left without a note. She still had that effect on him, the one that had him wanting to touch her soft skin and get lost in her fresh-after-a-spring-rain flowers-and-sunshine scent.

How many times had they slept twisted in the sheets with their bodies fused together in that very room? Exhaustion from making love sometimes two or three times in a row having zapped their energy and forced them to finally give in to sleep.

The memories were burned into his brain not just because the sex was mind-blowing—it was. Sex couldn't be this good with anyone else because he felt a connection to Faith that he'd never experienced with another woman. Sex was sex. The physical act was always good. No woman before Faith had ever fit his body the way she had. He'd never felt as content afterward with anyone else, either. And that had a lot to do with what happened in between rounds. Faith was easy to talk to. She was smart and had a quirky sense of humor. It didn't hurt that she was beautiful. She was just as attractive when she was fresh from the shower and her hair was pulled back in a loose ponytail, maybe even more so, than when she was all done up.

Thinking about their past and the times they'd spent together under this very roof stirred areas that didn't need to be awake at this hour and especially without the prospect of release. His body was keenly aware of her being in the next room.

Ryder took a sip of black coffee, hoping it would clear his thoughts and steer him away from the dangerous territory he was dipping into. It was the past, and best left far behind. They had a new reality to deal with. Five days of Nicholas missing.

The door to the bedroom opened and Faith stood there, wearing only one of his old T-shirts like she'd done countless times. His heart stirred at the same time blood flew south, awakening areas he'd have to work to ignore.

"I hope it's okay that I came back here," she said. Her voice had that low sleepy quality that was enough to tip him over the edge and make him want things he shouldn't. Another thing he couldn't afford to notice right now, since his better judgment had hit the trail, was how sexy her hair was when it was tousled and loose around her shoulders. Or how long and silky her legs were.

"I'm glad you did." Ryder took another sip of hot coffee, focusing on the warm burn on his throat. Holding his mug kept his fingers busy. And that was good because they wanted to do things that would get him into more trouble, like tangle in her hair and haul her body against his.

"You were right about my father," she said, taking a few tentative steps toward him. Her voice cracked like she was on the verge of tears.

And that was enough to dampen any sexual thoughts he'd been having. It was just as well. He forced his gaze away from the V that fell over her full breasts, exposing just enough skin for him to be able to remember planting kisses along that trail a few short months ago. Her breathing was erratic, and he felt electricity ping between them as she joined him in the small kitchen despite the fact that she was about to cry.

"You want a cup of coffee?" he asked, tamping down his own inappropriate thoughts.

"No, thanks. I can't." Her hand went to her stomach.

Right. He hadn't really thought about how much she'd already had to sacrifice for the pregnancy. How much more she'd be sacrificing when she had the baby. Her father would disown her for sleeping with an O'Brien. He'd cut her off financially in a heartbeat.

Not a problem, Ryder thought. He had enough money to take care of her and their child. It was just as much his doing as it was hers that she was in this situation, and no child of his would want for any necessities.

She stepped past him and his nose filled with her scent as she pulled a glass out of the cupboard. Ryder tried not to notice her sweet bottom or the silky-smooth skin of her thighs when the T-shirt rode up.

He forced himself to look in the other direction. It took considerable effort. She filled the glass with water from the sink and turned around to face him.

The two were in close proximity because the kitchen was built for one.

"Did you find something in his office?" he asked, needing to redirect his thoughts.

"He knows about Nicholas's disappearance, won't pay ransom, and I have no idea how I'm going to find my brother now. We had a confrontation," she said. "He doesn't care about my brother."

Talking about Hollister McCabe was sobering enough to quell any sexual thoughts Ryder had been having.

"Tell me what happened," he said, motioning toward the couch.

She shook her head, pacing in the small area between the kitchen and the living room instead.

"He caught me in his office and we exchanged a few heated words," she said. "I can't go home again."

"What makes you think you can't go back?" Ryder was relieved because he didn't want her there.

"He threatened me." Her gaze dropped down to her stomach and bounced up again. "It's no longer safe for me or the baby."

His grip tightened on the handle of his coffee mug and he clenched his jaw. At least she had that part right. Ryder didn't want his child anywhere near Hollister McCabe. "What did he say about Nicholas?"

"That he had no plans to give in to blackmail. He called Nicholas a bastard." She paced faster. "Can you believe that?"

Sadly, he could. That, and so much more about the senior McCabe. He wondered how Faith had turned out so normal given the family she'd grown up in. Her three brothers were trouble, and her mother seemed like a fragile woman the few times he'd seen her in town.

"I'm sorry." He could tell that she loved Nicholas

and he knew how much her father's rejection would hurt her.

"I mean, can you even imagine?" she asked, her voice rising in anger. "It's his own son and yet he called him a bastard. And Nicholas is the only good brother I have."

Becoming upset wouldn't be good for her or the baby. Ryder needed to figure out a way to calm her down…

Nothing immediately came to mind, since he'd never been much of a talker. So he pulled her into his arms.

"I know," he said, trying to soothe the frustration making her heart beat so rapidly against his chest. The man needed to be in jail, and yet he couldn't voice his opinion out loud. He could already see that it was hard enough for her to realize that her father wasn't the man she'd hoped he was.

Faith leaned into him and she looked up into his eyes. He sensed the second her body became aware of being fused with his.

Ryder should let go and back away slowly, because this situation was a powder keg. Logic flew out the window with common sense as she pressed harder against him. The feel of her full breasts against his chest spiked his blood pressure in an all too familiar way. He let his hands drop to her waist and then encircled her with his arms. No matter what else he felt toward her, Faith was a beautiful woman. Even more so now.

Her hands came up, palms flat against his chest. He wasn't sure if she was going to push him away, but his answer came in the form of her fists closing around his shirt and tugging him toward her. He was already hard and his erection strained against the zipper of his jeans as he breathed in her fresh-April-shower scent, all flowers and warmth.

He should probably stop himself before this went too far, or ask her if she thought this was really a good idea. He didn't do either. Instead, he dipped his head down and pressed his mouth against hers—something he'd been wanting to do far too long and had been denied. Her lips were soft against his, molding to his.

She raised her hands, tunneling her fingers into his hair. He brought his up, his fingers curling around the base of her neck, positioning her so he could really kiss her. In the space of one deep breath, her lips parted and his tongue slid inside her mouth. The taste of her, honey and mint, crashed down around him as memory merged with the here and now. How long had he been needing to do this?

Too long.

And that damn question resurfaced as to whether or not this was a good idea. Ryder had to force restraint, so he put a little physical space in between them first. That he could do easily because he didn't want to do anything that might hurt the baby growing in her stomach. Primal urge had him wanting to rip off her T-shirt and panties, lift her onto the counter, and drive his pulsing erection deep inside her. Her hands were all over him, roaming his arms and back. She was driving him insane with need.

But would it somehow hurt the baby?

With all the effort he could muster, he pulled back. "Faith—"

"Don't say it," she said breathlessly.

"You don't think this is a question we need to ask ourselves before…?"

"No. I don't." Faith crossed her arms, grabbed the hem of the T-shirt she wore and pulled it over her head. She let it go and it tumbled to the kitchen floor. Next, she shimmied out of her pale blue panties, and that nearly did Ryder in. She stood there, arms at her sides. There was enough light for him to see every curve of her body clearly. Her breasts were fuller than before, her hips a little more round, and he suspected that the changes had to do with the pregnancy. Her body had been beautiful before but he found her even sexier with a few more curves.

She was close enough for him to see her pulse pound wildly at the base of her throat. His groin strained as he took in her form. His gaze slid down her body, pausing at the small strip of hair at her mound.

"Don't just look at me. I'm right here. I want you to touch me, Ryder." She took a step toward him, cutting the space between them in half. Her delicate skin was flushed with desire and her honey-brown eyes glittered with need.

"You know I won't be able to hold back if you take one more step toward me," he warned, and it was more for him than her. Of course, he would stop at any point if she told him to or gave him a sign that she wasn't absolutely certain this was a good idea.

"Give me one good reason we shouldn't do this," she said, that defiance he loved about her twinkling in her eyes.

"The baby," he said.

"You can't hurt it, if that's what you're worried about," she said with confidence.

"How do you know?" He wasn't so sure.

"I've been going to the library and reading everything I can get my hands on about being pregnant, and that topic is more than covered. Didn't think I'd need to know any of it until right now," she said, her tone a low, sexy note. But then, he'd always liked the sound of her voice. His gaze roamed all over her throat, thinking of all the times he'd feathered kisses there. "At least, I hope I need to know that now."

She took another step toward him. Now she was so close that he could reach out and touch her. So he did. He took her by the hand and walked her into the bedroom.

By the time he turned around, her hands were already on the fastener of his jeans. He shrugged out of his shirt and then helped her with his pants. Those landed in a pile on the floor along with his boxers.

And then their mouths fused as hands roamed. He cupped her breast, and he could feel her nipple bead against his palm as she gasped. He rolled her nipple between his thumb and forefinger, and she released a sexy moan against his lips.

Her hands were all over his chest and then his arms, his back.

He followed the curve of her hip until her sweet bottom was in his hand. She ground her sex against his.

He had the fleeting thought that he should pull a condom from his side table. Guess it was a little too late for that. The thought of being inside her without a barrier between them sent a thrill rocketing through his body. He wanted to feel her silky skin.

They stood in the bedroom, moonlight streaming around them. He started with her lips and then roamed down, planting a trail of kisses along her chin. He was prepared to take his time even though his body hummed with an urgent need for release.

"I don't think so," she said, tugging him onto the bed. She had other ideas about the pace.

He supported his weight with his knees and arms as she wrapped her legs around his midsection. Her fingers curled around his erection, and he had to refocus so this whole thing didn't end before it even got interesting.

She guided his tip inside her, his tongue plunging in her sweet mouth as his erection dipped into her sweet heat. Her body tensed and he immediately pulled out.

"What's wrong?" He searched her face for signs of pain, panic beating his chest.

"Nothing. It feels a little too good. I told you that pregnancy hormones intensify everything, didn't I?"

"Yes." He remembered that she did.

"Well, I've been thinking about doing this with you for months, Ryder." Her hand was already guiding him back inside her…home. "You have no idea how much I need this."

Now it was his turn to tense. She was already wet for him. He eased his length inside with a groan as he teased her heat. He went as slowly as he could manage under the circumstances.

She stretched around him and he nearly exploded.

She matched his stride, stroke for stroke, until they worked into a frenzy of heated breaths.

And then she detonated around him, her body clenching and releasing, so he rode to the edge. He let himself think about how amazing she felt with that silky skin squeezing him.

With a final thrust, his entire body tensed and he exploded inside her.

She felt so damn good.

He didn't pull out right away as his erection pulsed until every last drop drained.

It might've been a costly mistake to look in her eyes right then, but he did it anyway. And he saw something mirrored in them that looked a lot like love.

Rather than overanalyze the emotion coursing through him, Ryder rolled onto his back and pulled Faith close. She fit perfectly as she turned on her side and threw her leg over his. Her head rested on his chest and his heart clutched.

This was going to hurt later.

For now, he planned to let himself get lost in the moment.

FAITH WOKE TO the smell of breakfast cooking in the kitchen. She stirred, a little sore from last night but the happiest she'd been since walking away from Ryder three and a half months ago.

Hadn't she told her father last night that there'd be consequences to his actions? She was going to try not to eat those words after spending the night in Ryder's arms. If she was going to go through with her plan, she needed some emotional distance.

There was no way she could let her brain go there… where it was trying to make sex with Ryder a bad thing. It wasn't. Sex with that man was nothing short of amazing. But she could be honest enough to realize that it was also a dangerous thing even if she couldn't allow herself to regret it.

She also knew that it couldn't happen again. Not under any circumstances.

Chapter Nine

"Sit. I'll make something to eat," Ryder said after telling Faith good morning. He handed her a cup of decaf.

"Since when did you start cooking?" Faith asked as she took the offering.

He'd already had the talk with himself this morning that sex was just that, sex. They both needed to blow off steam last night—and they did a damn good job of it—and it was the best way to stem the attraction between them that was driving them both to distraction. There was no way they could have sex again.

"Take a seat." He pointed to the small table and chair.

She did.

"I woke up thinking about what my father said last night," she said. "If he's being blackmailed and he doesn't care about what they're threatening him with, where does that leave Nicholas?"

"Good question. You won't like the first thing that pops into my head if I say it," he said, placing bread in the toaster.

"No. I won't. Because it's the same thing I'm thinking," she replied, and then took a sip of coffee.

"We need to figure out who is behind this," he said.

"Or I could just let them take me. Maybe that's why the guys were trying to kidnap me the other day. Whoever is in charge didn't get the leverage they expected with Nicholas so they decided to up the ante with an actual McCabe. I'm sure they'd take me to wherever Nicholas is being held," she said.

"Absolutely not. No way." He stopped what he was doing long enough to stare at her. "Don't even think about it."

"But he might be in trouble. Maybe I can help," she offered.

"Or maybe you can get all three of you killed."

She drew back with a pained reaction.

"I'm sorry. I'm not trying to be a jerk." Ryder didn't want to be so direct, but he needed her to make herself and the baby top priority.

"I know," she said quietly. "I would never do anything to hurt the little bean."

"If anyone goes in, it's going to be me," he said. "Promise me that you won't do anything without talking it over with me first and giving me a chance to figure out a better move."

She sat there for a long moment thinking. He wasn't sure if she realized that her hand came down over her stomach, but he took it as a good sign.

"You're right, Ryder. I won't be stupid," she said.

"You couldn't be. You're too smart for that. But I could see you running in to save him without taking your own life into consideration," he said. "Your heart is too big and you put yourself last."

"But it's not just my life anymore, is it?" It wasn't really a question, so he didn't answer.

"I keep thinking about my mom. How she's endured

so much from my father over the years. It's no wonder she relies on pills. She's been even more anxious lately, and I can understand why. Living with my father has to be getting to her."

Ryder grabbed the pieces of toast as soon as they popped up and then put a dollop of butter on each. "You liked it this way at the restaurant the other morning."

She nodded, smiling.

And that shouldn't make him feel proud of himself for putting a little sunshine on her face.

"I know your mother isn't like him. But you can't give up your life for hers. She made a choice to live with him and you're not responsible for that decision," he said.

Faith took a bite of the toast being offered and chewed on it.

"It's just hard because I've always been her safety net," she said. "Without me, she has nothing. She's the reason I came back from college to live here. I had no plans to stay in Bluff."

"Oh, yeah? Where would you go?" He couldn't imagine not living in Texas.

"There's this place up north that I fell in love with one summer. It's a small town in Michigan on the lake."

"You mean you didn't want to come back here for me?" He pretended that she'd just knifed him in the chest.

And that made her laugh.

That was the second time that morning his chest felt full. As it was, he needed to keep the mood as light as possible, especially since he didn't want her thinking she needed to run off and be valiant. He'd take finding Nicholas seriously but he didn't want her worrying. That wouldn't be good for her or the baby.

"Cut it out. The place actually reminds me of your ranch in a weird way. Everyone's friendly and neighbors know each other. I'm not haunted by my last name there, so no one treats me differently because I'm a McCabe. Not like here in Bluff." She said the last part under her breath.

"People treat you diff—"

She shot him a look before he could finish.

Of course they did. Even he'd had preconceived ideas about her because of her last name. "I never thought about that before. That must've been hard for you growing up in a town so biased against your family. The bias isn't for no reason, though."

"Of course not. I can see my father for the person he is now. All hope he was a better man came crashing down around me last night. Plus, pretty much everyone around here wants to be an O'Brien," she shot back, and he could tell that she was only half joking. "My best friend in high school was Susan Hanover, remember?"

"I never understood the two of you being friends after I got to know you better," he said. "She was always so manipulative, and that made me think you were the same."

"How many friends do you think a McCabe has in Bluff?" she asked, like he should've figured that out already. "It wasn't exactly easy growing up here with my family name. Don't get me wrong. We didn't go hungry and I'm grateful for small miracles. Plus, I had no idea what my father was truly capable of back then so I thought we were being targeted unfairly." She blew out a burst of air. "Little did I know."

She had a point. It must've been hard to grow up the only decent McCabe, and that was probably the reason she felt so close to Nicholas and protective of her mother. Ryder was beginning to have a better understanding of why she was so motivated to help out her little brother. "I'm gathering that you and Nicholas share a special connection."

"He's the most like me. The only brother I have anything in common with," she said. "I now know that there are others out there based on what I saw last night. I have no idea how many or who they are but there are more."

"One step at a time, okay?" he asked, seeing that her stress levels were picking up again. He pulled on all his self-discipline to keep a little distance between them and not repeat last night.

"I heard about what Susan did to Dallas," she said.

"Trying to peg him as the father of her son to keep her boy safe was wrong on every level, but I can understand a mother's desperate need to protect her child," he said.

"The funny thing that she didn't realize was that all she would've had to do was ask any one of you for help and you would've done whatever you could. It's just the way O'Briens are built," she said, and his chest filled with pride at the admiration in her voice.

"Susan doesn't think like a normal person," he said. "And I'm not a knight in shining armor. I've been a jerk plenty of times when I should've been a shoulder to lean on instead."

His cell phone buzzed.

"I have no idea who this is," he said when he checked the screen.

"Do you have any news?" the familiar voice started, and Ryder knew right away who was on the line.

"It's Celeste," Ryder said to Faith, holding his hand over the mouthpiece.

"Why did you take off the other day?" he asked Celeste.

"I was done talking. I reported Nicholas as missing, like you said," she responded. "Have you found out anything on my boy?" Lack of sleep and worry deepened her voice. She had that low smoker's quality and he figured stress had her doubling up on cigarettes.

"We're still digging around, but we know very little," he said. "We believe that a girl by the name of Hannah was recruited to target him at a place called Wired."

When no hint of recognition came, he added, "Here, let me put you on speaker so we can both explain."

"Is *she* there right now?" Celeste said.

"Yes."

"I didn't call to talk to her," she said bitterly.

"Okay. Just me and you, then," he said, not wanting to scare her off. "Wired is a gaming center where the kids go to connect and play popular computer games."

That must've sounded familiar because she grunted an acknowledgment. He nodded toward Faith, who was leaned forward with all her attention on him.

"The sheriff said he'd let me know if they found anything. Nothing so far." She sucked in a burst of air. "Sheriff said he can sometimes find missing kids using something about a satellite and a chip in phones. He didn't have no luck with Nicholas's. Sheriff also said that Nicholas hasn't used his phone since eight o'clock the night he went missing."

Ryder shook his head. Faith nodded that she understood there was no good news.

"Like we said before. Most teenagers wouldn't be caught without their cell phones," he said.

"And especially not Nicholas. I used to tease him all the time that that smartphone thing was going to grow out of his fingers when he slept." She sniffed back a tear.

"Faith discovered someone is blackmailing her father in connection with Nicholas's disappearance," Ryder said.

Faith shot him a look that said she wasn't happy with him for telling Celeste.

He'd deal with that in a minute. Celeste had a right to know.

"Figures that jerk would be tied up with this somehow," she said, the anger in her voice booming through the speaker.

"He's not behind it," he said. "We know that for certain."

"But he don't care about Nicholas. That boy could be dead for all Hollister would care. In fact, I'd go one further and say that it would do him a favor for Nicholas to be out of the picture. Then he wouldn't have to worry about me coming after him for support."

"Have you tried recently?" he asked, just in case.

"Not since Nicholas was a baby. Once I figured out that Hollister was just using me I didn't want anything else to do with him or his money. This may sound stupid but he told me that he was going to leave his wife for me. Made all kinds of promises that he probably made to every woman he wanted." There was a wistful and wise quality to her voice now. And Ryder suspected she was on point with all counts.

"Think we can swing by and check out Nicholas's room later?" he asked, hoping they'd find a clue there.

A long pause came across the line.

"I've been over his room and didn't find nothing," Celeste said on a heavy sigh.

"Fresh eyes might help," he said.

Another few seconds passed without a response.

"I guess letting you look around wouldn't hurt. The sheriff's already checked over it and didn't find anything," she conceded. "He didn't say I couldn't let anyone else have a look at it."

"I'd still like the chance," he countered, thinking that it might be time to bring in extra help in the form of a private investigator. Five days missing with no word wasn't a good sign.

"I go in to work at eight. You can come by before then. Just *you*. There's no room for a McCabe in my house," she said, leaving no room for question. "They've done enough to mess up my life."

"Just me," he repeated so that Faith could hear. If it were up to him, he'd bring her with him. He wasn't calling the shots and might just get lucky and find something that could lead them to Hannah or, better yet, Nicholas. But based on Celeste's tone when she talked about any McCabe, Ryder knew better than to push the issue of asking if Faith could go with him. Besides, he couldn't be sure she wouldn't offend Celeste again. Those two women together were fire and gasoline. Maybe he could help smooth some of that over for Faith and figure out a way for them to forge some kind of bond when Nicholas was home safe.

Celeste didn't say goodbye. She just ended the call. Her defenses were up.

"Of course she'll let you come and not me." Faith blew out a frustrated breath. She stood up and then started pacing. "You know, it might be her blackmailing my father for money since he refused support all those years ago."

"Yeah, I thought about that, which is why I asked. She said no. I believe her. I mean, why now?" he asked. "Plus, that doesn't explain the note."

"I don't know how a crazy person thinks," she shot back. "And she could've sent him off to camp for a week and written that herself. What mother doesn't notify the sheriff when her child goes missing?"

Faith was hitting on territory that Ryder didn't want to go over again. It was a dead end. Celeste wasn't involved.

"It might be best if you stay here and get some rest anyway," he said. "I won't stick around any longer than I have to."

Faith flashed her eyes at him. "I hope not. She's a black widow, that woman."

What was going on there? Was she jealous?

He couldn't afford to let himself feel the burst of pride. His new mantra was *stay objective* when it came to Faith. The baby deserved that much from both of them, and getting too attached would only muddy the waters. *Good one, O'Brien.* Like sleeping with her hadn't already done that. He told himself that it wasn't too late to salvage a friendship between them. Anything else had *disaster* stamped all over it. He had no plans to walk into that trap again no matter how right it had felt at the time. And it had felt damn right.

Of course it had. Faith was gorgeous. She was easy to talk to. He liked joking around with her. Naturally, mind-blowing sex would follow. His groin tightened thinking about it. And since there was no chance of a repeat, he said, "I'm going to take a shower. We can talk more when I get out."

WHEN RYDER STEPPED into the kitchen wearing jeans hung low on his hips and no shirt, Faith was determined not to watch a couple stray rivulets of water rolling down his muscled chest. Her fingers stretched, remembering the feel of his skin from last night. She forced her gaze away. Memories were as close as she planned to get to that toned, athletic, silk-over-steel body of his from here on out. Anything else was tempting kerosene with a lit match.

"Thunderstorm's coming," she warned, having checked her phone while he was in the shower. "They're saying it might be a bad one."

"Truck should be okay," he said, gulping down a glass of water in the kitchenette.

"Hope it doesn't get too bad. Route 453 might wash out." She didn't need to remind him there was only one way to the fishing cabin and one way out.

"I'll check before I head back home," he said, his voice a sea of calm.

Meanwhile, she hoped he couldn't hear her heart thundering. Not knowing if Nicholas was okay had her pulse making double time. And then there was Ryder. He'd always had that effect on her. Even when they were teenagers and he acted like he had no idea who she was. That was the only explanation for him smiling at her in the halls. No one else ever did that.

"Be careful out there just in case," she said.

He checked his phone. "Shouldn't be too bad. Believe me, I've driven through worse."

FAITH LOOKED AROUND for a magazine to read in order to pass the time. There were none. She played around on her phone, checking Nicholas's social media pages for the umpteenth time. Waiting for Ryder to return from Celeste's house was worse than watching paint dry.

She glanced down at her belly. A little boredom was worth it for this little bean growing inside her. Unless stress with no foreseeable outlet could actually kill a person, which felt like a very real consideration at the moment.

Now she was just getting punchy.

The sun was starting to fade. It got dark by seven thirty this time of year. Celeste's place was nearly an hour away, and Ryder had said that she left for work at seven thirty for an eight o'clock shift. He'd said that he would call as soon as he could and that he didn't want to upset Celeste by walking through her house with a cell phone glued to his ear.

She'd known he might be back late when he'd gone out and brought back groceries before he left. He'd offered to pick up takeout but Faith had refused. She'd needed something to do, and cooking dinner was busywork even though she didn't know how to make much more than soup and a sandwich.

Her mind wasn't easy to shut down. If she wasn't wringing her hands, worrying about Nicholas, her mind was going to places that she couldn't afford with Ryder.

So far, she'd avoided stepping into the bedroom. They'd spent a wild night in there and she didn't need to be reminded of what she'd be missing out on for the rest of her life. Sex with Ryder had been beyond amazing. Her body had needed the release, she tried to tell herself, and it seemed both had regained their senses after getting caught up in the moment and giving in to the heat between them. She'd chalk her desire up to rogue hormones but she knew in her heart that it was more than that. It was Ryder. Tall. Dark. Sexy. Ryder.

Okay, boredom really was taking a toll. There was no TV at the fishing cabin, so she showered, put on another one of Ryder's old T-shirts, and then wrapped herself in a blanket to sit on one of the rocking chairs out on the porch. There was a chill in the air tonight, and the weather app on her phone had predicted a nasty thunderstorm would be rolling in soon.

As she sat outside and felt the breeze in her hair, she saw the first wave of thick dark clouds forming as the sun dipped into the shadows across the horizon. Flash flooding could be a big problem this time of year, and she prayed that Ryder wouldn't get caught out in one as the first droplets of rain fell. He should be fine in his truck. He'd driven through much worse, she reminded herself.

The thought of being stuck at the cabin, alone, didn't sit well. She wouldn't risk driving if the weather turned out as bad as predicted. Of course, growing up in Texas she'd learned to take weather forecasts with a grain of salt.

Sitting on the porch, she was beginning to give in to her fears that the situation was completely hopeless.

Was there any way to get back into the ranch unseen so she could dig around a little more?

No. Her father was smart enough to find a better hiding place for the documents. He wouldn't risk Faith alerting her mother to what was going on. He wouldn't jeopardize what he already had. Thinking about her mother, how lost and alone she'd looked last night, brought fresh guilt washing through her. There was something else about her mother that had changed recently, too. Or maybe it was just stress catching up to her.

Experience had taught her that her mother most likely woke this morning with no recollection of what had happened last night and that was probably for the best. Maybe she could get a message to her mother before she left town. Some note to let her mother know that Faith was going to be okay rather than leave her to worry.

The air pressure changed and a wall of humidity hit as the hairs on the back of Faith's neck pricked. She searched the nearby tree line, trying to stem the creepy-crawly feeling that someone was watching her as large droplets of rain splotched the partially covered porch.

Lightning struck and thunder rocked.

Faith gathered her blanket around her and dashed inside to get out of the downpour. She peeked out the window, looking for any sign of headlights. It was getting late and there was no sign of Ryder. She checked her cell phone. No bars. The storm must be interfering with the signal. She bit back a curse.

Rain started coming down in sheets, reducing visibility to not much more than the end of the porch. She shivered under the wet blanket.

Thunder cracked and the lights blinked. She could start a fire in the fireplace in case she lost power. That would provide warmth and light.

She shrugged off the blanket and loaded a couple pieces of wood. She'd noticed a set of long matches in the kitchen earlier and she needed to find paper for tinder.

As she turned, she heard the wood floor groan behind her. By the time she registered an intruder, some kind of cloth was over her head and something like a rope was being tightened around her neck.

She tried to drop to the floor to break free from the viselike hands on her arms, but she was immediately hoisted back up. The hands were the size of a male's and she heard grunting noises as the men worked. There had to be at least two of them, one holding her upright and the other working the bag over her head.

Panic roared through her, robbing her breath. *Breathe.*

Before she could get her bearings she was being hauled off her feet. She twisted, trying to get them to drop her. These men were far stronger than the ones from the SUV. Bolder, too, she thought, given that they'd come to the O'Brien fishing cabin.

Faith screamed and fought even though there was no one around for miles to hear or help her.

Neither man spoke and all she could hear over the pounding rain was the sound of her own heartbeat. No matter how hard she twisted, there wasn't much give. The men who were taking her were strong. She remembered the threat that had worked so well earlier. But then, if these men were hired to take over for the others, they wouldn't care whose cabin this belonged to. Angering an O'Brien would roll off their backs. And she wondered who'd be crazy enough to do that.

Since her earlier attempts to break free had been fruitless, she needed to calm herself enough to bide her time. If she saw an opportunity, she'd run like hell. In the meantime, she'd conserve her energy. No way would she risk anything happening to little bean.

Fear rocketed through her body as she heard something scraping against the wood floors. And then suddenly she was being forced into a sitting position as her arms were being jacked up behind her body. Some kind of wire or thin rope was being twirled around her wrists, and real fear ripped through her. Terror squeezed her chest, making her lungs hurt.

Her fear of being abducted shrank as her feet were bound together and then tied to the chair. These guys had no intention of leaving with her. She had no idea what would happen next. Would they shoot her? Stab her? She grimaced, tensing her body as she expected the worst to hit at any second. Not knowing what would happen was far worse than any physical torture they could've done.

She strained to hear over the battering the cabin was taking from the rain. Feet shuffled across the wood. And she realized that the sound was…moving away from her?

What on earth?

Every muscle in Faith's body tensed as she waited for the men to return. Or worse yet, were they bringing in someone else to kill her?

Her heart battered her ribs as she tried to breathe slowly. Tremors rocked her body. She needed to get her blood pressure down. It was pitch-black as she felt around, trying to work the bindings on her wrists. It was no use.

She tried not to think about all the ways in which these men could do away with her. Calming her racing thoughts was next to impossible. It was impossible to hear anything over the rain on the tin roof. Impossible not to let fear grip her.

Faith prepared for the worst. Of course, there was the slight possibility that they'd take her to the same place Nicholas was being held. But then, wouldn't they have done that already?

What kind of torture was being planned that would take this long to prepare?

A door closed. Faith stilled, listening for footsteps. There were none.

This couldn't be it. Could it?

Chapter Ten

Ryder couldn't reach Faith on his way back to the cabin and he could admit that put him on edge. Making the drive out to Celeste's had netted a whopping zero, and now there was a tree trunk blocking the turnoff to the fishing cabin thanks to the storm. Not exactly the makings of a good day.

He jumped out of his truck and shivered in the freezing cold rain. Ryder could do cold or he could do wet. He couldn't do cold *and* wet.

Twenty minutes later, he returned to his seat soaked to the bone but with a clear road ahead. Water poured from his body as he put the gearshift into Drive and pressed the gas, taking it slow. He didn't want to risk getting stuck somewhere along the two-mile drive and have to hike his way to the cabin. It was too cold and he was drenched as it was.

His mood was pretty sour by the time he parked and cut off his lights. Either Faith was asleep, which he doubted, or the power was out. A common occurrence at the fishing cabin when it rained. And it had come down in sheets earlier. He took the porch steps two at a clip, opened the door and hit the light switch.

"Faith?" He rocketed toward the female figure

strapped to a chair in the middle of the room with a cloth sack over her head.

"Ryder, stop!" The words came out desperate, freezing him in his tracks. "They might still be here. Watch out!"

He scanned his surroundings as he backtracked to his truck to retrieve his shotgun. Anyone hanging around the cabin was about to get a big surprise. The fact that no one had jumped him so far made him believe whoever had done this was long gone, but there was no chance in hell he was planning to risk it.

After taking the sack off Faith's head, shotgun resting on his right arm and ready, Ryder pulled a knife from the kitchen. Ever alert, he sliced through the rope binding Faith's arms.

Moving around to face her, he put his index finger to his lips and motioned toward her ankles before placing the knife across her lap so that she could free herself.

There was only a bedroom, bathroom and closet to search. He checked the closet last, moving around the bed looking for any other spot where someone could hide along the way.

Faith joined him, rubbing her wrists, and he tucked her behind him as he finished with the bathroom.

The place was clear, so he locked the front door. He didn't bother lowering the shotgun and had no plans to until he got her out of there. He turned and hauled her against his chest.

"Are you okay?" he said in almost a whisper. A quick visual scan didn't reveal any signs of injuries. Her wrists were red and he figured her ankles would be, as well. He walked her toward the couch.

Faith sat on the edge, looking too stunned to speak.

Ryder brought her a glass of water. There was something on her lap and she was staring at it.

The burlap sack. And words. There were words scribbled on the burlap sack that had been placed over her head.

Leave it alone.

It was a warning delivered by bullies.

He seethed with anger at the thought anything could've happened to her while he was away.

"We can't stay here," Ryder said to Faith.

She nodded blankly.

"I'm taking you where I know I can protect you," he said. His voice was calm but left no room for doubt that there'd be no arguments. And he didn't expect any under the circumstances. As it was, she seemed to be in shock.

She looked up, her eyes wide and fearful. "Get me out of here, Ryder."

He didn't bother gathering up their things. Everything they needed was at the ranch, including better security than at the county lockup. Tommy had advised their parents on all aspects of security given that there were a lot of poachers in the area.

The rain was pounding the roof as Ryder closed and then locked the front door. All he could think of was that this had just become personal. The fight had been brought to his doorstep. And he had no intention of backing down.

"Why would they do that?" she finally asked when he'd secured her inside the truck. "I thought they were going to kill me and then they just left."

"Someone is warning you but they don't want you dead," he said.

"What kind of person does this?"

"They were showing us that they could get to you if they wanted," he finally said after taking his seat and thinking about it. "And that makes me think that whoever took Nicholas is keeping him alive."

"I felt at least two sets of hands on me. I tried to fight but they were too strong," she said, staring out the windshield, unmoved by the wipers' rhythm. "I was too surprised."

"Whoever is behind this might have been watching you for a few days. You said your father had pictures of you and Nicholas. This might be his twisted way of telling you to walk away," Ryder said, navigating onto the farm road.

Faith sucked in a burst of air. "I hadn't thought about the fact that my father might've been behind this attack. The whole time they were there—" she paused "—and it couldn't have been more than fifteen minutes in total, my mind was racing and I kept trying to figure out who would hurt me. Who would want me killed? Not once did I think of my father. And yet it makes perfect sense now that they walked away. I need to get my mother out of there and away from that lunatic."

"One step at a time. Your mother's safe as long as she doesn't stand up to him or get in his business."

Faith didn't think before she answered. "She won't. I can assure you of that. She's never gone up against that man a day in her life. I think she's too afraid of him."

"Then she's okay. Right now my only concern is you." Yes, he cared deeply about what could've happened to the baby but he couldn't think about that right now. Without Faith, there was no child.

No more unnecessary risks. Not on his watch. It was high time he brought in reinforcements.

"No one's truly safe in my family," she said through a low sob.

"Did you get a look at the men who did this to you? Anything at all?" Ryder asked.

"No. I was about to make a fire and then…*boom*. A bag was being shoved over my head and I was being picked up. I tried to fight back but they were strong. It all happened so fast that I didn't see anything and neither of them said a word. All I heard was a little bit of grunting when I tried to twist out of their grip. That's it. I have nothing to go on."

"Once we get to the ranch, I'll call a family meeting and we'll put our heads together," he said, gripping the wheel a little tighter.

"Do you have to bring everyone in?"

"I won't put anyone in my family at risk without their knowledge." He turned the wheel, navigating onto the road, watching to see if anyone followed.

"Is there anywhere else we can go then? There's already enough at stake and I'm pretty much the last person any O'Brien wants to see."

"That's not true. I'm here and I want to see you," he said, and he meant it. He cared about her, and the entire situation she was in with her family struck a bad chord. Even though he'd retreated into himself after his parents' murders he always knew that his family would be there if he needed them. Everyone might've processed the news differently but they were all on the same page when it came to support. "My brothers aren't going to treat you any differently than they would anyone else. If I bring you onto the ranch, they'll accept you being there."

"I can't begin to fathom that kind of loyalty," she said so softly he almost couldn't hear.

Being a McCabe had taken a toll on her. He had a fleeting thought that his child would never know that brand of rejection. Speaking of children, Ryder didn't like the fact that it had been five days since anyone had seen or heard from Faith's brother. "I need to touch base with Nicholas's mother and maybe get her out of town for a few days. I didn't find anything in his room and she's in danger."

"He'll hurt her, won't he?" Faith finally said.

"It's a possibility we can't ignore," Ryder said. The fact that Faith had been strongly warned but not injured pointed toward her father being behind what had happened tonight. As difficult as that was for Ryder to fathom, he figured he'd never understand the actions of Hollister McCabe and it was best not to underestimate the man.

Her hand came up to cover her stomach and he wondered if she even realized she did that every time she worried about the possibility of something happening to the baby. Faith was going to be a good mother.

RYDER HAD BRIEFED Tommy on the situation on the way to the ranch. Dallas and Austin were on their way. Joshua, Ryder's twin, was the first to arrive.

After a bear hug greeting, Ryder motioned toward the kitchen where a fresh pot of coffee had just finished brewing.

"What's going on?" Joshua asked.

"We'll wait for the others to arrive before we talk,"

Ryder started, "but you should know that this involves Faith McCabe."

Ryder's back was turned while he poured two cups of coffee, so he didn't see his brother's reaction to the news and that was probably for the best. He wasn't lying before when he'd said that his brothers would accept anyone he brought through that door. However, it would take some time for them to warm up to a Mc-Cabe.

If Joshua was shocked, he'd recovered by the time Ryder turned around. His brother took the mug he handed to him. "You know me. I'm up for pretty much anything as long as it's legal."

Joshua's grin was wide. Ryder knew his twin well enough to realize that he had questions—questions he was holding back.

"I know I have a lot of explaining to do," he offered.

"Well, this had better make for a good campfire story someday," Joshua quipped.

Ryder couldn't help but chuckle. "Believe me when I say that people around town will be chewing on this one for a long time when word gets out."

"Well, good. Maybe they'll stop talking about me and Tyler," Joshua teased, Tyler was one of their older brothers who'd recently had a scrape with criminals. Joshua was in the process of planning his wedding to Alice, a single mother with young twin boys and a teenage daughter they were planning to adopt.

"We've had more than our fair share of excitement on the ranch," Ryder said.

"That and a baby boom," Joshua retorted.

Ryder let that one go without a reaction.

Dallas and Austin arrived together before Ryder finished his cup of coffee.

"We saw Dr. McConnell's truck parked out front. You all right?" Dallas asked after a bear hug. The doctor was a good friend of the family.

"I'm good. It's not me," Ryder said. He'd convinced Faith to allow their family friend to examine her. Surprisingly, Faith hadn't put up a fight. The doctor had been in the guest room with Faith for longer than Ryder was comfortable.

He motioned for his brothers to follow him into the kitchen area.

"Either of you want a cup of coffee?" he asked as they greeted Joshua.

"I'll get it," Austin said after hugging his brother.

Ryder pulled Dallas to the side. His brother might not be thrilled that Faith McCabe was involved given that her onetime best friend, Susan, had tried to manipulate him into marriage and then claimed he was the father of her child. All of which turned out to be a ruse because she'd ended up in a relationship with a criminal. And Dallas deserved a chance to back out of this situation gracefully.

"I just want you to know the players involved and if you need to walk on this one, I'll understand," Ryder said to Dallas.

"If it involves you, I'm in. I don't need to know any other names," Dallas said without hesitation.

"Faith McCabe is in my guest room," Ryder said.

"Okay," Dallas said, unmoved. He started to say something else when Dr. McConnell walked into the room.

All four brothers stopped to hear what she had to say.

Dr. McConnell found Ryder. "You want to take this outside?"

"No. I'd been planning to tell my brothers anyway. Now's a good a time as any," he said.

"The baby looks good. Faith is tired, scared. She needs rest and no more stress. But everything should be fine. I still want to see her in my office tomorrow morning," Dr. McConnell said. "But I'm not seeing anything of concern."

Ryder released the breath he'd been holding.

"Thank you," he said to the doctor.

"If she has any more bleeding or cramping, I want to know right away," Dr. McConnell said.

"She's bled before?" Ryder asked.

"It can be perfectly normal. I'm ordering bed rest for the next few days.

"Will do, ma'am," Ryder said, and then showed her out the door after an exchange of hugs.

He returned to a silent room.

"Everyone knows what we've been through in the past year, so there's no need to rehash those tragic events. Faith and I started seeing each other during that time and now we're going to have a baby," he said, looking for a reaction from his brothers.

Calm-faced, they gave away nothing.

"Let me be the first to congratulate you both," Dallas said after a thoughtful pause. "Having Jackson is the best thing that ever happened to me, and I know you'll make a great dad."

The other brothers chimed in with similar sentiments.

"When did you find out?" Joshua asked first.

Ryder glanced at the date on his watch. "Two days ago."

"Is she in trouble with the law?" Dallas asked.

"No." Since Tommy had already been updated on the phone, Ryder figured it was okay to tell his brothers what was going on. "Faith has a fifteen-year-old half brother who disappeared five days ago. His mother works as a cocktail waitress a couple of counties over and she thought teenage hormones had gotten the best of him. According to Faith, he's a good kid. Not like the other McCabe boys. To make a long story short, her father denied paternity after the kid was born and wormed out of child support. His mother has been struggling to make ends meet ever since. Speaking of Nicholas's mother, I need to send someone from security over to pick her up. She could be in danger."

"You got an address?" Joshua asked.

Ryder pulled it up on his phone and handed the device over to his brother.

"I'll send Gideon to pick her up," Joshua said, referring to their head of security.

"Thank you," Ryder said before continuing. He could already see that it was going to make a huge difference to have full O'Brien support moving forward. "Faith confronted her father. He denies being involved but he mentioned being blackmailed."

"That doesn't exactly narrow down the suspect list," Austin stated. His brother was right.

"Exactly," Ryder agreed. "Faith and I have been investigating on our own while staying at the fishing cabin. Earlier, during the storm, someone broke in while I was away and tied her up. Did their level best to scare her away from continuing to poke around."

Dallas's jaw clenched. His brothers had similar reactions. There wasn't an O'Brien who would take something like that lightly.

"Whoever did this wrote a note on the bag they put over her head." Ryder unfolded the small sack that he'd placed on the counter.

"They could've killed her but they didn't," Joshua said, rejoining the conversation after making the call to Gideon Fisher.

"Why warn her to stop?" Dallas said. "They had her right where they wanted her and they could've silenced her permanently."

"Maybe they don't want blood on their hands. They're small-time," Joshua reasoned.

"Which gives me hope that Nicholas, her brother, is still alive," Ryder said.

All the men agreed.

Faith appeared at the entrance to the hallway. She stood there as stiff as if she was in front of a firing squad. It probably didn't help that all eyes flew to her.

Her tense posture eased a bit as Ryder moved beside her.

Dallas spoke first. "On behalf of all the O'Briens, congratulations."

The others chimed in, saying essentially the same thing. She smiled timidly. It was one of the few moments that Ryder felt that her guard was coming down.

"Do you want anything? Water?" he asked quietly.

"No. Thanks. I'm okay. I'm interested in hearing what's going on in here," she said with a small smile.

Joshua spoke first. "Someone is trying to scare you. This is a message telling you to back off."

"Good point." Dallas had started pacing.

"All we know so far is that a female is in charge," she said. "My father hasn't been faithful to my mother over the years and I'm sure he's hurt many women."

Ryder held a hand up. "We were followed after our first visit to Nicholas's mother. Two men abducted Faith at a gas station when I was inside the store. I went after them and as soon as Faith told them an O'Brien was involved they stopped in the middle of the road and let her go. Tommy knows about what happened. In fact, he's on his way over right now. I'm hoping he'll have some kind of information from the Braxton sheriff."

"So, it's someone who has ties to Bluff. Good luck with Sheriff Bastian. He isn't known for sharing," Joshua said. He had been law enforcement in Colorado before returning to Bluff to take his rightful place on the ranch.

Ryder nodded. "Celeste filed a missing persons report and Tommy said that nothing has come across his desk."

"No Amber Alert?" Joshua asked, sounding a little surprised. "Five days is enough time."

"Nothing," Ryder said.

"Which makes me think that the sheriff isn't taking this too seriously," Joshua agreed.

"So, this leaves us where?" Dallas asked. "We have an attempted abduction that gets nixed when they hear an O'Brien is involved."

"Faith had never seen the men before and they obscured their faces with scarves." Ryder said.

"All I remember is seeing dark eyes. The driver was wearing sunglasses so I saw even less of him," Faith supplied.

Ryder's cell phone buzzed. He pulled it out and

checked the screen. "It's a text from security. Tommy's here."

A few minutes later, Tommy was knocking on the door.

"I got this." Joshua answered the door and then ushered him into the kitchen.

"Any news out of Braxton?" Ryder asked.

"I just got off the phone with the sheriff," Tommy started, looking from Faith to Ryder.

Ryder put his arm around her without thinking and pulled her closer to him.

"Three bodies turned up this morning. All I'm being told is that they were found shot to death in a forest green SUV," Tommy said.

Chapter Eleven

Ryder tightened his grip around Faith as he absorbed the news. Even though the men weren't walking on the right side of the law, they'd done the right thing in letting Faith go. They didn't deserve to die. And then there was Nicholas to consider. Up until now, Ryder had counted on the fact that no one had been hurt. Faith had been in harm's way twice and had been released, which had everyone believing this group was into scare tactics.

This news changed everything. The third body could be Nicholas's.

"Did the sheriff in Braxton mention anything about my brother?" Faith asked. Chin up, determination in her eyes.

"An Amber Alert has now been issued and he's stepping up his investigation," Tommy said.

That was the first good sign that the third body wasn't male.

"What can we do to help?" Dallas asked.

"Right now? Something none of you are good at. Hold off and let law enforcement do our jobs," Tommy said.

The comment netted a few grumbles.

"It's my job to advise you of that," he clarified. "As your friend I have to tell you to be careful not to get in the way of the investigation."

"We have an issue that needs to be dealt with," Joshua said. "Faith is pregnant, and if word gets out—and let's face it, it always does—then we're going to have trouble on our hands."

"I'm not planning to tell anyone. We're cooperating fully with the Braxton County Sheriff's office and that means looking at everyone here locally who could be involved," Tommy said. He wouldn't be able to share much more than that.

"Any ideas who the shooter was?" Joshua asked.

"None. They're processing the scene now, hoping for fingerprints, but you of all people know how that goes." Tommy referenced the fact that Ryder's twin was former law enforcement.

Joshua nodded.

"We know as much as you do so far. A random girl by the name of Hannah shows up to Nicholas Bowden's occasional hangout spot. The two get together and then Nicholas goes missing. Hollister McCabe is then contacted with a demand for money or the relationship will be exposed. The question I can't answer is what does your father have to lose?" Tommy asked. He shot an apologetic look toward Faith. "He already has a bad reputation, so he can't be worried about that. Your mother could leave him."

"I highly doubt that. She hasn't left yet no matter what toll his antics take on her. This person might've made the mistake of thinking that my father cared about Nicholas," Faith said with so much sadness in her voice.

"Taking him might've been a warning," Tommy said. "Given that the description of the vehicle matches the one you gave me for your attempted kidnapping, I'm working off the assumption these are the same guys. Which gives me the feeling this whole situation is escalating."

"And what about the men at the cabin?" she asked. "They were stronger."

"The men from the SUV refused to take you based on an O'Brien being involved. They might've gotten scared and threatened to go to law enforcement," Tommy stated.

"Which could be why they were killed," Joshua added. "Whoever is behind this might be doing cleanup work."

"Could other McCabes be in danger?" Faith asked.

"Seems like the men from the cabin would've taken you," Tommy said.

Dallas, who had been listening patiently, said, "My gut is telling me these kidnappers are right under our noses. This is personal. They know us, or of us."

Tommy agreed.

"Which would also lead me to believe whatever your father did had to be recent," Ryder said. "Can you think of anyone he's had conflict with recently?"

"Like business affairs?" Faith asked.

"Could be. It would have to be fairly significant to net this kind of response," Tommy said. "The person behind this might believe they're owed."

"The largest deal my father was involved in was about two years ago and that was the Hattie ranch," she said. "It was bad. My father forced them off their land and I remember him being a little unsettled after.

I knew then that he wasn't struggling with a bout of conscience. I think the sons threatened him."

"Two years would be enough time for people to forget. They might've been biding their time, waiting for an opportunity for revenge," Ryder said.

"They would also be inexperienced at blackmail," Joshua added. "Thus, all the warnings."

"I remember when news of that deal broke. Your father bought out the interests from the bank, and then he foreclosed on them," Dallas said in a neutral tone. "The family left town and disappeared after that. I think Dad even reached out to them to help. Mr. Hattie was proud and said they'd be okay. They'd been through hard times before."

"Weren't there two sons?" Tommy asked.

"I believe so," Dallas stated.

"Anyone have any idea where they went?" Tommy asked.

"I didn't know the family, but then I tend to keep to myself," Faith said. "And it has been a long time. Surely they wouldn't still be carrying a grudge."

"You never know," Dallas said.

"Let's play this scenario out for a minute," Tommy said. "McCabe takes over the Hattie ranch and they disappear. What then? They wait for how long…"

"Almost two years," Faith supplied.

"Two years is a long time to wait for revenge," Tommy said. The small burst of hope they could be onto something fizzled.

"Unless something else happened to trigger a need, right?" Ryder asked. "Or they start working with someone else. A woman who has been scorned by McCabe could've known what happened and recruited them."

"I'll have Deputy Garcia do some digging to find out where they moved and what they've been up to. If there's a catalyst, he might be able to find it," Tommy said. He excused himself and then stepped outside to make the call to his deputy.

He returned a few minutes later. "Garcia is on it, seeing if he can find out anything about the Hatties."

"If the Hattie family is behind this they clearly didn't know my father very well," Faith said. "Or they would've taken one of my brothers. He cares more about those boys than anything else. It's twisted, don't get me wrong. But he'd be heartbroken if anything happened to one of them."

"Whoever did this didn't want to get caught and they might've wanted someone younger, someone who couldn't fight them off as easily," Tommy said after a thoughtful pause. "They tried to make Celeste Bowden believe that her son was disappearing for a few days to punish her. They probably expected to blackmail your father, get whatever they wanted and then return him safely home."

"But my father refused to pay and they started getting desperate," Faith said.

"Then we realized Nicholas was missing and started investigating. They got nervous and tried to snatch you," Ryder added. "But they didn't want to get into too much trouble because as soon as you dropped my name they let you go."

"All signs point to amateurs being involved so far," Tommy said. "And they would fit the bill. We also know there's a woman involved."

"What about the third person who was found in the SUV?" Faith asked, her bottom lip trembling, and

Ryder could see how much effort it was taking for her not to cry.

"Let's operate under the assumption that Nicholas is fine until we hear differently," Tommy said. "It's a good sign that the sheriff issued an Amber Alert."

The silence in the room was deafening.

"Okay. So tonight's attack. What does that mean?" Faith asked, rubbing her wrists again.

"You weren't hurt in any way and that's another good sign for Nicholas," Tommy said.

"Except that the people who tried to kidnap me are dead," Faith said.

"Your father refused to pay and plans are falling apart. People are getting desperate," Tommy agreed. "Let's follow the evidence and see where it leads."

"If the kidnappers are starting to panic," Faith said after a thoughtful moment, "that's not good news for my brother."

JANIS BROUGHT FOOD from the main house. There was no way Faith could eat until she knew if her brother was alive. Her nerves were on edge and she jumped every time someone's cell phone buzzed.

Most everyone made small talk while waiting for word from Tommy, who'd been called away for a different investigation. Ryder insisted that Faith stay seated on the couch if she wasn't willing to comply with complete bed rest. Under the circumstances, he seemed to understand why that was currently impossible.

The knock at the door had Faith ready to jump off the sofa. A woman came in with a baby on her arm, and a chocolate Lab followed them both. The mother and child were bundled up like it was Alaska in the dead of winter, and that made Faith smile.

"Who's this guy?" Faith asked Ryder as the hundred-pound Lab came toward her, tail wagging.

"That old boy is Denali," he said, bending down long enough to scratch behind the ears of the big dog who walked straight over to Faith and sat down at her feet.

Ryder was called into the kitchen while Faith took over ear-scratching duty.

After watching the woman peel off layer upon layer of outerwear, Faith recognized her.

"You must be Kate Williams. Congratulations to both you and Dallas. I hear you make a great couple," Faith said, extending a hand as the frazzled mom sat next to her on the couch. Dallas took the active baby from her arms, insisting it was his turn to hold the black-haired boy.

"It's really nice to meet you, Faith," Kate said after shaking hands. The woman wasn't tall but she seemed like the type who could hold her own, and Faith respected that. "I was just thinking how nice it'll be to have another woman on the ranch."

"Oh, we're not...actually..." Faith was pretty sure her cheeks had turned a dozen shades of red.

"I'm sorry," Kate quickly said. "I should know better than to assume. Dallas and I had an unusual courtship to say the least. And it's just that you and Ryder look good together, so I just assumed."

"We're friends," Faith said. "And we're going to have to figure out how to raise a baby together."

Kate looked at her with a slightly raised eyebrow. "That's as good a place to start as any."

Faith smiled, thinking it would be nice to have one genuine female friend. Then again, she didn't plan to stick around once Nicholas turned up, if he turned up. She just prayed that she wasn't about to have to ID a body. She shook off the thought before the walls crumbled around her.

"Your son is adorable," Faith said to Kate, refocusing.

"Thank you. He's nine months old now," Kate said. "I might be able to wrangle him away from Dallas if you'd like to hold him."

"Later?" Faith asked, not sure she was ready for that step. What if she upset him? Or he cried? No matter how much she already felt attached to the little bean growing in her stomach, she wasn't sure she felt prepared to care for a baby. Especially with the parenting examples she'd had.

Kate smiled and gave an understanding nod. Faith was grateful. She didn't want to turn off a possible new ally.

After the meal was set up buffet-style, Faith was surprised again by the O'Briens when everyone took a seat around the table to eat. It had always been her and her mother at the table. There had been plenty of days when a meal for her mother could be found in a cocktail glass.

She couldn't help but look at Jackson, especially as he was being held by Dallas. The bond between the two of them so evident. Would Ryder seem as natural with their child?

Joshua leaned over to Ryder and Faith could hear the conversation since Ryder kept her by his side.

"Did you hear about Uncle Ezra?" Joshua asked.

"Being brought in for questioning again," Ryder said, nodding. "Has Tommy said anything?"

"Ezra has a solid alibi for the night of our parents' murders," Joshua said.

"He and Aunt Bea were having it out over her chickens again," Ryder added. "I wonder what Tommy thinks he's going to find with Uncle Ezra? Are you questioning whether or not he's a suspect?"

"Tommy can't say one way or another and I wouldn't expect him to. Gets me wondering what he thinks Uncle Ezra might know," Joshua said.

Ryder's aunt and uncle were notorious for not getting along in a family as tight-knit as the O'Briens. But then, that closeness seemed to have come about because of Ryder's parents, both of whom had reputations for being good, honest people in Bluff. Faith could admit that she held the same high regard for the family. And they'd proved it once again now that everyone they'd broken the news to about the unplanned pregnancy seemed to accept it. The O'Brien brothers may have been shocked at first but they'd adjusted and genuinely seemed concerned about her safety.

The sentiment was almost unrecognizable to Faith. For a split second she wondered if they wanted something from her. It was silly, really, but she'd never seen that kind of acceptance in her own family.

A part of her was relieved that her child would be loved unconditionally by one side of the family. Except that also complicated everything...

No one in her family knew about the baby and she needed to keep it that way. Or be long gone by the time they found out.

Nothing was going according to plan. She'd been

holding back from leaving so that she could spend as much time with Nicholas as possible before she disappeared.

Thinking about family had her wondering about her own mother. Did she wake up wondering where Faith was? What would her father say to her? Anything?

Faith tugged on Ryder's hand and then flashed her eyes at him when he looked at her.

"You're worried about your mother, aren't you?" Ryder asked in a low voice.

"Yes," she admitted, thinking the strong connection she had with Ryder was odd to say the least. He knew her better than her own family even though they'd really only known each other for a short time. *Really* known each other and not just preconceived notions they'd had growing up in the same town because she was a McCabe and he was an O'Brien.

Ryder's cell phone rang. The room went dead quiet.

"It's Tommy," he said and then put the call on speaker after informing the sheriff.

"The Hattie family moved outside of San Antonio after losing their land to the McCabes. Once they left Bluff, the family declined. Their two sons, Douglas and Shaw, have criminal records for petty crimes in the past year. Turns out, they got involved in stealing cars and home invasions," Tommy said. "They're racking up quite a record. Shaw has a girlfriend who fits Hannah's description." There was a pause and voices could be heard in the background. "Hold on," Tommy said. "I have a positive ID on the bodies found in Braxton County this morning."

Faith held her breath, fearing this would be the news that she'd been dreading ever since Nicholas had gone missing. Even Ryder's comforting hand couldn't stop her body from shaking.

"Douglas and Shaw Hattie have been confirmed," Tommy said. "The third victim fits the description of Hannah."

Faith's breath came out in a sharp gasp.

She didn't have a chance to digest the news before Celeste walked through the door with Gideon, the head of O'Brien security. She faintly heard the call with Tommy being ended in the background.

"Why am I here?" Her eyes were wild, and fear was stamped all over the worry lines of her face.

"It's for your safety," Ryder said. "We have reason to believe you might be in danger."

"Oh." She thought about that for a moment. Her gaze intensified. "I'm taking it that you still haven't found my boy."

"No. But the men we believe were involved in his kidnapping have been found dead," Ryder said. "And so has the girl who lured him away."

Celeste gasped and her hand flew to her chest above her heart.

"We're doing everything we can to find your son," Ryder reassured. "So is our sheriff as well as Braxton's."

She gave a nod as she struggled against the tears welling in her eyes. Faith understood the mixed emotions that seemed to be running through Celeste, because she was feeling all of those and more. Relief that Nicholas wasn't dead. Scared that the people who'd abducted him had locked him up somewhere and he'd die of starvation or dehydration now that they were gone. Frightened that whoever killed them now had her brother. Faith absolutely knew that he would make contact with her if he was able.

"Can we talk outside?" Faith asked Celeste, knowing that walking into a room full of O'Briens was most likely overwhelming enough for her even before she heard the news.

Celeste didn't immediately respond. Her gaze bounced from Ryder to Faith before she nodded.

Faith ignored the look from Ryder, the one that worried she wouldn't be delicate with Celeste. After seeing the panic in the woman's eyes, Faith was starting to accept how much Celeste loved Nicholas. She could work with that and try to put the past behind them, if Celeste could. Besides, seeing Jackson had brought up all of Faith's fears that she wouldn't know what to do with a child, and for the first time, she could sympathize with a woman who had no financial backing and no emotional support. Nicholas could've done a lot worse.

The chilly air goose-bumped her arms as Faith led Nicholas's mother onto the back patio. She welcomed the cold but picked up a quilt for Celeste on the way out. The sky was cloudless and stars shone bright against the canopy of cobalt blue.

"You want to sit?" Faith motioned toward the rocking chair. A matching chair nestled on the other side of a small table. As crazy as the evening had been, Ryder's place felt like home, and she figured it was the small touches like the quilt that made it feel like she belonged there.

Celeste nodded and shivered.

Faith placed the quilt around Nicholas's mother's shoulders. "I'm worried about him, too."

"I didn't want to admit it at first but I can tell that

you care for Nicholas," Celeste said after a thoughtful pause.

"He's the only good thing that ever came from Mc-Cabe blood," Faith said, and then added. "And I think that's because he has you."

Celeste's smile didn't reach her eyes and Faith knew why. The woman was worried about her son. Even so, the acknowledgment meant a lot to her.

"It's not a good sign that his kidnappers are dead and they haven't found him yet, is it?" Celeste asked, looking out at the vast sky.

"I'm keeping my hopes up, thinking positive," Faith admitted.

"I've never been so scared before," Celeste said.

"Me, either." There was no reason to hold back. Maybe if Celeste knew how much Faith loved Nicholas she'd agree to let him move to Michigan with her.

"You think something's happened to him?" Celeste asked.

Faith shrugged. "I don't want to allow myself to think like that."

"You got a good man in there," Celeste said, thoughtfully.

"I'm pregnant," Faith admitted, and it felt good to be able to tell someone else. "It's the only reason he agreed to help in the first place. And I blackmailed him into doing it. He didn't know he was a father before I dropped that bomb on him."

Faith was a little baffled as to why she felt the need to confide in Celeste. She'd say that it felt good to talk to someone, anyone, but the truth was that she was beginning to actually like and respect Nicholas's mother—a woman who was bringing up a good young man on a shoestring budget with no support.

Celeste reached out and took Faith's hand in hers and the two sat quietly for a long time. It was a peaceful silence, a camaraderie that Faith had never felt before with another woman. A few moments ago with Kate on the couch was the closest she'd ever come.

"I've been in that situation before. With my Nicholas. A good man won't walk away," Celeste said.

"Ryder would do the right thing if I let him," she said. "Trapping him is unfair to everyone."

"Then you don't see what I do," Celeste said after another thoughtful pause.

"Yeah? What's that?" Faith asked.

"That man has real feelings for you. If he didn't, he wouldn't be here. He might do the right thing by his own child but he wouldn't be looking for Nicholas, pregnant or not."

"He's a good man. I basically blackmailed him into helping me find Nicholas. What kind of trust is that to build on?" Faith asked, listening for any trace of judgment in the woman's voice. She couldn't find any. There was sympathy and kindness. No judgment. And she felt like a jerk for being so hard on Celeste's parenting. Faith's child hadn't even been born yet and she could already see that none of this was going to be easy. And trying to make ends meet as a single mother who'd had no opportunity had to have been the worst feeling. Was Celeste perfect? No. Neither was Faith. It was time to jump off her high horse and keep her feet on the ground. See the truth.

"I can see why you'd think that," Celeste said. "And no one wants to feel like a man married them because he was forced to. There's nothing in that man's eyes that makes me think he wouldn't have helped you if you'd asked, baby or not."

Faith let that thought simmer. Could it be true? Or was she tempted to believe what she heard because she was pregnant and wanted to give her baby a family? Her hormones were so far out of whack she couldn't decide one way or the other.

"You've been a good mom to him," Faith said after a few minutes.

"I have not been anything of the sort," Celeste snorted. "I've done my best, don't get me wrong, but—"

"Nicholas is a great kid," Faith countered. "That didn't come from my side of the family."

Celeste looked up at the stars, seeming to contemplate what Faith had said. "You turned out all right."

Faith's cell phone buzzed before she could thank Celeste. She squeezed her hand and Celeste seemed to understand what that meant before Faith let go and fished her cell phone out of her pocket.

There was a text from her mother. Faith's heart skidded as she read:

I know what's going on with your father. I can help. Meet me at Farmer's Mill Road. You know where.

At the end of Farmer's Mill Road was a cornfield where her mother had taken Faith and her brothers the first of every October to kick off the Halloween season when she was a kid. There were hayrides and a pumpkin patch at the mouth of the corn maze. Her brothers had always immediately broken off, running into the maze and jumping out to scare her, except for Jesse.

He was the closest thing to a decent McCabe boy, and he seemed the most sympathetic to their mother. She hoped that he would take care of their mother once Faith disappeared.

"I need to show this to Ryder," Faith said. "You coming inside?"

"In a minute," Celeste said. "I like it out here."

Faith put her hand on Celeste's. "Thank you for what you said before."

"It's true. I meant every word."

"That means a lot to me," Faith said, wiping away a stray tear. "When we get Nicholas back, I'd like to be there for both of you." Faith's hand went to her belly. "I have a feeling that we're going to need all the family around we can get."

Celeste practically beamed. It was her first real smile since this whole ordeal had begun.

"We're going to find him and bring him home. I promise," Faith said.

"I hope so. He's my world."

"I know that, too." Faith made a beeline for Ryder the second she spotted him in the kitchen. He was holding baby Jackson, and her heart galloped at the sight.

He looked up and his face morphed as soon as he picked up on Faith's heightened emotions. He handed the boy over to one of his brothers and met her halfway across the room.

"What is it?" he asked.

She showed him her cell phone. "I have to go."

"We'll see what she knows," he said after reading the text. Ryder let everyone know what was happening before he and Faith left in his truck.

"Where on Farmer's Mill Road?" Ryder asked twenty minutes into the drive.

"Remember the corn maze entrance?" she asked.

Ryder nodded.

"We used to go there when I was little," she said. A spark of hope lit that her mother wasn't completely gone. Not if she'd mentioned the mill. The last night with her mother had Faith concerned.

There was a small gravel parking lot at the mill and no other cars.

"We must've beaten her here," Faith said, shivering against the cold as she stepped down from the cab.

"She wouldn't necessarily recognize my truck. If she knows something, she'll want to be cautious," Ryder said, catching up to her.

"Good point." Faith walked toward the entrance to the maze. It was too cold for corn stalks but the wooden entrance was clearly marked.

"Faith." Her mother stepped from the shadows. "Is that you?"

"I brought Ryder O'Brien with me," Faith said as her mother moved toward her. When she came into the light, Faith could see the bags under her mother's eyes. "I'm so glad you're okay."

They embraced. Her mother felt cold and bony. She was like hugging a skeleton, Faith thought, and there was an emotion present in her eyes that made Faith shiver.

"What's he doing here?" her mother asked. Was that disapproval or disdain in her voice?

Faith started to explain when she felt something hard, something metal press against her ribs.

"No one is going to mess this up for me, you hear?" Mother said and her eyes were wild. "I've lived with that man for thirty-seven years and I've had to endure humiliation after humiliation. Why couldn't you just leave this alone, Faith? It didn't have to be this way. Your father has to pay for what he's done to me. To us."

"You don't want to hurt me, Mother." Faith didn't hide her panic as the pieces clicked together in her mind. Had her mother used and then set up the Hattie boys? Had them shot? She wished there was a way to signal Ryder, who was standing by his truck, giving them privacy. "What have you done, Mother?"

"Everything's spinning out of control and you need to stop digging around." There was a desperate quality to her mother's voice.

"Put the gun down, Mother."

The snick of the bullet being engaged in the chamber dropped Faith's heart. Her mother was serious?

Ryder must've heard because he put his hands in the air as he leaned against his truck. "No one has to get hurt."

"Except maybe they do now because you two wouldn't leave things alone," Jesse said from the opposite direction.

Faith followed the sound of her brother's voice until she saw him. The barrel of her father's favorite Smith & Wesson was trained on Ryder's chest. Reality struck. Was he planning to set up their father for Ryder's murder? For hers?

"You?" Shock didn't begin to cover Faith's emotions at that moment. Her brother and her mother working together against her father? "What are you doing with Dad's gun?"

"That's right," Jesse said. "You should've listened to our warning instead of dragging the sheriff into it."

Chapter Twelve

"Where's Nicholas?" Faith managed to grind out through the whirlwind of emotions that had to be rushing through her. Ryder could almost see all the neurons that had to be firing in Faith's head with the news.

The Hattie brothers had been worried about a *she*. Karen McCabe.

All Ryder could focus on was the gun pressed against Faith's ribs. His heart stuttered at the thought of it going off. At point-blank range, Faith didn't stand a chance. He had to figure out a way to direct Karen McCabe's gun toward himself instead. He'd take a bullet before he allowed anything to happen to Faith.

"Move over there against the truck," Karen McCabe said to Faith. She took a few bewildered steps toward him before he could reach out to her. He tucked her behind him as best he could, shielding her with his six-foot-three-inch frame.

"Be careful," Ryder warned. "That thing might accidentally go off. You don't want that. You don't want to hurt your daughter."

"I might," Mrs. McCabe said, and her voice had a vacant quality to it.

"It was you all along, wasn't it? You sent those men to the fishing cabin to scare me," Faith said.

Her mother cackled.

"You didn't answer my question. Where is he?" Faith asked with a mix of sadness, anger and hysterics in her voice. She'd underestimated her father, and Ryder prayed she wouldn't make the same mistake with her mother or brother.

"I don't know. Shaw was in charge of that part," Mrs. McCabe said. Her voice was unsteady. She could be on heavy medication. A combination of alcohol and prescription drugs would dim her judgment. Was there anything Ryder could do while Faith was talking, distracting them? He'd had no idea the depth to which the McCabe family would go until that moment—the one where a gun was pointed at one of their own and neither was trying to talk the other one down.

She continued, "Nicholas was only supposed to disappear for a couple of days. Your father was supposed to pay or risk his bastard son being exposed. I thought he'd pay for a son."

"How could you do this to him? He's just a boy and he's good," Faith said.

"He was supposed to be my salvation." Mrs. McCabe was stone-faced. She was too far away for Ryder to make a move for the gun. With Jesse twenty feet to the other side, he'd get off a shot before Ryder could reach her.

Damn.

His shotgun was inside his truck. He couldn't get to it even if there was enough distance.

"I never thought I'd see you with an O'Brien," her mother sneered. "We're not so different, Faith. You'll do anything you have to in order to get out of the family, too."

"Ryder's better than any one of the men in our family," Faith retorted. "Except for Nicholas. He's good. And you've ruined that, too."

This wasn't a good time for her to defend the O'Briens. He shifted position, effectively blocking her line of sight with her mother. He knew full well just how high her emotions would be riding, had to be riding the minute she realized how quickly her mother would likely pull the trigger.

"It's not too late," Ryder hedged. He needed to dig around a little bit and figure out what was going on inside the woman's head if they were going to have a chance of getting out of there alive. "If you let us go and tell us where Nicholas is, you'll never have to see your daughter again. No harm. No foul."

An insidious laugh tore from Mrs. McCabe's throat. "I already said that was Shaw's part, and he couldn't do that right. I should've known better than to involve those idiots. They messed everything up. I can't go back now."

"I'm pregnant," Faith said, and Ryder didn't like the fact that she was playing that card. Based on her mother's reactions so far, she didn't care.

"I know," she said, and it was the first time her voice faltered.

Faith was left speechless, but recovered quickly. "How?"

"I heard you throwing up in your bathroom countless times, Faith. I had four kids, remember? I know the signs of pregnancy when I see them. But I didn't know who the father was until I had you followed," her mother said, and her tone was shaking. Maybe Faith's gamble to mention the baby was paying off.

"Mom, don't do it," Faith pleaded. "Don't hurt us. I'm carrying your grandchild. It doesn't have to be like this. If you're doing all this to hurt Dad, I'm fine with it. He doesn't care about any of us. I'm not the enemy. He is. I'm on your side. I've always been on your side."

A moment of hesitation crossed Mrs. McCabe's features. She looked to Jesse, who shot her an unsympathetic look as he stepped toward them.

"It doesn't matter. We threatened to kill her if he didn't pay and we can't let her walk out of here. He can't think she's alive or we'll get nothing," her brother said.

"Now you're using me as a pawn?" Shock reverberated through her.

"We'll disappear. You can tell him whatever you want about what happened to us." Ryder positioned Faith farther on his right; Jesse was to his left. Mrs. McCabe was dead center in front of them, still too far away to make a move. Maybe if Ryder could get around the right side of the truck with Faith…no, it was too risky. They had two shooters, and he and Faith were unarmed. One of them was likely to get off a decent shot at this range. His money was on Jesse.

"I can't. I have to find my brother," Faith said.

"He's not your family," Mrs. McCabe said.

"Yes. He is. How could you do this to us?" Faith said, and there was so much torment in her voice. "How could you use me? And I can't believe what you've done to the Hattie brothers and that girl. Are you planning to kill me, too?"

"What?" Mrs. McCabe seemed confused.

"The Hattie brothers and that girl," Faith said. Ryder squeezed her hand, warning her not to continue. "They're dead. They were shot."

Her mother's gaze intensified on Jesse as she let out a sob. "We should've just taken you when we had the chance. I thought we could warn you but your brother was right. You just won't let up. Let me tell you something. I won't end up with nothing from that man. I can't. I deserve so much more, and he won't give me a thing if I leave him. I tried all those years ago when you left for college and he tracked me down like I was some kind of animal and he was a hunter. He threatened to destroy me. And I've been waiting so long to have the last say. But you couldn't leave it alone, could you?" Her gaze locked onto Faith. "I didn't want it to turn out like this, Faith. I'm sorry."

"You have options, Mom. It doesn't have to be this way. I have a place where you can hide. I've been putting money aside in an offshore account. Dad doesn't know. You can have it. You can have everything. I set up a new identity and bought a house. If this is about money, you don't have to do this. I'll take care of you. It's perfect. You can have everything, all of it. I won't tell a soul." Faith sounded desperate, like she was pleading not just for her life but the life of her unborn child.

Mrs. McCabe looked tentatively to Jesse again. Faith was making ground. And yet her words were a punch to Ryder's solar plexus. In all the time they'd been together over the past couple of days she hadn't mentioned anything about a fake identity or a new life. And now it made perfect sense as to why she'd been holding back with him. She'd planned to walk away from the start. She wouldn't have even told him about the baby had she not needed his help. She'd been honest enough about that. But he'd believed that they'd made progress toward some kind of future involving a relationship. Just what that relationship would've been, he had no idea. So, she'd been using him the whole time to find Nicholas. And then she'd planned all along to disappear?

No need to jump to conclusions. One conversation could clear all this up.

"We can't risk it. He's a liability," Jesse said, glancing at Ryder. Then he fired his weapon.

Ryder didn't feel the bullet hit his arm as he pushed Faith back a step and toward the side of the truck. His knee buckled and he landed hard on the gravel.

Faith burst out from behind him and made a beeline toward her mother, who had raised her pistol.

From this position, there was nothing Ryder could do to stop Mrs. McCabe, but her shaky hands would help ensure an inaccurate shot. It was Jesse that Ryder had to focus on. Another step toward him and Jesse was close enough to grab. Ryder scrambled onto his knees and then flew toward Jesse, tackling him at the ankles. Jesse came down hard, his shoulder slamming into the gravel, his hand opening. The gun skidded across the gravel drive.

Blood was everywhere. Ryder needed to move fast before he lost too much, and, even worse, consciousness.

At least the gun was too far away for Jesse to grab it. He was clawing his way toward it when Ryder threw himself on top of Jesse. His six-foot-three-inch frame gave him an advantage over the smaller McCabe. However, all McCabe boys knew how to fight.

Jesse whirled around, knocking Ryder off him and onto the gravel. He sucker punched Ryder's bad arm, causing pain to shoot up his arm. Ryder sucked in a burst of air, dug deep and landed a hard fist to Jesse's chin. His head snapped back. Ryder grabbed his throat using his one good hand.

Jesse wriggled out of Ryder's grasp with the aid of a knee to Ryder's groin.

Coughing, wincing in pain, Ryder managed to grab Jesse's thigh. He battled fatigue, fighting to stay alert.

Jesse fired off a punch, landing it in the middle of Ryder's chest. Didn't help the breathing situation, and blood loss was beginning to be an issue. Ryder blinked blurry eyes as Jesse scored a fist to his face.

"I'M SORRY, BABY, but I can't go back."

"He doesn't know it's you. He'll never tie this back to you and Jesse," Faith offered.

"Faith will tell him or the sheriff." Jesse grunted. "If she leaves here, it's over for us."

"Oh, baby. It wasn't supposed to be like this." Her mother hesitated for a split second and then fired a shot.

Faith was close enough to capitalize on her mother's moment of hesitation. She managed to knock her mother's arm, causing the shot to go wide. Faith pushed her mother and the gun tumbled toward the ground.

A sweep of her mother's ankles had the woman on the ground, facedown. Her mother was still frail and Faith had always been the opposite, strong and capable. She'd do anything to save her child.

"Where's my brother?" Faith asked, using her knee

to force her mother to stay on the ground, praying that Ryder was holding his own. She didn't dare risk turning away from her mother, even for a second. "You have to have some idea. Where would they have taken him?"

Her mother reached around for the gun.

"I'm sorry, Faith. I never intended for anything to happen to you. Neither did your brother," her mother said, trying to squirm out of Faith's grip.

It didn't matter how sorry her mother was, or her brother. Either one of them would kill Faith in a heartbeat if she gave them the upper hand. They'd already proved that. Her mother was so lost.

No way would Faith allow her mother to hurt her child.

And Ryder? She could only hope that he was okay. She'd heard the gunshot and half expected to see blood running down her shirt, surprised when it didn't. She prayed that bullet had missed Ryder—the man she loved.

"Ryder," she shouted without taking her eyes off her mother.

By now, Faith was straddling her mother and holding her hands down. She couldn't check to see if Ryder was okay, and her heart pounded against her chest so hard she thought it might explode. Nothing could happen to him.

"Tommy's on his way." Ryder's voice sent a wave a comfort through Faith as he dropped to her side and secured her mother with flex-cuffs. "Joshua left a couple of these in my truck the last time he borrowed it."

Faith glanced around to see her brother on his side, his hands flex-cuffed behind his back.

Ryder was breathing heavy, and when she looked at him she saw blood everywhere.

He was sitting on his heels, over her mother, and she panicked when she couldn't see the source of his blood.

"You're shot," Faith said.

"Yep."

She made a move toward him but he pulled back. Fear assaulted her that he was protecting her from seeing how bad his injuries were.

"Are you hurt?" he asked.

"No. I think I'm fine, actually. Just shaken up," Faith said. He didn't make eye contact.

It didn't take long for a deputy to arrive.

"I'm so sorry, Faith," her mother said, looking just as lost and alone as she had the other night. Tears streaked her cheeks. "I never intended for any of this to happen. For any of this to go so far."

Ryder was leaning against the back of a cruiser, an EMT at work on his arm. Faith waited until he was done.

"I'd still advise you to go to the hospital," the EMT said to Ryder as she approached.

"I'll swing over when I get a chance," Ryder said before offering a handshake. "Still got work to do."

Tommy had arrived and he was standing next to Ryder.

"Nicholas could be anywhere," she said once the EMT walked away. "He might die from dehydration."

"Braxton County Sheriff's office is working on it," Tommy said. "You can ride with me. I'll wait for you in my vehicle."

He nodded toward Ryder as he walked away and Faith wondered what that was all about. The two had been talking and she figured she was about to find out. Based on Ryder's stony expression, it wasn't going to be good for her. Faith only cared about a few people: Ryder, Nicholas and her baby. And now, Celeste. Two of those could be gone forever.

Ryder leaned against the bumper of his truck, fixed his gaze on a point in the barren cornfield.

"How's your arm?" she asked for lack of anything better to say.

He didn't answer, didn't budge.

"You were planning to leave when we found him, weren't you?" he asked.

"Yes," she said honestly, "but—"

"I can't." He pushed off the bumper and walked away. There was no doubt in her mind that he meant those two words.

Faith had lost Ryder. Nicholas was out there—somewhere—going to die if they didn't find him. Her family was a mess. Her mom and brother were going to jail or a psych ward. And her father, the real criminal in all this, was a free man. There was no one left in the world that Faith trusted. Well, except for Ryder, and she'd messed that up royally. She couldn't blame him. McCabes were toxic and he was right to walk away.

Faith hated deception and lies. She knew without a doubt that Ryder did, too. She would come clean with him, with herself, with everyone. Living a lie, like her mother had, would only destroy her and everyone she'd ever loved. She had every plan to move away, but not before she found Nicholas and then confronted her father.

With his life hanging in the balance, her brother had to come before everything else. Now that she'd lost Ryder, nothing else mattered more than Nicholas and the safety of her child.

Where could Nicholas be? Without access to water, he wouldn't live three days. The Hattie brothers had been found this morning. Time was a ticking bomb, the enemy, and Faith struggled to conceal the tears streaming down her face.

She stared out the window of the cruiser as Tommy drove.

"Where are we going?" she finally asked.

"Ryder has asked me to take you back to the ranch. He'll stay in the main house," Tommy said quietly.

She expected his family friend to come off as judgmental but he only sounded sympathetic.

"I have all my available resources looking for Nicholas. They won't stop until every stone has been overturned," Tommy offered.

"Thank you," she said, sniffing back tears. She'd blame it on hormones, and that might be partially true, but the thought of losing Ryder forever hit so hard she could barely breathe. If it weren't for the need to find Nicholas, she'd curl up in a ball and cry. "I know my family hasn't been... They're messed up beyond belief. I just want you to know how much I appreciate you for helping me in spite of everything they've put you through over the years."

"Family is as much about who you chose to be with as it is about the blood running in your veins," Tommy said, thoughtfully.

She thought about the fact that he'd grown up practically an O'Brien and she couldn't help but wonder what had happened to his family. He'd moved in with his uncle, a ranch hand on the O'Brien property, when he was a little boy. Faith never knew what had happened to Tommy's family or why it had broken up. All she knew was that he was lucky to have had other people who cared about him as one of their own.

"I sent a deputy to get a warrant to search your parents' place," Tommy said. "We might find something there to reveal Nicholas's whereabouts. I'll keep you posted every step of the way."

"Can't say that I deserve your kindness," Faith said, unsure how she would cope until he was found.

"You didn't do anything wrong. I remember that you were the nicest one in your family," Tommy said. "Like I said, we can't decide who links us genetically. But we can determine who our real family is."

They pulled into the ranch and drove to Ryder's house. Tommy didn't make a move to get out.

"Are you coming inside?" Faith asked.

"Nah. I'm going back to my office so I can dig through the files that come in. See about finding your brother," he said.

"I can't thank you enough for everything you've done already."

Tommy nodded, half smiling. "The door's unlocked and Janis made the place up for you."

Tears streamed down Faith's cheeks at the thought of being inside Ryder's house without him.

"Give him time. He'll come around," Tommy said, sounding hopeful. There was no real conviction in his voice.

"No. He won't. But thank you for saying that." She closed the door to the cruiser and figured she needed to figure out her next step.

Inside Ryder's place, there was a note signed from

Janis. She'd put fresh-baked cookies on the counter and wanted Faith to help herself. There was a meal in the fridge that just needed to be microwaved. All the instructions were there. Faith doubted she could eat anything, but she recognized that starving herself wouldn't be healthy for the baby, either. Maybe she could find a way to get down a few bites if she kept that thought close to her heart.

The feeling of hopelessness was an oppressive weight on her chest. After everything she'd been through to find her brother, he was still missing. Her mother and brother had no idea where the Hatties had taken Nicholas. With the remorse in her mother's voice, Faith knew she would've told her if she'd known his location. Faith had acted quickly before, but her mother could've shot her a dozen times in that parking lot and didn't. And when she finally managed to pull the trigger, she'd missed.

"Everything okay?" Celeste's voice came from the hallway.

"No," Faith said. "It's not."

With those words, the dam broke and a flood of tears rocked her body.

Comforting arms embraced her as she put her head on Celeste's shoulder and gave in to the emotions overwhelming her.

Chapter Thirteen

"My father took everything from them, their land. He took everything that was good about my mother and shattered it," Faith said to Celeste. "That's what started all of this."

Celeste took Faith's hand.

"The Hatties wrote the note and then took Nicholas, thinking you'd be none the wiser. My mother was behind it all," Faith said. "They all figured he'd be home before you even noticed him missing. They thought my father would care. I have to believe that no one wanted Nicholas hurt. But the men who took him are dead along with the girl."

"If that's true and they had no intention of harming my boy, then he's somewhere tucked away safe," Celeste said. "And that means the sheriff or one of his men will find him."

"Everything's a mess because of my family," Faith said on a sob. "They ruin everything they touch."

"I can only imagine what your mother's been through," Celeste said, thoughtfully.

"She believed she could extort money from my father and get away from him. I'm not making excuses for him, for either one of them, but Jesse probably endured the most emotional abuse from my father because he was the oldest. And I think it warped him."

"Sounds like a hard situation to grow up in and one my boy escaped," Celeste said. "I believe Hollister did me and Nicholas a favor by turning his back on us."

"My mom has been fading away all these years. I saw it happening but couldn't do anything to stop it and yet I never imagined it would come to this. She'd take more medication and my brother started drinking heavily. I always wondered why she wouldn't just leave. I guess my father had a hold over her," Faith said. Now that the dam had broken, she couldn't stop unloading.

"He manipulates people and gets what he wants from them. Sounds like your mother finally cracked. Your brother, too," Celeste said. "People can only take so much."

"It's sad what my father's done to our family—" she glanced up at Celeste "—and to others. He destroys everything he touches."

Tears free-fell and Faith didn't have the strength to hold them in any longer.

"He didn't break us," Celeste said. "You and me are too strong. And he didn't break Nicholas. Hollister McCabe might take down weaker people, but he can't touch the three of us. Four counting the little one who's on the way."

"No, he can't."

"Come on. I want to get you into a warm tub," Celeste said.

"I can't—"

"You have to. All this stress isn't good for that little one." Celeste pointed to Faith's belly.

She was right and Faith shouldn't want to argue.

Under the circumstances, it was difficult to worry about herself when her brother might be in danger. She needed to think of the little bean growing in her stomach and dig deep enough to find the strength to take care of herself.

"Besides, you'll think better once you wash off all that dirt."

Celeste made a move toward the master bathroom.

"I'm sleeping in the guest room," Faith said.

"That may very well be, but you're soaking in the big tub," Celeste said. "There was a woman here earlier, Janis, and I already asked. She said it'd be fine and put out some of those good-smelling candles for you."

Faith didn't argue. A warm bath sounded good and she figured that she could go over everything that had happened in her mind while she soaked. Maybe figure out a connection or something that might help find her brother. As it was, she was drawing a blank on what to do next. The sheriff had an address for the Hattie brothers and was checking there. And then there were the parents. Another deputy was being sent to speak to them. An Amber Alert had been issued.

Celeste stayed with Faith long enough to fill the tub with water. "I'll be in the next room if you need anything. Don't hesitate to shout."

"I will."

"Okay then." Celeste turned to leave.

"Celeste…"

She turned.

Faith wrapped her in a hug. "Thank you. I don't know how you've managed to comfort me with everything you're going through, too, but I don't know what I would do without you tonight."

"You're welcome, hon. Us tough girls have to stick together, right." She winked.

"Right." Faith could see where Nicholas got his quiet strength from now.

Celeste patted Faith on the back before reminding her that she'd be in the next room if she needed anything. Having an ally was the only comfort Faith had to hold on to. She'd messed everything up between her and Ryder. If she closed her eyes, she could see the look of hurt in his eyes and she understood why he'd feel that way. She'd cut him out of her plans again. Between the two of them, he was going to be far better at communication than her. If they were going to get along for the sake of their child—and really that was the best scenario she could hope for at the moment—then she needed to get better at talking to him about her plans.

She wished he would walk through the door so she could apologize. Okay, not walk through the door right then while she was stark naked in his bathroom, but after she was out and dressed.

Faith slipped into the warm water and put her head on the rolled-up hand towel/makeshift pillow on the side of the oversize tub. There was enough room in here for her and Ryder, but she highly doubted that he'd want to be anywhere near her now or in the future. And that was probably just as well because she'd only been around him for a couple of days—a couple of extreme, intense days—and she could already see how easy it would be to lose her heart to him again. The pain that had followed walking away from Ryder had been the most intense she'd ever experienced. There was no physical ache that compared.

Now he would most likely never want to see her

again. They could arrange visitation without ever having to speak. They could communicate through emails or lawyers.

Michigan had never sounded better. Or did it? What had changed in the past forty-eight hours that made it feel more like running away, hiding?

The small bungalow on the lake suddenly felt less like an escape and more like being banished. And that was silly, really. Or was it? Because she figured it had a lot to do with the fact that she might never see Ryder again.

THE CLOCK READ one twenty in the morning and Faith couldn't sleep. Not even a warm bath followed by a glass of warm milk had done the trick.

No Nicholas.

No Ryder.

But there was plenty of stress. She pushed off the covers and stepped into the robe Janis had brought for her. The cotton nightgown had fit perfectly, but it was too cold to walk around in only that.

She wandered into the living room and stopped. Celeste was curled up on the couch, flipping through a horse magazine.

"How are you doing it?" Faith asked. "How are you so calm?"

"Looking after you is keeping my mind busy. I learned a long time ago that it's no good to make yourself sick with worry over things you can't control," Celeste said, sitting up.

Faith took a seat across from her. "Can't sleep."

Celeste smiled and nodded.

"I didn't know he was married at first," she said

after a pause. "Looking back, I should've. I was barely twenty at the time. When I found out, he said they had a bad marriage and he was leaving her. I believed every word. What did I know?"

Faith's father needed to pay for all the hurt he'd caused. "I'm sorry for the way he treated you."

"Thank you. I mean it. For everything you've done for Nicholas." Celeste closed the magazine and set it on the couch beside her. "I hope you don't mind my saying but you're nothing like your father."

"That's the best compliment anyone could pay me," Faith said with a melancholy smile.

The door opened and Ryder walked through. He made a straight line to the kitchen without acknowledging Faith. He gave a nod toward Celeste.

"I put on a fresh pot of coffee a little while ago," Celeste said. "Hope you don't mind."

"Help yourself as long as you're here," Ryder said, pulling a mug from the cabinet and filling it with the brew.

He stopped at the threshold of the living room and looked straight at Faith. "Can I talk to you?"

Celeste got up and stretched. "I'm tired. I'll just go to bed."

There was so much tension radiating off Ryder. He'd showered and washed the blood off him. He was wearing a clean pair of jeans and a flannel shirt rolled up on the left side. There was white gauze covering his left arm and she was grateful that the bleeding had stopped.

Celeste stopped in front of Faith.

"You okay?" she asked.

"Yeah," Faith said.

"You need me, I'm in the next room," Celeste said.

She was a good person to have Faith's back. She'd never had that feeling before Ryder.

"I'm okay."

A few seconds of silence passed after Celeste left the room. Ryder took a sip of his coffee and then set it down on the counter. His muscles were corded and his jaw clenched and released a few times before he spoke. "We need to talk."

"Before you say anything, Ryder. I owe you an apology," Faith said. She did. She owed him that and so much more. "I dragged you into this situation by blackmail. You're hurt and it's my fault. And worst of all, I didn't tell you the truth. I know you're angry and I don't blame you. All I can say is that I'll try to get better." She put her hand on her stomach. "I know what's at stake and I want to get along for the baby's sake. I also know that it's my fault we aren't. I should've told you everything about Michigan."

He stood there, looking momentarily stunned. And she could tell that he was contemplating what she'd said. She'd meant every word, and if he gave her a second chance she would do her best to include him in every way.

Ryder took in a sharp breath. "Everyone thinks my family is perfect. Well, I have a news flash. We're far from it. But we love and accept each other for who we are. We're honest with ourselves and each other. And that's good enough."

"I know," she said quietly.

"I can also see, especially after tonight, that you've never had anyone you could trust in your life before," he said, and her heart galloped with hope. "But we have to change if we want this to work. We have to learn to let each other in and talk about the future. I get that we've had a lot thrown at us in the past few days and we haven't exactly had time to process any of it and come up with a plan. But I need to know that you're not going to up and disappear on me. That we're doing this together. I think our child deserves that much from us, don't you?"

"I couldn't agree more," Faith said, wiping away a stray tear. She'd cried enough. She didn't want to cry again, hormones be damned. "I don't want us to end up anything like my family. Promise me that we won't let that happen."

"It's impossible. You're nothing like your family and I'm nothing like your father," Ryder said without hesitation, and that convinced her that he believed it. She would've hated if he'd believed that she was just another McCabe.

Their tentative agreement wasn't what Faith really wanted—she realized that she wanted Ryder—but this would be good for the baby and that was something to hold on to.

"You must think my family is crazy," she said. "I know I do."

"Lost maybe," he said, "not crazy. I don't think your mother or brother really thought this through. They could've killed us at any time tonight but they hesitated. Even your brother's shot was wide and he knows better."

"I blame my father for all of this. If he'd treated my mother like a human being none of this would be happening. He's a monster," she said simply.

"No. He's just a man. We all have darkness and light inside us. It's up to us to decide which one we chase."

Those words made her father seem beatable.

"When we found Nicholas, I'd planned to disappear," she said, figuring it was high time she came clean.

"And now?"

"I was afraid of my father. Still am. I'm scared of what he'll do when he finds out his daughter is carrying an O'Brien baby," she admitted, and it felt good to say those words out loud. She'd been holding so much inside for so long.

"I can see why you'd feel that way," Ryder said. "I'd never let any harm come to either one of you."

"He's sneaky. He manipulates. No one can guarantee my safety, Ryder. And, so, after I found out that I was pregnant, I got scared and stepped up my plans to disappear. I hated what I did to you, hated myself for lying and making you think that I'd walked away…that I'd gotten over you."

"You hadn't?" he asked.

"No, of course not. What we had was real to me. My father is powerful and he won't accept this. I'd hoped to disappear. Problem solved. Or, at least one problem was. I created another because I knew inside my heart that it wasn't fair to you or our child to keep you in the dark. I was too afraid to tell you what was really going on. You're a good person and you'd think that you could help."

"I could've and I can."

"I don't know. You can't watch over me 24/7. I have to go outside the ranch sometime. I didn't see a way out. And then Nicholas disappeared before I could execute my plan and I had nowhere else to turn."

"It's not a good feeling to be someone's last resort," he said.

"If I'm honest, I'd been stalling anyway. My home has been ready for weeks and I'd started stashing money in an offshore account a long time ago. Small amounts so my father wouldn't notice what I was doing. If he figured me out, it was over. I guess my mother was trying to do the same thing in her own twisted way. She was just doing it all in one shot. Now I have no idea what will happen to her."

"I'm surprised you care," he said.

"There's no way she should've missed at that close range," Faith said. She'd been brought up Texan, and that meant she knew her way around guns.

"I know." He held up his arm. "Your brother couldn't fake that bad of a shot. He tagged me anyway and I think it was meant to slow us down. He could've done a lot worse damage."

"The two of them working together? I never saw that coming," she said. "I guess they've both had enough. Jesse was always the most compassionate of my brothers. He'd been drinking more and more recently. I guess I've been too caught up in my own troubles to notice. And when I saw him earlier, I just saw desperation in both of their eyes."

"Like caged animals," Ryder agreed.

"I know I should probably hate both of them for what they did, but it makes me sad more than anything else that they've been pushed to this point. I know how desperate they feel because I've lived with it every day, too."

"And yet you didn't react in the same way," Ryder said.

"We're different people." She shrugged. "They made

their choices. I just can't bring myself to hate them for trying to get away from my father. It blinded them to everything else and it made me realize that I have to face him. Going behind his back and hiding isn't me. He needs to know that I'm cutting him out of my life. I never want to see him again and he's no grandfather to my child."

"It's a risk I don't plan to take with you or the baby," Ryder said.

"You can come with me."

"I would. I'm just hoping that you'll listen when I say that you don't owe him anything. His emotions are going to be heightened when he realizes your mother and brother masterminded this whole plot against him, if he doesn't already know. I don't want you to leave the ranch for a while. I need you to be safe, and Dr. McConnell ordered bed rest," he said.

"Okay," she said after a thoughtful pause. "I don't have to deal with him right now if you're not comfortable with that. I'll face him once the baby's born. I need him to see that he can't break me." The look of relief on Ryder's face was worth giving in. She couldn't deny his points. Once Nicholas was found healthy and alive—because she wouldn't allow herself to think any other outcome was possible—she planned on focusing on having a healthy pregnancy.

"I have a question to ask…a favor," he started.

She nodded.

"Would you consider sticking around the ranch?" he asked. "At least until the baby's born, and then we can figure the rest out."

She didn't immediately respond. She hadn't given much thought to a plan B. Now that her entire life had

changed she probably needed to learn to be more flex-
ible. She also had some ground to make up with Ryder,
and taking his ideas seriously would surely go a long
way toward showing that she was ready to change, to
let him in so he could begin to trust her. The threads
were still very fragile. Plus, his suggestion had a nice
ring to it. She'd be safe at the ranch and everything she
needed would be provided. Maybe it was time to learn
to go with the flow.

"Yes," she finally said, liking the smile that one
word put on Ryder's face.

RYDER NEEDED TIME to figure out what he was going
to do about his relationship with Faith. He saw a new
maturity in her, and he was ready to take a few tentative steps toward working together for the sake of their
child. Trust was still an issue but he could work toward
finding a way to trust her again.

The past few hours without her had been pure hell.
He told himself it was because he needed to know
that she was okay for the sake of the baby. Anything
more would just add to his confusing feelings for her.
Confusing because Ryder didn't normally do second or third chances when it came to people he cared
about. They let him down once and he'd always been
more than willing to walk away. Faith was different.
He wasn't ready to explore all the ways just yet. All
he knew was that he felt more at ease when she was
around and he knew she was okay.

"You should try to get some sleep," he said. "Everything that can be for Nicholas is being done tonight.
Tommy said it's a good sign that the Hattie brothers

saw him as innocent in all this and so wouldn't want to hurt him."

"My biggest fear is that he's out there, somewhere, alone. Scared. With no food or water," she said.

"We'll find him, Faith. Between us, my brothers, and two sheriff's offices, we'll bring him home safely."

Faith stood and started toward the guest room wing.

"Take my room," Ryder said. "McConnell was called in to check on a patient at the hospital and wants to stop by to check on my arm on her way home."

Besides, he had no plans to use his bed. He intended to stay up and go over the possibilities until he figured out where they'd keep Nicholas. In this process, Ryder had come to care for Celeste and couldn't turn his back on her any more than he could walk away from Faith.

Chapter Fourteen

Dr. McConnell had come and gone. She'd pressured Ryder into taking pain relievers for his arm that would also help him sleep. Faith crashed on the couch, her phone on her lap. The last thing he remembered was popping those two little pills in his mouth and then he'd gone down for the count.

So what was with feeling like he was being bounced around in a dryer?

Blinking his eyes open, Ryder tried to focus. Everything was a haze of yellow and orange, no doubt due to the pain meds. Concentrating was problematic.

There was a humming noise in his ears that he couldn't shake. McConnell must've given him strong medicine, because Ryder couldn't will his arms to move. What the hell? Was he even awake?

A burst of light passed over him and for a split second, he saw clearly.

Faith was across from him, eyes wide, tape secured over her mouth.

Ryder tried to speak, but couldn't. Then it dawned on him that he had tape over his mouth, too. He bit back a curse because he also realized that his hands were tied in front of him.

Somehow, and he had no idea how this could happen, there'd been a security breach at the ranch. Anger ripped through him that Faith was in danger once again.

They were traveling in some type of vehicle. Based on the size of the back area, an SUV. Thoughts of the Hattie brothers and Hannah crashed into Ryder's thoughts. A moment of sadness for the senseless loss of life pricked at him. It was replaced by determination.

Something was digging into his back. Hard. Metal.

Another burst of light revealed that someone was on the other side of Faith. His first thought was Celeste and that probably was right. If anyone managed to get inside the ranch and into his house, they'd had three people to deal with.

Ryder needed a plan. His ankles were bound together, so walking wasn't an option. Where were they being taken? He had no idea how long they'd been in the SUV. Figuring out which road they were on was useless for now. As soon as the vehicle slowed, he'd try to pop up and get his bearings.

On second thought, the element of surprise was all he had going for him.

Ryder fought his instincts to blindly react to the situation.

Patience.

The SUV made a soft right. He'd heard the *click-clack* noise of blinkers so whoever was behind the wheel was being careful not to break any laws that could get him pulled over. Ryder was reasonably certain that the driver was male. It would take someone with superior strength to haul his dead weight into the SUV. Or the driver had help of some kind. Maybe someone who knew the ranch. He'd circle back with his brothers to discuss tightening security when he got through this ordeal. He refused to believe any other outcome besides survival was remotely possible.

Ryder listened for voices.

The SUV was quiet save for the purr of the engine, normally a sweet sound. This time, it felt like background music for attempted murder.

He kept the fact that he was awake from Faith. One wrong move, her eyes diverting a second too soon, could give him away. He'd keep her as much in the dark as the driver hopefully was. Of course, he'd prefer that she wasn't involved at all. Since that option was outside his control, he'd work with what he had.

After a bumpy ride through what Ryder had to believe was woods, the SUV stopped. It was pitch-black outside, so they were obviously somewhere remote with no street lighting. The driver had veered off the main road at least fifteen minutes ago, which would be a safe enough distance to bury them alive if he wanted to without anyone noticing for weeks, months, possibly years.

The hatch slowly opened.

As soon as the bastard leaned in, he was going to get Ryder's heels in his face. If he could connect in the right place…

He shot his feet toward the blurry mass leaning toward him.

"Oh, no you don't," Hollister McCabe said as he caught Ryder's ankles.

McCabe? That thought didn't have nearly enough time to settle in as Ryder realized the man had a surprising amount of strength for being in his early sixties.

Faith tried to scream through the duct tape. Ryder

needed to communicate to her that she had to stay strong. He'd figure a way out of this mess. No way was Hollister McCabe going to be Ryder's downfall.

"Think you're going somewhere? Think again. Many people have tried to bring me down and failed," McCabe said, agitation clear in his voice. He would know by now that his wife and eldest son had betrayed him.

Ryder wished he could say, "Like your wife?" but the reminder might make McCabe even more determined to take his frustration out on Faith. Ryder couldn't afford to let that happen. McCabe's emotions would be even more raw now.

The next thing Ryder knew, he was being hauled out the back of the SUV. He dropped onto the ground with a thud and a grunt, having landed on his sore arm. He'd ducked so his head didn't slam into the bumper.

Feet hauled in the air, he flipped onto his back as he was being dragged into a wooden building of some sort, fighting against the pain shooting up his arm. A light flipped on and Ryder could see this place housed mowing and extra farm equipment.

Curled in a ball, bound and gagged, was another male frame. Even on his side, Ryder could see that the figure was tall and thin, the body of a boy who had yet to grow into his height. Nicholas.

McCabe mumbled unintelligible words as he tossed Ryder's feet toward the dusty wood floor and then disappeared. No doubt he was leaving to get Faith and the other person in the SUV Ryder believed to be Celeste.

He scooted toward the frightened teen.

Eyes wide, tearstained cheeks, there was no doubt

this was Nicholas. The resemblance to Faith was evident.

Not being able to speak to calm the teen was frustrating. Ryder glanced around the room, looking for something—anything—he could use against McCabe. He tried to work the bindings on his arms with no luck. His legs netted the same result.

He had to slow down, to think. Joshua had told him how to break free from duct tape years ago when he was in some kind of law enforcement training. There was a way, if Ryder could remember. He hadn't been paying close attention, hadn't thought he'd ever need to know.

Another body was dragged in, kicking and fighting. Celeste.

A wave of panic shot through Ryder in thinking that McCabe would disappear with Faith. He forced steady breaths through his nose to keep his heart rate down. Fear would only feed the beast and cause him to make a mistake.

Ryder repeated his new mantra. *We're making it out of here alive.*

He thought back to his brother, to the duct tape.

The tape was easy to rip from an angle, he remembered, as McCabe disappeared again. He didn't close the door, and that was the first sign of hope that he was coming back.

Celeste was still kicking and screaming. Ryder needed to calm her down. Or maybe not...

Faith was dragged in next, and then positioned sitting up next to the door.

"You think you're going to betray me?" McCabe

said. His voice had an eerie detachment to it as he ripped the tape off Faith's mouth.

"Say it," he demanded. "Tell them how you turned on me with that filthy mother and brother of yours. Did you really think you could use the Hattie family to out-smart me? I didn't want it to come to this, Faith. After all, you're my only girl. But you've turned on me."

"I have nothing to do with Mother and Jesse," she stated.

A menacing laugh tore from his throat. "You expect me to believe that? All three of you can burn in hell for all I'm concerned."

"Fine. Punish me. You won't believe that I'm not involved anyway. But the others here had nothing to do with it. None of this is their fault."

McCabe reached up high and then backhanded her across the cheek. Her head snapped left. She let out a cry that nearly broke Ryder's heart and renewed his resolve in the same beat.

"Everyone will pay for your betrayal." He sneered. "Just remember, all this is your fault."

"Please," she begged, "don't hurt them."

Ryder remembered what he needed to do. He needed to sit up in order to break out of the duct tape, re-membering that his brother had said too often people freaked out and gave up when it didn't come off easily. Others fought it until they were too exhausted to keep going. Ryder had to admit that he'd fall into the sec-ond camp if he didn't know better. Many had died be-cause they didn't know how easy it could be to rip. The method was specific, though. And Ryder needed space.

It would be impossible with Hollister McCabe in the room.

"I'm pregnant," Faith said, turning her face toward her father. Shock had been replaced by anger.

Ryder didn't need her saying anything else to agitate her father, and those two words would surely do it.

"You think I don't know about the secret doctor's visits? Sneaking around behind my back? You put on a good show, though." His lip curled. "And now I know who the father is."

"How did you…wait, you had me followed. How long have you known?" she asked, so much anger in her voice. Which was another thing that could set Mc-Cabe off.

"For a while," he snapped.

Ryder was close enough to nudge Nicholas with his toe to get his attention. As it was, the boy lay on his side, crying.

Celeste tried to inch her way toward her boy. Ryder needed her to cause a scene in a different direction. He just needed a chance…

His opportunity came when McCabe stomped out of the shed, barn, whatever this building was. Using every ounce of energy he could muster, Ryder sat up. His abs burned but he managed it. He poked Nicholas's shin with his toe in order to get his attention. He had no idea how long he had before McCabe returned but he'd put money on not long enough.

With a bad arm, Ryder grunted as he put his arms over his head and pushed his elbows together. A forceful, downward motion and a quick burst out should rip the tape.

His first attempt netted zero unless he considered the intense pain.

"I don't hear him," Faith said quietly. "What can I do?"

Ryder shot her a look that said, "Stay put."

She took in a sharp breath and then scooted a little more toward the door.

Thankfully, with the explosion of pain came a burst of adrenaline. Celeste was still making her way toward Nicholas but he'd been focused on Ryder and was trying to break free of his bindings.

Ryder repositioned his arms, elbows together, hands above his head and gave it another try. Nothing. He was getting nowhere and McCabe could walk through that door at any second. With duct tape over his mouth he couldn't tell Faith to alert him the instant she heard footsteps. He assumed she would.

He squeezed his elbows together, hoping to create a tight seal. Hands high above his head and with a burst of energy, he pulled down and out. The rip echoed at the same time Faith warned that her father was coming.

Ryder glanced at Nicholas, who was still struggling with the tape. Damn. It would've been useful to have his help. At least Ryder's arms were free even if the pain was blinding and blood covered his elbow and ran down his arm. He dropped to his side, as did Nicholas, and put his arms together in front of him so McCabe wouldn't realize what was going on.

McCabe stomped into the room and straight to the opposite corner, which had several cans of gasoline. Nicholas must've realized, too, because his crying amplified and Ryder had no way to calm him. He could only hope that he wouldn't anger McCabe further.

They had exactly three things going for them right now. One, Ryder's arms were free. Two, McCabe didn't know. Three, the old man was working alone.

How he got inside the ranch was a topic for another

day. As for now, Ryder needed to make sure they'd be around to ask the question.

"You think I didn't know what you were up to, little girl," McCabe mumbled as he went about shaking the contents of the first gasoline container from the corner toward Ryder and the others in the middle of the room. "You're going to watch everyone you care about burn before you die."

"How did you find Nicholas?" she asked.

"The Hattie brothers sang like birds right before they died," he said and his voice had a hysterical quality to it.

Ryder pulled on all the strength he had to stay completely still, reminding himself of the stakes. Make a move too early and he'd give himself away. Give himself away and they had no chance of survival.

Unaware, McCabe moved closer, splashing the contents of the container on the floor in front of him as he walked. The contents were making a wide splatter as McCabe dragged his feet across the floor. He sprinkled some on Nicholas and Celeste. And then, Ryder. A few more steps.

Let him get close enough…

In one motion, Ryder swept McCabe's feet out from underneath him. The elder man came down hard with a grunt as he hit the wood floor.

Ryder's arm hurt like hell and the pain weakened him, but he couldn't allow himself to think about that right now. All he could focus on was bringing down McCabe. Grinding his teeth, Ryder pushed through the ache and used both arms to secure McCabe. The older man kicked and cursed, trying to wriggle out of Ryder's grip. The left arm was giving him trouble; the pain medication did little more than make him want to vomit and he was losing strength because of the blood loss.

On a normal day, McCabe would be no match for Ryder. Today was far from normal.

A boot slammed against Ryder's chin and his head snapped to the right. He caught a glimpse of Nicholas sitting up, trying to break his arms free. *Hurry.* Momentum was shifting in McCabe's direction and Ryder had no idea how much longer he could hold on.

Faith was shouting, and from the corner of his eye he could see that she was trying to break her hands free, as was Celeste. Any one of them succeeded and this fight would be over.

Gasoline was everywhere and had splattered them, which didn't help with the bile burning his throat, trying to force its way out. Ryder couldn't afford to let McCabe gain an inch. The older man's arms were free and Ryder had him by the thighs. He needed to hold on. Fists flew at him and then hands were grabbing at his face, poking at his eyes, pulling his hair. Ryder curled downward, angling his face away from McCabe. If they went up in flames, the old man was going with them.

McCabe was pulling out all the stops to try to break free. With Ryder's ankles still bound there'd be no way he could catch the old man if he broke out of Ryder's grasp. Worse yet, there was enough gasoline to light up the building with a single match. He could strike a match and lock the door behind him.

Ryder was losing strength. His arms felt like rubber. It was taking all his power, all his energy to hold on to the old man's legs. And then he heard the rip.

The hand gripped around his skull made it impossible to turn his head and look to see who was free.

A few seconds later, the hand was gone. Ryder looked up in time to see Nicholas on top of his father, holding his arms. Ryder held on to the man's thighs, making it impossible for him to kick, but he was trying to head-butt his son.

"What should I do?" Nicholas shouted.

Faith was scooting toward him, as was Celeste. There wasn't much either woman could do while they were tied up, and Ryder had exhausted all his strength getting this far. He wished he could tell Nicholas to grab something hard and bash his father in the head. That should slow McCabe down enough to set one of the women free.

He didn't have to. Faith did.

"I can't do it," Nicholas said, anguish in his voice.

In the big picture, it was probably for the best because it said a lot about the boy's character. However, in the moment it was problematic.

"He doesn't deserve to live," Faith said, managing to push up to her knees. "But if you can knock him out, we'll make sure he goes to jail for a very long time."

Faith was finally close enough to rip the duct tape off Ryder's mouth. His adrenaline was pumping too hard to feel the effects from the burn. Later, he'd pay for all of this.

"I can't hold on much longer," he said to Faith. "Put your hands up to my mouth."

She did.

He bit a small tear in her duct tape and she managed to free herself the rest of the way.

"You okay?" he asked with a glance toward her belly.

She nodded and then tore the tape from his ankles before freeing herself. She worked quickly and within thirty seconds had freed Celeste.

The scorned woman had no problem wielding the makeshift weapon. She stood over Hollister and said, "Your daughter and Ryder are going to make a beautiful family. You're an idiot not to see that Ryder will be more of a father than you'll ever be to any of your children. And I hope you enjoy your nap."

She winked at Nicholas and then swung the weed-whacker like a golf club. The casing cracked after making contact with the back of McCabe's skull, and he was immediately knocked unconscious.

He'd come around later behind cold, metal bars and have one hell of a headache to show for it, Ryder thought wryly.

They'd done it. Faith was safe. That was the only thought Ryder held on to as he gave in to the darkness pulling him under.

Chapter Fifteen

"Where's Faith?" Ryder broke through the fog long enough to ask. His body ached and he was being bounced around again. A sense of dread settled around him until he blinked his eyes open and realized he was in the back of an ambulance. There was an oxygen mask strapped over his mouth.

He lifted it and asked again.

"You're okay," the EMT said, obviously not understanding his question.

"Faith McCabe," Ryder said through searing pain, "where is she?"

"Ms. McCabe is fine. You, on the other hand, have lost a lot of blood." The man hunkered over Ryder was barely out of his twenties. "And I need you to put that back on."

He motioned toward the mask.

"I need to see her." Ryder tried to sit up but was easily pushed back down by the strong EMT.

"You will," he said, and introduced himself as Carl. "She's in the car following us and we're almost there. As for now, I need you to let me do my job."

Ryder didn't have the strength to argue. He would

take Carl on his word that Faith was okay, especially
considering the fact that he was too weak to fight.

A few minutes later, the ambulance stopped and
Ryder was being wheeled out the back strapped to a
gurney.

"Hold up," Carl said to his partner and then winked
at Ryder.

"Ryder," Faith shouted, as Carl waved her over.

Seeing her face gave Ryder new reason to fight the
darkness tugging at him. He wanted to be fully awake
so he could ask her the question that had popped into
his mind the moment he considered the possibility that
they both might die.

Nicholas was next to her and Celeste behind him as
he took her by the hand.

"I'd get down on one knee if I could," Ryder started,
suddenly unsure of himself in a way that he'd never
experienced before. He'd push through the lack of confidence because she needed to know how he felt about
her. "Because I don't want to live another minute without knowing you'll be there beside me every morning
when I wake up. When I'm with you, I don't need to
search for a thrill because just being with you makes
me feel like I'm diving off a cliff, no safety net, in a
way that I want to last forever. So I'm asking you to
take me as your husband, your partner in this life. In
turn, I promise to celebrate all the good times and be
there to help you up every time you fall. Will you do
me the honor of agreeing to marry me?"

Her moment of silence gripped him with fear that
they'd never be able to get past their differences.

And then the wide smile broke across her face when
she uttered the only word he needed to hear. *Yes.*

He tugged her down for a kiss before Carl broke it up and wheeled him into the ER and to the OR nurse waiting.

When Ryder woke the second time in a hospital room he was surrounded by everyone he loved. Faith sat on the edge of the bed. His brothers stood around, talking quietly. Nicholas and Celeste sat together in the chair by the bed.

He squeezed Faith's hand and she turned to him with a mix of worry and hope.

"Remember what you said earlier," he said with a wink. "Because I plan to hold you to it."

"Good. Because for a minute there I thought you were delirious before and wouldn't remember. I had no intention of letting you get away with it," she quipped. And her smile was all he needed to see. The rest of the people in the room were icing on a cake.

"Look who's finally awake," Joshua teased. And the others mumbled similar sentiments. They might be joking but Ryder knew just how worried they'd all been based on the lines creasing their foreheads and drawn around their mouths.

He thanked everyone for coming, and then reassured them that he was okay.

"Good. We didn't want to stand in line to see whose blood type matched up," Colin, one of his middle brothers, joked. Humor was the best stress reducer.

"You all should know that I've asked Faith to marry me," he said. "I love her and can't wait to be a family. I hope you'll be able to accept her in time, even if her last name is McCabe."

"Correction. Her last name is O'Brien," Dallas shot back. "And we wouldn't care what it was…she looks like she can keep you out of trouble and that's all that matters to us."

Congratulations broke out as each of his brothers hugged her one by one.

"You guys have never made me feel like an outsider," she said, wiping tears from her eyes. She glanced at Celeste and Nicholas. "And I hope you'll do the same for my family."

Dallas turned to Celeste. "Ryder filled us in on your situation and we'd like to offer you a job on the ranch. Janis is lonely in the big house and she's already preparing rooms for the both of you in hopes you'll accept."

"Wait. Hold on a minute," Ryder said to his brother. "How did you know I'd bring Faith home with me?"

"We're not stupid," Dallas said. "And neither are you, but you would've had to be to let her go."

"You guys really are going to make me cry like a baby," Faith said, turning to Ryder. "I've never felt so accepted or so much like home than when I'm with you."

"I don't want to be no charity case," Celeste said.

Nicholas started to protest, but she shushed him.

"I didn't say that I wasn't taking the job. I just meant that I'll work harder than anyone else to prove I'm capable," she said.

"I have no doubt that you will," Ryder said.

Dallas agreed, kicking off another round of hugs and congratulations.

"Welcome to the family," Dallas said to Nicholas and Celeste. "One thing I've learned this year is that families only grow in love as they expand. I'm looking forward to growing ours with the two of you."

A nurse scurried into the room and then stopped when she saw the small crowd.

"I'm sorry to do this but I need everyone out," she said. Her name tag read Adeline.

"We'll be downstairs," Dallas said, leading the way out of the room.

"My future wife stays or I go with her, Adeline," Ryder said with a wink, pulling out all his charm. It must've worked because she fussed a little before agreeing.

Adeline checked his blood pressure and a few other things he didn't care about as he focused on the thought that he and Faith were going to be parents together.

A few minutes later, Adeline warned him about doing anything that would spike his blood pressure before she scurried out the door.

He laughed.

"We should probably check on your mother and Jesse," he said.

"Tommy called and said they were in trouble but since they hadn't intended for anyone to get hurt that the courts will most likely go light on them," she said. "He even said that he'd speak on their behalf if I wanted him to."

"And?"

"I do. My father will do everything in his power to make sure that she ends up with nothing, so I'm planning to offer my escape route to them once she serves her time." She looked at him and he could see warmth in her eyes. "I don't need it now that I have you."

"I meant every word of what I said before," he said to her. "I'm head over heels in love with you and I can't wait to make our family official."

"Want a shock?" she asked, and he couldn't read her expression.

Tears streamed down her cheeks when she rubbed her belly and said, "I think I've been in love with you from the very first day we met in second grade…and I can't wait to be Mrs. Ryder O'Brien."

Ryder pulled her down on the bed next to him and kissed the woman he loved, the mother of his child and his future wife.

* * * * *

Look for more books in USA TODAY
bestselling author Barb Han's series
CATTLEMEN CRIME CLUB *in 2017.*

*You'll find them wherever
Mills & Boon Intrigue books are sold!*

Inhaling deeply, she selfishly enjoyed another tantalizing breath warmed by Chris's skin, perfumed by his masculine scent. Then she pushed herself back to sitting, forcing him to move back and drop his arms.

He studied her intently, his dark eyes boring into hers. "You do know that I'm going to protect you, right? You seem. . .scared, or maybe worried."

Unable to stop herself, she caressed his face. Her heart nearly stopped when he rubbed his cheek against her hand. Oh, how she wished her life were different, that she had met this man in another place, another time.

He smiled, a warm, gentle smile she felt all the way to her toes.

"Everything's going to be okay, Julie," he said. "We'll figure this out. Together."

"Thank you," she whispered back. Her gaze dropped to his lips, and hers suddenly went dry. She automatically leaned toward him. Her hands went to his shirt, smoothing the fabric.

A shudder went through him and she looked up, her eyes locking with his. The open hunger on his face made her breath catch. And then he was leaning toward her slowly, giving her every chance to stop him, to pull away, to say no.

But she didn't.

MOUNTAIN WITNESS

BY
LENA DIAZ

First Published in Great Britain 2017
By Mills & Boon, an imprint of HarperCollins*Publishers*
1 London Bridge Street, London, SE1 9GF

© 2017 Lena Diaz

ISBN: 978-0-263-92859-4

46-0217

Our policy is to use papers that are natural, renewable and recyclable products and made from wood grown in sustainable forests. The logging and manufacturing processes conform to the legal environmental regulations of the country of origin.

Printed and bound in Spain
by CPI, Barcelona

Lena Diaz was born in Kentucky and has also lived in California, Louisiana and Florida, where she now resides with her husband and two children. Before becoming a romantic suspense author, she was a computer programmer. A former Romance Writers of America Golden Heart® Award finalist, she has also won the prestigious Daphne du Maurier Award for Excellence in mystery and suspense. To get the latest news about Lena, please visit her website, www.lenadiaz.com.

Thank you, Allison Lyons and Nalini Akolekar.

For my family. . .George, Sean and Jennifer.
I love you so much.

And in loving memory to the family member who has
passed over the rainbow. I'll always love you, Sparky.

Chapter One

Blood, there was so much blood. Julie stood over him, one hand braced on the bed's footboard, the other still holding the gun. The blood soaked his shirt, seeping between his fingers as he clutched at the bullet hole in his side. Air wheezed between his teeth, his startlingly blue eyes blazing with hatred through the openings in the ski mask. The same eyes that had once stared at her with such love that they'd stolen her breath away.

Right before he'd said, "I do."

Julie Webb shook her head, blinking away the memories, wishing she could put the past behind her just as easily. Her hands tightened on the steering wheel as she sat in the driveway, the thin pale line on her ring finger the only tangible reminder of the diamond that had once sat there.

Stop it. He can't hurt you anymore. It's time to move on.

Unfortunately, with most of her assets frozen while the courts did their thing back in Nashville, moving on meant hiding out in the tiny—aka affordable—rural town of Destiny, Tennessee. And with the limited rentals available in Blount County, she'd chosen the lesser of evils, the one place with some land around it—an old farmhouse that had sat vacant for so long that the owner had been desperate to rent it. Desperate equaled cheap. And that was the only reason that Julie had taken it. Well, that and the fact that Destiny was a good three hours from Nashville. She wasn't likely to run into anyone she knew in the local grocery store.

The sound of a horn honking had her looking in her rearview mirror, reminding her why she was in her car to begin with. The moving truck sat idling in the gravel road that ran past the expansive front yard, waiting for her to back out so it could back in. After two days of living out of a suitcase and sleeping on the floor, having a couch and a bed again was going to feel like heaven.

She put the car in Reverse, hesitating when she noticed that her only neighbor had come out onto his front porch. Long, unpaved road, dead end, surrounded by acres of trees and pastures, and she still had a neighbor to contend with. A handsome, sex-on-a-stick kind of guy to boot. Which was going to make ignoring him difficult, but not impossible. She'd had her own sex-on-a-stick kind of man before. And look what it had gotten her.

He flashed her a friendly smile and waved just as he'd done every time he'd seen her in the past two days. And once again, she pretended not to notice. She backed out of the driveway.

Rhythmic beeping sounded from the truck as it took the place of her car, stopping just inches from the porch that ran along the front of the white clapboard house. It was a much smaller, one-story clone of the place next door. There weren't any fences on either property, so she wasn't sure where his acreage ended and hers began. But clearly he had a lot more land than her rental. The mowed part of his yard extended for a good quarter of a mile to the end of their street.

She didn't care, didn't want to know anything about him. The only way to survive this temporary exile was to keep to herself and make sure that none of her acquaintances figured out where she was. Which meant not associating with the hunk next door or anyone else who might recognize her name or her face, in case any of the news stories had made it out this far. She fervently hoped they hadn't.

The movers had the ramp set up by the time she'd walked up the long gravel driveway. It would allow them to cart the boxes and furniture directly to the top of the porch without having to navigate the steps. That meant everything should go quickly, especially since she didn't have much for them to unload—just the bare essentials and a few things she'd refused to leave in storage.

She risked a quick look toward the house next door. The friendly man was gone. A twinge of guilt shot through her for having ignored him. He was probably a perfectly nice guy and deserved to be treated better. But her life was extremely complicated right now. By ignoring him, by not letting him get involved in any way in her problems, she was doing him a favor.

"Ma'am, where do you want this?" one of the movers asked, holding up a box.

Apparently, the thick black letters on the side that spelled "kitchen" weren't enough of a hint.

She jogged up the steps. But, before going inside, she hesitated and looked over her shoulder at the thick woods on the other side of the road. The hairs were standing up on the back of her neck.

"Ma'am?" the mover holding the box called out. He lifted the box a few inches, as if to remind her he was still holding it.

"Sorry, this way." She headed inside, but couldn't shake the feeling of doom that had settled over her.

Chapter Two

Chris shaded his eyes against the early afternoon sun and watched through an upstairs window as the curvy brunette led one of the movers into the house next door. He didn't know why he bothered waving every time he saw her. Her standard response was to turn away and pretend that she hadn't seen him. He'd gotten the message the first time—she wanted nothing to do with him. Too bad the good manners his mama had instilled in him, courtesy of a well-worn switch off a weeping willow tree or his daddy's belt, wouldn't allow him to ignore her the way she ignored him.

He leaned against the wall of the corner guest bedroom, noting the car that his neighbor had parked on the road. He couldn't remember the last time he'd seen a BMW. Most of the people he knew had four-wheel drives. Come winter, that light little car would slide around like a hockey puck on the icy back roads. Then again, maybe she didn't plan on sticking around that long. Summer was just getting started.

A distant rumble had him looking up the road to see a caravan of trucks headed toward his house, right on time to start his annual beginning of summer cookout. The shiny red Jeep in front was well ahead of the other vehicles, barreling down the road at a rate of speed that probably would have gotten the driver thrown in jail if he wasn't a cop himself, with half the Destiny, Tennessee, police department following behind him.

Dirt and gravel spewed out from beneath the Jeep's tires as it slowed just enough to turn into his driveway without flipping over. The driver, Chris's best friend, Dillon Gray, jumped out while the car was still rocking. He hurried to the passenger side to lift out his very pregnant wife, Ashley. Chris grinned and headed downstairs.

He'd just reached the front room when the screen door flew open and Ashley jogged inside, her hands holding her round belly as if to support it. The door swung closed, its springs squeaking in protest at the abuse.

"Hi, Chris." She raced past the stairs into the back hallway and slammed the bathroom door.

The screen door opened again and Chris's haggard-looking friend stepped inside.

"Sorry about that." Dillon waved toward the bathroom. "Ashley was desperate. She had me doing ninety on the interstate."

Chris clapped him on the back. "How's the pregnancy going?"

Dillon let out a shaky breath and raked his hand through his disheveled hair. "I'm not sure I can survive two more months of this."

A toilet flushed. Water ran in the sink. And soon the sound of bare feet slip-slapping on the wooden floor had both of them turning to see Dillon's wife heading toward them. Her sandals dangled from one hand as she stopped beside Chris.

"Sorry about the bare feet. They're so swollen the shoes were cutting off my circulation." She motioned toward Dillon. "Let me guess. He's complaining about all the suffering he's going through, right? He keeps forgetting that I'm the one birthing a watermelon." The smile on her face softened her words as she yanked on Chris's shirt so he'd lean down. She planted a kiss on his cheek and squeezed his hand. "Don't worry. I'm taking good care of him."

He raised a brow. "Him? You're having a boy?"

"No, silly. I mean, yes, we might be. Or it might be a girl. We're waiting until the birth to be surprised about the gender. I meant Dillon. I'll make sure he survives fatherhood."

Dillon plopped down in one of the recliners facing the big-screen TV mounted on the far wall. "It's not fatherhood that I'm worried about. It's the pregnancy, and childbirth." He placed a hand on his flat stomach. "Every time she throws up, I throw up. Last week, I swear I had a contraction."

Ashley clucked her tongue as she perched on the arm of his chair. "Sympathy pains." She grinned up at Chris. "Isn't it wonderful?"

Chris burst out laughing.

Dillon shot him a glare that should have set his hair on fire.

"Did you remember to bring the steaks?" Chris headed toward the abused screen door, assuming the food was in the Jeep.

"The chief has them," Dillon said. "I didn't feel well enough to go to the store so I called him to do it, instead." He pressed his hand to his stomach again and groaned as his head fell back against the chair.

Ashley rolled her eyes and plopped down onto his lap. In spite of how green Dillon looked, he immediately hugged her close and pressed a kiss on the top of her head. Dillon started to gently massage his wife's shoulders and she kissed the side of his neck. Chris had never seen two people more in love or more meant for each other. Then again, they'd only been married for close to a year. They were still newlyweds.

"Where do you want all of this stuff?" someone called from outside.

Chris turned away from the two lovebirds and looked through the screen door.

"Those two are enough to make you sick, aren't they?" fellow SWAT officer and detective Max Remington, holding a large cooler, teased from the porch.

"Hey, Max." Ashley waved over Dillon's shoulder.

"Hey, Ash." Max dipped his head toward the cooler and glanced at Chris. "This beer and ice ain't getting any lighter. Where do you want it?"

"Around back, on the deck, well away from the grill. It's hot and ready."

Max carried the cooler back down the steps. Twenty minutes later, Destiny PD's entire five-man-and-one-woman SWAT team was on the large back deck, plus Chief William Thornton, his wife, Claire, Ashley, their 911 operator—Nancy—and a handful of other support staff.

Steaks sizzled on the double-decker grill, which was Max's domain. On one side of him, SWAT officers Colby Vale and Randy Carter chatted about the best places to fish. On Max's other side a young female police intern helped load foil-wrapped potatoes and corncobs onto another section of the grill.

"Two weeks." Dillon grabbed a beer from the cooler at Chris's feet.

Since Dillon was watching Ashley talk to SWAT Officer Donna Waters a few feet away, Chris wasn't sure what he meant. "Two weeks until what?"

Dillon used his bottle to indicate the pretty young intern who was earning college credits for helping out at the Destiny police department over the summer.

"I give her and Max's fledgling relationship two more weeks, at the most," Dillon said. "They have absolutely nothing in common and she's young enough to be his…niece…or something."

Chris shrugged and snagged himself a beer from the cooler. The rest of the team laughed and talked in small groups on the massive deck. The chief and his wife were the only ones not smiling. They were too intent on discussing the best placement of the desserts on the table at the far end. Chris grinned, always amused to see the soft side of his crotchety boss whenever his wife of forty-plus years was around. He hoped someday that he'd be lucky enough to be married that long, and be just as happy. But so far he hadn't met the right woman. Given Destiny's small size, he just might have to move to another town to expand the dating pool.

The sound of an engine turning over had him stepping closer to the railing. The moving truck headed down the driveway next door, then continued up the road. His new neighbor stood in the grass beside her front porch, watching it go. Unless she was deaf, she had to hear the noise in his backyard. Was she going to ignore *all* of them?

He waited, watching. As if feeling the force of his gaze upon her, she turned. Their eyes locked and held. Then she whirled around and raced up her porch steps, the screen door slamming as she hurried inside.

"What's her name?"

Chris didn't turn at the sound of Dillon's voice. His friend braced his hands on the railing beside him.

"I have no idea," Chris answered. "She's been here two days and she hasn't even acknowledged that I exist."

Dillon whistled low. "That's a first for you. Must be losing your touch."

He slanted his friend a look. "Yeah, well. At least I'm not puking my guts up every time someone says fried gizzards."

Dillon's eyes widened and his face went pale. A second later he clapped his hand over his mouth and ran inside the house.

Judging from the way Ashley was suddenly glaring at Chris, she'd obviously noticed Dillon's rapid retreat. She put her hands on her hips. "What did you do?"

"I might have mentioned 'fried gizzards.'"

She threw her hands in the air and shook her head in exasperation. Then she ran inside after her husband.

Chris winced at the accusatory looks some of the others gave him. He shouldn't have done that. He knew that Dillon's sympathy morning sickness could be triggered by certain foods, or even the mention of them. But teasing Dillon was just too easy—and way too fun—to resist.

He supposed he'd have to apologize later.

But right now there was something else bothering him, a puzzle he was trying to work through. He turned back toward his mysterious new neighbor's house, trying to fit the pieces together in his mind. There'd been something about her that was bothering him, the way she'd twisted her hands together as she'd stared down the road, the look in her eyes when she'd met his gaze.

And then it clicked.

He knew exactly what he'd seen.

Fear.

Chapter Three

Judging by the empty beer bottles and bags of trash sitting on his deck, Chris reckoned the annual summer-opening bash for his SWAT unit had been a success. Everyone had seemed to have a good time, even Dillon, once he'd gotten over being mad. They'd probably still be partying if the mosquitoes and gnats hadn't invaded after the sun went down.

He probably should have invited everyone to go indoors. But he'd been too preoccupied to even think of that earlier. He'd spent most of the cookout worrying about a woman he'd never met, who'd made it crystal clear that she wanted nothing to do with him.

After another glance at the house next door, he cursed and forced himself to look away. He grabbed two bags of trash in one hand and a bag of recyclables in the other. Then he headed down the deck steps and around the side yard toward the garage. He slowed as he neared the front. Behind the dark blue BMW next door was a silver Ford Taurus that hadn't been there earlier.

He shook his head. It was none of his business who the woman next door invited over. Judging by the plates on the Taurus, it was from out of town. Maybe some of her friends were helping her unpack and set up the place. Again, none of his concern.

Rounding to the front of his house, he keyed a code into the electronic keypad to open the garage door. After stowing the trash and recyclables in the appropriate bins, he closed the door again and took the front porch steps two at a time. If he hurried, he just might catch the start of a baseball game on TV.

A few minutes later, he was sitting in his favorite recliner with a beer and a bowl of popcorn on the side table. He was looking forward to a relaxing few hours vegging out before going to bed early, even though it was Saturday.

Come dawn, he had a date with a tractor and a Bush Hog and over an acre of brush to clear for Cooper, a neighbor laid up in the hospital. After that, he had his own chores to see to, including repairing some fencing to keep cows from wandering into his yard again from the farm behind his house. Sunday definitely wasn't going to be a day of rest for him. And he'd still have to catch the Sunday evening service at First Baptist or his mom would hear about it and start praying for his soul.

A piercing shriek sounded from outside, then abruptly cut off. Chris jumped up from his chair, grabbed his pistol from the coffee table. Standing stock-still, he listened for the sound again. Had a screech owl flown over the house? Maybe one of the baseball fans on TV had made the noise. Maybe. But he didn't think so. The volume on the television hadn't been turned up very loud. He pressed the mute button on the remote. Still nothing. Everything was silent. So what had he heard?

As if pulled by an unseen force, his gaze went to the

window on the east side of the great room. The front of his home was about ten feet closer to the road than his neighbor's. He had a clear view of her porch, dimly lit by a single yellow bulb now that the sun had gone down. Everything looked as it had earlier when he'd dealt with the trash. Two cars were still parked in her driveway. There was no sign of any people anywhere. But he couldn't shake the uneasy feeling in his gut and the memory of the fear he'd seen in her eyes.

Cursing himself for a fool, he headed toward the screen door, gun in hand. His neighbor was probably going to think he was an idiot for checking on her. But he had to see for himself that she was okay. He shoved the pistol into his waistband at the small of his back. No sense in scaring her with his gun out. After jogging down the porch steps, he strode across the lawn to her house.

The sound of breaking glass made him pause before he reached the bottom step. An angry male voice sounded from inside. Chris whirled around, changing direction. He went to the side of the porch, where he wouldn't be visible from the front door, then hauled himself up and over the railing. Crouching down, he edged to the first window, then peeked inside.

The layout of the house was basically a one-story version of his own. He'd been in it dozens of times helping out old man Hutchinson before his family moved him to an assisted-living facility. The front door opened into the great room. The kitchen was to the left, through an archway. Both homes had a hallway that ran across the back, with two bedrooms and a bath. The only true difference was the size and the fact that Chris's home had a staircase hugging the wall on the right.

Boxes were stacked neatly across the left end of his neighbor's great room. A couch and two chairs sat in a grouping on the right. Standing in the middle of the room was a tall, lean man, his face a mask of anger as he said something to the woman across from him. Pieces of a broken drinking glass scattered the floor. But what captured Chris's attention the most was what the man was holding in his right hand—a butcher knife.

Chris ducked down, his hand going to the gun shoved into his waistband. No. He couldn't bust in there pointing his gun. The other man was too close to the woman and might hurt her. What he needed was a distraction, some way to put more distance between the two.

He also needed backup, in case this all went horribly wrong. He didn't want the woman left facing the man with the knife all by herself. He had to make sure she'd get the help she needed, no matter what.

After silencing his phone, he typed a quick text to dispatch, letting them know the situation. As expected, the immediate response was to stand down and wait for more units. Yeah, well, more units were a good thirty minutes away, best case. That was part of the price of living in the country. Like it or not, he had to go inside the house. If he waited, his neighbor could get hurt or killed by the time his fellow SWAT team members arrived.

He shoved the phone into his pocket, then hopped over the railing and dropped down to the grass. His hastily concocted plan wasn't much of a plan. It basically involved making enough noise to alert the two inside that he was there, and then going all hillbilly on them. If they were typical city slickers, as the BMW and out-of-town plates on the Taurus suggested, they might take the bait and think he was a redneck without a clue. If his gamble paid off, he'd manage to insert himself between the two and wrestle the knife away—hopefully without getting himself or anyone else killed.

Yeah, not much of a plan, but, since he couldn't think of another one, he went with it.

He wiped his palms on his jeans, then loudly clomped his booted foot onto the bottom porch step.

Chapter Four

A hollow sound echoed outside. Julie jerked around to see the sexy guy from next door stomping up the front porch steps.

"Who is that?" Alan snarled, closing the distance between them.

She swallowed, watching the knife in his hand. "My neighbor. I don't know his name."

"Get rid of him."

He edged halfway behind her, his left hand—the one holding the knife—hidden from view. Its sharp tip pressed lightly between her shoulder blades, just piercing her skin. She gasped and arched away, but the threat was still there. Her only chance was to try to appease him. If she didn't, he'd kill her, and try to kill a stranger whose only crime was that he lived next door.

A knock sounded. The tall, broad-shouldered man who'd given her so many unreturned smiles and friendly waves peered through the screen door, grinning when he saw her standing in the middle of the great room.

"Hello, there," he drawled. "I'm Chris Downing, from the house next door. Hope you don't mind me coming over. I figured it was high time I introduced myself."

"Um, actually, I don't—"

He pushed the door open and stepped inside, his white teeth gleaming in a smile that would have been charming if she wasn't so scared.

She shot a pleading look over her shoulder, then glanced back at her neighbor. "Mr. Downing, this really isn't a good—"

"Chris," he corrected, striding toward her. "No point in formalities between neighbors."

The knife pressed against her spine, a warning that she needed to do something. Fast.

"You sure are pretty, ma'am." His grin widened. "Welcome to the neighborhood." He took one of her hands in his. "And what lovely name did your mama gift you with?" He waited expectantly, his green eyes capturing hers, looking oddly serious in spite of his silly grin.

She could almost taste Alan's simmering anger, his impatience.

"I'm…ah… Julie. Julie Webb. I'm sorry but you *really* need to—"

"Can't remember the last time I met a Julie. Beautiful name for a beautiful woman." His head bobbed up and down while he vigorously shook her hand, pulling her off balance. She was forced to step toward him to keep from falling over.

Alan made a menacing sound in his throat and plopped his right hand on her shoulder, anchoring her and keeping her from moving farther away from him. But her neighbor misinterpreted the gesture. He let go of Julie's hand and offered his hand to Alan, instead.

"Didn't mean to ignore you back there," he said.

"Where are my manners? Are you my new neighbor, too, or just visiting?"

The pressure on her shoulder tightened painfully, making her wince. She tensed, fully expecting to feel the bite of the knife sliding between her ribs at any moment. Most people would have read the tension between her and Alan and realized they were intruding. But her neighbor seemed oblivious, his hand still in the air, waiting for Alan to take it.

She could have sworn Alan said "stupid redneck" beneath his breath before he released her shoulder and reached around her to shake the other man's hand.

As soon as Chris's much larger hand closed around Alan's, he gave a mighty, sideways yank, ripping Alan away from Julie. Alan roared with rage and slashed at Chris with the knife. Chris twisted sideways, the blade narrowly missing his stomach. He grabbed Alan's left wrist, both men twisting and grunting with their hands joined crosswise in front of them.

"Get back," Chris yelled at Julie, twisting sideways again.

She jumped out of the way, pressing her hand against her throat. The two men grappled like a couple of grizzly bears. Alan was shorter, but both men rippled with muscles, their biceps bulging as they strained against each other. Chris's extra height seemed to be a handicap, though. He was bent over at an impossible angle. And his hold on Alan's knife hand appeared to be slipping.

"Julie, run!"

Chris yanked Alan again. Alan countered by ducking down, trying to pull Chris off balance.

Julie couldn't seem to make her feet move. She was frozen, her throat so tight no sound would come out.

"I'm a cop," Chris bit out as he and Alan jerked and shoved at each other. "Drop the knife and we can work this out. No one needs to get hurt."

"Work it out?" Alan spit between clenched teeth. "You're the intruder. I can kill you and no one will even question me."

Chris risked a quick glance at Julie. "*Go.* Get out of here!"

She stepped back, ready to do what he'd said. But then she stopped. The room seemed to shimmer in front of her, and she was back in her bedroom five months ago. All she could see was blood, its coppery scent filling the air. It was everywhere. The floors were slippery with it. Her hands, sticky.

No. Don't think about the past. Stay in the present.

She blinked and brought the room back into focus.

"Please." She stepped forward. "Please." Another step. She stared at Alan, willing him to look at her. "Don't do this."

Something in her voice must have captured Alan's attention. His head swiveled toward her. Bloodlust shone in his eyes. Julie knew the exact moment when he took the bait.

He gave Chris a mighty shove backward, catching him off guard. Chris stumbled, his hold on Alan broken. Julie tried to scramble back, but Alan was already lunging at her with the knife. She brought her arms up and turned her head, bracing herself.

Boom! Boom! Boom!

Alan dropped to the floor, inches away from her, unmoving. She stared at him in shock, not quite sure what had happened. Then blood began running in rivulets across the worn, uneven floor, reaching out from beneath his body like accusing fingers, pointing at her. She stumbled backward, a sob catching in her throat.

A piercing scream echoed through the room. And suddenly she was clasped tightly against Chris's chest, his arms wrapped protectively around her. He turned, blocking her view of the body lying on the floor. The screaming stopped, and she was mortified to realize that she was the one who'd been screaming.

"It's okay." One of his hands gently rubbed her back as the other cradled her against him. "He can't hurt you now."

He can't hurt me now. He can't hurt me now. She drew in a shaky breath.

Sirens wailed in the distance. How could there be sirens? She hadn't called anyone, never had a chance to call when Alan had burst into the house. But her neighbor had come inside. Chris? And he'd…shot… Alan? Yes. Those had been gunshots she'd heard. She shivered again.

"The police are on their way," he continued, speaking in a low, soothing tone. "I called them when I saw him through the window holding the knife."

The police. He'd seen Alan threatening her. Wait, wasn't *he* the police?

"I don't… I don't understand," she whispered. "What happened? Who are you?"

He gently pushed her back, his hands holding her upper arms. "I'm Christopher Downing, a detective and SWAT officer from the Destiny Police Department. I called for backup before I came in here." He scanned her from head to toe, as if searching for injuries. "Are you okay? Did he cut you?"

She blinked, her jumbled thoughts starting to come

together again. "N-no. I mean, yes, he did. My back. But it's not—"

He carefully turned her around.

His fingers touched her cuts through her shirt, making them sting. She sucked in a breath.

"Sorry." He turned her to face him again. "There isn't much blood. You probably won't need stitches. Did he hurt you, in any other way?"

She frowned, trying to understand what he meant. Then she got it. He was asking whether she'd been sexually assaulted. Heat crept up her neck.

"No, he didn't…ah…do…anything else." She pulled away, rubbing her hands up and down her arms.

The sirens had stopped. Red-and-blue lights flashed through the front windows. She was vaguely aware of a door opening, footsteps echoing on the hardwood. Chris guided her to the couch and she sat down, her gaze automatically going to the body on the floor. Deep voices spoke in quiet tones. Another voice, a woman's, said something in reply.

Blood. There was so much blood. How could one person bleed that much?

She wrapped her arms around her middle.

The couch dipped beside her. A policewoman. She was dressed in black body armor. Bright white letters across the front of her vest read SWAT.

"Hello, Ms. Webb." The woman's voice was kind, gentle. "I'm Officer Donna Waters." She waved her hands at her uniform, the gun strapped at her waist. "Don't let this gear bother you. We came prepared for a possible hostage situation." She patted Julie's hand. "An ambulance is on the way to take you to the hospital to get checked out. But you're safe now. You're going to be okay."

The woman's words seeped slowly into her brain as if through a thick fog. "Hospital? No. No, no, no. I'm not hurt. I don't want to go to a hospital."

"Ms. Webb?"

The now-familiar masculine voice had her turning her head. Chris Downing, the man who'd risked his own life for her, knelt on the floor, his expression full of compassion and concern.

"We'll take your statement after you've seen a doctor. Is there anyone I can call—"

"Is he dead?"

Her question seemed to startle him, but he quickly smoothed out his expression. "I'm afraid so, yes. Do you want me to—"

She grabbed his hands in hers and stared into his eyes. Could she trust him? Would he tell her the truth?

He frowned. "Ms. Webb—"

"Are you sure? Are you absolutely positive that he's dead?"

He had to think she was crazy. But she'd been here before. She'd been the woman sitting on the couch while the policeman told her that he was dead. And then he… wasn't. And then…and then. She shuddered.

"Is he dead?" She held her breath, waiting for his reply.

He exchanged a look with the female officer before answering. "Yes. I'm sorry. Yes, he's dead."

She covered her mouth with her hands, desperately trying to keep from falling apart.

He's dead. Oh, my God. He's dead.

"Someone will take your official statement after

you've been checked out at the hospital. But can you tell us anything right now about the man who attacked you? Did you know him?"

"Know him?" A bubble of hysterical laughter burst between her lips. "I married him."

Chapter Five

Chris exchanged a startled look with Donna as he knelt in front of the couch. His neighbor, Julie Webb, had just announced that the intruder Chris had killed was her husband. And, instead of being angry or crying or… something that made sense, she was rocking back and forth with her arms around her middle, eyes squeezed tightly shut. The rocking wasn't the part that was odd. What had the hairs standing up on his neck were the words that she kept whispering over and over in response to him telling her that her husband was dead.

"Thank you, Lord. Thank you, thank you, thank you."

Her callous words didn't seem to match the fragile, lost look in her deep blue eyes, as if she were caught in a nightmare and couldn't find her way out. He instinctively wanted to reach for her, pull her into his arms, tell her that everything would be okay. But the words she kept chanting sent a chill up his spine and started alarm bells going off in his suspicious detective's brain.

If she'd been abused by her husband, which seemed likely given that he'd held a knife on her, Chris could understand her relief that her husband couldn't hurt her anymore. And he'd seen the fear in her eyes earlier today, which lent more evidence to the abuse theory. But he'd also seen many domestic violence cases, and almost without fail, the abused party would defend her abuser. If a cop tried to arrest the husband, or hurt him while trying to protect the wife, nine times out of ten that wife would immediately leap to the husband's defense. Julie's actions were nothing like what he was used to seeing in those cases. The whole situation just seemed...off.

"The chief's motioning for you." Donna kept her voice low. "Go on. I'll sit with her until the ambulance arrives."

He hesitated, feeling guilty for wanting to jump at her offer. He'd created this mess. He should have to stay and deal with the fallout, including whatever was going on with Julie Webb.

"It's okay. I've got this," she reassured him. "Go." She put her hand on Julie's back, lightly patting it like she would a child. Julie didn't even seem to notice. She just kept rocking and repeating her obscene prayer.

As if drawn by some invisible force, Chris's gaze slid to the body of the man who was dead because of him. This wasn't the first time he'd killed someone in the line of duty. Being on the only SWAT team within a hundred miles of Destiny meant he was often called out to help other small towns or unincorporated areas when violence landed on their doorstep. But every time he'd had to use lethal force, the what-ifs and second-guessing haunted him for a long time afterward. He didn't expect this one would be any different.

He wished he could put a sheet over the man, afford him some kind of dignity in death. But the uniformed officer standing near the body was his reminder that the scene had to be preserved until the Blount County coroner arrived. And since Destiny shared their coroner with a handful of other rural counties, that could be a while from now. Two more uniformed officers stood near a stack of boxes on the left side of the room, probably to keep Julie and others from contaminating the scene.

"Downing."

Chief Thornton's gruff voice had Chris finally standing and turning around. His boss stood just inside the front door, still wearing the khaki shorts and polo shirt that he'd worn to the cookout a few hours earlier.

"Powwow, front lawn. Now." The chief headed outside.

Chris followed the chief down the porch steps to where three members of the SWAT team who'd also been at the cookout stood waiting. Max, Randy and Colby were dressed in full body armor just like Donna, back inside the house. It occurred to him that they must have raced like a mama sow protecting her piglets to have gotten here so fast. None of them lived close by, except for Dillon, and he was noticeably absent.

"Is Ashley okay?" he asked no one in particular, assuming the worst. He couldn't imagine his best friend not responding to a call for aid from Chris or any of their fellow officers unless something had happened to Ashley.

"She's at Blount Memorial in Maryville." Max held up his hands to stop the anticipated flood of questions. "When your 911 call came in, Dillon and Ashley were halfway to the hospital because she'd started having contractions. I assured him we could handle—"

"It's too soon," Chris interrupted, worry making his voice thick. "She's only seven months along."

"I know that," Max said. "Like I was saying, I told Dillon not to worry about you, that we had your back. And, before you ask, I spoke to him a few minutes ago. They were able to stop her labor, but they'll keep her there for observation overnight, maybe even a few days. But she and the baby are both fine."

Chris nodded, blowing out a relieved breath.

"You okay?" Max put his hand on Chris's shoulder. "You look greener than Dillon did when you mentioned fried gizzards."

"I killed a man. No. I'm not okay."

Max winced and dropped his hand, immediately making Chris regret his curt reply.

"Tell us what happened," the chief said, impatience etched on his features. "Take it from the top and don't leave anything out."

Chris began reciting the events that had led to the shooting, being as detailed as he could. Since everyone on the SWAT team performed dual roles as detectives in the fifteen-officer police force, they all listened intently, taking notes on their phones or the little pads of paper most of them kept handy.

Dillon was normally lead detective, with Chris as backup. But obviously Chris couldn't investigate a case where he was a primary participant. He wasn't sure who would run with this one.

After Chris finished his statement, the chief motioned to Max.

Max pulled a brown paper evidence bag from his rear pocket and awkwardly cleared his throat as he held it open. "Sorry, man. Standard operating procedure. Gotta take your sidearm as evidence."

Chris knew the drill and had been vaguely surprised

that no one had taken his gun the moment they'd arrived. But even after putting his pistol in the bag, the weight of his now-empty holster seemed heavier than before, a reminder of what he'd done, the life he'd taken.

Max closed the bag and stepped back beside Randy. Since Max looked miserable about taking the gun, Chris gave him a reassuring nod to let him know that he understood.

"You said they were arguing when you approached the house," the chief said. "Did you hear what they were arguing about?"

He replayed the moment when he was crouching by the window, trying to remember what he'd heard.

"Seems like they both said something about 'keys,' or maybe it was 'please.' I definitely heard the man mention a gun. But he was holding a knife, so that doesn't seem right." He shrugged. "I was too far away to hear them clearly. I was more focused on what he was doing with the butcher knife and how to get it away from him."

The low wail of a siren filled the air as an ambulance turned down the road and headed toward them.

"About time," the chief said. "I was thinking we'd have to wake up Doc Brookes if it took any longer."

Chris couldn't help smiling. Even though it was only a few hours past sundown, it was probably Doc Brookes's bedtime. The town's only doctor was getting up there in years. And he made sure everyone knew not to bother him after hours unless there was arterial bleeding involved or a bone sticking out. Unfortunately, with the only hospital nearly forty-five minutes from Destiny, ornery Brookes was who they were stuck with most of the time.

"I'd better move my truck," Max said.

"Ah, shoot," Colby said. His truck's front bumper was partly blocking the end of the driveway. "Me, too."

They hurried to their vehicles to make room before the ambulance reached the house.

"Chief, got a second?" Chris asked.

Thornton looked pointedly at Randy, who took the unsubtle hint and awkwardly pounded Chris on the back before heading toward the house.

As soon as Randy was out of earshot, the chief held up his hand to stop Chris from saying anything.

"I know we still have to process the scene, and get the coroner out here, perform due diligence and all that. But honestly, son, it looks like a clean shoot to me. I can tell it's eating you up inside, but you need to let that go. You saved a life tonight. That's what you should focus on."

They moved farther into the grass while the ambulance pulled into the driveway. The EMTs hopped out of the vehicle and grabbed their gear.

"I appreciate that, Chief," Chris said. "I feel like hell for taking a life. But I know I did what I had to do. That's not what I wanted to talk to you about."

Colby and Max jogged up the driveway, having parked their trucks farther down the road. They started toward Chris and the chief, but a stern look from Thornton had them heading toward the house, instead, and following the EMTs inside.

Still, Chris hesitated. Putting his concerns into words was proving harder than he'd expected.

"Well, go on, son. Spit out whatever's bothering you. The skeeters are eatin' me alive out here."

As if to demonstrate what he'd said, the chief

smacked his arm, leaving a red smear where a mosquito had been making a buffet out of him. He wiped his arm on his shorts, grimacing at the stain he'd left behind, before giving Chris an impatient look. "Well?"

"It's Mrs. Webb," Chris said. "The thing is, after the shooting, she asked me whether the guy I'd shot was dead. No, what she asked was whether I was *sure*, as if she thought I was playing a cruel joke on her, as if she *wanted* him to be dead. The guy is, *was*, her husband. And it seemed like she was…relieved…that I'd killed him."

"Well, he did hold a knife on her. Makes sense she'd be happy to be alive and that she didn't have to worry about him attacking her again."

Chris scrubbed his face and then looked down the dark road, lit only by the occasional firefly. Crickets and bullfrogs competed with one another in their nightly symphony. All in all, everything seemed so normal. And, yet, nothing was the same.

"You think there's more to it than that, don't you?" The chief was studying him intently. "Why?"

"Because she didn't ask me just once whether he was dead. She asked several times. And it was more the way she asked it that spooked me. You know how it is. If there's a domestic dispute, a husband beating his wife or trying to kill her, we cops intervene and suddenly we're the bad guys. Happens almost every time. But I shoot Mrs. Webb's husband and she starts praying out loud, thanking God. I don't know about you, but that's a first for me."

Thornton was quiet for a long moment, leaving Chris to wallow in his own thoughts, to wonder if saying anything was the right thing to do. He hated the unflattering picture that he'd just painted of Julie Webb. It didn't seem right, as if he was spreading rumors, gossiping—something his father would have rewarded with an extra long switch applied liberally to his hide. But this wasn't high school. This was the real world, a death investigation, where actions and words had consequences. They mattered. And he couldn't ignore something just because it was uncomfortable.

"How did she seem before all of this?" Thornton finally asked. "If her husband had a history of violence against her, she might have joined a support group and got the help she needed to cut all ties. Maybe she moved here to escape him, thought she was safe. But he figured out where she was, came after her. Seems to me that'd make her mighty grateful that he's never going to hurt her again."

"Maybe." He wanted to believe that was it. But even he could hear the doubt in his voice. He shrugged. "Hard to say what her state of mind was prior to this incident. She kept to herself, didn't even wave. I did get the feeling earlier today, when I saw her on her porch, that she was afraid of…something. And that was before her husband showed up."

"There, see? It's like I said. Her behavior could very well make sense, given those circumstances. And she's lucky you were close by to save her."

"Yeah," he mumbled. "Lucky for both of us."

The chief gave him a knowing look. And it dawned on Chris that Thornton might know firsthand how he felt. Chris had joined the force right out of college, thirteen years ago. But Thornton was already chief by then. There was no telling what horrors he might have faced as a young beat cop, or even in his detective days, what burdens he might have accumulated like an invisible weight that no one else could see. All Chris knew for sure was what *he* felt, which was all kinds of uneasy about this whole thing.

It was bad enough that he'd taken a life. Even worse if there was something else going on here. The "something else" that kept running through his mind was so prejudicial against Julie Webb that he couldn't voice it to the chief, not without proof, something concrete. All he had was a disturbing series of impressions that had begun to take root in his mind from the moment he'd seen her reaction to the shooting.

Suspicions that maybe this wasn't "just" a case of a domestic dispute with tragic consequences.

That maybe Julie Webb knew she was moving in next door to a cop all along.

That she had planned this whole thing from beginning to end.

That she'd just used Chris as a weapon to commit murder.

Chapter Six

Standing in the Destiny Police Department at midnight on a Saturday wasn't exactly where Chris imagined his fellow SWAT team members wanted to be. But not one of them had even considered going home. Max, Colby, Donna and Randy stood shoulder to shoulder with him in a show of solidarity while they watched their boss interview Julie Webb through the large two-way glass window.

Behind Chris and his SWAT team, two more officers sat at desks on the other side of the large open room that was essentially the entire police station. One of them, Blake Sullivan, was a recent transfer and would eventually be a detective and member of their SWAT team. But not yet. For now, he was learning the ropes of Destiny PD as a nightshift cop, which included filling out a lot of mundane reports.

There were fifteen desks in all, three rows of five. And other than a couple of holding cells off the back wall and a bathroom, there was just the chief's office, his executive washroom that the team loved to tease him about and the interview room.

The entire night shift consisted of the two officers currently writing reports and two more out on patrol.

Destiny wasn't exactly a mecca for crime. The town didn't boast a strip of bars or clubs to spill their drugs or drunks into the streets. A typical night might mean lecturing some teenagers caught drag racing, or rescuing a rival football team's stolen mascot from a hayloft.

Tonight was anything but typical.

Tonight a man had died.

And Chris wanted, *needed*, to find out what had precipitated the violence by Alan Webb, leaving Chris no choice but to use lethal force. The chief had officially placed him on administrative leave, pending the results of the investigation. He'd expressly forbidden Chris from going into the interview room. But since the chief would've had to fight his own SWAT team to force Chris to leave the station, he'd wisely pretended not to notice him in the squad room, watching the chief interview the witness.

Along with her counsel, assistant district attorney Kathy Nelson.

Plus two administrative lackeys—Brian Henson and Jonathan Bolton—that Nelson had brought with her from Nashville. She'd left the two men sitting at one of the desks on the opposite side of the squad room like eager lapdogs waiting for their master to give them an order.

Chris studied Henson and Bolton for a long moment before looking back at the interview window. "If she felt she needed a lawyer, why call an ADA? And since when does an assistant district attorney have an entourage? Or drive with that entourage for three hours in the middle of the night for a witness interview, let alone one that's way outside her jurisdiction?"

"Right? Doesn't make a lick of sense," Donna said beside him.

After dodging another barrage of questions like the polished politician that she was, Nelson shoved back her chair and stood.

"Wait, what's she doing?" Max asked.

Nelson motioned to Mrs. Webb. She picked up her purse from the table and stood.

Chris stiffened. "They're leaving."

Donna was clearly bemused. "But they didn't answer hardly any of the chief's questions."

"Screw this." Chris stepped toward the interview room door.

Max grabbed his shoulder. "Don't do it, man. The chief will—"

Chris shoved Max's hand away and yanked open the door.

JULIE HURRIEDLY STEPPED back to put more distance between her and the imposing man suddenly filling the open doorway of the interview room—her neighbor, Detective Chris Downing. With his clenched jaw and hands fisted at his sides, he seemed like a tautly drawn bow, ready to spring.

Before Kathy could say anything, Thornton held his hand out to stop her and confronted his officer.

"I warned you, Chris. You can't be in here." His gravelly voice whipped through the room. "What do I have to do, arrest you? Lock you in a cell?"

Twin spots of color darkened Chris's cheekbones. His heated gaze flashed to Julie, then back to Thornton. "I need answers. And, so far, you're not getting any. Let me interview her. I'll make her talk."

Julie flinched at his harsh tone. She'd retreated to her chair, but even with a table between them, his anger seemed to fill the room, crowding in on her. Where was the gentle, concerned man who'd knelt in front of the couch earlier this evening, reassuring her that everything was going to be okay?

Kathy didn't move. Her only concession to Chris standing so close was to tilt her head back to meet his gaze. "Are you threatening Mrs. Webb, Officer Downing?"

Thornton aimed an aggravated look at Kathy. "It's *Detective*, not *Officer*. And he's not threatening anyone. Stay out of this."

The shocked look on Kathy's face was almost comical. Julie doubted that anyone, except maybe Kathy's husband, had ever dared to speak to her that way before. She seemed to be at a loss as to how to respond.

"Don't you be questioning my methods, son." Thornton jabbed his finger at Chris's chest. "I was interviewing witnesses when you were knee-high to a mule. Since you're the one who fired the gun, you can't be involved in the investigation. Until this is over, you're a civilian. And civilians have no business questioning witnesses. Now, turn around and—"

"No." Julie jumped up from her seat.

Everyone stared at her in surprise.

She cleared her throat, just as surprised as they were at her outburst, but she now acknowledged what her subconscious had already known—that this was the right thing to do.

"I want him to stay," she said.

The expression on Chris's face turned suspicious.

"What did you say?" Thornton's question sounded

more like he was daring her to repeat her request, a request he had no intention of fulfilling.

"Julie—" Kathy began.

She waved her hand. "Taking a life is a heavy burden that no one should have to bear, even if taking that life was necessary. Letting Detective Downing ask questions about why he was put in that situation is the least that I can do to show my gratitude for his saving my life. So, Chief Thornton, either you allow him to stay, or the interview is over."

While Thornton stood in indecision, Chris firmly closed the door and then straddled the chair directly across from her. He gave her a crisp nod, as if to grudgingly thank her. She nodded in return, just as stiffly—two adversaries facing off before a fight.

The other two gave up their vigil. Kathy sat down while Thornton stared pointedly at his chair, the one Chris was currently occupying. Chris ignored him. After grumbling something beneath his breath about "seat stealers," the chief finally sat down. But the table's small size and Chris's broad shoulders had forced the chief to the end of the table, which had him grumbling again.

Julie waited expectantly. Rather than attack her with a volley of questions, Chris simply stared at her, as if sizing her up. If he was trying to figure out how to intimidate her, the effort was unnecessary. She'd been intimidated since the moment he'd stood in the open doorway like a fierce warrior looking for a dragon to slay.

And she was the dragon.

She clasped her hands beneath the table so he couldn't see that they were shaking. It wasn't just Chris that had her so nervous. Being in an interrogation room again, after all these months, stirred up a host of horrific memories. The past few months had been rough, brutal. But at least she'd survived. Her husband hadn't. And even though she was relieved she no longer had to fear him, she still grieved that it had come to this. There'd been a time once, long ago, when she'd loved him.

He'd been a good man back then—handsome, kind, sweet, helping her move forward after the tragic loss of her family just a few months before she'd met him. She grieved for *that* Alan, the one she'd pledged to honor and love until death do they part. The man who had, or so she liked to believe, loved her, too, once upon a time, until the fairy tale had twisted into a tragedy.

"Mrs. Webb?" Chris's deep voice intruded into her thoughts. "Please answer the question."

She blinked. "I'm sorry. What did you ask me?"

"I'll answer your question," Kathy interrupted. "Mrs. Webb came to Destiny to hide from her abusive husband."

Julie shot the other woman an irritated look. She made it sound like Julie had stayed with Alan through a long, abusive relationship. In truth, before today, Alan had been abusive only once, five months ago. After that one horrific night, she'd filed for divorce and ended her three-year marriage. She supposed she was lucky. Some women ended up caught in cycles of violence from which they could never escape. But Julie wasn't feeling particularly fortunate at the moment. Everything was in turmoil. And Alan had lost his life. There was no way to feel good about what had happened.

"Her husband somehow found out that she was here, in Destiny," Kathy continued. "And he broke into her home and assaulted her. The rest you know. Detective Downing had to use deadly force to protect her."

"How about we let the witness give her own statement," Chris said, closely watching Julie. "Mrs. Webb—"

"Julie, please," she corrected, so tired of the awkwardness and formalities of this never-ending interview. At this point she just wanted it over.

"Julie," he corrected. "Do you agree with the assistant district attorney's version of this evening's events?"

She hesitated, then nodded.

Kathy let out a breath, as if relieved.

"Except for the part where she made it sound like my husband had a history of violence," she said. "Alan and I never had a perfect marriage. But until…recently… he never lifted a hand against me. Something…happened to make him snap." She finished in a near whisper, her defense of Alan sounding weak when she said it out loud. Still, she hated to paint him as a bad person when, for most of the time that she'd known him, he was kind and good to her.

Kathy put a hand on top of Julie's and gave her a sympathetic look. "You're being far too kind to a man who tried to kill you."

Julie swallowed and looked away.

Kathy sighed and turned in her seat to face Julie. "For the record, are you stating that your husband wasn't dangerous? That you weren't afraid of him?"

"No, of course not. He was definitely dangerous. You know what he did in Nashville."

Kathy groaned and closed her eyes.

"I was wondering why you hadn't brought that up yet." Thornton jumped on her statement. "I ran your husband's name through the computer before the interview. Why don't you tell us your version of the first attack?"

Chris shot a surprised look at his boss. Julie figured he must not have been told what Thornton had found.

Kathy checked her watch, probably calculating how late—or early in the morning now—it would be by the time this was over and she could start the long drive back.

"You might as well tell them," she said. "Now that you've brought it up. Then I'll take you back to Nashville and—"

"I'm not going back."

Kathy frowned. "Why not?"

"I just got here. I don't want to move again. Not this soon."

"You were here to hide out from Alan. Obviously, that's not necessary anymore."

"We don't know if he was the one flattening my tires, salting my yard, and everything else. What if it was his family? I wouldn't put it past them."

"I don't think they're dangerous," Kathy said.

"We both know what they can be like," she said. "I'd much rather stay here until everything is settled. Then maybe they'll finally leave me alone and I can return home and live in peace."

Kathy shrugged. "Maybe it does make sense to stay here, at least until the civil case is over."

"Civil case?" Thornton's voice had risen again and he looked like he was ready to explode with frustration. "This is supposed to be an interview, a police interview. You two need to start talking to *us*, instead of to each other. You need to answer our questions."

"Chief—" Kathy began.

"What did he do to you?" Chris's deep voice cut through the conversation, silencing everyone in the room. His brow was furrowed with concern, his tone gentle, almost a whisper, just like back at the house. "How did he hurt you?"

Her stomach did a little flip. Part of her was tempted to throw herself in his arms and beg him to take her away from the nightmare that her life had become. She must be more exhausted than she thought. Chris had shown his true colors when he'd barged into the room, looking like a bull ready to charge after a red flag. He wasn't really interested in helping her. She'd do well to remember that, and not let her exhaustion and longing for someone to lean on after all these months of being alone influence her decisions.

She straightened her spine and focused on Thornton as she answered. If she looked at the supposed concern on Chris's face one more time she just might shatter.

"The reason I moved to Destiny was to hide from my husband, as Kathy said. He disappeared after posting bail. And there have been some…incidents, annoyances really, that made me wonder if he was stalking me. While it's true that he doesn't have a…*long* history of being abusive, he did attack me about five months ago, which you obviously already know. We were separated. He'd moved out and left the house to me. And then he broke into our home in the middle of the night. He was dressed all in black and wore a mask. And that night, like earlier today, he had a knife. Today, Detective Downing saved my life when he shot Alan. And I deeply appreciate his sacrifice. But there wasn't anyone else around months ago to protect me. So I saved myself. I grabbed my husband's gun, the one he'd left in the nightstand before moving out, and I shot him."

Chris blinked in surprise. "You shot your husband?"

"I did."

Thornton and Chris exchanged a glance. But Julie had no clue what they were silently communicating to each other.

Kathy said, "Mr. Webb was charged with breaking and entering and attempted murder. He had duct tape, a knife and gloves. He attacked Mrs. Webb, pulled her out of the bed and onto the floor. She was able to get away and grab the gun or she wouldn't be sitting here today. She'd be buried six feet under. However, in spite of the overwhelming evidence in the case, the judge went against our recommendations and set bail at one million dollars, which Mr. Webb immediately paid. Then he—"

"He paid a million-dollar bail?" Thornton asked. He and Chris both looked at Julie with renewed interest. "Just how much money did he have? And who's the beneficiary?"

She closed her eyes and squeezed her hands together in her lap. This was what she'd wanted to avoid. Now they would look at her the way Alan's family did. They'd never believed her side of what had happened and had accused her of trying to kill him for his money.

Kathy said something to Thornton but Julie tuned it out. She just wanted the interview to be over. How had it come to this? As she often did when thinking about the past year of her life, when her marriage had started to fail, she tried to pinpoint that one decision, that one pivotal event that had led to her entire life being turned upside down. But she still didn't know what had happened. One day she was happy, *they* were happy, her and Alan. The next, everything had changed. Alan had become moody, angry, and it continued to go downhill from there. A tear ran down her cheek. Then another. She drew a shaky breath and wiped them away.

"Here." Chris was crouching beside her chair, holding a box of tissues. And in his other hand was a bottle of water, which he held out to her. "They're so busy arguing with each other over there that they didn't even notice I'd left the room to get you the water and tissues."

He jerked his head toward the corner by the window where Thornton and Kathy were standing, having a heated argument. Apparently, Julie had been so lost in her own thoughts, she hadn't noticed anything that had happened over the past few minutes, either.

She wiped her cheeks with a tissue, then took the bottle. He'd already opened it and had set the cap on the table.

"Thank you," she said.

"You're welcome." He gestured toward the corner again. "I think they're going to be at this for a while. Want to get out of here?"

She blinked. "I thought you wanted to interview me? Or is that your plan, to take me somewhere else and ask me questions without Kathy present?"

He cocked his head, looking every bit the handsome, sexy neighbor again instead of the angry, hardened cop. "Do you trust me?"

"No."

He laughed. "Score one for honesty."

"Sorry."

"Don't be. Never apologize for telling the truth." He glanced at the chief and Kathy, completely consumed in their argument, before looking at Julie again. "I'd like to remind you that I'm a police officer, sworn to protect and serve. And if that doesn't make you trust me, I'll resort to blackmail."

"Blackmail?"

His grin faded, and he was once again staring at her with an intensity that was unnerving. "Like you said before, I deserve answers. So how about we ditch this place and I take you somewhere safe, where no one will bother you? We'll both get a good night's sleep. No questions. No talking unless you want to. Then tomorrow, we take a fresh look at the situation and figure out where to go from there. Sound good?"

"Sounds too good, actually. Why are you offering?"

"Because somewhere along the way this interview turned into an inquisition. The chief and I both want answers, so I don't want Nelson convincing you to leave and never come back. But it's late, we're all tired and you aren't a criminal being interrogated. You're a witness, a victim. You deserve to be treated better than you have been. I'm offering a truce. What do you say? Will you let me get you out of here?" He stood and held out his hand.

This time it was her turn to glance at Thornton and Kathy. Both their faces were red. Whatever they were arguing about, it didn't look like they'd stop anytime soon.

She put her hand in Chris's. "Let's go."

Chapter Seven

Chris glanced at his passenger as he turned his pickup off the highway onto a gravel road. Thanks to his SWAT team, he'd managed to get the witness out of the station without Henson or Bolton being able to give chase. It was hard to follow someone when the only exit door was blocked by three cops with guns. But he was already having buyer's remorse.

The chief was going to kill him for this.

Julie sat stiffly, clutching the armrest as if it were a lifeline, staring through the windshield. Was she also regretting the decision to flee? Wondering if she'd gotten herself into worse trouble than she was already in?

"This isn't the way I go to my house." She leaned forward to peer at the narrow gravel road and trees crowding in that were revealed in the headlights. "I assumed you were taking me home. Is this a back way?"

"Your home is still taped off as a crime scene. You can't go there until it's released."

Her shoulders slumped, but she nodded. "This seems awfully far from town to be leading to a hotel."

"It's called Harmony Haven. You'll see the place over that next rise. See how the sky is lighter up ahead? That's from the security and landscape lights."

"A bed-and-breakfast then?"

He steered around a pothole, surprised the road was in such poor condition. Then again, there'd been a lot of rain this past month, and he hadn't been down this way in quite a while.

"Chris?"

He shook his head. "It's not a B and B. It's a private home on a horse-rescue farm. It belongs to my friends Dillon and Ashley. They're not here right now and I figured they wouldn't mind us crashing for the night."

Any argument she might have been about to give was forgotten as they topped the rise and Dillon's property came into view. Julie stared in wonder at the beautiful vista laid out before them. It pleased him that she seemed so awestruck. He felt that way every time he came here, especially at night because of the way the lights cast an ethereal glow on the place.

With the sweat equity he'd invested to help Dillon get this place up and running over the years, he couldn't help feeling proprietary about it. But with Dillon married now, Chris's visits had become less frequent. Newlyweds needed their privacy, even more so now with a baby on the way. His jaw tightened. If it weren't so late, he'd call the hospital for an update on Ashley. He'd have to remember to call first thing in the morning and check on her.

He pulled the truck to a stop beside the two-story white farmhouse and took a moment to enjoy the view himself. Soft floodlights that Ashley had insisted upon, which were more for ambience than security, dotted a long, pristine, white three-rail fence and acres and acres of lush green pastures that went on forever.

The enormous stable was partially visible behind the

house. He parked at the end of the home's enormous wraparound front porch that boasted white rockers and an old-fashioned swing hanging from chains.

"It's beautiful," Julie whispered, seemingly mesmerized as the light breeze teased the swing back and forth, the chains creaking in rhythm with the sound of cicadas.

"I reckon it is." He cut the engine, admiring her profile. The lights from the yard sparkled on the honey-blond highlights in her brown hair. She had a small, pert nose and pale skin with a smattering of freckles across both cheeks. A lock of her hair hung forward and he barely resisted the urge to brush it back.

"Harmony Haven," she whispered, as if testing the name on her tongue. "You said it's a horse rescue?"

He waved toward the stable, the main doors sealed up for the night. "There are a couple dozen horses in there, another dozen or so out in the pasture. Ashley and Dillon run horse camps every summer and adopt out most of the herd. Then rescues trickle in throughout the year and they work on rehabilitating them, regaining their trust. A couple months from now this year's first campers will arrive. There's a bunkhouse farther out for the farmhands and a second bunkhouse for the campers."

"Ashley and Dillon are married?"

He nodded. "Almost a year now."

"Then who's Harmony?"

Chris's smiled faded. "Dillon's baby sister. She loved horses even more than he does, which seems impossible."

"Loved? Past tense?"

"She died a long time ago. Hang tight. I'll help you down."

Before she could ask him any more questions or

dredge up memories of the past, he hopped down from the truck and hurried to the passenger side. Although his black four-by-four was suspended a lot higher than the average pickup, it wasn't quite a monster truck. It was just high enough for his six-foot-two frame to be comfortable climbing in and out. But Julie was almost a foot shorter than him, which meant he'd had to lift her up into the truck back at the station. Something he'd realized he didn't mind one bit. She sure was a pretty thing.

She'd just opened her door when he reached her. With a mumbled apology, he put his hands at her waist and lifted her down. As soon as her shoes touched the ground, she stepped back, forcing him to drop his hands. She seemed awkward, uncomfortable as she smoothed her blouse over her khaki pants.

"Why didn't we go to a hotel?" She followed him as he led the way toward the front porch. "Why drive so far from town?"

He stopped with his boot on the bottom step. "There's only one hotel in Destiny. Nelson would have looked for you there."

Her brows shot up. "I didn't know we were hiding from her."

He smiled. "We're hiding more from my boss than from your ADA. I'm on administrative leave, which means I'm not even supposed to talk to you."

"But you want answers, like you said at the station."

He nodded.

"You aren't too good at following orders, are you?"

"Not when I'm shut out of a case where I had to kill a man."

She swallowed and looked away.

"Look," he said. "I'm not going to force you to do anything you don't want to do. For now, we're just escaping the inquisition back there and getting a good night's sleep. As a bonus, I ensure that Nelson doesn't whisk you off to Nashville overnight."

She stood on the first step, then moved up one more, making her almost eye level with him.

"You seem to think that if Kathy tells me to do something, I jump to do it. What gave you that impression?"

He shrugged. "I think it's more that she drove three hours to come to your rescue. Allowing you to talk anymore to us would have pretty much defeated the purpose in her driving down here. Lawyers don't want their clients to talk. Ever."

He took the stairs two at a time and paused at the door.

When she joined him there, he added, "This place has the best security around. No one is going to sneak up on you while you're here. You're safe."

Her lips parted in surprise.

He shook his head, exasperated. "Did you really think I was buying the picture that Nelson was painting? It's as obvious as the day is long that you're both hiding something, holding something back. And if you moved to Destiny just to hide from your husband, or little high school-type pranks, you wouldn't still be scared."

She stiffened. "What makes you think I'm scared?"

He glanced at her hands, which she was twisting together.

She jerked them apart, her face flushing again.

"I guess the real question is whether Nelson knows whatever secrets you're hiding."

Her expression went blank, as if she'd thrown up a

wall. He'd been fishing, but now he knew for sure that she really was hiding something. What could she be hiding that even her ADA friend didn't know about? And why?

She looked at the truck as if debating whether to demand that he take her back to town. Sensing that if he pushed her on it, if he argued to get her to stay, that she'd push back and demand to leave, he remained silent and waited.

"Your friends Dillon and Ashley—they know we're here? You have keys to the house?"

In answer, he separated the keys on his key ring and held up one. "If Dillon is awake, he knows. The security system texted him our picture as soon as we turned down the private road to the farm."

Her eyes widened.

"I'm sure they don't mind," he continued. "But I'll call in the morning and explain the situation."

"Okay, then. I'll stay. Just for the night."

He unlocked the door and waved her inside before she could change her mind.

Chapter Eight

Of all the reckless, crazy things that Julie had ever done, sneaking off with Detective Chris Downing was probably the most outrageous and stupid. She couldn't believe that she'd had the gumption to tiptoe out of the conference room, pausing only briefly as he whispered to his SWAT team members, and then getting into his pickup truck.

When he'd handed her that tissue in the conference room to wipe her tears, it was as if they were co-conspirators, the two of them against the world. And she'd been just desperate enough to take the lifeline that he'd offered, tricking herself into believing that he was someone she could trust. He'd been what she'd needed most at that very moment—someone to lean on, someone who would keep her safe, be a friend, if only for one night.

She was such a fool.

They had a truce, more or less, but she knew the limits. The moment she got up tomorrow he'd probably barrage her with questions, and she wouldn't have Kathy here to deflect them. She might as well have stayed at the police station.

As she followed him inside, he paused beside a beeping security alarm keypad and keyed in the security code, disabling it. After locking the door, he set the alarm again and waved his hand to encompass the large open room.

"This is it," he said. "Dillon took down most of the walls to give it an open floor plan. As you can see, the kitchen is on the back left. Feel free to grab something if you're thirsty or hungry."

She nodded, noting the granite-topped island that separated the kitchen from the great room. A straight staircase was in front of them, with a small dark hallway opening behind it on the main floor. The room was an eclectic mix of masculine and feminine touches, with dark chunky wood furniture softened by pastel throws and pillows, and rugs scattered across the hardwood floor.

"Your room is through there." He led her through a doorway on the right, just past the front door. "This is the in-law suite, with its own private bath. Ashley's expecting her parents to stay here for a few weeks after the baby is born. So I'm sure she's already got it stocked with everything you could possibly need—shampoo, toothbrushes, stuff like that. But if there's something else you need, let me know. I can check upstairs."

"I'm sure I'll be fine." She hesitated by the four-poster bed. "I didn't even think about packing a bag when I left my house."

"We wouldn't have let you anyway."

Her gaze shot to his in question.

"Your house is a crime scene," he reminded her.

"Oh." She twisted her hands together, then remembered him noticing her doing that before when she was nervous and she forced her hands apart.

"We'll call Donna in the morning. She's one of the SWAT officers. You met her, just after…"

"I remember," she said, thinking back to the kind woman who'd sat beside her on the couch, while Alan lay on the floor not far away. She swallowed against the bile rising in her throat and rubbed her hands up and down her arms.

Looking uncomfortable, Chris shifted on his feet. "She can get you whatever you need from the house."

She nodded. "What about you? You'll need a bag, too."

He shook his head. "I stay here sometimes when Dillon and I brainstorm cases, or when we have to get an early start during hunting season. Don't stay nearly as often as I used to. But I've still got stuff in a guest room upstairs." He waved toward the doorway to the great room. "If you want, we can see if Ashley has a nightgown that will fit you. I'm sure she wouldn't mind. You two are close to the same size, although you're a bit shorter."

"I don't want to impose any more than I already have."

"You're not imposing. Trust me. Ashley and Dillon would give the shirts off their backs to someone in need."

Trust him. She wished it were that easy. But she'd given her trust before, and it had nearly killed her.

She forced a smile. "I'll be okay without borrowing any clothes. Where will you stay? The guest room you mentioned upstairs?"

His gaze dropped to her hands, and she realized she was twisting them together again. She tugged them apart and tried to keep her expression neutral. She didn't want him to know that she was already getting scared again. It was stupid, ridiculous, to be worried about anyone finding her way out here. But Alan had found her. And that meant that anyone could. So what was she going to do? Going home to Nashville didn't seem like a good option. But neither did staying here. She hadn't been thinking clearly when she'd told Kathy that she wasn't leaving. She should go somewhere else. But how could she leave without a destination in mind?

Chris was studying her. What did he see? Again, she tried to keep her expression neutral, to hide the doubts, the questions, even the fear roiling through her mind.

Finally, he said, "I like the couch down here just fine. If you need anything, just holler."

The couch. This house was huge, probably had four or five bedrooms upstairs, and he was taking the couch. Either he was an old-fashioned Southern gentleman and truly wanted to be close by if she needed him, or he suspected something and didn't want to let her out of his sight. She thought about arguing with him, to try to get him to go upstairs. But that would probably only make him suspicious, if he wasn't already.

"Thank you," she said.

He tipped his head as if he were wearing a hat, but continued to stand there.

The silence drew out between them.

She motioned toward the cell phone on his belt. "I'm surprised your boss hasn't called you by now."

"Ringer's off. What about Nelson?" He waved at her purse. "I assume you've got a cell phone in there. But she hasn't called you."

"Ringer's off."

They both smiled.

He motioned toward the clock on the bedside table.

"The sun will be coming up sooner than you think. I reckon we'd better get some sleep while we can." He tipped his head again. "Good night, Julie."

"Good night... Chris."

His smile broadened, and then he stepped through the doorway. He'd just grabbed the doorknob when she called out to him.

"Chris?"

He glanced back in question.

"Tomorrow, when news of my husband's death spreads, when Kathy tells his family what happened, they'll demand justice. They'll accuse me of orchestrating his death. They'll say some really awful, terrible things about me."

His brows furrowed.

She took a step toward him, then another, until the tips of her shoes pressed against the tips of his boots. "But I promise you, I didn't plan any of this. I would never have placed you in the position that you were in today if I could have prevented it. I'm so sorry that you got involved."

He slowly raised his hand toward her, giving her every chance to step away.

She didn't.

He feathered his fingers across her cheek, pushing back some of the hair that had fallen across her face. But, instead of dropping his hand, he cupped her cheek, as he stared down into her eyes. She felt the warmth of his touch all the way to her toes.

"Who else are you afraid of?" he whispered.

She wanted to trust him, to ask for his help. But this wasn't his fight. She couldn't involve him any more than she already had.

She gently pulled his hand down, squeezed it, then let it go.

"Good night, Chris."

He hesitated, then nodded. "Good night, Julie."

The door closed behind him. She sat down on the bed, listening to the sounds of the house settling around her, to the sound of him going upstairs, probably to get sheets and pillows for the couch. Water ran in the bathroom down the hall a few minutes later. And not long after that, the light under the door went dark.

She continued to sit on the bed, thinking about what had happened, about what would happen tomorrow, about what she needed to do. She twisted her hands in her lap, watching the minutes tick by on the clock. When the clock struck two, she stood and grabbed her purse.

Chapter Nine

Chris used the tongs to put the last piece of bacon onto the paper-towel-lined plate with the others and turned off the stove. He shoved the hot pan of grease into the oven to be cleaned later once it cooled, then stepped back to make sure he hadn't forgotten anything.

Other than throwing the occasional steak or ribs on a grill when he had friends over and Max wasn't there as the master chef, cooking wasn't his thing. He tended to live on cereal, sandwiches and an occasional hot meal of catfish and grits at Mama Jo's Kitchen back in town. But since he'd practically kidnapped Julie last night, he figured paying her back with a stick-to-the-ribs breakfast was the least he could do.

Dillon's wife, Ashley, was one of the best cooks he'd ever met. Her kitchen was stocked with everything he could possibly need to prepare a feast—or, in this case, scrambled eggs with cheese, fried bacon and toast. He'd looked for canned biscuits to cook, but premade dough was probably an affront to someone like Ashley. She probably made them from scratch, which was beyond his capabilities. He'd had to settle for whole-wheat toast.

Now, all he had to do was go wake Julie. He checked his watch. Seven-thirty. On a normal day he'd have been at the office for a good hour by now. Maybe Julie wasn't an early riser like him. They had been up awfully late last night. And goodness knew she'd been through a terrible ordeal. He'd assumed the smell of bacon and freshly brewed coffee would bring her into the kitchen. But if she was too exhausted for those delicious smells to lure her out of bed, maybe he should give her just a little bit longer to sleep. Everything could be reheated. And he did have some calls to make.

He covered the food with paper towels to keep it from getting cold and plopped down at the table. The first call he made was to Dillon. After getting an update on Ashley and the baby, he explained to Dillon about what was going on with the case and why he'd crashed at Harmony Haven for the night. As expected, Dillon didn't mind one bit and had already seen the security camera text to let him know that Chris was there.

The second call didn't go nearly so well.

"What the hell were you thinking?" his boss yelled.

Chris winced and held the phone several inches from his ear. He waited until the yelling stopped before risking holding the phone closer. After suffering through a chastisement that had him feeling like a five-year-old, he explained his reasons to his boss and agreed that he'd go ahead and bring Julie to the police station after breakfast.

Nelson had left for Nashville late last night after the chief had essentially lied to smooth things over. He'd made it sound like it had been his idea all along for Chris to take Julie to some safe house for the night and that they'd escort her to Nashville today once she'd had a good night's rest. The chief said Nelson had seemed more than happy to believe him as she had a heavy caseload back in town.

Of course, Chris and the others had no intention of taking Julie to Nashville. Not until they'd gotten to the bottom of their investigation. But Nelson didn't need to know that.

He hung up and checked his watch again. The chief, of course, wanted them at the station ASAP. But with the ADA out of the picture, at least temporarily, there wasn't as much of a rush in Chris's opinion. He'd let Julie get a little more sleep, give her a hot breakfast, then they'd head back to town. Until he knew for sure just how "innocent" she was in what had happened at her house, he was going to try to give her the benefit of the doubt and treat her as a victim and a witness rather than like someone with more skin in the game. But he wasn't going to let those soft, doe eyes of hers make him let down his guard, either. Maybe he could ask her the questions he was dying to ask on the way to the station, too. This administrative leave thing was going to make it next to impossible to get answers once he turned her over to his boss.

He shoved his phone back into the holder on his belt as a knock sounded at the back kitchen door. Recognizing the silhouette of Dillon's main farmhand behind the filmy white curtain covering the glass, Chris waved in greeting. He hurried to the door and reached up to key the security code into the electronic keypad by the door. But the light wasn't red. It was green.

The alarm was already disarmed.

He yanked his backup gun out of his ankle holster, since the chief had made him turn over his primary gun, and held it down by his thigh. He had two more pistols locked in the pickup. He'd have to remember to strap one of those on his belt when he left. On duty or off, he didn't want to get caught without enough firepower if the need arose. Especially if someone was still after Julie Webb—which seemed possible based on the fear he'd still seen in her eyes last night.

He threw the door open. "Griffin, you seen anyone skulking around here?"

The answering smile on Griffin's sun-browned face was replaced with concern as he glanced around. "Just the workers, feeding the horses, mucking stalls. I saw your truck and thought you might have an update on Miss Ashley."

"Stay here."

Without waiting for the older man to reply, Chris hurried from the kitchen, through the great room to the still-closed door of the front guest room. He didn't stop to knock. He threw the door open, sweeping his pistol out in front of him, fully expecting to see an intruder standing over Julie's bed or perhaps already holding her hostage.

There wasn't anyone there. The bed didn't even look like it had been slept in.

"Chris?" Griffin had obviously ignored his order to stay put and was behind him in the doorway.

Chris ignored him and cleared the closet, then the attached bath, before turning around. He strode across the room, the gun still at his side.

"What's going on?" Griffin asked, quickly backing up to let him through the doorway. "Should I call 911?"

"Not yet." He headed to his right, beside the staircase to the back hallway and the room at the back right corner of the downstairs. He headed inside and pulled up a chair in front of the main security camera console.

"Is Miss Ashley okay? Did something happen?"

The worry in Griffin's voice as he ran into the room finally sank in and Chris turned to face him. Last year Ashley had nearly been killed by some very bad people who were after her. Griffin had probably seen Chris's gun and thought the worst.

"She's fine. She and the baby are both fine. Dillon's with them at the hospital. They were able to stop the contractions, but they're keeping her for observation for a few days."

"*Gracias a Dios*. Thank God," Griffin whispered, making the sign of the cross on his chest. "I thought the bad men were back again to hurt Miss Ashley."

A pang of guilt shot through Chris for not taking a few extra seconds at the back door to reassure the old man. From what Dillon had told him, Griffin still had nightmares about the siege that had happened here when the men had caught up to Ashley last year.

Chris flipped on the computer monitors and entered the password into the menu to access the security footage. "Like I said, Ashley and the baby are fine. I'm here for another reason entirely." He keyed in some commands and accessed the recording from the cameras on the front and kitchen doors, with both displays side by side on the monitor in front of him. It didn't take long to find what he was looking for.

He cursed and pressed a key to pause the footage. Then he shoved his gun into his holster.

"Detective Downing? What's going on?"

Chris forced a smile. Griffin was always polite, but

for him to call Chris "Detective" meant he was getting really worried.

"It's okay, Griffin. Everything's okay. When I went to open the kitchen door to let you in, I realized the security alarm was off. I thought something might have happened, so I had to check things out. But everything is fine."

The look of relief that swept over the older man's face was palpable. "Good, that is very good. Dillon will tease you about forgetting to set the alarm then." He grinned.

Chris smiled back. "Yeah, he'll get a kick out of that. Was there anything that you needed?"

"No, no. Just saw your truck, wanted to check on you and see about Miss Ashley. If you don't need me, I'll get back to work."

"Thanks, Griffin. Good to see you again."

"You, too."

As soon as Griffin left the room, Chris turned back to the monitor. It showed a picture of the front door opening a crack. From the inside. He pushed Play and the image expanded to show Julie Webb sneaking out the front door. Which meant she must have watched him key in the security code yesterday and she'd shut off the alarm.

He watched the video until she disappeared from the camera shot. He punched up several other videos, examining angles from other cameras. Then he turned off the monitors and pulled out his cell phone.

"You on your way?" Chief Thornton asked, recognizing Chris's cell phone number.

"Actually, no. There's something I need to take care of. It'll be a couple more hours before I can bring Julie to the station."

CHRIS DROVE HIS pickup across the field toward the weathered gray barn on the right side of Cooper's farm. The older man's white pickup was sitting beside the barn where he must have left it before going into the hospital. After last night, Chris had planned on calling someone else to clear the land he'd promised Cooper he'd clear. But after seeing the security video, and seeing Julie climb into the back of his pickup and hide under a tarp early this morning, he'd changed his mind.

He was going to make her tell him what she was hiding and why she'd snuck out of the house. To do that, he needed some time alone with her. His boss would think to check Harmony Haven if he got impatient waiting on him to bring Julie in. But he'd never think to look here. The only question now was how long Julie would let this little farce play out before she came out of hiding. She was about to find out that Chris could be a very patient man.

He parked next to the white pickup and killed his engine. He waited, checked the rearview mirror, waited some more. When the tarp didn't move, he let out an exasperated breath and hopped out of the truck, shoving the keys into his jeans pocket.

Two blood-bay mares and a palomino gelding idled lazily in the corral attached to the barn. Cooper's small farm was several miles from the nearest neighbor, but all of them were pitching in until he was back on his feet. One of them must have come by this morning already and fed and turned out the horses. That was the sum total of livestock on the farm. Cooper kept the horses for his grandkids when they came visiting. Otherwise, he rotated tobacco and hay in his fields, to augment his pension and keep himself from being bored.

Thousand-pound round bales of freshly cut orchard grass dotted the field behind the barn and the little one-story farmhouse a few hundred yards away. The grass was already drying to a golden brown that would become hay. In a few more days, another neighbor would bring equipment to gather up the bales. By the time Cooper was home, all he'd have to do was tend the summer garden he wanted for his own personal use. Which was why Chris was here.

Unless Julie quit being stubborn and made herself known, he'd be just as stubborn and go ahead and clear the acre of brush close to the house to make it easier for the owner to tend without having to walk so far. Cooper was getting a hip replacement, which meant exercise was good for him. But there was a limit to just how far he should have to walk and Chris aimed to help him out in that regard.

After another glance at his truck, he headed into the barn that housed Cooper's tractor and other farming equipment. He was just about to hook up the Bush Hog mower attachment to the back of the tractor when his phone vibrated. When he took it out of the holder and saw who was calling, a mixture of worry and dread shot through him.

"Dillon, did something happen? Are Ashley and the baby okay?"

A tired sigh sounded through the phone. "They're no worse than when you and I spoke earlier this morning. We're still fighting to keep the baby in the oven. Ashley's going stir-crazy, wanting to get out of bed. But the doctors won't let her move and they've been pumping her with meds to stop her contractions."

"Sorry, man. Is there anything I can do? Do you want me to bring something to the hospital?"

"You already have."

"What?"

"That ADA, Nelson? She sent two henchmen to the hospital an hour ago to ask me if I knew where you'd taken the witness. This is the first chance I've had to call and tell you."

Chris tightened his hands around the phone. "Henchmen? Are you talking about Henson and Bolton, her admin assistants? They should have gone back to Nashville with her."

"Well they didn't. I don't suppose you noticed they're both over six feet tall and built like bodyguards? You don't really think they're Nelson's gofers, do you?"

"Honestly, I'm embarrassed to say that I didn't pay them much attention at all last night. Other than noting they both had dark brown hair and wore matching gray suits, I probably couldn't pick them out of a lineup. I'm sorry they bothered you."

"Oh, I didn't let them bother me. When they knocked on Ashley's door and introduced themselves, I introduced them to hospital security and had them escorted outside. I didn't like the vibe I got from either of them. You might want to run a background check and see who they really are and why they're hanging with an assistant district attorney."

Chris leaned against the tractor. "You have a working theory?"

Dillon paused before continuing. "Not based on any facts. It's more of a feeling. I didn't trust them. Which makes me not trust Nelson, either. I think your next-door neighbor has landed you in the middle of something really bad. And since you're going to be my daughter's godfather, I just wanted to tell you to be careful."

Chris couldn't help grinning. "So, you're having a girl."

A chuckle sounded through the phone. "We'd planned on being surprised during the delivery, but they've been doing so many ultrasounds and checkups that we really couldn't avoid finding out the gender. So, yeah. We're having a girl."

"That's great. Any ideas on names yet?"

"We don't want to jinx anything, so we're waiting on that. Taking it one hour at a time. The doctor wants the baby to cook at least a couple more weeks, if possible. Until delivery, Ashley's on complete bed rest."

"She's going to go nuts lying around that long."

"Tell me about it. Hey, Chris. Back to this Julie Webb person and the goons who showed up this morning. I watched them from the hospital room window when they left. They were in two separate cars, which seems odd enough since they're both allegedly from out of town on a business trip together. What was even odder was that both cars were muscle cars. What's that sound like to you?"

"Like you said earlier, bodyguards. But the ADA wasn't with them?"

"No sign of her," Dillon said.

"Which means they aren't guards. We're back to the henchman theory."

"Pretty much. Be careful, all right? I mean it. Watch your six."

He glanced at the barn's huge double doors, made large enough to accommodate the tractor, and thought about his truck outside—and what was *in* the truck— or rather, who. His little game of outwaiting Julie was no longer viable, not if there were two thugs looking for her. He pushed away from the tractor and headed toward the doors to get her out of her hiding place. The bush hogging would have to wait.

"Thanks, Dillon. I'll check back later."

He ended the call and pushed through the double doors, just in time to see Cooper's white pickup truck bumping across the field toward the road.

With Julie Webb in the driver's seat.

Chris swore and ran toward his truck. He skidded to a halt at the driver's-side door, his boots sliding in the dirt. The front left tire—which had cost a cool five hundred dollars because it was so big—was completely flat. He whirled around in time to see the white pickup reach the road and turn north toward town. A moment later, Julie had rounded a curve and thick stands of pine trees hid her from sight.

A whinny had Chris turning around. The palomino brushed against the corral fence, its head extended over the railing as it tore chunks of sweet clover out of the ground.

Chris ran into the barn. Less than a minute later, he had a harness and reins on the palomino. No time for a saddle. He led the gelding out of the corral, grabbed a fistful of mane and vaulted onto its back.

"Yah!" he yelled, squeezing his thighs against the horse. The gelding squealed and took off at a bone-jarring gallop across the field. Right before the horse reached the road, Chris yanked the reins, sending them both crashing into the woods.

Chapter Ten

Gravel seemed to roll beneath the wheels like a wave as Julie fought to keep the truck on the road. She eased her foot off the gas and the pickup straightened out. Too fast. She was going way too fast for these bumpy country roads. If she didn't slow down she'd end up in a ditch.

Easing off the accelerator even more, she glanced in her rearview mirror. She'd caught a glimpse of Chris running out of the barn when she'd stolen his friend's truck. Thank goodness she'd let the air out of one of his tires. Facing him when he looked that angry wasn't something she hoped to do anytime soon.

Guilt swept through her as she sped up again on a straightaway. From the moment she'd met her sexy neighbor, he'd been nothing but nice. He'd done everything he could to protect her. And how did she repay him? She'd snuck out of the house before dawn, using the security code that she'd seen him enter into the keypad when they'd gotten there. And then, when she'd realized she was in the middle of nowhere with no hope of escaping on her own, she'd hunkered down in the back of his four-by-four, hoping he wouldn't notice.

Her plan had worked. Except for the part where he

didn't take her into town and, instead, drove to a farm even farther out in the boonies than the horse-rescue place had been.

It didn't matter. Now that she had transportation, she'd head to Destiny and leave the truck parked somewhere obvious so the owner would find it. And leave a wad of cash hidden inside as an apology for taking it.

The trees seemed to encroach on the narrow road as she slowed for another one of the hairpin turns. At this rate, she might get there faster by walking.

She came out of the curve and onto another straightaway. A dark blur suddenly burst from the trees on the right and leaped onto the road fifty yards ahead of her truck. A horse! She slammed the brakes and desperately turned the wheel. The pickup began to slide sideways like a jackknifed semi.

Oh, God, oh, God, oh, God. She was going to hit the horse.

The animal gave a high-pitched whinny and bolted toward the trees on the other side of the road just as the pickup slid to a stop.

Julie's heart hammered in her chest, her breaths coming in great gasps as she stared through the windshield. Her hands gripped the steering wheel so tightly she could feel her pulse thumping in her fingers.

What in the world had just happened?

She blinked, drew a ragged breath and scanned the road, looking for the horse. There, thirty feet away on the left, it stood with its head down, calmly munching on the tall green grass beside the road. Reins hung down from its harness. But it wasn't wearing a saddle. She frowned. Had someone been on the horse when it dashed in front of her? Everything had happened so fast. But she was almost positive she'd seen something, someone, bent low over the horse's neck.

Her door flew open. She jerked around and let out a squeal of alarm.

In the opening stood a very angry looking Chris Downing.

His dark eyes seemed almost black as he glared at her. "Get. Out."

CHRIS STALKED ACROSS the road toward the gelding, leaving Julie standing beside the truck, minus the keys this time, which Cooper had been foolish enough—or trusting enough—to leave in the cab. Then again, around these parts, people didn't make a habit of stealing their neighbors' vehicles. Unlocked doors were the norm. The only reason that Chris and Dillon were so security conscious was because in their role as police officers they saw more than the average citizen of the dangers that lurked out there.

Like from out of towners passing through, such as Julie Webb.

He cursed beneath his breath and forced himself to act as calmly as possible so he wouldn't spook the horse. He spoke to it in low, soothing tones as he took off the harness and scratched its velvety nose. Then he steered the horse around to the other side of the road and slapped its withers, sending it off at a trot back into the woods.

Julie's eyes widened as he strode toward her. She glanced at the harness in his hand, then the horse as it disappeared into the trees. He wasn't going to tell her that the horse would find its way back home just like a cat would. Let her wonder, and maybe worry just a bit about the havoc she'd caused.

He tossed the harness and reins in the bed of the truck and popped open the driver's door.

"Get in."

She glanced longingly toward the trees where the horse had gone, then at the road that led toward town.

"You just told me to get out."

He grabbed her around the waist and lifted her into the cab of the truck. Not giving her a chance to hop back out or argue with him, he climbed in after her, forcing her to slide over.

She glared at him and kept sliding, then grabbed the passenger-door handle.

Chris yanked her toward him and anchored her against his side with his arm around her shoulders.

"Let me go." Her eyes flashed with anger.

He leaned down until his face was just inches from hers, intentionally using his much larger size to get his point across.

"I'll let you go if you give me your word that you won't try to hop out of the truck."

A shiver went through her as she stared up at him, uncertainty replacing the anger in her eyes.

And just like that, Chris's own anger began to fade. Intimidating a young woman who'd been through what Julie had been through didn't make him exactly feel proud of himself. He swore yet again and released her.

"All you had to do was ask me to take you back to town and I would have." He shoved the keys in the ignition and started the engine. "Slashing a five-hundred-dollar tire and stealing my friend's truck was completely unnecessary."

She was silent as he did a three-point turn in the middle of the road and headed toward Cooper's farm.

"I didn't slash your tire."

He glanced at her.

"I just let the air out," she clarified. "I don't have a knife." She held out her hands in a placating gesture. "Not that I would have cut the tire if I'd had a knife. I just needed a head start. I didn't want to hurt anyone, or their property. I would have left this truck parked in town for the owner."

"The owner is in the hospital recovering from surgery. He doesn't need the stress of being told by someone that his one and only truck has been stolen and then found downtown. Why did you do it? Why did you sneak out of Dillon's house and then hide in the back of my truck, only to steal Cooper's truck and make a run for it? It's not like you were under arrest. And you have a phone, don't you? If you'd wanted a cab, you could have called for one."

She snorted and gave a little laugh. "I would have called a cab, but I forgot the name of your friend's farm. And the GPS on my phone couldn't figure out where I was. Apparently, that horse place doesn't exist in whatever maps my not-so-smart phone has."

He steered around another curve. "It's called Harmony Haven." He glanced at her. "Are you afraid of me?"

"What? Afraid of you? Why would you think that?"

He shook his head in exasperation. "You snuck away, stole a truck to avoid me. Call it a hunch."

This time it was her turn to roll her eyes. "Okay, okay. I may not completely trust you, but I trust you more than I've trusted anyone else for a long time. It's just that the longer I sat in that guest room thinking about the questions you'd be asking me in the morning, the more I realized I didn't want to involve you further. This is my battle. Not yours."

He turned onto the long dirt driveway up to Cooper's farmhouse. When he reached the house, he threw the truck into Park but left the engine running to keep the cab cool. The summer heat was already uncomfortable even this early in the morning.

Turning to face her, he put his right arm across the back of the bench seat.

"Let me see if I have this all straight in my mind. Your husband tried to kill you—twice. I'm the police officer who had to kill him to save you. I think I'm already involved almost as deep as I can be."

Her face flushed a light pink. "Well, when you put it that way, it does sound like too little, too late. But at least I can protect you from here on out by not involving you anymore."

"What part of *I'm a police officer* did you not hear? Julie, I'm a detective and part-time SWAT officer. It's my job to protect you, and to find out what's going on, administrative leave or not. And if you're still in any danger, it's my job to figure out why and who is after you."

Her eyes widened.

He shook his head and let out a deep sigh. "I've been a cop since I got out of college thirteen years ago. I can read body language. And right now yours is screaming that you think there's more to your husband's attempts on your life than typical domestic violence, if there is such a thing as typical in these cases."

When she didn't say anything, he shut the engine off

and shoved his door open. "Come on. At least let me take you inside while we talk this out. And, once we do, if you still want to go into town, I'll take you myself. In *my* truck."

She didn't agree with his plan, but she didn't try to run either. He supposed that was progress.

They were heading toward the front porch when the sound of galloping hooves reached them. He immediately shoved her behind his back and drew his gun. The palomino gelding appeared around the corner, tossing its mane and blowing out a snort as it stopped a few feet from him.

Chris holstered the gun and opened the front door.

"Go on in," he said. When she didn't move, he added, "Please?"

She hesitated, then stepped inside.

Chris started to pull the door shut but she stopped him with a hand on his.

"What are you doing?" she asked.

"I'm going to put the horse back in the corral. I'll be right back."

Chapter Eleven

A few minutes later, Julie sat at the kitchen table in Cooper's house, watching a shirtless Chris sit down across from her. His shirt had been soaked with sweat from his ride on the horse, so he'd washed it out in the sink and hung it on a chair to dry. He'd also rinsed his hair under the faucet. Julie had freshened up in the bathroom as much as possible without taking a real shower. And now she was desperately trying to pretend he wasn't completely distracting her.

His thick hair was beginning to dry in waves of cinnamon brown that made her fingers itch to touch it. But far more enticing was his golden-skinned, impressively muscled chest.

Chris Downing had a mouthwatering body to go along with his handsome face. And she was in no way immune to his appeal. The only thing keeping her from blatantly staring at the dips and valleys of his muscular chest and abs was the fact that he was grilling her with questions—questions that were going a long way toward dampening her enthusiasm for the incredible male specimen sitting across from her.

He'd asked her to give him more details about her husband attacking her five months ago. She told him about that night and that right after he'd paid bail, he'd disappeared, gone off grid, only communicating through his lawyer. Which had left Julie looking over her shoulder all the time, worried he'd try to come back and finish what he'd started.

"The first month after he disappeared, things were okay. But then his family filed a civil suit, alleging I was lying about the attack. And little things started happening, like someone slashing my tires. I was convinced that either Alan, or his family, was harassing me. The ADA's office didn't have the budget to offer 24/7 protection, which I needed if I was going to stay in Nashville. Since most of my accounts have been frozen as a result of the civil case, I can't afford that kind of security, either. So I'd moved here until the criminal case against my husband was settled, or until I had to go back to fight the civil case. I was trying to keep a low profile."

"That worked out really well," Chris said, his tone dry. "Why do you think your husband's family is suing you? Sounds to me like there's plenty of evidence against your husband."

"Kathy said it's a device to try to undermine the criminal case against him."

Chris nodded. "The threshold for proof in a civil case is much lower than in a criminal case. A civil judgment could sway the media in their favor, maybe turn a juror, even though they're supposed to ignore things like that.

He tapped a hand on the table. "So the reason you called the ADA after the shooting is because of the criminal case? To keep Nelson in the loop?"

She nodded. "That and I really didn't know anyone else to call. It's not like I have a lawyer on retainer. I wanted her advice, and she immediately said she was on her way."

"Awfully nice of her."

"I guess."

He studied her for a moment. "What were you and your husband arguing about when he found you in Destiny?"

"Arguing?"

"I heard you scream, twice, heard voices raised in argument before I confronted your husband. The screams, I get. He threatened you, cut you with the knife. But what was it that you were fighting about?"

"I remember he was angry that I'd shot him in Nashville, and that I ran away, as he called it. He threatened me, grabbed my arm, shook me. I probably cried out when he did that. Mostly I just kept telling him to go away and leave me alone."

He stared at her as if he didn't believe her. She tried to remember what she and Alan were saying when Chris had barged into the house. But she'd been so scared. The angry words they'd exchanged were all jumbled up in her mind.

"The last time he confronted you, you shot him. Was he worried about a gun this time?" Chris asked.

"I don't have a gun. I had to surrender it as evidence when the police arrived at my home that night."

"Did your husband know that?"

"Probably. We never talked about… I can't be sure. Actually, I seem to remember him asking if I had my gun. So, yeah, I guess he was concerned about it."

Some of the suspicion seemed to leave his face, as if he'd been testing her and she'd passed. What would happen if she hadn't passed?

"Did he have the knife with him when he came inside? Did he take it from the kitchen? Or did he take it from you?"

So much for him not being suspicious anymore. "What are you talking about?"

"Are you the one who had the knife first? Did your husband wrestle it away from you?"

"I never had the knife."

"Then we won't find your fingerprints on it?"

She held her hands out to her sides. "I don't know."

"You don't know?" He sounded incredulous.

"When I came out of my bedroom, Alan was standing there, holding the knife. I don't know if he brought it with him or grabbed it from my kitchen."

"You have to know what knives you brought with you when you rented the house. Judging by all the boxes I saw, you didn't have time to unpack before your husband got there."

"True, I didn't get to unpack everything. But I did unpack the boxes for the kitchen. I was looking forward to preparing my first decent meal since arriving in Destiny. I really don't know whether he'd grabbed one of my knives or brought his own."

"What were you arguing about?" he asked again, barely giving her a chance to catch her breath between questions.

"I told him to leave me alone. Why are you badgering me?"

"Because things aren't adding up. If your husband's goal was to kill you, he'd have snuck up on you, stabbed or shot you before you even knew he was there. Instead, he confronted you. So here's the real question. What do you have that your husband wanted so badly that he was willing to risk getting killed?"

Chapter Twelve

Chris checked his shirt hanging over the kitchen chair beside him. It was finally dry enough to wear, so he pulled it over his head and smoothed it into place.

"I think Alan might have been talking about the key to the safe," Julie said from her seat across from him.

"Safe? What safe?"

"When Alan and I separated, about nine months ago, I had all the locks changed while he was at work. He'd been angry, moody, aggressive—like, in your face aggressive but never actually hitting me. I'd never seen him like that before and it scared me. So I got a restraining order. And had the locks changed. That made him even angrier. Over the months that followed, he kept calling. He would say he needed different things from the house. Every time he'd mention something, I'd pack it up and ship it to his apartment. But he was never satisfied. It seemed like he was making excuses to try to get me to let him come over. That whole back and forth arguing went on for four months. Then he broke in one night and you know the rest."

"Was there a specific incident that made you separate from him nine months ago?"

She considered his question, then shrugged. "More

like a series of them. In the first years of our marriage, he never mentioned my family. But this past year, he started bringing them up for seemingly no reason. He asked if I had anything to remember them by. I told him I had what mattered, memories. That seemed to make him really angry. Then I said all I had of them, physically, was a box of pictures and junk. He demanded that I show him what I had. If he hadn't acted so odd, I probably would have. But he'd been acting so strange, I refused. He went ballistic. The next day I changed the locks."

"You mentioned a safe. Is that where you put this box?"

"No. The pictures, costume jewelry, Naomi's hair clips, my dad's baseball cards—they're all in a safety deposit box that I haven't opened since their deaths. The safe I'm talking about is in our house in Nashville. When Alan broke into my house here in Destiny yesterday, after calling me vile names and ranting about the shooting and me leaving, at some point he demanded that I give him the key."

"What key?" Chris asked.

"I was about to ask him the same thing when you came in and things spiraled out of control. I got the impression he had a lot more he wanted to say. But he never got a chance. If he thought I had something in the safe that belonged to him, he was wrong. The thing is, I filed for divorce after Alan attacked me. And I gave him everything that was listed in the pending divorce decree, on top of what I'd already given him. So all I can figure is that he lost something, maybe some important papers that he didn't want anyone to know about. I'm not sure. But, like you said, it had to be important. It just occurred to me that he might have been talking about the floor safe in the house in Nashville. It was there when we bought the place and I remember him saying it would be a good place to keep our birth certificates and passports, things like that. But then I forgot about it. I never used that safe, but maybe he did. And maybe he thought I had the key."

"Do you?"

She shrugged. "I honestly don't know. Alan was practically a hoarder. I was all about keeping things neat and simple. Any time he left stuff lying around the house I'd put it up. It's very likely if he left a key somewhere that I might have thrown it in a junk drawer. But even if he thought I had the key, wouldn't it be easier for him to break into the house and try to, I don't know, pick the lock? Seems crazy that he'd track me down out here just for a key."

"It probably depends on what's in the safe, if indeed that's why he came here. Floor safes are generally extremely heavy and require special equipment to install. He couldn't have just broken into your house and taken the safe with him. And unless he's a master lock-picker, he'd need a locksmith to help him break into the thing. It would be hard for him to get a professional locksmith to pick the front door lock and a safe lock. They'd know something was up and would probably call the police."

She nodded. "When you put it that way, I suppose that coming here might be worth the risk—if we're even going down the right path. There could have been another reason entirely for him coming here. But that's the only key I can think of."

"Have you told Nelson about the safe?"

She shook her head. "Why would I? You asking me

about what Alan said is the only reason I thought of it now."

"Don't."

She frowned. "Don't tell the ADA? Why?"

"How well do you know her?"

"Again, why?"

"Because she's the one who told you to leave town, to hide so your husband wouldn't find you. And yet, he did. Besides her, who knew you were here, in Destiny?"

She grew very still. "There isn't anyone else. Kathy is the only person I told. But she wouldn't tell Alan where I was. Kathy is the one who's been helping me fight him in court."

"Then how did your husband find you?"

"You're the detective. You tell me."

Her sarcasm and obvious frustration had him smiling. He was pushing her hard, probably harder than the chief would have if she were back at the station undergoing an official interview. But this was probably his only chance to ask her questions before turning her over to the team, and he intended to get as many answers as he could.

"Did you come directly to Destiny after leaving Nashville?" he asked.

"No. I wasn't sure where to hideout. I drove around the state, checking out several small towns before settling on this one. It took me about a week of exploring to decide that Destiny was where I wanted to land."

"The car you drove here, is it yours?"

"It's mine."

"How have you bought gas and food since leaving your home?"

"All cash. I've seen enough TV crime shows to know not to leave an electronic trail."

He nodded. "Good. How did you lease the house here in Destiny?"

"Cash again. I saw the place in an ad, called the number, met the landlord in person, paid cash and signed a fake name." Her face flushed a light red. "Probably not legal, exactly, but again I was worried about Alan being able to find me. I suppose if the landlord had pushed for ID I'd have been in trouble. But he didn't."

"Around here, people aren't as suspicious as they might be in a big city. You never answered my question about Nelson. How well do you know her?"

"We're casual friends, just barely. I met her and Alan a couple of months into my senior year in college." Some kind of emotion flashed in her eyes. Sorrow? Pain?

"You okay?" he asked.

She drew a bracing breath. "Yes, sorry. Just…thinking. Anyway, I…was…having a tough time in school and pretty much kept to myself. Kathy was in one of my classes. I knew her name but that was about it. I think she took pity on me. We started hanging out every once in a while. One day, I guess she could see how down I was and she insisted that I go to the school's football game that night. She had an extra ticket because a friend had canceled. When we got there, we sat by Alan. Neither of us knew him, but he introduced himself and we got to know each other a bit during the game. After that, we'd occasionally go to movies or other college events."

"So it's fair to say the three of you became friends?"

"More like acquaintances than friends. I clicked pretty well with Alan and Kathy, but they were like oil and water with each other. She tolerated him but didn't really like him. I tried to stay friends with both of them, but Alan and I got serious pretty fast. He... helped me through a really tough time. And, well, when you're guy-crazy you sometimes forget about your other friends. Kathy and I didn't ever get very close because I was usually with Alan. We got married right after graduation. Or, well, my graduation anyway. Alan had failed a few courses and never finished his degree. After I graduated, he stopped taking classes and decided to go into his family's business, Webb Enterprises." She waved her hand. "Not that any of that is relevant."

Chris didn't want to assume anything wasn't relevant at this point, but he did have other questions he wanted to ask right now. "Did Nelson attend your wedding?"

"No. We didn't invite her." Her cheeks flushed a light pink. "It's embarrassing now to say that. I mean, she was a friend, even if we weren't really close. But like I said, Alan didn't like her. So, no invitation. I guess you'd say I chose Alan over her."

"Maybe you only thought she and Alan didn't get along. Maybe she liked him and resented you. After all, you did both meet him at the same football game."

She shook her head. "She was never anything but kind to me, never expressed any resentment. And Alan never looked twice at her. She wasn't his type."

She held up her hands as if to stop him from arguing. "Before you say it, I know—she's tall and blonde, which most guys like, while I'm short and a brunette. But even if he and Kathy had been able to get along, he just wasn't attracted to women like her, with her kind of forceful personality. Everything about her set him off, irritated him. And he showed me pictures of some of his former girlfriends. Every one of them was like me—short, brunette."

Chris could certainly see Julie's appeal over the glossier, more made-up look that Kathy Nelson sported. Nelson was sophisticated but seemed fake, whereas Julie seemed the girl-next-door type, a beautiful girl next door but still down to earth, approachable. Still, that didn't mean Alan couldn't have been attracted to both of them.

"If neither of you kept up with Nelson, then why is she so invested in your case that she drove all the way out here from Nashville?"

"We didn't keep up with her at all. The first time I had seen her since college was the night that Alan was arrested. And the reason she's taking this case so personally is because Alan is…was…something of a celebrity in Nashville. He comes from money. His family is well-known in high-society circles and he was a respected philanthropist. Kathy is a career muckety-muck looking for a way into the governor's office. She made no secret to me that she felt if she could win against someone as high profile as Alan Webb, she'd prove she was in nobody's pocket and was tough on crime. She'd make a name for herself and be well on her way to establishing her political career."

That part didn't surprise Chris at all. Even in Destiny, people had heard of Kathy Nelson and her political aspirations. But there might have been another reason, too. If Julie was wrong—if Kathy did like Alan and felt he'd chosen Julie over her—maybe being in charge of the case against him was a way to get even for him passing her over in college. That seemed unlikely, though, to hold that kind of a grudge over three years later. Especially since Kathy was married.

Chris made a mental note to check with his team to see if they were looking into Kathy as a potential suspect. Just to cover the bases.

"Let's get back to the night your husband attacked you in Nashville. When was that?"

"About five months ago, on my twenty-fifth birthday."

A sick feeling twisted in Chris's gut. "Not that there's a good day to try to kill you, but on your birthday? Really?"

"Yes. Really." She was twisting her hands together again. "Like I said earlier, we'd been separated for about four months. Looking back now, the marriage was never what I'd hoped it would be. He'd doted on me in college. But as soon as that ring was on my finger, things cooled off, changed. At first, I thought it was because he'd quit school and took over the family business. He was under a lot of stress. And I figured he was frustrated that he never got to work in the field he loved."

"What field was that?"

"Botany. He absolutely loved working with plants. He could talk for hours about their medicinal properties and how to get more yield from organically grown crops. He'd planned on having his own career for a while before having to take the reins of the company. But it didn't work out that way. He's an only child, and his father's health was failing. He had to step in much sooner than he'd hoped. Once he started working at Webb Enterprises, that's when he started getting depressed and closing himself off from me. Then again, maybe I'm making up excuses for him. Maybe it was just me he didn't like."

The hurt was there again, in the tightening of her jaw, the way her lips thinned. She'd loved her husband once upon a time—that was obvious. And even now, she couldn't fathom why he'd turned on her.

Neither could Chris.

Why had Alan tried to kill her? Twice?

She waved her hands again, as if waving away her words. "Shortly before we separated, I remember him coming home one night in a sour mood after work and shutting himself up in his office for hours. Wouldn't even come out for dinner. And once he did emerge, it was almost as if...as if he were a different person. He was...serious, angry. He insisted that I call in the next day and take a week's vacation, said we needed to get away. I couldn't just drop everything like that. People count on me." She twisted her hands. "At least, they used to. I had to quit work once the media got hold of the story about Alan attacking me and me shooting him. I became a liability to my coworkers at that point."

"Where did you work?"

She hesitated, looked away. "I started a nonprofit foundation, figured it was a good use of my business management degree and I could help people. The office was in downtown Nashville. We fought to raise awareness and money to fight orphan diseases—illnesses that are so rare that it isn't profitable enough for a drug company to devote money researching possible cures or even treatments. But the diseases are devastating to the victims and their families."

He studied her. Her voice was a little too bright, like the emotion was forced. She was hiding something.

He'd sensed it from the moment she'd begun talking about the tough time she'd been having right before she'd met Alan. There'd been a flash of pain in her eyes then, the same flash of pain in her eyes right now.

"Julie?"

"Hmm?" She was staring toward the front window, at the acres of green grass that would need mowing soon.

"What was the name of the nonprofit?"

She swallowed hard. "Naomi's Hope Foundation."

Again, she wouldn't look at him. And then he got it.

"Was Naomi a friend or a family member?"

Her startled gaze shot to his. She stared at him so long he thought she wasn't going to answer. But then she sighed heavily, looking defeated.

"She was my sister, a year older than me. My parents went broke taking her to hospitals, flying around the country to different specialists. They even went down to Mexico once, looking into alternative medicines. Nothing helped. She had a condition so rare it didn't even have a name. It baffled every doctor who tried to treat her. It struck her during her senior year in college, my junior year at the same school. She died four months later. At least she wasn't in pain anymore. She was free. But my parents…"

She shook her head. "They were immigrants, my mom and dad. Star-crossed lovers from London. Both sets of their parents, my grandparents, didn't approve of them dating. So as soon as they were of legal age, they married and moved to this country. They left their families, their history, everything familiar to them to have a fresh start, to build a legacy of their own. They were Romeo and Juliet, basically, coming here for the American dream.

"They didn't have any money, their families had disowned them and they had to fight for everything they had, which was never much. Their entire life savings was built around sending Naomi and me to college. But when Naomi…" She shook her head. "Naomi was a daddy's girl. When she died, my father couldn't handle it. He shot himself. The day after his funeral, my mother took an overdose of sleeping pills and alcohol."

Tears were running down her face now. Her bottom lip trembled.

"I always wondered what went through their minds when they did it. I know they were devastated. We all were. But, somewhere along the way, they forgot they had another daughter. They left me all alone. I had no one to turn to. But I couldn't let their sacrifices be for nothing. Naomi died in the summer after my junior year, my parents right after that. A month later I enrolled for the fall session of my senior year. I felt I owed it to my parents to get my degree. But I was miserable, couldn't concentrate on my studies. A couple of months later, I was about ready to give up. And that's when I met Alan. He turned my life around. He was there for me, encouraged me. And then he…then he…"

She covered her face with her hands, her shoulders shaking as her misery overtook her.

Chris stood and crossed to her. He couldn't bear doing nothing, so he took a chance and damned the consequences. He pulled her to standing and wrapped his arms around her.

"I'm so sorry, Julie," he whispered, resting his cheek against the top of her head. "I'm so very, very sorry."

She'd stiffened when he first touched her. But then she seemed to melt against him, putting her arms around his waist and clinging to him while tears tracked down her face, soaking his shirt.

They stood there a long time while he whispered soothing words against her hair. The storm finally subsided, her tears stopped and she was no longer shaking.

Finally, with one last sniffle, she pushed back and gave him a watery smile. "Thank you."

The pain in her beautiful blue eyes had him wanting to pull her back into his arms. But he fought the urge and instead allowed himself only to gently push her tousled hair out of her eyes, then wipe the last of her tears from her cheeks before dropping his hands to his sides.

"Anytime." He smiled and stepped back to put some much-needed space between them.

She drew a shaky breath. "I don't think my heart or your shirt can take much more of this. You might as well finish asking your questions right now."

"We don't have to—"

"Yes. We do," she said. "I want to know why Alan did what he did. And you need the investigation resolved. Both of us need this case closed in order to get on with our lives. So go on. Ask whatever else you want to know."

"All right. What about the movers?"

"Movers?" She frowned. "What about them?"

"Yesterday afternoon, they brought your furniture and belongings. I assume they drove down from Nashville. Did you pay them cash, too? Or did you use a credit card when you hired them?"

"I went to the bank the day I left and withdrew several thousand dollars from my checking account so I could live on cash for a while. I paid the movers in cash like I did everything else."

"Several thousand dollars—from checking, not savings?" he asked. "I'm not exactly living paycheck to paycheck, but I'd have to dip into savings to pull out several thousand in cash."

"Even with the civil suit freezing our joint accounts, I still have plenty of money in my personal accounts. As long as I'm not too extravagant, I'll be okay until the case is settled. Money has never been a problem for Alan and me. Like I said, he took over the family business, an import/export empire. Even without receiving his botany degree, he'd taken enough classes in his minor—business management—to do really well running the company. And he was smart, really smart. The company was struggling when the economy went south. But within weeks of Alan taking it over, the profits soared."

That didn't sound right to Chris. A young kid, freshly flunked out of college, was able to turn around the family business? A lot of things about Alan didn't sound right. The next time Chris called his boss he was going to see how the background check on Julie's former husband was going. He wanted a complete history on Alan Webb, from birth to the grave.

Julie shoved her chair up to the table and remained standing, wrapping her arms around her waist. "That's what allowed me to work at the nonprofit instead of getting a job that paid real money. I'd offered to work at his family's business, to help him manage it. But he didn't want me to worry about that, insisted that I chase my dream of getting the government to devote resources to research orphan diseases like my sister's. It truly was the most decent thing he ever did."

The bitterness in her voice told him there was a lot

more water under the matrimonial bridge, but he decided to steer clear of that for now. Making her miserable wasn't his goal. He'd only delve into that earlier line of questioning again if it was absolutely necessary.

"All right. Back to the moving company then. I'm surprised they took cash. Most companies like that require a credit card."

"Yeah, well. You'd be surprised what a few hundred dollars under the table can do for you."

"You bribed them."

"I did what I had to do to stay under the radar. It's not like Alan was involved in some kind of nefarious criminal activity and the government was giving me a new identity to testify against him. He was just a husband who'd tried to murder his wife. I was on my own. I would have used a fake name if I could. But they required ID, wouldn't budge on that. So, as soon as I decided that I wanted to leave Nashville, I had them put the things I would need into storage and left everything else in the house to deal with at a later time. Like I said before, about a week later I knew where I wanted to settle. After renting the place in Destiny, I called them to arrange a date and time for them to deliver my things."

"There's a direct link from your house to the moving company to here if someone wanted to follow it. That could be how Alan tracked you. But it's not like he could have watched the storage unit 24/7. He had to sleep sometime. If the movers had loaded up the unit while Alan was asleep, he'd have missed that link to you and wouldn't have been able to find you—assuming that he did find you through the movers. I'm betting he had a partner. He wasn't working alone in his quest to locate you." He studied her carefully. "And you're not surprised by that. Why not?"

She shrugged. "When your husband tries to kill you, trying to figure out why he wants you dead pretty much consumes your thoughts. The fact that he found me so fast this second time shocked me. And it made me think he had to be working with someone else. He had to have help. And I couldn't see him hiring a private investigator, not with the criminal case hanging over his head. That could look bad in court. Like he was stalking me. I figure it has to be someone bad, a criminal, someone likely as dangerous as Alan became. So, no, it doesn't surprise me. I figured he had a partner. The only question is who, and of course, whether they still want me dead now that Alan's gone."

Listening to the pain in her voice, the confusion and anger pretty much obliterated his earlier concerns that she might have intentionally used him as a tool to kill her husband. She was consistent in her answers. She didn't hesitate like she would if she was making up lies as she went along. And her body language struck him as honest, too. He'd bet all of his years of experience at interviewing witnesses that everything she was telling him now was true.

Or at least what she thought was true. But there was still one more thing bugging him.

"Have you told me everything?" he asked.

"Yes, of course."

"Then why are you still running? Why stow away in the back of my truck, and steal Cooper's truck, to get away from me if you've done nothing wrong and have nothing to hide? You said you think your husband has a partner who might be after you. So why wouldn't you trust the policeman who risked his own life to save you yesterday? It doesn't make sense, unless the real reason you want to be on your own is because you want to get even."

She blinked. "Excuse me?"

"You don't want some cop hanging around when you figure out who was working with Alan against you. Because you want revenge."

"That's ridiculous. I want to be safe, that's what I want."

"Then why run from me? I can protect you."

"I've known you for all of two seconds," she said, her voice shaking with anger. "I knew Alan for three and a half years, was married to him for three of those years. You tell me. Why should I trust you when I couldn't trust him?"

And that was the last piece of the puzzle he'd been looking for. It had been in front of him all along. He'd quit thinking of her as a conspirator and was thinking of her solely as a victim. But he still hadn't understood why she'd run. It all came down to trust. She'd been hurt, horribly hurt, and here he was berating her for not being willing to put her faith and her life in his hands when, as she'd said, she'd known him for all of "two seconds."

He'd been a complete ass and hadn't even realized it.

"Julie."

When she didn't reply, he moved a step closer and took her hand in his. She tried to tug it away, but he held fast.

"Julie, maybe you don't trust me completely yet. I get that. I understand it after everything you've been through. But look at this objectively. We both want the same thing. We want answers. The answer to why Alan tried to kill you—twice—will enable you to go back and live your life without having to look over your shoulder and worry that someone else is out there trying to hurt you. That same answer will help me resolve this case so I can go back to my life, to being a cop. We both want the same thing, to end this. So how about we work together, as a team, and end this once and for all."

He could see the indecision on her face, in the way she chewed her bottom lip as if debating her options. For a moment, he thought she'd turn and walk away. But then, very slowly, she put her hand in his.

He couldn't help but notice how soft her skin was and how good it felt to thread his fingers with hers. And from the way her blue eyes widened at the contact, he had a feeling she was thinking much the same thing—that it was nice holding his hand, too.

A tiny red circle of light appeared on her forehead.

He shouted a warning and yanked her toward him just as the front window exploded in a hail of rifle fire.

Chapter Thirteen

"Stay down." Chris yanked his gun out of his holster.

Julie couldn't have gotten up if she wanted to, not with two-hundred pounds of protective male squashing her against the hardwood floor.

He rolled off her and jumped up in a half crouch, sprinting toward the window with his gun out in front of him.

Bam! Bam! Bam!

He fired through the gaping hole that used to be the front window, then dove toward the floor. Whoever was shooting at them outside let loose with another round of shots.

Julie covered her ears and squeezed her eyes shut. Bits of plaster and wood rained down where the bullets strafed the walls above her. When the chaos of noise and dust had settled, Chris was once again crouching over her, his gun pointed up at the ceiling. In his other hand was his phone.

"You okay?" he asked her.

She felt as if she'd inhaled a lungful of plaster dust, but nodded to let him know she was at least alive. As for "okay," she'd reserve judgment on that.

"It's Chris," he said into the phone. "I'm over at Cooper's farm, holed up in the house with Julie Webb. We're taking rifle fire."

Julie looked toward the shattered front window while Chris talked police codes that made no sense to her. This low to the floor, she couldn't see the road or even the acres of grass outside. All she could see was the wall of trees at the edge of the cleared portion of the property. Where was the shooter? Was he making his way toward the house even now? Ready to lean in through the opening and gun them down?

She should have been terrified, melting into a puddle of tears and nerves. And maybe if this was the first time someone had tried to kill her, she would have been. But after everything she'd been through, and everything she'd lost, the only emotion flowing through her veins right now was rage.

She was absolutely livid.

If the shooter did lean in through that window, she'd try to tear him apart, limb by limb, with her bare hands. Assuming he didn't shoot her first, of course. She was so sick of people trying to hurt her. And what about Chris? Once again his life was in danger because someone had decided to go after her, or at least that was what she had to assume. It made sense that between the two of them, she was the target. And here Chris was in the wrong place at the wrong time, again.

"Give me your backup gun," she snapped, as he ended his call.

"My backup gun?"

If their situation wasn't so dire, she'd have laughed at the stunned look on his face.

"You do have one, right? All the cops in movies and on TV have them. It's probably strapped to your ankle.

I may not be an expert marksman, but I do know how to shoot. I've been to gun ranges. I want to help."

He said something under his breath and she was pretty sure she didn't want to know what it was from the exasperated expression on his face.

"Unless you have law enforcement or military experience that I don't know about, I'll keep my alleged backup gun where it belongs. Come on. You can help us by getting out of the line of fire so I don't have to worry about you. Our friend out there is going to get braver anytime now and I don't want you catching a bullet when he does."

"Or she."

He nodded. "Or she. Come on."

He crouched over her, shielding her body with his as he duck walked with her out of the main room and down a short hallway. No more gunshots sounded from outside, which had her even more nervous. Judging by his worried look, it made him nervous, too.

"In here." He pushed her through a doorway into a bathroom.

An old-fashioned claw-foot tub sat against the far wall, beneath a small, high window.

"Get in."

He didn't wait for her to figure out what he meant before he was lifting her and settling her inside the tub.

"This is cast iron. It's the best protection from stray bullets that I can give you."

The idea of bullets ripping through the walls hadn't even occurred to her. The anger that had helped her stay calm earlier began to fade, leaving her shaking so hard her teeth chattered.

"Wh-what a-bout you?" she asked between chatters. "Sh-shouldn't you g-get in, too?"

He'd been half-standing, peeking through the bottom of the window. But when she spoke he ducked down, an amused, half smile curving his lips.

"As much as I'd love to join you in the tub," he teased, "the timing isn't right." He added an outrageous wink and even managed a chuckle.

She couldn't believe he was flirting with her at a time like this—or that she found him utterly charming. She was about to tell him to knock it off and get into the tub with her before he got shot, when the sound of gunfire echoed through the house.

Chris dove to the floor.

A loud pinging noise had Julie throwing her hands over her ears and squeezing her eyes shut. The shots seemed to go on forever. When they finally stopped, she lay there, her breaths coming in great gasps, her hands still covering her ears.

Forcing her eyes open, she pulled herself up to sitting. Sunlight slanted through small round holes riddling the outside wall. Paint chips lay scattered on the floor—the same color as the tub. That pinging sound she'd heard must have been a bullet hitting the tub. And she'd been safe, just as Chris had promised.

But where was he?

She looked through the open door into the hallway, but it didn't have any windows and was too dark for her to see anything.

"Chris," she whispered, not wanting the shooter to hear her if he was close by. "Chris? Where are you?"

No one answered. No footsteps sounded on the

hardwood floor from the other rooms. Had he left her? Alone?

She swallowed, hard, trying to tamp down the rising panic that had her pulse hammering in her ears. It was too quiet outside. Had Chris gone out there to confront the shooter? Had he been forced to dive into the hall-way to avoid getting shot, only to catch a stray bullet? If he was lying past the open doorway, injured, he could be bleeding out right now. She couldn't sit here and do nothing. She had to check on him, and if he was hurt, somehow she had to help him.

Her whole body shook as she started to pull herself up on her knees in the tub. Something shifted against her leg and she let out a squeal of surprise before she could stop herself. She looked down. Chris hadn't left her alone, after all.

He'd left her his backup gun.

CHRIS EDGED HIS way around the back of the house, pis-tol sweeping out in front of him. He kept to the grass to make as little noise as possible. Leaving Julie alone inside had nearly killed him. But as soon as the bullets started coming through the wall, he knew it was only a matter of time before the shooter breached the house. Julie had a much better chance of survival if Chris could intercept the shooter outside.

She'd have an even better chance if his SWAT team would get here.

He checked his watch. It had only been ten minutes since he'd called them. Donna, Colby and Randy had probably been at church, which was a good half hour away. Max usually went to the evening service like Chris. But Max lived even farther out than the First

Baptist Church. Hopefully, his team was speeding toward him like a moonshiner running from a revenue officer. Still, best case, the first of them might arrive in another ten minutes.

He and Julie didn't have ten minutes—not against someone with a rifle and a laser scope.

He ducked down and peered around the corner of the house. The side yard was empty and he couldn't see anyone out front. But thick trees to his right marched all the way down to the gravel road. There were a million places for someone with a rifle to hide. If Chris couldn't reach cover, and get up close and personal with the shooter, his 9mm was just about useless. What he needed was a way to draw the gunman out and keep him away from the house, and Julie.

He eased back behind the wall, glancing toward the barn, his truck, the corral with the horses. They were nervous, agitated, running back and forth because of the gunfire. Too dangerous to try capturing one, let alone riding it to create some kind of diversion—assuming he could even make it that far without being picked off by the rifle. No, he needed something else to get the gunman's attention.

His gaze slid to the large silver propane tank set about fifty yards back from the house. It was slightly toward the right side of the property, close to one of the round hay bales drying in the sun. Acres and acres of wide-open field with more hay bales opened off to the right. And, past that, the barn and the horses—far enough away that they would be safe from harm, but close enough that the animals would be terrified and make their own racket. Dillon and Ashley would kill him for even considering what he was about to do. But he figured three traumatized horses in exchange for saving Julie's life was a bargain he was willing to make.

To his left, a deadly sprint from the house, the line of thick pine trees and oaks beckoned as cover—*if* he could reach them. Then he could circle around, locate the shooter and end this dangerous stand-off.

He raised his pistol and aimed it at the propane tank. *Bam! Bam!*

Chris jerked around at the sound of gunfire to his right. Julie was crouching in the back doorway, shooting toward the closest round hay bale. The long end of a rifle appeared at the left side, pointed right at her.

"Get back!" Chris squeezed off several shots toward the rifleman to give Julie cover to head inside.

But, instead of running into the house, she ran toward him, her eyes wide, face pale.

Wood siding exploded close to her head. Chris fired toward the hay bale again and ran toward Julie. The rifle jerked back. Chris grabbed Julie around the waist and shoved her down against the foundation of the house while he kept his gun aimed toward the hay.

"You need to get back into the house," he hissed, without turning around. "Get into the cast-iron tub until I take this jerk down!"

"Can't." She sounded out of breath. "I was worried you were hurt or needed help and was coming to look for you when the front door creaked open. Someone else is inside."

The rifle shoved through the hay. Chris and Julie both started shooting. Julie's gun clicked empty.

As soon as the rifle jerked back, Chris reloaded.

"I need more bullets." Julie ejected the spent magazine like a pro and held out her hand.

"The extra ammo for that gun is in my truck."

She gave him an aggravated look that would have made him laugh at any other time. Most people he knew in this situation would be cowering in fear. Not Julie. She was full of surprises.

A hollow echo sounded from inside the house. Whoever was in there was probably searching for Julie. If they came out back, the two of them were done for. They had to get to cover—now.

He grabbed her around the waist, jerking her up to standing and pointing her toward the trees.

She instinctively tried to crouch back down against the house. Chris pulled her up again.

"Run," he ordered. "I'll cover you. Get to the trees. Go!"

She took off running.

The rifle shoved through the hay. Chris fired off several shots, drawing the rifle bore toward him. Bullets pinged against the house right beside him. He swore and dove to the side. The sound of running feet sounded from inside the house, coming toward the back door. In desperation, Chris swept his pistol toward the propane tank and squeezed the trigger.

An explosion of heat and sound engulfed him, knocking him backward. His skull cracked against the wood siding, making his vision blur. He shook his head, trying to focus. A wall of thick black smoke and flames blasted toward him, offering him much-needed cover. Pushing away from the house, he took off in a wobbly run toward the trees.

Chapter Fourteen

Julie peered around the same tree as Chris, looking toward the house and the burning remnants of the propane tank.

"I think the explosion took out the rifleman," Chris said. "The hay bale where he was hiding is obliterated. The question is, where's the second intruder?"

A shiver ran up Julie's spine. "I suppose it's too much to hope that the first gunman just got knocked out."

Chris looked at her over his shoulder, his brows raised. "You're worried about a man who tried to kill you?"

She shrugged, feeling silly. "I just don't like the idea of being responsible for someone's death."

A shuttered look came over his face. "Seems like I remember you thanking God yesterday after your husband was killed."

She jerked back, feeling his censure like a physical blow. "I never wanted Alan to die. I was thanking God that Alan couldn't hurt me again. But I didn't mean I was glad he'd been killed."

Chris's face softened. "It's not my place to pass judgment either way. I shouldn't have said anything." He turned back to the house, intently watching for signs of any gunmen.

Julie felt sick inside that he'd thought she was grateful for Alan's death. That was an awful thing to think about someone. Yet, here he was again, protecting her.

"Why?" she blurted out before she could stop herself.

"Why what?" Again, he didn't turn around, just kept his gun trained toward the house.

"Why are you helping me if you think I'm the kind of person who would rejoice over my husband being killed?"

He sighed heavily and reached toward her. "Take my hand, Julie."

She hesitated.

"Please."

His tone was gentle, imploring. She shoved her useless empty gun into the waistband of her khaki pants and put her right hand in his left one.

He tugged her up beside him, still not taking his gaze from the dying fire and the building.

"I'm a cop," he said. "A detective. It's my nature to doubt everything, to assume the worst. It's how I stay alive. Yes, I thought you were happy that your husband was dead." He glanced at her. "I also thought you might have planned the whole thing, moving in next to a cop and arranging that confrontation when you knew I'd be home."

She gasped and tried to tug her hand out of his grasp, but he tightened his hold.

"I don't think that anymore. Okay? I saw the truth in your eyes, heard it in your voice back in the house when you answered my questions."

His thumb lightly brushed the underside of her wrist, doing crazy things to her pulse and her breathing.

"You're a victim—"

"No. I am *not* a victim."

He squeezed her hand. "You're right. You're not. You're a witness, and a strong woman. Most people I know, most men I know, would have stayed in that bathtub. They wouldn't have gotten out because they were worried the police officer protecting them might need help. And the moment they heard someone else in the house, they would have frozen or run screaming. Instead, you covered me. You kept that rifleman busy when I was focused on shooting the propane tank. I might have saved you yesterday. But you saved me today. You're one of the bravest women I know. And, trust me, my respect for you has grown exponentially this morning."

"Thank you," she whispered, her throat tight. "And I do trust you."

He smiled and faced the house. Then he stiffened and pulled his hand from hers. "The second gunman's making a run for it. He's heading for the barn."

Julie leaned sideways, trying to see what he saw.

"Wait here!" Chris sprinted past her, arms and legs pumping as he ran toward the house. He stopped at the far corner, sweeping his gun out in front of him.

The horses let out shrill whinnies and bolted to the other side of the corral, as far from the barn as they could get. A dark figure seemed to materialize from out of nowhere, running around Chris's pickup toward the barn.

Chris dropped to his knees, aiming his pistol with both hands.

The sound of a distant siren filled the air, coming up the road.

"Yes, hurry. Please," Julie whispered, praying that help arrived soon. It was killing her watching Chris risk his life like this.

He fired off several shots. A metallic ping sounded from the truck where a bullet buried itself in the driver's-side door, narrowly missing the gunman.

The man returned fire. Chris let loose with a volley of shots. The gunman clutched his shoulder and spun around, dropping to the ground.

Chris took off, legs pumping like a champion sprinter as he ran toward the truck. Julie clutched the tree as she watched, bark cutting into her fingertips. The siren was much closer now.

The gunman rolled beneath the pickup, firing a couple of quick shots of his own. Chris dove toward the questionable cover of the fence, bringing up his pistol again. But the gunman had rolled out the other side.

Another pickup suddenly barreled into view, gravel and dirt spitting out in a dark cloud from beneath its wheels as it raced toward the corral. Lights flashed in the grill and its shrill siren filled the air. Julie recognized the driver as one of the SWAT officers she'd met after her husband was shot—Randy Carter.

Chris jumped up, motioning in the direction where the gunman had disappeared.

Another cloud of dust billowed up as a black Dodge Charger raced from the other side of the barn where it must have been parked. It took off across the open field, bumping and weaving like a drunk between the enormous hay bales.

Julie heard Chris's shout as he waved for Randy to

pursue the Charger. More sirens sounded from somewhere out front. Chris watched the truck chasing the
Charger across the field. Julie could no longer see them
because of the trees. When she looked back at Chris,
he was jogging toward the ruins of the exploded propane tank and what was left of the rifleman's last hiding place.

Her fingers curled against the tree trunk again as
she waited like he'd asked.

Two vehicles—an old black Camry and a white Ford
Escape—pulled up on each side of the house, parking sideways at the far corner where the side yard and
backyard met.

The drivers, a man and a woman, hopped out in full
SWAT gear, both of them crouching down behind the
engine blocks of their respective vehicles. They kept
their long guns pointed up toward the sky in deference
to Chris, but obviously they were there to support him
in any way he might need.

He slowly straightened from crouching over something on the ground and motioned for both officers to
join him. They rushed forward in unison, their motions
well-rehearsed and sure, as if they'd practiced this type
of situation hundreds of times.

After a brief consultation with Chris, the officers
took off their helmets. Julie recognized them as having
been at her rental home and later at the police station.
She couldn't remember the man's name, but the woman,
the one who'd arrived in the Escape, was Donna Waters.
She'd sat beside Julie after the shooting.

And heard Julie praying her thanks.

She winced as Donna started toward her, apparently

at Chris's request. Officer Waters probably thought Julie was a horrible person, as Chris had.

Straightening her shoulders, Julie pushed away from the tree to meet her halfway.

Donna was probably only a few years older than Julie, maybe twenty-eight or twenty-nine. Her blond hair was cut in a short, wavy style that flattered her heart-shaped face. They met in the side yard. Contrary to the chilly reception that Julie had expected—given the misunderstanding over her prayer after Alan's death—Donna gave her a sympathetic smile and hugged her.

"Bless your heart," the officer said when she pulled back. Genuine sympathy stared back from her blue eyes. "Not the best reception Destiny has ever given a newcomer. I'm so sorry, sweetie. How ya holding up?"

"Um, fine, I guess. Thank you."

Donna squeezed her shoulder. "I really hate to ask this. But Chris wants you to ID the body."

Julie took an instinctive step back. "The body?"

"You don't have to. It's totally okay, and understandable. But we think you might know the guy who tried to shoot you two. He was apparently facing away from the blast when Chris shot the tank. So…"

"His face wasn't burned up."

Donna nodded. "It'll just take a second. Only if you're okay with it. Chris told me to make sure you know you don't have to do this."

She swallowed the bile rising in her throat. "But he thinks, you all think, that I know the man who…the rifleman?"

"We do."

"Why?"

"It's something you'd have to see to understand." She waited, then nodded again, smiling. "It was a lot to ask, after everything you've been through. Just wait here and I'll tell them you can't—"

"I'll do it." Julie hurried past her, walking at a brisk pace. For some unfathomable reason, Chris wanted her to look at a dead man. So that's what she was going to do. And if she didn't do it fast, before she had time to think, she knew she couldn't go through with it.

Donna rushed to catch up to her. Together they approached the two men. Julie kept her gaze trained on Chris. He was watching her like a hawk, looking as if he would grab her and pull her away if she showed any signs of faltering.

She stopped a few feet in front of him, sensing more than seeing the body on the ground at her feet.

"You don't have to do this," he said.

"I know. But you want me to?"

He slowly nodded. "I do."

She drew a shaky breath. "Okay. Then I will."

The man standing beside him—Max maybe?—gave them both a surprised look. She could see him in her peripheral vision, as if he was puzzled by their exchange. Was it unusual for a witness to trust a cop the way she did Chris? Maybe, probably. But she'd been through more trials and tribulations in the past twenty-four hours with him than she'd ever been with most of the people in her life. And every single time she needed him, he was there. She did trust him, completely. And that had her so scared she was shaking inside.

She closed her eyes, gathered her courage, then did what he'd asked.

She looked down at the body.

And then she knew why he'd asked her to come over here, hoping she could identify the man who'd most recently tried to kill her. Sadly, no, she didn't recognize him. Had, in fact, never seen him before in her life. Because if she had, she'd never have forgotten him.

He could have been her twin.

Chapter Fifteen

Chris thanked the restaurant manager and closed the door to the private dining room. Several tables had been pulled together in the center of the room to accommodate Julie, the chief and the entire SWAT team minus Dillon—who was staying at the hospital with his wife.

Surprisingly, the chief was treating Chris just as if he was on active duty and had yet to gripe at him over spiriting Julie away from the station. Maybe the chief was giving him a break for surviving another close call. Or maybe he was rewarding Chris for getting Julie to really talk to them. Then again, it could just be that without Dillon the department was stretched too thin. Regardless of the reason, Chris was glad to be part of the team again.

A banquet of fried chicken, mashed potatoes, corn, lima beans and corn bread was laid out in front of them—the perfect Sunday lunch spread after a long morning at church. Or, in Chris and Julie's case, a morning spent dodging bullets and blowing up propane tanks.

He sat beside Julie, who seemed a bit stunned at the volume of food in front of them.

"Go on," Chris urged. "You haven't had anything to eat today."

She nodded and accepted a bowl of mashed potatoes from Donna, who was sitting on her other side.

Everyone was quiet as they ate, without the usual conversation or gossip they usually shared when all of them ended up at the same table—an event that was rare and usually enjoyed. But not today. Today food was just that—food, energy to get through whatever else was going to happen during this investigation.

Since Cooper's farm was a crime scene, it had been cordoned off and a dozen CSU techs and police officers were processing it for clues. Only five of those officers were Destiny police. The rest had been "borrowed" from the state police and neighboring counties, as often happened whenever there was a major crime scene.

Julie set a chicken leg on her plate and offered the platter to Chris. He murmured his thanks and put a breast and a thigh on his own plate before handing the platter across the table to the chief.

"So, the guy in the Charger got away?" Julie asked.

Randy winced beside the chief. "He got off a lucky shot and took out my left front tire. I overcorrected the resulting skid and slammed into a tree."

"I'm so sorry," Julie said. "You're okay?"

He nodded, looking pleased that she'd ask. "I'm fine. My truck needed a new paint job. Now I get it for free, courtesy of the Destiny Police Department."

Thornton frowned his displeasure at his officer, but didn't deny that the department would pick up the tab.

Chris noted that Julie played with her food more than she ate. Not that he could blame her. His own usually healthy appetite—especially when it came to fried chicken—was nearly nonexistent. There were too many questions rolling around in his head. Plus the worry that something could happen to Julie. There was zero doubt now that more than one person was after her, trying to kill her. Whatever was going on was bigger than a soon to be ex-husband wanting to settle the score.

Several minutes later, Chief Thornton pushed back his plate and wiped his hands on his napkin. That seemed to be the signal that everyone had been waiting for. They all put their forks down.

"Before anyone asks," Julie said, "I've been racking my brain about the rifleman, like you all told me to do before we left Cooper's farm. I still don't know who he is…was."

"He sure had an uncanny resemblance to you," Chris said. "Just how sure are you that he wasn't a long-lost brother?"

She rolled her eyes. "If I had a brother, I'd know about it."

"Doppelganger," Randy said, with the solemnity of a sage oracle, as if he'd just figured out the secret to life.

Julie frowned. "Doppelganger?"

"Don't," Chris warned.

"Don't what?"

"Encourage him. He's got all kinds of crazy theories. We try not to get him started."

Randy pressed a hand against his shirt, feigning hurt even as he winked at Julie. "A doppelganger is an evil twin. They say everyone has one somewhere in the world. Today you met yours."

"Evil twin?" Julie asked.

Donna shook her head. "That's not what a doppelganger is. A doppelganger is a ghost, an apparition who's the spitting image of you. Obviously, if you'd met your doppelganger it would be a woman."

Randy crossed his arms over his chest. "Then how do you explain the gunman? He looked just like Mrs. Webb. But she insists she doesn't have any long-lost brothers. So what other explanation is there?"

Chris tossed his napkin on top of his plate. "Obviously, Julie is related to the gunman somehow. The CSU guys submitted his prints. Hopefully, we'll get a hit, and get it soon. In the meantime, we need to shake the Webb family tree and see who falls out. Julie, you can help by giving us some background on your family."

"I already told you about my sister, and what happened to my parents."

The pain in her voice had him hating himself for having to ask her even more questions. But worse would be standing at her graveside while they lowered her casket. To help, he briefed everyone on what she'd already told him.

Donna took a small notebook and pen from her purse. Like the others, she was still dressed in her Sunday best. But her dark blue dress was horribly wrinkled because of the body armor she'd worn earlier. She didn't seem to mind.

She made some notes and smiled at Julie. "Can you tell me your parents' names?"

Julie looked at Chris. "This is supposed to help you figure out the gunman's identity?"

"It's a starting place, victimology," Chris said. "In order to find out why your husband tried to kill you, and who else is after you, we need to know as much as we can about your history. That includes your family, your friends, your work—everything."

She let out a long-suffering sigh. "Okay. Fine. My mom was Beatrix. My father was Giles Linwood. They were both born and raised in London, England. But their parents didn't approve of them dating. Well, mostly my mom's parents didn't approve. Mom said they had some money and thought my dad was a gold digger. After my grandfather died, my grandmother—Elizabeth—took an even harder stance against my mom and dad dating. They ended up getting married anyway. Grandmother disowned my mom and she and my dad moved to America to start a new life.

"Disowned," Donna said. "Sounds old-fashioned."

Julie shrugged. "I don't know much about my grandmother, but old-fashioned covers it. She was big on loyalty and felt my mom had turned her back on the family by marrying my father."

"Did you ever meet her?" Chris asked.

"No. I've never heard from her or any of my parents' relatives. But my mother had a necklace that was given to her by my grandmother when Mom turned eighteen. She passed it on to my sister, Naomi, on her eighteenth birthday, saying it was a family tradition and that she must promise to always keep the necklace safe. When Naomi…when Naomi died, my mom told me to take the necklace, that it was mine now."

She shook her head. "That's all I have of my English heritage, just a stupid necklace. Once my parents died, I had an estate sale, got rid of the furniture, clothes, things I figured someone else might need. I've never been much of a packrat. But I couldn't bear to let go of some things—pictures mostly, my mom's costume jewelry that she loved so much, Dad's baseball card collection. And the few things I had of Naomi's, including that necklace and her hairclips."

The earlier tortured look in her eyes faded as she smiled at the memory of her sister. "She had a fetish for the darn clips, snatched them up at flea markets and estate sales, the gaudier the better. If you pasted rhinestones or fake gems onto something to put in your hair, Naomi would drool over it. I'd forgotten about that. I put the box away for safe-keeping, but haven't looked at it even once since then. I think…looking at their things would make it too real that I'll never see my family again."

Chris was about to ask her more about her sister when the chief's phone rang. The chief apologized and stepped away from the table to take the call.

A few seconds later, Max's phone rang, too. Conversation stopped while both men took their calls. When they were done, Chris glanced back and forth between them.

"Well?" he asked. "Something about the investigation?"

The chief nodded. "Mine was. Kathy Nelson said she needs Mrs. Webb to return to Nashville in order to wrap up the loose ends of the criminal case that was pending against Mr. Webb. She's demanding that we escort her there right away." He arched a brow at Julie.

"I don't see why I need to be there. She already has my statements about Alan breaking into our home in Nashville. What happened here doesn't change the case."

"I agree," the chief said. "Which is why I told her not to hold her breath, that you'd leave if and when you were ready."

Julie blinked, looking half-horrified that he'd talk to an ADA that way, and half-amused. "Um, thanks. I think."

Detective Max Remington leaned forward, resting his arms on the table at his seat on the end. "My call was about the case, too. The license plate check on the black Dodge Charger came through. The car is owned by a rental company. You'll never guess where it's based."

"Nashville," Chris said. "Do I get to guess who rented it?"

"You could, but I'd rather tell you. The car was rented by assistant district attorney Kathy Nelson."

Julie let out a gasp of surprise.

"She wasn't driving," the chief said. "The call I just took was from a landline in Nashville. I know because it was the ADA's receptionist who put the call through. And she told me Nelson was in court all morning, with another ADA, and they'd both just gotten back into the office. No way could she have done that and been driving through hay fields a few hours ago."

"Agreed," Chris said, still watching Max. "But I don't think the car was rented for her use. The Charger was rented for one of her assistants, wasn't it, Max?"

"Yep. The winning answer is Brian Henson. A second car, also black, this one a Chevy Camaro, was rented by Nelson for her other assistant, Jonathan Bolton."

"I don't remember seeing a Charger or a Camaro parked in the police when they were at the station," Chris said. "All I saw was Nelson's silver Mercedes. Why would she rent cars for her assistants—separate cars—but all three of them arrive together at the station?"

The chief stood and pulled out his phone again. "You don't have to say it. I'm calling Nelson back right now to ask about her assistants and her rental-car habits. This is getting really weird is all I have to say." He headed to the other side of the dining room.

"I don't understand," Julie said. "We're saying that Kathy's employee, Henson, tried to kill us this morning? And that because Kathy drove both of her administrative assistants to the police station for my interview, that she was—what—planning the attack and didn't want us to know what cars her men drove? That doesn't make any sense. She's an assistant district attorney. An old college friend. What would she have to gain by having me killed?"

"I'm not sure we're ready to make all of those leaps in logic, yet," Chris said. "We're just gathering facts. But if we do assume that Nelson is behind the attempt on your life this morning, then it makes sense to also assume that she could have been working with Alan and that together they may have orchestrated both times that he attacked you."

She pressed her hand against her throat. "I don't... I don't see how that's possible. She and Alan couldn't stand each other."

Chris leaned forward. "You sure about that? For all you know, Kathy and Alan may have been far more than friends in college and hid it from you. Maybe they already knew each other when you and her supposedly first met him."

Julie shook her head. "No. No, that can't be. I'm telling you, they really didn't get along in college. Besides, even if I were wrong—which I'm not—if they were interested in each other, all they had to do was date and leave me as the third wheel. We're the same age. We were all struggling college students, with nothing to gain or lose by becoming friends or hiding any attractions. What would be the point? If Kathy liked Alan, and vice versa, they'd have become an item instead of Alan and me." She spread her hands out in front of her. "On top of that, if Kathy liked Alan, it would have been in her best interest to let him know back then, not hide it and encourage me in my relationship with him, which is what she did."

"She encouraged you to date him?" Chris asked.

"Basically. I mean it wasn't like she pushed me toward him. But she seemed happy for me and made sure that I knew she didn't mind when I did essentially choose my boyfriend over spending time with her."

"You said it would have been in her best interest to date Alan," Chris continued. "Why?"

"Money, of course. He wasn't exactly flush in college, but he wasn't hurting either. Everyone knew he was the heir to Webb Enterprises, his father's import-export business, and that he was expected to take the reins of the company one day. Whoever ended up marrying Alan would have come into a lot of money. If this is about Kathy and Alan being some kind of partners, they would have become partners in college and gotten married. I had nothing to offer anyone. There was no financial benefit for Alan marrying me."

"I'm not so sure that's true," Max said from the end of the table, just as the chief resumed his seat.

The chief waved toward him. "I got some silly run-around answer from Nelson about her men wanting to explore the countryside, thus the rental of two cars. And she'd driven them to the station because they were all at the hotel together and it made sense to share a ride to Mrs. Webb's witness interview." He rolled his eyes.

"I'm still not buying it," the chief continued. "Especially since they didn't end up staying overnight at the hotel. Naturally, her response to my question about that was that they changed their minds after Julie left the interview. But unless the city of Nashville has money to burn in their budget, I don't see them reimbursing an ADA for renting her admin assistants cars." He waved at Max again. "Go on. You were about to say something else you found out?"

Max nodded. "Mrs. Webb, you mentioned your mother's family had some money. Any idea how much?"

Julie shook her head. "My mom didn't talk about her family very often. I got the impression they lived comfortably, but not anything crazy. It's not like they were millionaires, or however many pounds sterling it takes to make someone rich." She smiled, but Max remained stoic.

"You didn't mention your mother's maiden name earlier," Max said.

"Abbott, why?"

He nodded, as if that was what he'd expected. "Your grandmother was Elizabeth Victoria Abbott, correct?" Max asked.

Julie frowned. "Yes, that's right. Is there a point here somewhere?"

"Your grandmother's late husband was Edward. They were from old money and built that inheritance into an extremely lucrative corporation they simply named Victoria and Edward. Your grandfather died many years ago. But your grandmother is still alive and thriving. She's the CEO. And you're right that she's not worth millions. Her net worth is in the billions. About two-point-six billion, to be exact."

The room went silent.

Julie's mouth dropped open.

"There's one other piece of information I got from that call," Max said, shifting his glance to Chris and then the chief. "The fingerprint search on our dead rifleman got a match based on a passport-database search." He looked back at Julie. "His name was Harry Abbott."

Chapter Sixteen

Julie yanked the comb through her wet hair, wincing when it caught on a tangle. She freed the comb and tossed it into the duffel bag that Donna had gotten for her from the rental house. The chief had been nice enough to let Julie take a shower in the bathroom attached to his office here at the police station. This luxury had surprised her and elicited a few snickers from the SWAT team.

Julie braced her hands on the countertop and stared into the mirror above the sink, thinking about what she'd learned during lunch. Her mom had painted Julie's grandmother as being ancient, in poor health. Julie had always assumed the woman had passed away by now. But now she knew her grandmother was alive and well, and at the helm of a multibillion-pound enterprise.

Not that it made any difference. Julie would have loved to have a grandmother, regardless of her grandmother's financial situation. She longed for someone to help fill the holes in her heart left by the loss of her family. But obviously that sentiment wasn't returned. If Elizabeth Abbott had really loved her only daughter, she'd have done something over the years to reach out to her. And she'd have discovered she had two granddaughters to love, as well. But she never had. Which told Julie that her mother was right all along, and that she'd made the right choice in fleeing across the pond when she was just a girl herself.

Julie shoved her hair back from her eyes, straightened the bathroom, then grabbed the duffel and headed into the chief's office. She stopped short when she saw Chris writing on a whiteboard hanging on the wall opposite the desk.

He turned and smiled a greeting. Then his smile died as he looked at her. "Julie? What's wrong?"

She glanced at the closed door, relieved that no one else was in the office right now. She sat in one of the guest chairs in front of the chief's desk.

"I'm not normally a whiner. But I'm beginning to seriously dislike my grandmother even though I've never met her. I can't get past the fact that she's as rich as Midas but could never forgive her daughter and provide the help that Naomi needed, the help my parents could never afford. If she had, maybe Naomi would still be alive."

Chris crossed the room and crouched in front of her chair, taking her hands in his. "Are you saying your grandmother contacted your mother? That she knew she had granddaughters, and didn't do anything to intercede when your sister got sick?"

She clung to his hands, to the strength and support he offered, grateful to have one person she felt comfortable with, one person she could lean on right now.

"No. But I just can't see my loving, wonderful mother not reaching out to *her* mother to save her dying child. If there was anything humanly possible that could be done to save Naomi, my mom would have done it. So

I have to believe that she did contact my grandmother, told her the situation and asked for her help."

Julie shook her head, tears tracking down her cheeks. "No help came. My grandmother chose her feud over trying to save the life of her eldest granddaughter. How can I ever forgive that?"

He pulled her into his arms and held her tight. Embarrassed to be crying on him again, she tried to think of something else—anything else—to stop her tears. But blanking all her troubles from her mind left far too much room to think about how good his arms felt around her.

The last time she and her husband had held each other like this had been too long ago to remember. That had to be why she felt so drawn to this man. She was lonely, starved for affection, desperate for someone who seemed to care what happened to her. But, really, who wouldn't be drawn to him?

His strong arms felt wonderful around her. His chest was the perfect pillow for her cheek. And he smelled so darn good. But of course there was so much more to him than the physical. He was brave, protective, loyal— the qualities that meant the most to Julie, probably because those were the qualities of a tight-knit family. And family meant everything to her. Which was why losing hers had been so devastating.

For just a moment, she allowed herself the fantasy of pretending that Chris was her family, that he was hers to hold and to keep and treasure. It was a delightful fantasy, and one that would be over far too soon. Because even if he felt the same draw, the same attraction—heart, soul and mind—to her that she felt to him, what kind of a future could there ever be for a relation-ship between so very different people?

She'd seen how close he was to his SWAT team, how they acted like their own little family. He could never give up something like that, give up the friends he was loyal to and cared about. And she wouldn't want him to. But she couldn't see herself in a small town like this for the rest of her life. Her work meant far too much to her, and it relied on charity, the kinds of donations she could only get by working in a large city with affluent pools of people to draw upon—a city like Nashville. Moving here, to Destiny, permanently, would mean giv-ing up on finding cures that would help so many fami-lies like hers. That was something she just couldn't do.

Inhaling deeply, she selfishly enjoyed another tan-talizing breath warmed by Chris's skin, perfumed by his masculine scent. Then she pushed herself back to sitting, forcing him to drop his arms.

He studied her intently, his dark eyes boring into hers. "You do know that I'm going to protect you, right? You seem…scared, or maybe worried."

Unable to stop herself, she caressed his face. Her heart nearly stopped when he rubbed his cheek against her hand. Oh, how she wished her life were different, that she had met this man in another place, another time.

He smiled, a warm, gentle smile she felt all the way to her toes.

"Everything's going to be okay, Julie," he said. "We'll figure this out. Together."

"Thank you," she whispered. Her gaze dropped to his lips, and she automatically leaned toward him. Her hands went to his shirt, smoothing the fabric.

A shudder went through him and she looked up. The

open hunger on his face made her breath catch. And then he was leaning toward her, slowly, giving her every chance to stop him, to pull away, to say no.

She didn't want to say no.

She wanted his lips on hers, his arms around her, wanted to feel her breasts crushing against the hard planes of his chest. She wanted this. She wanted him, needed him.

His breath warmed her as he kissed first one cheek, then the other, before lowering his lips to hers.

Heaven. She'd died and gone to heaven, and it was far better than she'd ever thought it could be. His mouth moved against hers, softly, gently, a warm caress that made her feel cherished, wanted, needed, the way that she needed him. The kiss was so beautiful it made her want to cry all over again, this time with joy. And then the kiss changed.

Gone was the gentle lover. The hunger she'd seen on his face, in his eyes, she now felt in his touch, in the way his arms crushed her against him, the way his lips slanted across hers. His tongue swept inside her mouth, a hot, wild mating, urgent and demanding. Her pulse rushed in her ears, her heart beating against her ribs as she slid her arms up around his neck.

He groaned deep in his throat and lifted her out of the chair, turning with her in his arms and never taking his lips from hers. He pressed her back against the whiteboard. She lifted her legs, wrapping them around his waist. The kiss was hot, ravenous, full of need and longing for more, so much more.

She pulled her arms down to his shirt and began working the top button, then the next. When she reached the third, she slid her hands inside his shirt, reveling in the feel of his hot skin against hers. And just like that, they both broke the kiss, staring in shock at each other.

"Oh, my," she breathed. "I think I was about to tear your clothes off."

"I was about to help." He chuckled and pressed his forehead against hers. He drew a ragged breath before pulling back and smiling down at her. "Where did that come from?"

She shook her head. "I have no idea. But it probably happens to you all the time."

His eyes widened. "Why would you say that?"

She slid her arms up behind his neck, then realized what she was doing and forced them down. He eased back and helped her stand, keeping his hands on her shoulders as if she needed steadying—which she definitely did.

"Why did you say it happens all the time to me?" he repeated.

She rolled her eyes and waved toward the three undone buttons on his shirt. "Because of…that. You're gorgeous. And charming. And smart. And a dozen other things. Women probably throw themselves at you so much you have to fight them off."

Her cheeks grew hot under his incredulous stare. "What?" she demanded, feeling extremely self-conscious.

"Have you seen yourself in a mirror lately, Julie? You can't tell me that you didn't notice how Max and the others kept looking at you during lunch. You're beautiful."

It was her turn to stare at him with an incredulous expression. "Now that I think about it, I remember seeing you bump your head after the propane tank exploded. Isn't that right? Now it all makes sense."

He laughed and buttoned up his shirt, much to her sorrow. And then she laughed, too, because this was the lightest she'd felt in months. Which made no sense at all considering that someone was trying to kill her.

That thought helped sober her up and, unfortunately, killed the good mood Chris had managed to put her in. Her gaze fell to the duffel bag, forgotten on the floor, and just like that all of the horrible things that had been happening since that night that Alan had broken into their Nashville home flooded back.

A gentle touch beneath her chin had her looking up into Chris's eyes. He gave her a sad smile. "You're back to worrying again, I see. I wish there was something that I could do to convince you it's all going to work out."

"Me, too." She pointed at the whiteboard. "What is all of that?"

He picked up a pen and piece of paper from on top of the desk and held them out to her. "I'll tell you in a minute. First, though. I'd like your written permission to search your home in Nashville and to open the safe. The chief will notarize the document. We'll need the house keys. And we'll use your written permission to get a locksmith to open the safe."

She took the paper, skimmed the two paragraphs of legalize. "How did you know the address?" She set the paper on the desk to sign it, then grabbed her purse from another corner of the desk.

"The night the chief interviewed you, the paperwork you filled out gave your basic info, including addresses. You don't remember?"

She worked the required key off her key ring as she shook her head. "Not really. Everything that night is kind of a blur at this point. And I'd prefer to keep it that way."

She set the house key on top of the form she'd signed and tossed the rest of her keys into her purse. "Do I need to sign anything else?"

"Not at the moment. I'll get one of our guys working on this right away." He picked up the key and paper and strode out of the office.

Julie crossed to the whiteboard, trying to make sense of what Chris had written on it. There were several columns, in varying colors, with bullets beneath each column.

"I'm a list maker," he announced as he came back into the office and shut the door. "If I can make a list out of something, it organizes my thoughts, helps me form a big picture and then put all the pieces together."

She smiled. "I'm a list maker, too. What does all of this mean?"

He walked her through it, and she noted how he'd used different colored markers for different categories. Suspects were written in green.

Kathy Nelson.
Brian Henson.
Jonathan Bolton.
Alan Webb—Deceased.
Harry Abbott—Deceased.

She rubbed her hands up and down her arms. "I thought Kathy had an alibi for when we were at Cooper's farm?"

"She does. But if she put out the hit, she's just as guilty. Even without evidence, that seems like the simplest explanation for everything. And usually the most straightforward explanation is the right one. I also don't believe in coincidences. When looking at this as a whole, Kathy and Alan working together against you is the basic premise that makes the most sense. But we have to figure out what they were after, which leads me to my next column."

He wrote on the board—Motive. And beneath that he created another list.

Love.
Money.
Revenge.
Hatred.
Hide something.

He turned around. "Every case I've ever worked fell into one of these categories, often more than one. At the heart of every murder, one of these overrides all else and drives the killer. Looking at Alan first, we know that he wanted to kill you. But it seems like he was also after something else—perhaps this key that you mentioned. So which of the motivations seems to make sense as to why he did what he did?"

She cocked her head, studying the list, thinking about how her relationship with Alan had started, how it had been so warm and loving in college, and then how it had changed shortly after they got married. She grew still, trying to figure out what, if anything, that might mean.

"What is it?" Chris asked. "You've thought of something."

"You said you don't believe in coincidences. And

yet Alan just happened to appear the moment when I needed him the most. Just a few months after I lost my family, and my support system, when I was at rock bottom, he was there. Strong, understanding, helping me work through my grief. Given everything else, that just feels…wrong."

Chris slowly lowered the dry-erase marker that he was holding. "Tell me how your family died again. Don't leave anything out."

She frowned. "I don't see how that—"

"Humor me."

She shrugged. "Okay. Naomi got sick—"

"And the doctors couldn't figure out what was wrong with her."

"Right."

"Why not?"

"Excuse me?"

He set the marker onto the ledge. "Doctors used to have to rely on their memories, or look up symptoms in some thick medical tome to try to figure out what illness or disease matched them. Nowadays, they can plug symptoms into any number of online tools and get a list of possible causes. Doesn't it seem strange that they couldn't do that in your sister's case?"

She shook her head, uncomfortable with where the conversation seemed to be heading. "It's not strange. That's the thing about orphan diseases. They don't come up in internet searches if they're so rare that no one has input any information about them into a computer. The doctors said she must have had an orphan disease."

"But they couldn't give it a name?"

"No, they couldn't."

"Again, why not?"

She spread her hands in a helpless gesture. "I suppose because her symptoms kept changing. And each symptom came on so suddenly. Really, by the time my parents realized how seriously ill she was, and that she wasn't getting better, she only had a few weeks left. She died four months after the first day she got sick. But my parents had only started hounding the doctors about six or eight weeks before that. I think that's why it hit them so hard. They felt guilty for not seeking help sooner."

"I can totally see that, a parent thinking their child had a cold or virus, expecting it to go away on its own. It would be particularly difficult to realize how bad it was if the symptoms changed."

"Exactly. That's why my dad spiraled into a deep depression after her death. He felt he should have done more." She twisted her hands together in her lap. "We all felt we should have done more."

She braced herself for his sympathy, not wanting him to feel sorry for her. But, as if sensing how she felt, he gave her one quick empathetic look before grabbing a dry-erase pen and moving to the right side of the board. He wrote "Naomi" and "Symptoms" on top of a new column.

"Tell me her symptoms, in the exact order in which they appeared, and tell me how long they lasted."

"I don't understand. Why do you want me to relive that pain again?"

His jaw tightened. "I don't want to hurt you, Julie. But more importantly, I want to save your life. If that means I have to cause you a little pain to do it, then I will."

Had she really thought of this man as her fantasy-hero a few minutes ago? Her perfect man? Because right now, she just wanted to walk out of this office and turn her back on the wounds he was opening inside her.

"Julie, you told me that you trust me. Was that a lie?"

His gentle, soothing voice wrapped around her heart like velvet. "No," she finally said. "That wasn't a lie. I do trust you."

"Then work with me on this. Tell me Naomi's symptoms. What was the first thing you or your parents noticed?"

She worked with him for over half an hour on the list. Each time she thought they were done, he'd ask another question, force her to delve deeper into her memory, try to associate each appearance or disappearance of a symptom with some event in her life to help her make sure she had it right.

Finally, he stepped back from the board, taking it all in. He seemed deep in thought. And when he turned around, Julie could have sworn she saw a flash of anger in his eyes. But the emotion was quickly masked with one of his kind, gentle smiles. He took her hands in his and led her to the door.

He pulled it open, and she looked up at him in confusion. "You want me to leave?"

He waved at Donna, who was sitting at one of the desks, typing on her computer. She hurried over, raising a brow in question.

"Donna, can you show Julie the kitchenette and get her something to drink? I need to make a phone call."

Donna smiled and put an arm around Julie's shoulders. "No problem. Come on, sweetie. Calories don't count during murder investigations. And thanks to Ashley, Dillon's wife, we've always got all kinds of goodies over here. I'll pull a batch of her banana nut muffins out of the freezer and heat them up. They're amazing."

She led Julie to what Chris had called a kitchenette but that was really just a long counter against the wall to the right of the chief's office door and to the left of the main door into the station. It was loaded with cookies and all kinds of other baked goods, with a coffeemaker on one end and both a small refrigerator and a freezer underneath the counter on the other.

"Soda, coffee or water?" Donna asked. "Pick your poison."

"Um, soda, I guess. Something with a lot of caffeine. Thanks."

"You got it." Donna opened the refrigerator.

Julie looked toward the chief's office, but Chris had already closed the door.

"SORRY TO BUG you again, Dillon. But this is really important," Chris said into the phone as he stared at the white board. Just thinking about what he now believed to be true had him wanting to go to the morgue and kill Alan Webb all over again

"Not a problem," Dillon whispered. "Give me a second."

Chris heard the sound of muted footsteps, as if Dillon was trying not to make any noise. A moment later, a click. "Okay. I'm out of Ashley's room. This is the first real sleep she's had since we got here and I didn't want to disturb her."

"Does that mean what I think it means?"

"We think this scary episode is over now, yes. She hasn't had any contractions in quite a while. Go ahead. Tell me what you've got."

"I'm asking you to go way back to your college days, to all those fancy medical classes you took when you wanted to be a large-animal vet."

"I'll pay you back for calling me old the next time I see you, especially since we're the same age. What classes specifically are you talking about?"

"Did you take any botany classes?"

"Of course. I needed to know what kinds of plants were poisonous and recognize the symptoms in case of accidental ingestion by an animal. Why?"

"That's what I figured. I've got a list of symptoms for you, and then I want you to tell me what comes to mind."

There was a long pause before Dillon spoke. "Shouldn't you be calling an actual botanist or doctor about this?"

"I will, or I'll have one of the guys follow up. But I figured this would be faster and you could at least tell me if what I'm thinking is crazy."

"All right. I've got my pen and notebook out. Go."

It didn't take long. The anger that had been building inside Chris was now ready to explode.

"What was this Alan Webb guy's major in college?" Dillon asked.

"Botany."

"You know what you need to do."

"Yeah. I need to exhume Naomi's body."

Chapter Seventeen

Julie was backed into a corner, literally—the one in the chief's office between the window and the door to the bathroom. It was the farthest away she could get from everyone else in the office, because they'd all lost their ever-loving minds.

She shook her head, raking the chief, Max and Chris with her glare. She'd have glared at the very nice Donna, too, and even Randy or Colby, except that they were in the squad room handling other cases that had come in.

"I won't do it," she repeated. "Naomi's gone. Digging up her body won't change that." She looked at Chris. "I can't believe you would ask me to do this."

"Did you understand what I explained about the plants? How someone can extract solanine, glycoalkaloids, arsenic—"

"Oh, I understand just fine. What you're saying is your police buddy Dillon studied plants in vet school, even though he never became a vet. And based on a short phone call and a list of symptoms I may very well remember wrong you two have come up with a crazy theory that my botany-major husband poisoned my sister. You think he switched up the plants he used so he could confuse the doctors. One set of symptoms would go away, a new set would begin, all so he could make it look like a natural death when there wasn't anything natural about it at all. Did I get that right, Chris? Did I explain your theory correctly?"

Tears, again the blasted tears, were running down her face. But this time they weren't tears of grief or fear. They were tears of anger.

"Did I get it right?" she demanded.

Chris slowly nodded. "Except for the part about this all being a crazy theory. I had Max confirm everything by calling a real botanist. We're not wrong about any of this, Julie. The botanist told us exactly how he could reproduce the same symptoms with plants that are easily available."

"Good for you. You get a gold star. Now, if you're through trying to rip my heart out, I'm leaving." She shoved away from the wall and strode toward the door.

Chris glanced at his boss, then moved in front of Julie, blocking her way.

"Move," she said.

"Not until you hear us out."

"I've heard all I want to hear and then some. I don't want to hear any more." She swiped at the tears. Dang it. Why couldn't she stop crying?

"Julie, please. We need to talk through this. I believe Alan poisoned your sister. If we can exhume—"

"No. I told you, no. I'm not changing my mind. And what you're saying doesn't make sense anyway. Alan never even met my sister. I didn't meet him until two months after my parents died, three months after Naomi died."

"I know." His voice was ridiculously calm. He motioned to Max. "Do you have that printout handy?"

Max pulled a sheet of paper out of his suit jacket pocket and handed it to Chris.

Julie tried to grab the doorknob, but Chris planted a foot to his left, again blocking her. He opened the paper and started to read what amounted to a short bio about Alan.

Julie shook her head, her hands fisted at her sides. "Some investigators you people are. You've got his birthdate wrong. He wasn't two years older than me. He and I were the same age."

"Max," Chris said in that infuriatingly calm, soothing voice. "Where did you get Alan's birthdate?"

A look of sympathy crossed Max's face as he answered. "Mrs. Webb, I know your husband told you he was your age. But it was a ruse so he could enroll in the same classes as you without raising red flags. Even more damning, the classes he took at your college were all audited, meaning they weren't graded and didn't apply toward a degree. That's because he'd already graduated. He already had his degree from another school. That's the real reason he told you he was dropping out. He couldn't pretend to be getting a degree when you graduated. Dropping out was how he covered up that he was never a degree-seeking student at your school."

She shook her head. "No." But her voice was barely above a whisper. Panic was closing her throat.

"In addition to his school records, which had his correct birthdate, I pulled his birth certificate and cross-referenced his information in the social-security database. And if that's still not enough proof, I had a librarian pull a copy of his high-school yearbook. He graduated high school two years before you did."

He pulled another piece of paper from his jacket and handed it to Chris. "Even more importantly, I tracked down one of your sister's friends from college. That's her written statement in response to my questions. I texted her a picture of Alan off the internet from when he attended a ribbon-cutting ceremony at one of the offices for his father's company."

Chris held the paper up for Julie to see. She refused to look at it.

"The friend remembered Alan, said he went to a lot of the same bars that she and Naomi went to during Naomi's senior year, just two months before she got sick. Naomi couldn't stand Alan. He kept hitting on her and wouldn't take no for an answer. A month after she first met him, she filed a complaint against him with the local police."

"But she never...she never told me about him," Julie whispered.

He shrugged. "Maybe she didn't want to worry her family and figured filing the police report would end the problem."

With that, Max pulled another piece of paper out and handed it to Chris.

"It's the arrest report," Chris said.

The room went silent as they all waited. She stared at Max and slowly took the paper from Chris. The paper rattled because her hands were shaking so much. It was a brief report, printed on the police department's letterhead, with details like the date and the name of the officer who'd taken the statement, a statement signed by Naomi Linwood, their father's last name, Julie's maiden name.

There, at the end of the report, highlighted in yellow, was the name of the man who'd been essentially stalking Julie's sister—Alan Blackwood Webb. Exactly one month after the complaint was issued, Naomi called their mother to tell her she couldn't come home for a planned family dinner because she had an upset stomach and had thrown up three times. Four months later, Naomi was dead. And when Julie met Alan Blackwood Webb three months after that, he'd told her how sorry he was that he'd never had the pleasure of meeting her sister or her parents.

Julie lowered the piece of paper. A low buzz started in her ears.

"My father," she said, her throat so tight she could hardly talk, "killed himself, shot himself, shortly after Naomi…died. The funny thing is, he was always so vocal against guns. He didn't even own one. But no one questioned that. We were all too grief stricken. The police assumed he'd bought it off the street. There really wasn't much of an investigation."

"Julie." Chris reached for her, but she shoved his hand away.

"Now, my mother," she continued, "was devastated when my daddy died. She'd handled Naomi's death like a soldier. But Daddy—my mom just couldn't take losing him. Couldn't sleep. Got a prescription for sleeping pills. They say she drank down the whole bottle of pills with a glass of wine."

She choked on the last word, had to cough to clear her throat. "Most people would assume the woman in a household is the wine drinker, and that the beer in the refrigerator is for the man of the house. But my mama…" Julie shook her head. "My mama was the beer drinker. I always thought it was odd that she chose to end her life drinking something she didn't even like."

She looked up at Chris through a wall of tears she could no longer stop. "He killed them. All of them. And I never even asked any questions. I accepted their deaths like everyone else. And then I married their killer."

The room began to spin around her. The buzzing got louder and louder until it was all she could hear.

Until she couldn't.

CHRIS SWORE AND caught Julie's crumpled form in his arms.

"She's passed out. Get Dr. Brookes," the chief ordered, waving at Max.

"No," Chris said, settling her higher against his chest. "She doesn't need a doctor poking at her. She needs rest, and peace and quiet. Everything about her life has come into question and she needs time to process it. Max, shove her purse into that duffel and take it out to my truck, will you?"

"You got it." Max hurried to do what he'd asked, leaving the office door open behind him.

Chris followed him out.

"Hold it," the chief ordered behind him. "You can't just walk out of here with the witness. Again."

Chris ignored the surprised look on everyone's face as he strode through the squad room. Max waited at the door, holding it open.

The chief stubbornly followed Chris into the parking lot and rushed to get in front of him when Chris stopped at his truck.

"Detective Downing, I'm ordering you to stand down. Take Mrs. Webb back into the station."

"Max, mind getting the door, please?" Chris asked.

Max seemed to be struggling to hide his grin as he held the passenger door open.

Chris settled Julie inside and fastened her seat belt before shutting the door.

"Detective," the chief barked, his face turning red.

Chris stepped around him and climbed into the driver's seat.

The chief stood in the open doorway. "If you do this, you're as good as resigning."

Chris hesitated and glanced at Julie's tear-streaked face. Somehow, in a ridiculously short amount of time, he'd gone from suspecting her of being a murderess to respecting and admiring her more than any woman he'd ever met. He'd seen her fight when others would have given up. And now, without meaning to, he'd finally ground her down to the point that she'd shut down just to survive. Taking her to a doctor or leaving her at the station to be confronted with the facts and interviewed yet again wasn't the way to heal her, to make her better. She needed to get away from the trauma she faced at every turn. And he was going to make sure she got exactly what she needed and deserved.

He turned back toward the chief. "Move."

The chief's face turned so red it looked as if he might have a stroke. Instead of moving out of the way, he called Chris every curse word that Chris had ever heard. And then he reached for his gun.

Max rushed forward. "Hey, hey, chief. Let's not get carried away."

"Shut up, Officer Remington." The chief glared at Max before looking back at Chris. "Here, take it. Yours is still locked up in evidence." He reached in his back pocket and took out a magazine, then slapped that in Chris's palm, along with the gun.

"Chief?" Chris wasn't sure what to say. And he didn't bother telling his boss he had other guns in the truck. He had a feeling that wouldn't go over well in the chief's current mood.

"That's all the ammo I got with me," the chief continued. "It's enough to keep the rattlers and bears away if you're heading up into the mountains, which is what I'd do in your situation. But if you run into any other kind of trouble, you call me. Hell, you call anyway. I want regular reports until we get all of this sorted out. You hear me, son?"

Chris was so surprised by the chief's gesture that he didn't have the heart to tell him that in addition to the weapons in his truck, he'd had Donna and Max both load up the duffel with plenty of ammo along with the clothing they'd gotten from Julie's and Chris's houses. At the time he'd assumed they'd end up in a hotel, perhaps one town over. But, as hot as this case was getting, the mountains sounded like a far better plan.

"Yes, sir," he finally said. "Thank you, Chief."

"For what? When the ADA calls asking where Mrs. Webb is, I don't know nothing. You can't thank me if I didn't do anything. You got me?"

"Yes, sir. I got you." He glanced at Max. "Keep working those angles we talked about. I'll call you later."

Max grinned. "You and Dillon always were the favorites. I'd be out on my ass if I pulled a stunt like this."

"You may still be if you don't get back in that station and follow up on those leads." The chief glared at both of them before whirling around and stalking back toward the front doors.

"Stay off the main roads as much as possible when you head out of here," Max warned. "I heard Alan Webb's family is hot over his death and might pay us a visit soon."

"When did you hear that?"

"A few minutes ago. One of my contacts warned me."

"You sure have a lot of contacts. Maybe we need to share some of them sometime."

"Nope. They're all mine." He gave Chris a jaunty salute and closed the door.

Chris checked Julie once more, then backed out of the space and took off down the road toward one of the lower peaks in the Smoky mountain range. There was a hunting cabin he and Dillon used up there during deer season. It was the perfect spot to let Julie process everything. And it also had a satellite dish, which meant that Chris could continue helping with the investigation, plus keep a tab on the efforts to locate the driver of that Charger, Brian Henson.

Chapter Eighteen

Julie rolled over in the soft bed, sighing at the fresh, clean smell of the sheets. The bed was ridiculously comfortable. The pillows fluffy, down filled. Wait, her down-filled pillows were still in boxes. Weren't they?

She gasped and bolted upright in bed. Clutching the covers to her chest, she scanned the room. A lamp was on beside the bed, casting a soft yellow glow. The walls were polished, a honey gold, and the floor beside the bed was knotty pine. Other than the lamp, the night-stand it sat on and the bed, there was nothing else. Not even a chest or dresser. None of it looked familiar. So where was she? And how had she gotten here?

"Don't panic. You're safe."

She let out a squeak of surprise, then flushed at the embarrassing sound when she recognized Chris standing in the doorway.

"Are we back at Harmony Haven?" she asked. "I don't recognize the bedroom."

"I wanted you to have some rest, some peace and quiet. So I drove us to a cabin in the mountains."

He waved his hand to encompass the room. "The rest of the place is a bit more modern, not quite this rustic. But this is the only bedroom on the first floor and I wanted you close by so I'd hear you if you woke up in a panic. You were pretty much out of it. I wasn't sure how much you'd remember of the drive up here."

She didn't remember any of it.

She blew out a long breath and shoved her hair back. A quick look down confirmed that she was still dressed in the white blouse and khaki pants that she'd been in after her shower in Chief Thornton's office. Chris must have taken her here after leaving the police station. So why couldn't she remember any of that?

All of the memories of the last confrontation in the chief's office suddenly flooded back. She squeezed her eyes shut, fighting down the panic she'd felt earlier.

He killed them.

Alan, her husband, had killed her family.

And then he'd built a life—with her.

"It gets better."

Her eyes flew open. He'd stepped beside the bed, still dressed in the jeans and casual shirt he'd changed into after his shower. The words he'd just said sat like stones in her stomach.

"What do you mean, it gets better? Your wife murdered your family, too?"

He winced, making her regret her sarcasm. She drew a deep breath, trying to calm down.

"Not exactly," he said. "I've never been married. I do know what it's like to lose someone you love. But what you're going through right now is way worse than anything I've been through. I shouldn't have said that. Sorry, I really am."

He turned as if to leave.

"No, wait. Please."

He gave her a questioning look.

She shifted in the bed, making room beside her. "Tell me about whoever you loved, and lost. Maybe...maybe it will help. Both of us."

He slowly sat down, facing her. "I've never talked about it with anyone else."

"Never?"

"No. I couldn't. I was too busy trying to be there for my best friend, to help him face his own grief. Announcing that the love of my life had just been killed in a car accident—when I'd never even told him about her—wouldn't have helped him. So I kept it inside. As the years went by, it got easier to just never talk about it."

"Your best friend? Isn't Dillon your best friend?"

"Yes."

"Then his grief—it was for the woman he named his farm after, his sister?"

"One and the same."

"That's the woman you loved and lost?"

He chuckled. "I loved Harmony, but not romantically. She was still a kid when she died, six years younger than Dillon and me." His smile faded. "But, yes, Harmony died back home, in Destiny, when Dillon and I were both away at college—separate colleges. The woman I loved, Sherry, was killed a week before Harmony. I stayed for Sherry's funeral, and to pull myself together enough to come home and tell my family and friends about her. Only, once I got here, I found out about Harmony. And Dillon was already home, and devastated."

He shook his head. "If I'd told him my own sorry tale he'd have tried to be there for me. It wouldn't have been right. I'd only been in love with Sherry for a few months. Dillon had lost his baby sister, a whole lifetime of memories. It wasn't the same."

Her heart ached for the loss Chris had suffered and for how he'd lived with it all of these years, keeping it inside. She reached for his hand and clasped it in both of hers.

"I'm so sorry, Chris. You shouldn't have had to bear that pain alone."

Slowly, ever so slowly, he leaned in toward her and placed the softest, sweetest kiss against her lips before pulling back.

"And you shouldn't have to bear your pain alone. That's why I brought you here, Julie. You've lost so much. Suffered an enormous amount of trauma, found out devastating secrets, all in a very short amount of time. I want you to know that you're safe here and I won't badger you with any more questions. We'll stay on the mountain until you're ready to come down. And in the meantime, my teammates will figure the rest of it out. We…they…will find out who's after you. And they'll stop him. I can't take away the pain you feel about what we believe happened to your family. But I can take away some of the stress, or at least try. Do you need anything? Are you hungry?"

"What I need right now is to feel normal. I don't want to talk about the case or my past or any of this. Just… talk to me, for a few minutes. About something, anything, other than the investigation."

He cocked his head, a half smile playing around his lips. "Where did you grow up? Nashville?"

She nodded.

"Ever been to the Smoky Mountains before?"

"Hasn't everybody? I've ridden on the three-story

go-kart tracks in Pigeon Forge, seen Dolly Parton perform in Dollywood, gone to the stores in downtown Gatlinburg."

He grinned. "Typical tourist. You think you've seen everything, when you haven't seen anything." He stood. "Come on."

She flipped the covers back and took his hand.

He tugged her through an archway that she had assumed led to a closet. Then he unlocked and opened a door at the end. She could see blue sky and the dark green leaves of towering trees beyond.

"Wait, my shoes—"

"You don't need them."

"Easy for you to say when you're wearing shoes."

He pulled her through the doorway onto a balcony. She barely noticed the door closing behind them. Her mouth dropped open as she stared at the incredible beauty that stretched as far as she could see. Tall green pine and oak trees framed the vista to the left and the right, but directly below them the mountain steeply dropped away. A deep green valley stretched out below, and beyond that, going on for miles and miles were the blue-gray silhouettes of the Great Smoky Mountains. Little puffs of white mist rose in dozens of places, as if someone was making smoke signals. All of it combined to create a soft, beautiful haze of color and "smoke." It was as if an artist had painted the mountains, then softened everything with a light color wash.

"It's beautiful," she said. "I can't believe I've never come up into the mountains before, not like this."

"The best places in the Smokies are the ones the tourists don't know about, the little turnoffs that lead deep into the forest. There are hundreds of waterfalls all through the mountains, pristine, looking as if no one has touched them or even seen them for thousands of years. It's all unspoiled beauty. Paradise."

He leaned past her, pointing down toward the valley below. "Look," he whispered, "to the right, just coming out of the tree line."

She watched in awe as a group of three deer emerged from the forest, a doe with two fawns. The mother sniffed the air, her large ears flicking back and forth as she scanned for signs of danger. Her young pranced around her on wobbly legs, oblivious to how hard their mother worked to keep them safe. A yellow butterfly rose and dipped around them, much to the delight of the fawns, who scampered after it.

"They're so…innocent…and happy. They're gorgeous," she said, keeping her voice low, not sure if it would carry down to the deer and scare them away.

He gave her a nod of approval. They stood beside each other until the deer disappeared, until the sun began to sink behind the mountains. Tiny little lights blinked on and off down in the valley, close to the tree line.

She laughed with delight. "Fireflies. I haven't seen those since I was a little girl."

A half smile played around his mouth. "They've always been here. You just have to know where to look."

"You grew up here?" She waved her hand to encompass the incredible vista surrounding them. "With all of this?"

He nodded. "Tennessee, the real Tennessee, the one the tourists never stop long enough to appreciate, is heaven on earth. I can't imagine any place more beautiful. I left for a few years to go to college, see a bit of the world. But my heart was always here. No matter where I go, I'll always come back to Destiny."

"You haven't mentioned a family." As soon as she said it, she worried that she might have stumbled into bad territory, that he might have memories in his past he'd like to forget, like she did. But the smile on his face told her otherwise. Family wasn't a bad memory for him. The love shining out of his eyes told her that, even without the smile.

"I reckon I'm related to half the people on this mountain," he teased. "I can't go anywhere without running into a second or third cousin, twice removed. And that's on top of my parents and three brothers. At church the Downings take up three pews. And we usually get together a couple of times a month at someone's house—potluck, everyone brings a dish. We roast marshmallows over an outdoor fire pit, tell ghost stories, swap lies about who caught the biggest fish last."

His smile faded as he looked at her. "I'm sorry. I shouldn't have gushed like that."

She shook her head. "Don't apologize. I asked. And I love hearing about your family, about your life out here. It sounds…wonderful. Tell me more."

The moon was high in the sky and the stars burning bright by the time they retreated inside, driven in by the no-see-ums, gnats and other flying bugs that descended onto the balcony, attracted by their presence.

Chris stopped beside her bed and gave her a soft kiss on her forehead. "You have to be starving by now. Are you a carnivore or one of those vegan people?" He shuddered, as if not eating meat was a fate worse than death.

"I can eat a steak with the best of them," she reassured him. "But I'm not hungry just yet. I think I'll just lie down a little bit longer, if that's okay."

"Of course. I'll be in the next room, just a knock on the wall away."

He started to turn away, but she tugged his hand, keeping him there. His brows raised in question.

She stood on her tiptoes and reached up and cupped his handsome face in her hands. The aching need she'd felt for him back in the chief's office, when they'd shared that soul-shattering kiss, was nothing compared to the way her heart yearned for him now.

There was something so adorable about this man, something that called out to her in every way. He was so kind, took such joy in the world around him. Her bruised and battered soul, even with everything still going on, seemed to feel better, to heal just a little bit more, every time she was around him. She couldn't just let him leave without knowing what he meant to her at this moment. Or how amazing it was to meet a man who put everyone else first, no matter what. That kind of selflessness was rare, a true gift, to be treasured, cherished.

She angled her lips up toward him, waiting, hoping. He was too tall for her to reach unless he wanted this, too. His eyelids dropped to half-mast, need and hunger reflected in his eyes as he leaned down and pressed his lips against hers.

But this was her kiss. She wanted to lead, and he let her. She kissed him, softly, gently, as he'd kissed her back at the station. She poured all the sweetness into her kiss, the raw, new emotions she felt for him but couldn't yet define. She tried to show him that she cared, that he mattered to her, so much that it confused her. All she knew was that he'd saved her life, but he was also saving her soul.

When he would have deepened the kiss, it nearly killed her to pull away. But she wasn't ready for more, not yet. She needed to think and rest and try to make sense of things.

The question was there in his eyes. She fanned her fingers over his cheeks, smiling up at him.

"I wasn't ready for you," she whispered. "You're a surprise. My heart..." She shook her head and smoothed her fingers across his shirt. "Thank you."

The poor man looked just as confused as she felt.

"Thank you for saving me, several times," she said. "Thank you for being there for me no matter what, for sharing the joy of your childhood, your family, your love for this mountain. But most of all, thank you for sharing your pain. I'm so sorry that you lost someone you loved. But it means more than you can possibly know that you shared that with me. It gives me hope that I can work through my own losses, move on and be...happy...one day. So, thank you."

She kissed him again, then dropped her hands and got into bed. She pulled the covers up to her chin. "I really am tired. I think everything that's happened has exhausted me. I'll just lie here awhile longer, okay?"

He looked like he wanted to say something, then sighed and changed his mind about whatever it was.

"I'll be in the next room if you need anything." He waved toward a closed door beside the nightstand. "That's the bathroom. The bag that Donna packed for you is in there."

After he left and pulled the door closed, she shut her eyes. All of his talk about family and happy times had lifted her up, but it also had her thinking about her own family, and feeling like a traitor for laughing and smiling after what had happened to them.

She tried to remember her family the way they'd been before her mother's alleged overdose, before her father supposedly shot himself, before Naomi's mysterious illness. And, mostly, she just tried to remember her family before Alan Webb injected himself into their lives and destroyed them all.

CHRIS HAD BEEN standing over the cabin's kitchen table for about an hour now, moving papers back and forth, like pieces of a puzzle, but so far, he wasn't able to see the big picture.

The background information was pouring in, thanks to the emails and phone calls from his team. But, no matter how he looked at everything or how he classified it into various lists, he wasn't seeing the connections that he needed to make.

He straightened and rubbed the back of his neck. It looked like the only thing to come out of tonight's research session was an aching back and a crick in his neck.

The sound of feet padding across the carpet had him turning around to see Julie coming toward him. She'd changed into a tank top and shorts, revealing a mouth-watering amount of smooth, pale skin. Normally he was all about eyes, lips and curves. But Julie's legs were incredible and had him picturing how they'd feel wrapped around his waist while he—

"Turn around," she said. "And sit. I can help you with that stiff neck you were rubbing."

Since he didn't think he could speak right now without his tongue lolling out, he decided to do what she said. He sat. The moment he did, she slid her hands onto his shoulders and began rubbing and kneading them in slow circles, working out the tension that had coiled in his muscles without him even realizing it.

When she moved her hands to his neck and began massaging him again, his head dropped toward his chest and he let out a groan of pure ecstasy.

She laughed and continued her ministrations.

"You're really good at this." He closed his eyes, hoping she'd never stop.

"I'm good at a lot of things."

Her sexy whisper near his ear had his eyes flying open. Did she realize how her words sounded? The double meaning his suddenly lust-fogged mind had latched on to? He waited, barely breathing. When she didn't say anything else or lead him toward the bedroom, he silently berated himself for even thinking of her that way. He desperately wanted to make love to her, but that would be completely inappropriate.

The few kisses they'd shared were just as inappropriate, but he blamed them on the fact that they were both tired and not thinking straight. He couldn't use that excuse now. It was nearly ten o'clock at night, which meant she'd taken a three hour nap. And he'd slept for at least two hours on the couch before coming into the kitchen to work on the case.

Julie was a witness, and she needed time to work through the topsy-turvy changes in her life. Chris had no business thinking of her except as a woman he was duty-bound to protect.

Too bad his traitorous body wasn't listening.

His phone buzzed on the table. With Julie's hands

still massaging his neck, he carefully leaned forward and picked up the phone. And just like that, the lust-induced fog evaporated. He reached up and took one of her hands in his, pulling her away from him.

"Thanks. Really," he told her. "But I've got to answer this."

The disappointment in her eyes had him wondering if maybe he *hadn't* imagined the sexy double entendre of her earlier words. And that made taking this call feel like torture.

He cleared his throat, gave Julie a pained smile as he held the phone against his ear. "Hi, Mom."

Julie's eyes widened. Then she started to laugh.

He frowned at her, which only made her laugh harder.

"No, Mom. No, I'm, ah, working." He listened to her next question and shook his head. "No, that's not Donna that you just heard. You don't know this woman." He shook his head again as his mother continued to badger him with questions. "No, it's not Nancy the 911 operator either. Nancy works from home, Mom. Yes, you can route 911 calls remotely these days." He rolled his eyes.

Julie grinned and blew him a kiss before retreating into the bedroom.

Chris groaned.

His mother demanded to know if he was hurt or something.

"What? Oh, no, sorry, Ma. I'm fine, promise. Are you okay? It's awful late. What? You can't sleep? Okay. Me? Just working a case—you know, same old, same old. Church? Oh, sorry. I forgot." He closed his eyes. Shoot. He had completely forgotten to call her and tell her he wouldn't make it to church.

While he listened to his mother go on and on about how important it was to go to church, he settled back and rested his head against the wood slats of the chair. Missing church was a cardinal sin in his mother's book. She would probably be up all night praying for his eternal soul. And if she had her way, he'd be up, too, listening while she prayed.

He sighed and shoved back from the table. The cool night air this high up on the mountain had put a definite chill inside the family room. He knelt down by the fireplace, saying the occasional "Yes, ma'am" into the phone whenever his mother paused for breath. Once he had a roaring fire going, he settled onto the massive sectional couch and rested his head on one of the throw pillows.

This was going to be a long night.

Chapter Nineteen

The deep, husky sound of Chris's voice had faded long ago. He must have finally finished his phone call. But, unfortunately, he hadn't taken Julie's hint and joined her in the bedroom. Or maybe he had taken the hint, and the answer was no.

Sighing, she stared at the ceiling above her bed, the moonlight flooding in through the high-set windows giving her plenty of light to see by. The idea of making love to Chris Downing, once it had settled in her mind, wouldn't go away. She didn't need to know him for years to know he was a good man and that she was wildly attracted to him. In a matter of days she knew he was a far better person than she could ever hope to be, and had her thinking all kinds of what-ifs.

She looked toward the doorway. The kitchen light had been turned off long ago, replaced with the flickering of firelight. While her bedroom was warm with the heavy comforter surrounding her, the appeal of that fire beckoned, if only because Chris was out there, too.

Thumping the bed impatiently, she debated her options. Lie here all night, unable to sleep, wishing she was with Chris. Or go see whether he wanted her as much as his kisses implied. The worst he could do was say no. She'd be mortified, but she'd never heard of anyone really dying from embarrassment. And at least she wouldn't be lying here for the rest of the night wondering whether she'd blown her chance.

Decision made, she tossed back the covers before she chickened out and changed her mind. She opened the nightstand drawer, knowing what she would find. She'd looked in it earlier while hoping that Chris would follow her. After grabbing one of the foil packets, she padded across the carpet and into the family room.

The gorgeous fireplace was like a beacon, the flames dancing across real wood logs, heat flooding into the room. It was beautiful and made the gas-burning fireplace in her Nashville home seem like a pathetic pretender in comparison. But when she rounded the end of the brown leather sectional that faced the fireplace, she froze in awe.

There were so-called masterpieces hanging in her home, but none of them came close to framing the incredible male beauty before her. Chris must have gotten overheated from the fire. He'd shed his clothes, all except his boxers. With one arm crooked over his head, the muscles of his chest were displayed to advantage, golden light flickering across his skin.

A light matting of dark hair furred his chest and marched down the center of his abs to disappear beneath the waistband of his underwear. One of his legs was drawn up, his other hand draped over his knee. Thickly muscled thighs tapered to his calves. Even his feet were sexy. Everything about him was enticing and, yet, so perfect, so beautiful, she could have stood there forever just drinking him in.

No, no, what she was doing was wrong. Watching

him without him knowing it was like being a voyeur, a Peeping Tom. She should either wake him up and risk his rejection, or go back to her room. Option number three, standing here all night marveling at him as he slept, while incredibly appealing, was not an option at all. She needed to do something. Soon. Now.

Good grief, the man was gorgeous.

She sighed and bit her lip in indecision.

An intake of breath had her gaze shooting to his face. His eyes were open and he was watching her. He made no move to cover up or sit up. Instead, he simply waited, his jaw tight, his pupils dilated. Like a hungry panther, languidly watching its mate. Any thought of being rejected died in the face of such raw need. He wanted her, needed her, as much as she wanted and needed him.

Slowly, she crossed the room, devouring him with her eyes, her fingers clenching at her sides. The foil crinkled in her grip. His gaze went to her hand, and when he saw what she was holding, his nostrils flared.

When she stopped in front of the couch, he held out his hands to her, an invitation she was helpless to resist. And then she was beneath him, the delicious weight of his body pressing her down, his lips greedily moving across hers in an openmouthed kiss that had her moaning and panting even before his tongue swept inside.

A draft of cold air across her shoulders told her that he'd taken off her top. The man was an expert at undressing a woman. That both delighted and dismayed her. She didn't want to think about anyone who'd come before her—or the woman he'd professed to love back in his college days. She wanted this man completely to herself.

Before long they were both naked, heated skin sliding against heated skin. His hands were everywhere, caressing, molding, stroking, making her shiver with delight. She wanted to touch him as much as he wanted to touch her. They twisted and strained against each other, kissing and being kissed, touching and being touched.

Then he was pressing her down again, claiming her mouth with his. She vaguely registered the sound of the foil packet being torn. He must have taken it from her at some point. She didn't remember. He lifted off her, rolling the condom into place while he continued to make love to her mouth with his. And then, just when she thought she would die if he didn't take her, he moved between her thighs, pressing against her.

She eagerly lifted her legs, cradling him against her body. When he didn't press into her, she opened her eyes to see why.

He was staring at her, his face inches from hers. He smiled, gently kissed her, then framed her face in his hands.

"You're so beautiful, and strong, and brave," he whispered. "Are you sure about this? We haven't known each other that long. I'm supposed to be protecting you, not…doing this."

She slid her fingers across his ribs, making him shudder against her. "I'm more sure about this than anything in my whole life. Don't stop, Chris. Love me. Please. Just love me."

He shuddered again and swooped down to kiss her, his tongue thrusting between her lips as he thrust inside her body. The pleasure, the pressure of him filling her so completely while he did amazing things with his mouth and his hands had her arching off the couch, whimpering against him.

He tore his mouth from hers, his eyes squeezed shut, his jaw tight as he pumped into her, over and over, drawing her body into a tight bow of pleasure. She kissed the column of his throat, scored her nails down the muscles of his back, encouraging him with the words of lovers passed down through the generations.

Higher and higher he drew her up on waves of pleasure so exquisite she didn't think she could possibly go any higher. And then, with one clever stroke of his fingers, a deep thrust of his body inside hers, he took her to a new level.

He let out a savage growl and captured her mouth with his before sliding both hands beneath her bottom and angling her up. He withdrew once more, then plunged into her so deeply she exploded, shouting his name as she clung to him, her body shuddering with the strength of her climax. He thrust into her again, riding her through the waves of pleasure until he tightened inside her and came apart in her arms, his breath rushing out of him in a groan of ecstasy and making her climax all over again.

Like embers from a wildfire, they both slowly floated back to earth, wrapped in each other's arms, skin slicked with sweat. She could feel his heart hammering in his chest, feel the rush of her own pulse slamming in her veins.

He shuddered again, then slowly withdrew, turning her in his arms, spooning her with a thigh draped over hers as he turned them toward the fireplace. Her eyes fluttered closed. Her body felt boneless, cradled against his. He curled an arm over her belly, his fingers idly caressing the undersides of her breasts. She fell asleep with him whispering erotic love words in her ear and telling her how beautiful she was.

Chapter Twenty

Chris fanned the papers out on the kitchen table, trying again to refocus on the case and look at all of the clues in light of the latest reports he'd gotten just after the sun came up.

He glanced toward the ground floor bedroom. Julie was still getting ready to face the day, putting on makeup that he'd assured her she didn't need. For some reason, that had only made her more determined to fix her makeup and do something with her hair. He shook his head and looked down at the papers.

After making love twice more during the night, they'd both been exhausted and famished. They'd cooked omelets at four in the morning, taking turns feeding each other, laughing like a couple of newlyweds, before hopping into the shower together. If he wasn't careful, he could easily fall in love with the amazing woman.

The thought of his first love, Sherry, shot through his mind. Losing her had been devastating. Losing Julie? He couldn't even go there. It would destroy him. Maybe it was already too late to guard himself from caring too much. But it wasn't too late to protect her. He had to figure out who her late husband had been working with and why. If he didn't do that, he could never guarantee her safety.

He studied the newest list he was making, the same one that he'd started in the chief's office but never finished. This time he had more information.

Love.
Money.
Revenge.
Hatred.
Hide something.

Those were the possible motives he was working with.

Love. He hesitated. Did Julie love someone else? Was she involved with someone in Nashville? As soon as those thoughts went through his head, he discarded them. She was so honest with her feelings. There was no way that she could have made love with him last night, giving herself to him so completely, if she loved someone else. Her ex hadn't tried to kill her because of some love triangle. He crossed that one off the list.

Next possible motivation—*money.* Yesterday, he'd have been inclined to cross this one off the list, too. But that was before he'd received the in-depth financial study on Alan Webb and his family's import-export business. Everything was coming together now. And money seemed to be at the root of the whole damn thing.

"You look like you've got the weight of the whole world on your shoulders."

He looked up to see Julie crossing the kitchen toward him. Today she was wearing a blue blouse tucked into blue dress slacks, showing off all her curves. Her shoulder-length hair hung in glossy waves, with a simple side part. She didn't seem to be wearing much makeup, but what she did have on emphasized her eyes and her dark lashes, making him want to sit for hours just staring at her.

"Have I told you how beautiful you are?"

Her face flushed a delightful pink. "About a dozen times. Thanks." She cleared her throat. "What are you working on?"

He forced his gaze to the paper in front of him. "Finances. Specifically, you and your husband's. Did you know that his family's business was teetering on the brink of bankruptcy before you married him?"

She frowned. "That can't be right. Alan always had money in college. I think that's how he got a lot of people to like him—free drinks all around whenever he was in a bar. He never once said anything about running short on cash, or mentioned concerns about his father's company."

Chris shoved the financial report on Webb Enterprises across the table as she sat across from him.

"The company got a huge influx of cash from another corporation a few weeks after you got married."

Her brows furrowed as she skimmed the pages of the report. "What was the payment for?"

"It was listed as cash flow from an investment. But the state cops working on the financial side of the investigation can't find where any companies have invested in Webb Enterprises to produce revenue anywhere close to that amount. And the payments have continued, once a month, for years. Until recently, when they suddenly stopped."

She glanced up. "They stopped? When?"

"On your twenty-fifth birthday."

Her eyes widened. "My birthday? That's...a coincidence. Odd, but what other explanation could there be? What was this other corporation?"

"Victoria and Edward."

She blinked, her face going pale. "My grandmother's business?"

He nodded.

"Let me get this straight. My estranged grandmother, Elizabeth Victoria Abbott, the one who disowned my mother and never made any attempt to have anything to do with us, has been making cash payments to my husband ever since I got married? Is that what you're saying?"

"That's exactly what I'm saying."

"But... I never heard anything about it. Wait, wait." She held up a hand as if to stop him, a panicked look entering her eyes. "You said Webb Enterprises was going broke. But then my...grandmother...began making those payments. Then, all this time, Alan wasn't the wealthy one. It wasn't his business that was buying our fancy house and fancy cars. It was my distant relative in London?"

He nodded. "That's what it looks like."

She fisted her hands on the table. "Money. You said one of the motives for murder is money. And you said that you don't believe in coincidences."

"Right." He watched her work through what he'd been working through all morning. He didn't have all the answers, but this was the biggest piece so far. It had to be the key. He waited to give her time to process everything, and to be there for her once she did.

Several minutes went by. When she looked at him

again, the tears that he'd expected to see weren't there. Instead, she looked almost…relieved.

"So that's the answer then," she said. "That's why our marriage was so rocky, right from the start. Alan didn't marry me for love. He married me for money. Which is incredibly ironic considering his parents always acted like they thought I'd married him for his money." She shook her head. "This is crazy. Alan had to have been insane, a psychopath. He somehow knew about the link between my family and this corporation of my grandmother's and…what? Tried to figure out how to get the money? Oh, God above. It all makes sense now."

She pressed a hand to her stomach.

"What you said yesterday," she continued, "everything on the board—it's all true, and it all makes a horrible, macabre sense. Alan needed money. He found out about my grandmother, somehow. Then he hit on my sister. But she didn't like him. He must have realized he couldn't manipulate her so, instead, he killed her, and then my parents, leaving me as the one link to my grandmother. Let me guess. She regrets disowning my mother and set up a trust or something, right? You said she's still alive, so it can't be a simple inheritance. But it must still be set up to pay the heir—which, with the rest of my family dead—is me. Did I get it right, Chris? Alan knew he could manipulate me, so he killed everyone else? That's it, isn't it?"

Her voice broke and she closed her eyes, drawing in deep breaths.

Chris hurried to her, crouching in front of her. He wanted to draw her into his arms, hold her. But her stiff posture and the expression on her face told him she wouldn't welcome his touch right now. She needed time to work it through. He would wait all day if he had to. And when she needed him, he would be here.

She sat there, her back ramrod straight, for several minutes, before finally opening her eyes. She blinked at him, her eyes dry, her look determined.

"I need to hear you say it," she said. "Tell me I'm right, or tell me I'm wrong. Just say it."

"I'm sorry, Julie. But I think you're absolutely right. The finance guys are trying to contact your grandmother and representatives at Victoria and Edward Corporation to get more details. But it might take a while to get that information. On this side of the pond, they've confirmed the amounts of the payments, when they began, when they stopped, the financial troubles at Webb Enterprises, which is again having trouble, by the way. They haven't been able to make payroll this past month. The company is again in jeopardy of going bankrupt."

Her lips curled with disdain. "Because, for some reason, the payments Alan was getting stopped on my birthday. Now his company, his parents' company, doesn't have that cash cushion every month so they're failing again."

"Seems like it, yes. The question of course is why the payments were made in the first place. What triggered them to start if your grandmother had disowned your mother? Somehow she or her lawyers must have found out about you and Naomi and she decided to send you money. Maybe the payments were contingent on college graduation, or getting married." He shrugged. "If the payments were meant for you, why did someone set them up to go to Alan? And, more importantly, why did they stop on your birthday? If we can answers to those questions, we'll understand why Alan tried to kill you after you turned twenty-five."

"And why someone is still trying to kill me," she finished. "Alan's not the only partner in this endeavor. You've been saying all along that he had to be working with someone else. That would explain why those men tried to kill us at Cooper's farm. They have to finish what Alan started. And if it's been about the money all this time, I have to think their goal is to get the payments going again."

"I doubt that's their goal."

She crossed her arms, resting them on the table in front of her. "I thought we agreed this is all about money."

"Oh, absolutely. It's definitely about money, even if some other motivations are coming into play. But if you've been—pardon my analogy—a cash cow all this time, why kill you if it's about the monthly payments? They've stopped already, and yet your life is still in danger. That has to mean some kind of cash payout. Maybe the monthly payments were part of a trust, and you're to get the full lump sum at age twenty-five."

She nodded. "Okay, okay. That could make sense. If there's a trust and I'm the sole heir, when I turn twenty-five I have to…do something? To get the lump-sum payout? But since I don't know, or didn't know, about the trust, Alan had to do something else." Her eyes widened. "He would be *my* heir. If I died, he would get the lump sum. Isn't that how these things work?"

Again, Chris shook his head. "In general, yes. But I don't see that as the explanation here. If it were as simple as killing you and making Alan the heir, he—"

"Would have killed me right after we got married," she finished.

He nodded. "Yes. I think he would have."

She got up and began pacing back and forth. "Alan needed me alive to get the original payments. That implies proof of life to the trustees. How would he do that without me knowing about it?"

"I think we're back to the partner theory again. Someone, perhaps working with the trust, had to be working with Alan. Maybe he provided proof to that person and they claimed to have seen you in person. Here, take a look at this."

He shuffled through a stack of papers and pulled one of them out. "I printed this from an email this morning. Randy drove to Nashville last night and worked with the local PD there to search your house. He brought a locksmith, too, who opened the safe. And this paper shows the contents."

She read the paper. "Birth certificates, for my parents, my sister, me." She pressed a hand against her throat. "Death certificates for my family. My marriage license?"

"I imagine these are what he used to get the payments started. But he wouldn't need them after that. So I doubt this is what he wanted when he came to Destiny looking for you."

"No, probably not," she agreed. She swallowed hard. "I'm not an expert on trusts. But I'm thinking they can be written up any way the maker of the trust wants. If my grandmother was holding wealth for my mother's heir, these birth and death certificates prove that I'm the heir. And the marriage license proves that Alan was my husband. Since my grandmother never made any attempt to see me or my family in person, she was probably perfectly willing to accept that I would feel the same way. Her trustees, or perhaps the partner we keep theorizing about, were fine accepting Alan as their surrogate. Pay Alan, they were paying me. The requirements of the trust are satisfied without any messy family reunions."

The bitterness in her voice had Chris pulling her into his arms without thinking. Instead of stopping him, she sank against him, holding on to him as he rocked her and stroked her hair. They sat that way for a long time, until she let out a shuddering breath and pulled back.

She kissed him, a sweet, soft kiss that rocked him to his soul.

"Thank you," she said. "I don't think I could get through this without you. It's a heavy burden, a lot to take in. If it weren't for you, I probably would have curled up in a fetal position long ago and given up."

He shook his head and squeezed her shoulders. "No. You wouldn't have done that. You're far too strong. Alan used you, he destroyed your family. Now he's dead. And I'm not going to apologize for saying that I'm glad he's dead."

She smiled. "I think I'm kind of glad he's dead, too, even though that sounds terrible." Her smile faded. "Where do we go from here? I still don't understand why someone else is after me or how Alan got this started without someone verifying it with me."

"That's definitely a piece we need to figure out. Plus we need to find out what's required by the trust once you attained age twenty-five to get the lump sum payout, which is the only thing that makes sense to me. Alan wanted you alive to get payments, but once you reached twenty-five, something changed and the payments stopped. At that point, he was still trying to get something from you. So that implies you have something he needed in order to get the lump sum."

She nodded. "But now that he's dead, his partner needs me dead. Why?"

"To cover their tracks I'm guessing. Since they're trying to kill you, not talk to you like Alan tried, then they've either found another way to get the money or they've given up on that and just want to ensure you can't lead anyone to them. Did your husband have your power of attorney? That could help explain how he got the trust to give him the payments in the first place."

"I never gave him a power of attorney. He never even asked."

Chris nodded. "It probably would have raised red flags to you if he'd asked right after you got married. I'm guessing he already had that part covered. Maybe he had a forger produce one for him. As much diabolical planning as he did in regards to your family, a simple power of attorney couldn't have been more than a blip on his radar."

She sighed. "True."

"When our finance guys cut through the red tape and get a copy of the trust document, that should clear up a lot of our questions and hopefully will point us in the right direction to figure out who was Alan's partner."

"One of the main things bugging me," Julie said, "is Harry Abbott. It can't be a coincidence that he shares my last name. Have you found anything else about him?"

"He appears to be your distant cousin, on your mother's side obviously, hence his last name. The team is still working on how that might figure on the case. Brian Henson, the one driving the black Charger, has to be another hit man your husband hired. Which means this still all seems to tie into the ADA somehow since Henson was her assistant. The team will need to look into Bolton, too, the other admin assistant, just in case he's part of this. If Nelson was Alan's partner, she may be tying up loose ends to make sure none of this comes back to bite her, especially given her political aspirations. Maybe she's the one who hired the hit men instead of your husband. Maybe she's protecting herself."

He gently lifted her off his lap and set her on her feet. "I'm going to talk all this through with Max. He's managed to cull some amazing contacts by networking at seminars and conferences. Maybe one of those contacts can put some pressure on your grandmother or the attorney's running the trust to get the information that we need. Maybe she can answer questions about Harry Abbott, too. Plus, we need to look into Kathy Nelson, see if we can tie her to any of this."

She nodded and moved to stand by one of the windows, looking out onto the mountains.

Chris called Max and brought him up to speed.

"Hold on," Max said through the phone. "The chief wants to tell me something."

Chris shoved back from the table and meandered around the furniture to Julie's side. He put his arm around her shoulders and pulled her against him as they looked at the achingly beautiful day, how the sun shone down onto the trees and mountains.

He was glad that he'd brought her here. He'd never intended to talk shop in the cabin, but they'd made a lot of progress. They could sit back now, enjoy the seclusion, enjoy each other and let her continue the healing process while his team caught up to Henson and looked into Nelson's dealings. A few days in the mountains without any other cabins for miles around could be exactly what Julie needed. Chris too. Because he was finding out that she was exactly what he needed.

As soon as Max came back on the phone and told him what the chief had said, Chris swore and grabbed Julie's hand.

"We're leaving—now," he told Julie and Max at the same time. He pulled Julie toward the bedroom while he worked out the planned route with Max. "That's right, we'll head down now and meet you in—Max? Max? You still there?"

He pulled the phone away from his ear. The signal still showed strong, but the phone had only static. He swore again, shoved the phone into the holder on his belt and grabbed the duffel from beside the bed.

"What's going on?"

The fear in Julie's voice made him hesitate. "A state cop was killed a few minutes ago after pulling over a speeder at the bottom of this mountain. Another cop saw the patrol car on the side of the road and found the dead trooper. When he viewed the dash cam he saw that the cop had pulled over a black Camaro. As he was walking up to the driver's window, a black Charger raced past and the driver shot the officer. The Camaro pulled out behind the Charger and they both took off down the road. It was Henson and Bolton. And the road they were on is the only one up this mountain."

"Oh, my God."

"Put your shoes on. We're leaving." After double-checking the guns and ammo in the duffel bag, he zipped it up and slung it over his shoulders like a backpack. He tightened the straps so it was snug and secure.

Julie had just put on her second shoe when the throaty roar of a powerful engine sounded from outside, then abruptly shut off.

Chris raced to the window.

The Charger was in the driveway. The Camaro was parked a little farther down the road.

Both cars were empty.

Chapter Twenty-One

Julie was shaking so hard she could barely keep her balance on the balcony stairs. Chris was right behind her, pistol in his right hand, left hand gripping the waistband on the back of her pants like a lifeline in case she lost her footing.

The front door to the cabin had burst open right after Chris had looked out the bedroom window. He'd fired several shots through the bedroom doorway and thought he might have nicked Henson on the shoulder. Chris had slammed the door shut and shoved the nightstand against it. Then he was urging Julie through the back hallway to the balcony.

It was bad enough knowing two hit men were looking for them and could suddenly appear from out of nowhere. Worse was trying not to panic at what waited for them down below. Julie tried to keep her eyes on the stairs, not the stilts under the house to her left that kept it from plunging down the side of the mountain. And certainly not on the fact that the stairs appeared to end several feet above the ground—ground that was steep and littered with razor-sharp-looking rocks. One wrong move and both of them would be killed.

"Stop," Chris ordered, jerking her back toward him.

She froze, her foot suspended in the air above the last step. He eased down to the stair beside her, then slammed his shoe against the step she'd been about to use. It exploded in a rain of sawdust and splintered wood.

"Dry rot," he whispered.

She shivered, wondering what would have happened if she'd been standing on that step when it collapsed. Since the pieces of wood from it were still bouncing down the side of the mountain, she really didn't have to wonder all that much. She swallowed, hard.

"Why do they even have these stairs if they don't reach all the way to the ground anyway?" She knew she sounded like a petulant child, but she was so tired of running and being shot at and having the constant threat of death hanging over her head. Surely she was allowed to complain every once in a while.

"There were probably another half-dozen stairs at one time. It's to provide access for examining the structure beneath the house and the foundation, to make sure it's secure."

He looked up behind them. Julie didn't see any signs of a gunman, but Chris's jaw tightened and he looked around, back toward the stilts, as if time was running out. One last glance down the mountain, then back to the stilts.

"Hold on to the railing," he whispered. "Don't move." He lifted his leg and grabbed a gun from his ankle holster, then shoved it into her front left pants pocket. "Just in case."

She made a choking sound in her throat. "In case of what?"

He looked back at the stilts again.

"Wait," she called out. "That's a six-foot leap, at least. And if you miss the tiny strip of land below us, you'll plunge off the side of the mountain. Please tell me you aren't going to try to—"

He jumped from the stairs, pushing off so hard the entire staircase wobbled.

Julie sucked in a breath and clung to the railing, staring in horror as Chris clung to the bottom stilt, trying to pull himself up on a crossbar. Dots swam in her vision and she realized she was still holding her breath. She forced herself to draw in some air while she sent up an anxious prayer for his safety.

He managed to get his fingertips around the crossbar, then pulled himself up to standing. He was about a foot above her now, but still a good six feet away. It might as well have been the Grand Canyon.

"Keep an eye out," he warned as he began unfastening his belt.

She looked at the balcony above them. "I don't see anyone."

"Good. Slide over to this side of the stairs. Hurry." He yanked out his belt and threaded the end through the buckle, then looped the other end of the belt around his wrist and back on itself, grasping the end in his palm.

She did as he'd asked and looked down. "The ground isn't too far away. Maybe I can jump."

"No. It's too rocky, too steep. Your momentum will throw you right off the cliff."

"Cliff?" She leaned over, then jerked back. "Oh. Yeah. The cliff. This is why I love Nashville and don't live in the country. I remember now."

He grinned. "You might have a point. It's not really a cliff. More like a really steep hill with lots of rocks. Still, taking a ride down there wouldn't be my first choice."

"Or mine."

After another quick glance up, he looked over his shoulder toward the house where the stilts were cut into the side of the mountain, essentially bolting the house in place. What was Chris's plan, for them to both cling to the stilts until help arrived? That might be great for him, but she'd never make it. Her legs were too short.

"You can make it," he said, as if hearing her thoughts. "I'm going to swing my belt toward you. Catch it and slide your hand in the loop. Then tighten it back until it hurts. I'm serious. Make it as tight as you can. I don't want your hand falling through."

"Maybe I could just go up the stairs and take my chances inside. They might not expect me to have a gun."

"They're hit men, Julie. They kill people for a living. They're probably better shots than I am. You really want to take that chance?"

She clutched the railing and looked down again. "Not really. But I don't want to become a human pancake, either."

He laughed. "You're adorable, you know that?"

"I'll bet you say that to all the women you drop down the sides of mountains."

"Counting you? You're right." He shrugged, then winked. "Come on. The only reason Henson hasn't come out that door with guns blazing already is he's giving me more credit than I deserve. He probably thinks I'm waiting on the balcony with a plan to ambush him."

"That might work."

"If it was just me, that's what I'd do. But there's no

cover. You'd end up shot in the cross fire. Come on, Julie. Grab the belt."

Before she could think of another argument, he dropped down, hanging from the crossbar by his knees and swung the belt toward her. She grabbed it on the first try and quickly shoved her arm through the loop like he'd told her.

The belt was taut between them, pulling them toward each other, her left wrist looped in one end, his left looped in the other.

"Is your hand tight?" he called out. "So tight it feels like it's cutting off the circulation?"

"As a matter of fact, yes. I probably should loosen—"

The belt jerked and she was falling through the air. She would have screamed, but she slammed against Chris so hard the breath was knocked out of her. He grabbed her with both arms and shoved her up toward the beam, grunting at the effort as he hung upside down.

She gasped and scrambled onto the wood, grabbing another piece perpendicular to the one she was on and clinging to it for dear life. The belt slackened on her wrist. Chris had pulled his hand out of the other end. Then he swung himself up beside her and grinned like a little boy at Christmas after getting a new bat and ball.

"That was cool, wasn't it?"

"Cool?" she muttered. "We could have died. That was the scariest thing I've ever done in my life."

His eyes widened as he looked past her.

She whirled around to see a man bent over the top of the balcony, holding the biggest, scariest-looking gun she'd ever seen. And he was pointing it at her and Chris.

"Hang on," she heard Chris yell as automatic gunfire exploded all around them.

She grabbed for the crossbar.

And missed.

Suddenly she was free-falling into open air.

CHRIS LEAPED AFTER JULIE, twisting in midair, firing his pistol toward the gunman on the balcony. The rocky side of the mountain rushed up to meet them. He twisted again, jerking the end of the belt as hard as he could. She screamed and fell against his chest. He grabbed her just as his back slammed against the rocky side of the mountain.

Red-hot fire scraped across his back in the places unprotected by the duffel bag as they half skidded, half fell down the steep face. He used every ounce of his strength to try to keep Julie on top of him to protect her from the rocks, while scrabbling with his boots to try to slow them down.

"Chris!"

Julie's choked-out scream of warning had him twisting again to see a tree rushing up to meet them. He jerked sideways, rolling to avoid the deadly obstacle. A garbled yell told him she'd been scraped hard. Again and again, he twisted, jerked, shuffled his arms and feet, fighting against physics and the forces of nature to try to protect his precious burden.

Finally the rolling and twisting slowed. Their shoes slammed against the earth, pulling them both up short. They flopped end over end, like rag dolls, into the tree line. The sudden cessation of sound and movement did nothing to stop the world from spinning. Chris squeezed his eyes shut, willing the dizziness to go away.

A pained moan had him opening his eyes. He was flat on his back and what was left of the duffel. Julie was clutched in his arms, her hair a tangled mess of leaves and twigs. She moaned again, and he forced himself to roll over, hissing in a breath at the throbbing fire his back and side had become.

He laid her down on the grass and smoothed her hair. A tiny line of blood trickled from the corner of her mouth. Her eyes were closed.

"Julie, can you hear me, sweetheart? Julie?"

Crack!

The ground kicked up beside him in a puff of green and brown.

He jerked back, looking up toward the house, high upon the mountainside above them. A lone gunman stood on the balcony, leaning over the railing, calmly aiming a rifle.

Chris swore and scooped Julie into his arms. He dove behind a tree as more rifle fire cracked around them. On hands and knees, he shuffled deeper into cover until he was certain they were protected. Then he carefully laid her down once again.

He tried to wake her up, but she didn't respond other than to moan in pain if he moved her.

Please, God. Don't let her die. Please.

He pressed his hand against her chest, judging her breathing. It was steady, strong. A check of her pulse reassured him it, too, was strong. Then why wasn't she awake? He ran his fingers through her horribly tangled hair, feeling for bumps. When he touched behind her right ear, she gasped and arched away from him.

He almost cried in relief.

That little arch of her back told him at least she wasn't paralyzed.

Thank you, God.

His hand came away bloody. He leaned down, clamping his jaw shut to keep from crying out himself. His back was on fire, mostly on his left side. But he'd worry about that later.

Bending over her, he pulled her hair away from her neck. The cut on her scalp wasn't deep, but it was ragged and bleeding heavily, as head wounds usually did. He worked the duffel bag off his back and dropped it beside them on the ground. When he saw the first-aid kit in the bottom, he couldn't help smiling. He owed Max big-time for packing the duffel, and doing it right.

A few minutes later, he had Julie's head wound packed and bandaged. The bleeding already appeared to be slowing down from the pressure of the wrap. He continued searching for other injuries. Her side had been badly scraped, probably from when he'd had to roll to avoid the tree. Nothing much he could do about that except to spray it with antibiotics for now. Like a burn, if he tried to cover it up, it would just lead to infection.

A sharp intake of breath had his gaze shooting to Julie's face. Her eyes were open.

He let out a shaky laugh as he leaned over her.

"What's your name?" he asked.

"Chris."

"That's my name. What's your name?" he asked again.

She shook her head, then pointed. "Chris, my God. Your side."

He frowned and looked down.

A piece of tree branch the diameter of a quarter had impaled him, from back to front, and was sticking out of his left side.

"Guess that explains why my back's on fire." He tried

to laugh, but of course as soon as he saw the wound, it started throbbing and burning far worse than it had before.

"Tell me your name," he insisted yet again. He held up three fingers. "How many fingers do you see?"

"Julie and three. I'm fine. You're the one who's hurt." She started to get up, then groaned and lay back down. "The whole world is spinning."

"Concussion. We need to get you to a doctor."

She kept her eyes closed and sat up, then slowly opened them again. "It's better. What in the world happened? We fell over the cliff?"

"More like you fell and I dove." He'd probably aged thirty years watching Julie fall off that crossbar and fly down the mountain. If he'd jumped even a half second later he doubted he'd have reached her in time to cushion her fall when she hit the highest swell of ground. If the mountain had been any steeper, neither of them would have survived.

"Can you stand?" he asked.

"I think so."

Together they pushed and pulled until they were both on their feet.

Julie started laughing. "If I look half as bad as you do we won't have to worry about the wildlife out here. They'll run away as soon as they see us."

He grabbed the duffel, and half the contents fell out. The material had been shredded. Since he'd lost his pistol in the fall, he was relieved to see one in what remained of the bag. Unfortunately, the extra magazines were scattered somewhere on the mountain.

He holstered his gun and checked Julie's pocket where he'd put his backup gun. Amazingly, the gun was still there. It would have been perfect if there was a knife in the duffel, but the two knives he'd seen in it earlier had escaped somewhere during their wild ride.

Looking at the sun, he tried to get his bearings. "We'll head that way." He pointed to his left. "That's east. It should lead to the nearest road. But we'll have to be as quiet as possible and keep a lookout the whole way."

"Why? It's not like the gunmen are going to leap off the balcony and try to free-fall down the mountain like we did. There's no way they'll catch up to us."

"There was only one gunman on the balcony—Henson. Bolton is still out there somewhere. And if I were him, I'd be heading down the mountain road right now to cut us off."

"Then shouldn't we go west or north or something, anywhere but east?"

"If you didn't have a concussion, I didn't have a tree in my back, and we had supplies to last a week or two, absolutely. East is our only option. It's just a few miles. Let's go."

Chapter Twenty-Two

She was worried about him.

The injury in Chris's side looked excruciating. How was he even walking, let alone stepping over the downed trees in their path and keeping his balance on the uneven ground?

After a terse argument about not having time to tend to his wound, Chris had finally given in and let her do what she could in sixty seconds, no more. She'd sprayed it with the antibiotic he'd used on her earlier, then stuffed some gauze around the piece of branch where it protruded both in back and front.

He'd stood stiffly, barely moving through her ministrations, and then he'd gone about three shades paler. His eyes had been glazed with pain by the time she'd stopped. Even with the packing, he was bleeding steadily.

"We should stop. You're losing too much blood."

He shook his head and plodded on, occasionally looking up when the sky could be seen through the thick canopy overhead. The man was incredibly stubborn and amazing and wonderful. And it was tearing her heart into pieces watching him, knowing he would die before he'd give up, all because he wanted her to be safe.

Tears clouded her vision, but she briskly wiped them away. He'd told her she was strong and brave. She was neither of those things, but for him, she was damn well going to pretend. He didn't need one more thing to worry about, like trying to console her. Somehow she had to hold everything inside and protect him.

The weight of his backup gun, now strapped on her ankle courtesy of Chris's ankle holster, wasn't very reassuring. How was she supposed to protect Chris in a gunfight, against a man who killed for a living? Somehow, she'd have to figure it out though. Because Chris was getting weaker and weaker. No way was he going to be able to protect himself if the gunman caught up to them.

He wobbled, falling against a tree. She reached for him, but he shook her off, straightened and started forward again. How long could he keep this up? How long could he survive? And where the heck was their backup?

Chris's phone hadn't survived the fall down the mountain. But he'd spoken to Max right before Henson and Bolton had arrived. She and Chris were heading toward the same road that Chris had told Max they'd go to, albeit on foot instead of by car. Still, if the SWAT team cared about their friend and fellow officer, they should bring the cavalry up the mountain to find him. So where were they?

A small cracking noise sounded from somewhere up ahead.

Chris froze, reaching out his right hand to stop her. But she'd already stopped. They both stood as still as possible, breathing through their mouths to make as little noise as they could, waiting, watching, listening.

There. Another crack, slightly to the right, like some-one's shoe crunching a dead, dry leaf or a twig.

He looked down, then to their left, motioning for her to follow. She walked where he walked, careful not to stray from the path. The woods, this mountain, was his domain. But she was learning fast, emulating him, doing whatever it took to survive.

They stopped behind two thick trees, peering through the crack between them toward the sounds they'd heard. Chris slowly raised his pistol, leveling it in the opening, sighting his target.

A deer stepped out from the bushes.

Julie laughed and relaxed against the tree.

Chris frowned but kept his pistol trained, not mov-ing.

Julie turned back toward the deer.

A dark shadow moved behind the bushes.

Bam! Bam! Bam! Chris fired six or seven times be-fore he stopped.

Julie held her hand over her mouth, frozen in place. A man staggered out onto the path, both hands red with blood as he held his stomach.

It was Henson.

"Help me." His plea was barely above a whisper. Then he dropped like a rock to the ground.

Chris grabbed Julie when she would have run to the other man.

"Don't. There's nothing you can do for him. And there's still one more gunman out there. Henson was on the balcony. He's the one who fired at us. If he found us, then the other guy has to be out here somewhere, too. And he's stalking us right now." He looked up at the sky. "Five, ten more minutes and we'll be at the road. If my team isn't already looking for us, we'll flag someone down. We're going to make it, Julie. Trust me."

He looked so haggard, so drawn, his complexion ashen. She wanted to weep. Instead, she smiled.

"I do. You'll take care of me. You always do." She looped her arm through his as if in comradery, when, really, she was just trying to hold him up.

His pistol was in his hand. She hop-skipped a few steps so she could grab hers from her ankle holster without stopping. Together, they headed deeper into the woods, side by side.

Rat-a-tat-tat-tat-tat-tat!

Chris shoved her to the ground and dove on top of her. Bark and leaves exploded around them. Deafening automatic gunfire chewed into the trees near where they'd been standing.

Julie tried to bring her gun up, but his weight was pressing her wrist hard against the ground and she could barely move.

He fired toward the trees where the gunfire was coming from until his gun clicked. Out of bullets. He threw the gun to the ground. Then he was on his knees, lifting her, half-dragging her behind a tree.

Bullets sprayed the forest floor and the bark on the tree where he'd pulled her.

Then, suddenly, they stopped. Everything went quiet.

Chris was on his knees in front of her, his chest heaving with each breath he took. Blood coursed down his side, coating his arms, his hands. Julie was backed against the tree, holding the little ankle gun in her hands.

Crunching noises sounded to their left, their right.

Was there more than one shooter now? And then the noise sounded directly behind Chris.

He stiffened.

Julie's breath froze in her lungs as Bolton stepped out from between the trees. The gun he held looked heavy, lethal, horrifying. It was a machine gun or something like that. All she knew for sure was that it was aimed at Chris's back.

"What do I do?" she whispered.

He gave her a half smile. "Live," he whispered. "Just live." He grabbed her gun and twisted around, using his body to shield her as he fired at Bolton.

Bam! Bam!

Boom!

The gunman blinked in shock, blood pouring from a hole at the base of his throat. Then he slowly crumpled to the ground.

Suddenly the woods filled with people: Randy, dressed in his SWAT gear, bending down to check the Bolton's pulse, shaking his head. Donna, also in SWAT gear, directing several state police, pointing back toward the path where the other gunman had gone down. Colby, staring in shock at Chris's side. And, finally, Max, dropping onto his knees beside Chris, who wasn't moving as Julie clutched him against her.

"Mrs. Webb, Julie, you have to let him go now." Max's voice was kind, gentle, like Chris's. "Let him go, so we can help him."

She looked at the precious man in her arms. His eyes were closed. Blood covered his back and made her arms sticky where she held him.

"Medic," Max yelled, as if they were in the middle of a combat zone.

Maybe they were.

Two EMTs rushed through the trees with a gurney.

"Julie. Let them help him," Max said. "You have to let him go."

His words seemed to reach her through a fog of pain and grief.

"Julie? Julie, are you okay?"

Max's voice had changed. He swore and again yelled, "Medic."

Julie surrendered to the darkness around her.

Chapter Twenty-Three

Julie couldn't believe that a month had passed since the shooting. And she also couldn't believe that she was once again sitting in the interview room at the Destiny Police Department, alone, waiting for others to join her.

She rubbed her left shoulder, trying to ease the ache where Bolton's bullet had passed through Chris's torso and buried itself in her upper arm. Both Chris and Max had shot Bolton. And since both of their bullets caused fatal injuries, they argued all the time over who should get the credit.

She smiled, glad to be alive, glad that Chris was alive. They were both still stiff and sore but would heal completely with time. She'd been released from the hospital a few days after admittance. But she'd still stayed, sleeping on a cot in Chris's room. Not that the two of them had any privacy.

Chief Thornton had assigned Detective Colby Vale to shadow her every move. He was essentially her bodyguard until they figured out who was trying to kill her. Thankfully, Colby was outside in the squad room right now, instead of in the interrogation room with her.

Chris had been released from the hospital yesterday. The skin on his back had been flayed away during their terrifying tumble down the mountain. He'd undergone several skin grafts. But at least he was up and walking, and finally allowed to leave the hospital.

She loved him. She'd realized that weeks ago during one of their many whispered talks in his hospital room, talks about everything from where they'd gone to kindergarten to their hopes and dreams. They hadn't talked about love yet, and she wasn't sure what the future held for them or if he felt about her the way she felt about him. The last month had focused more on recovery, and on wrapping up the case.

Which was why she was here. Chris had asked her to meet him at the station to discuss some new findings. She just wanted the case to be over and hoped this discussion meant that it finally was.

The door opened, and Chris stepped in, smiling as he crossed to the chair beside her.

"Hey, you," he said.

"Hey, yourself."

"Thanks for coming in," he said. "The chief will be here in just a minute."

"I can't believe you're already back at work. You aren't fully recovered yet. You should be home resting."

He shifted in his chair, the tension lines in his face telling her she was right, that he was in pain, and had no business being here.

"I'm going to tell the chief to send you home. This is ridiculous. You need more time to heal." She started to push her chair back, but he stopped her with a hand on her arm.

"Julie, I'm not back at work, not full-time. I've only been working over the phone with the chief and the others trying to tie up the loose ends on your case. And we just got some crucial information that I believe is going to help us wrap this up once and for all."

She slowly settled back against her chair. "You know who's behind everything? Who sent the hitmen after me?"

"Not exactly."

She was about to ask him to explain what he meant when the chief stepped into the room and closed the door behind him.

He nodded in greeting. "Mrs. Webb. Thanks for coming in." He sat at the end of the small table.

"Okay," she said. "The suspense is killing me. And, although I really appreciate that you've got Colby playing bodyguard, I'd love to be able to walk down the street without having a policeman shadowing my every move. Is it Kathy? You've found evidence to prove she's behind everything?"

Chris took one of her hands in his. "We don't have definitive proof yet. But I've got an idea of how to get it. And it's based on information the team has pulled together over the past few weeks, plus some surveillance photos they've taken of Kathy Nelson. It all starts with your cousin, Harry Abbott."

Julie frowned. "I don't understand. It starts with him?"

"He's the key to this whole thing and how your husband was able to begin receiving payments from the trust without you ever knowing about it. Harry Abbott was a small-time lawyer. He worked for the law firm that your grandmother hired to handle the trust. Apparently your grandmother was very ill shortly before Naomi got sick. I don't know if that made your grandmother more aware of her mortality, or what. But that's when she sent Harry Abbott to try to locate her daughter and find out if there were any grandchildren. By the time she got information back, your family was gone. So she created the trust for you. It was supposed to start payments upon either college graduation or marriage."

"Seriously?" Julie said. "So if I didn't get enough education, or decided my life was perfectly fine without a man in it, she wouldn't have deemed me worthy of receiving any money?"

He shrugged. "She's old-fashioned. What can I say?"

"She sure is. Go on."

"Your grandmother said she hired that particular law firm to handle the trust because of your cousin. He was family and she preferred to keep things like that in the family."

"You've actually spoken to her?"

He nodded. "On the phone, yes. Once we got through the layers of assistants and bureaucracy to get to her, she was quite forthcoming. Like I said, Harry was assigned the task of tracking down your grandmother's American relatives on behalf of the trust. But the temptation of all that money was too much. He resented that his side of the family wasn't in the direct line to inherit, and he planned on getting his hands on that money, probably felt he deserved it. Once he located your family, he looked around for someone as diabolical as he was, and found Alan. They made a pact—that if Alan could marry into the family and help Harry provide proof to the trust regarding the heir, then they could share the monthly proceeds."

"How do you know all of this? Harry's dead."

The chief tapped the table to get her attention. "Extensive research and interviews with people who'd interacted with Harry when he was in the States. I don't like unsolved puzzles, and I'm not about to let some ADA abuse the trust of her constituents and give police a bad name without paying her debt to society. I threw half my police force at this. And we got results."

"Thank you," she said. "I sincerely appreciate it. But I'm even more confused than ever. I thought we were talking about my cousin. Now we're back to Kathy?"

Chris looked to the chief, who nodded, as if giving him permission to take up the story again.

"I'll try to get to the point," Chris said. "Harry colluded with Alan. But Alan wasn't having much luck with your family. Naomi didn't like him, so he decided you were his best chance. After eliminating your family, he apparently tried flirting with you but you were too distraught to notice. You did, however, have a friend you associated with—Kathy."

"So they did know each other before I met Alan," Julie said.

"Yes. The meeting at the football game was a setup. Alan and Harry were getting desperate so they brought her in as a way for Alan to get your attention. We believe, and it's backed up by financial records of Harry's accounts, that the monthly payments were split into thirds."

"Harry's accounts? Not Kathy's?"

"She's too clever for that. We think she's hiding her money offshore. She's slick. Hard to pin anything on her. But she's the only person who makes sense as a surviving partner who has something to lose if her role is exposed, thus the hitmen. Plus, now that we know the full requirements of the trust—including a clause about your twenty-fifth birthday that your grandmother amended four months before your birthday—we have a theory about what Kathy is trying to do to get that final lump sum."

"Four months before my birthday? Wait, that's when things in my marriage took a nosedive, got really bad."

He nodded. "I know. I think that's when Harry broke the news to Alan."

She looked back and forth, from the chief to Chris. "What news?"

"That the payments would stop on your birthday unless you personally traveled to England to visit your grandmother, and that you bring the Abbott necklace with you—the one your mother gave to Naomi that used to belong to your grandmother. I'm pretty sure that's what Alan was looking for when he attacked you. He wanted the key to the safe so he could destroy the documents he had at your house. But he also wanted you to tell him where you had Naomi's things so he could get that necklace."

She held her hands up. "Wait. So not only did I have to finish college or get married in order to inherit, I also had to hold on to a necklace? What if I'd sold it, or lost it? I'd be out of luck?"

"Looks that way. Your grandmother is…a bit strict, uptight I guess. She really seems to value family and loyalty. I guess that's why it hurt her so much when your mother ran off with your father. It felt like a betrayal to her. And putting that stipulation about the necklace in the trust was her way of rewarding her heir only if they valued the history and legacy that necklace represented."

"You almost sound like you admire her," Julie accused.

"She's from a different generation, a different country, with a unique upbringing I could never understand. Let's just say that I'm trying to keep an open mind and see it from her perspective. Regardless, you can imagine Alan's reaction when he found out those details from Harry."

"He was probably furious. He couldn't take me to England, not without revealing what he'd been doing all this time. And, the necklace? No wonder he kept badgering me about my family's things. He needed to get the necklace without making me suspicious by specifically asking for it. Wait. It wouldn't do him any good without me though." She shook her head. "Did he think he could force me to lie to my grandmother? To not admit that Alan had been receiving the payments all along?"

Chris shot another look at the chief, then took both her hands in his this time. The concern on his face put her on edge.

"You're scaring me, Chris."

"I don't mean to. But the questions you're asking are exactly what I asked. And I don't believe for one minute that you would have meekly gone along with Alan's plan if that's what he wanted you to do. That's why Alan and his co-conspirators came up with a new plan. Alan was supposed to get the necklace from you. I think he was trying to get you to tell him where you kept your family's things without making you suspicious enough to kick him out or anything. Then, when you never revealed that information and you turned twenty-five—"

"He got desperate. Planned to kidnap me to force me to tell him."

"Right," Chris said. "But you foiled the first attack.

I foiled the second. He never got a chance to get the necklace."

"Where does that leave us?" she asked.

The chief pulled a photograph from his suit jacket pocket. Chris let Julie's hands go and took the picture, placing it face down on the table in front of her.

"Hypothetically, if Alan could have gotten the necklace, then there was only one more thing he'd need after that—to take you to England with him. But he knew that wasn't an option, that you wouldn't go. So he and his co-conspirators had to make plans months ago in anticipation of your twenty-fifth birthday, for another way to fool your grandmother. Remember I said that the chief had someone performing surveillance on Kathy?"

She nodded, a sick feeling settling in her stomach. "Yes."

"She rented a house out in the country about three and a half months shy of your twenty-fifth birthday, two weeks after your grandmother changed the conditions of the trust. Apparently Kathy rented it for another woman, someone whom neighbors said was recovering from some kind of trauma, based on the bandages and the fact that nurses used to stop by every few days. She's fully recovered now. And this is what she looks like."

He flipped the picture over.

Julie pressed her hands against her mouth.

The woman in the picture looked exactly like Julie.

A WEEK LATER, Julie opened the front door of her Nashville home to admit her visitor. "Thank you for meeting me here. So many things have happened in the past few months and I've only been back in Nashville for a couple of days. It's good to see a familiar face." Julie stepped back, pulling the front door open for Kathy Nelson.

"Of course, of course." Kathy stepped inside. "I'm just so relieved that everything is settled. No more looking over your shoulder and wondering if someone is out to hurt you. I still can't believe Alan was after your money all along, and willing to kill you for it. I'm so very sorry that the men Alan recommended to me as assistants ended up being such horrible people, hitmen of all things. Of course I had no idea."

Julie forced a smile. "Yes. How could you have known? The whole thing is so hard to believe. I didn't even realize you and Alan had kept in touch over the years."

Kathy's eyes narrowed a moment, then she seemed to realize what she was doing and her face smoothed out, her eyes widening innocently. "We didn't, not really. But he is, was, an important businessman in town. When he saw that the ADA's office was looking for help, he reached out to offer a suggestion. I don't know who was more surprised when he found out I was the ADA and when I found out that he was the one calling."

Nodding, as if she bought the rather thin story, Julie absently played with the gold chain around her neck, partially lifting it from beneath her shirt so some of the distinctive jewels showed.

Kathy went still, her gaze riveted on the jewelry. She cleared her throat and smiled stiffly. "My, what a lovely necklace you're wearing. I don't think I've ever seen anything quite like it."

Julie pulled it the rest of the way out from under her shirt. "It was passed down through my mother's side of the family. I kept it in a safe-deposit box for years along with other family mementos. But after everything that's happened, well, I just want to feel closer to her." She undid the chain and pulled off the necklace. "Then again, I'm told the gems are real. I probably should put it back in the bank to keep it safe."

She crossed to the desk in the front hallway and placed the necklace in the top drawer. "I'll do it tomorrow." She turned around. "Where are my manners? I asked you here for lunch. I doubt a busy attorney like you has a lot of time on her hands. I've got soup and salad waiting in the dining room. Let's enjoy a nice meal and catch up, shall we?"

Kathy took both of Julie's hands in hers. "It really is good to see you again. I'm so glad you're back. And you're right, I'm starving, and don't have a lot of time. Let's eat."

Julie tugged her hands free, forcing another smile as she led Kathy to the dining room.

Less than an hour later, she stood on the front stoop, waving as Kathy drove away. Then she stepped inside, and into Chris's arms.

"You're shivering." He pulled her close.

"You have no idea how hard it was to sit across from that woman making small talk, knowing all along that she conspired with my husband and my cousin against me. Either way, she had her tracks covered. If Alan had been able to get the necklace, she'd have used that poor woman she'd bribed to have plastic surgery to look like me. Then what? Kill her? Probably. And then kill me of course. Imagine how elated she must feel now, patting herself on the back for keeping my look-a-like alive just in case she could figure out how to use her to get the money, even without the necklace. It must feel like Christmas to her now, seeing me wear that piece of jewelry."

He pulled her back and smiled down at her. "You've baited the trap," he said. "Now, all we have to do is wait."

"There's still so much that could go wrong. That poor woman trusts Kathy. She doesn't know that Kathy will probably kill her as soon as she gets the lump-sum payment."

"We're not going to let that happen. You have to trust me."

She slid her arms up behind his neck. "I do. I trust you. I always have."

He grinned. "Always? Really?"

"Well, okay, maybe not always. It took a few hours."

She kissed him, but all too soon the kiss was over.

"Speaking of a few hours, we don't know how long it will take Kathy to make her move. Go upstairs like we agreed. We'll take it from here."

"Okay. Be careful, Chris. Promise?"

"Promise."

She headed up the winding staircase.

The break-in, when it came, was done so swiftly and professionally that the alarm didn't even go off. But Chris and his men were waiting, and watching. And when the burglar handed Julie's necklace through the open limousine window, they followed at a discreet distance.

Assistant district attorney Kathy Nelson was apprehended at the airport, along with a woman who bore an uncanny resemblance to Julie Webb. Chris was astonished at just how alike the two appeared. But the imposter's eyes gave her away. They were dull, a window to a dead soul inside, a woman who'd seen the worst of what life had to offer and had been broken down many years ago and expected nothing better for herself.

After talking to Julie, the woman agreed to take a plea deal and testify against Kathy. In return, she would go under the knife again to get her old face back. That was something that Julie insisted upon. In addition, she'd get the therapy that she needed. And Julie would help her get an apartment and a job, plus provide her a small nest egg to help her start a new life.

The chief thought Julie was crazy to do all of that for a woman who, because she was going to pretend to be Julie, had given Alan, Kathy and her cousin the ability to complete their master plan and then kill Julie to cover their tracks. But Chris understood. Julie was too kindhearted not to help someone who'd been willing to give up her own identity out of desperation for a new life. It was the girl's background that had convinced Julie that she wasn't the hardened criminal the chief thought her to be. The girl was a runaway, had sold herself on the streets just to survive. Julie felt the imposter deserved another chance.

Chris loved that about Julie, that she saw the good in people. That she put others' happiness above her own. She was the kindest woman he'd ever met, and he was deeply in love with her. And that's what made this so damn hard.

He was about to let her go.

As she entered the coffee shop a block from her Nashville home, she looked around for him. She thought he was here to say a temporary goodbye now that the court case was over and he didn't have to testify again.

They hadn't talked about long-term plans yet, even though she'd tried to bring it up several times. He'd kept dodging the conversation, knowing she would agree in a heartbeat to move back to Destiny with him. After all, her grandmother was funding Naomi's Hope Foundation now and there was nothing else keeping her here in Nashville.

That had been another surprise to some, that Julie would want to continue the Foundation even though the eventual exhumation had proved that Naomi didn't have an orphan disease. But it didn't surprise Chris. Finding cures for orphan diseases was a cause Julie believed in and she couldn't turn her back on those in need. Apparently, her grandmother agreed. She'd been more than willing to fund the charity.

But she'd decided not to go through with the trust's lump sum payment.

Not without some stipulations, at least. Stipulations that she'd told Chris, but hadn't yet told her granddaughter. Julie was going to find out the terms for herself very soon. And there were about a billion reasons for Julie not to go back to Destiny. Or to Chris.

She just didn't know them yet.

When she saw him, her face lit up and she smiled, as she always did. He watched with a heavy heart as she approached his table. She gave him a quick kiss as he held out her chair for her, a kiss that nearly killed him.

He sat across from her while a waitress took her order. As soon as the waitress moved away from the table, he pulled the envelope out of his pocket and handed it to her.

"What's this?" she asked.

He pushed his chair back and stood. "It's a letter

from your grandmother. I wanted to deliver it in person, make sure that you got it. My cab's waiting out front. I've got to go now. The chief is anxious for me to start a new case."

She frowned. "You're leaving Nashville? Right this minute?"

"Right this minute." Unable to stop himself, he leaned down and kissed her. "Goodbye, Julie."

And then he walked out of the coffee shop, and out of Julie's life forever.

Chapter Twenty-Four

Steaks sizzled on the double-decker grill on Chris's back deck. Once again, Max presided over the cooking. And once again, another young intern from the Destiny Police Department helped him load potatoes and foil-wrapped corncobs onto another section of the grill.

"One week." Dillon grabbed a beer from the cooler at Chris's feet.

Since Dillon was watching Ashley show off her and Dillon's new baby girl, Letha Mae, to half the police force crowding the deck, he wasn't sure what his friend meant.

"One week until what?"

Dillon used his bottle to indicate the intern. "I give this new intern and Max one week. I said two weeks last time and lost the bet."

Chris shrugged and snagged himself a beer. "Looks like we need more ice. I'll get some from the freezer in the garage."

Dillon stopped him with a hand on his shoulder. "Why don't you just get a ticket and fly to London and sweep Julie off her feet? We're all tired of you moping around like a lovesick calf. It's depressing."

Chris shoved his hand off his shoulder. "A billion

dollars, Dillon. Julie's grandmother offered her a billion dollars if she'd agree to live in London with her. And the cherry on top is the old woman wants to pick Julie's next husband. If Julie refuses, she loses all that money. Now you tell me. What woman would give up a billion dollars to marry some redneck cop in Nowhere, Tennessee?"

"This woman would."

Chris froze, then slowly turned. Julie stood at the bottom of the deck stairs, staring up at him. She looked so…damn…good. He hadn't seen her in well over a month, and he couldn't quit drinking her in. God, how he loved her. But, wait, what had she said?

He took a step toward her, then stopped. "What are you doing here?"

She rolled her eyes and marched to the top of the deck. "If that's a proposal, I've heard better. And considering my first husband, that's saying something." She crossed her arms and tapped her shoe.

He took another step toward her, then another, until he was standing right in front of her.

"I didn't think I'd ever see you again."

"Why not?" she asked. "Because you thought I loved money more than I loved you? Seriously? I would think you knew me better than that after everything we've been through. And you should also know that I thought it was wonderfully romantic that my mother and father gave up everything for a future together, and didn't let my grandmother choose who they should love. So why would I, for even one minute, consider letting her choose who I should love?"

By the end of her speech, the deck had fallen silent

and she was jabbing him in the chest with her pointer finger.

Chris winced and pulled her hand down. But instead of letting go, he entwined his fingers with hers.

"Can you say that again, please?"

She frowned. "My entire speech? I didn't memorize the darn thing."

"No, just the part where you said you loved me."

Her frown faded, and a smile slowly grew in its place. Then she frowned again. "Wait, that came out all wrong. You're supposed to tell me you love me first. Forget I said that. What I meant to say is that you're too stubborn for your own good and you shouldn't have walked away in that coffee shop. You should have known that, of course, I'd go visit my grandmother, because she is family, after all, and old, and deserved to know about what kind of person Naomi was and—"

"I love you."

She sputtered to a stop in the middle of her sentence. "What did you say?"

"I love you." He framed her face in his hands. "I'm stubborn, stupid and shouldn't have doubted you. I'm sorry. And I love you. And I want to marry you."

He dropped to one knee.

Her mouth fell open and she pressed her hands against her chest.

"No, wait." He stood up. "Wait right here."

He turned around and ran into the house.

JULIE BLINKED AND looked around the deck. What had just happened? Everyone was staring at her, looking just as shocked as she felt. She'd flown from half the world away to get here, fully expecting Chris to beg her forgiveness and ask her to marry him. A little groveling might have been nice, too. Instead, he'd dropped to his knee, then ran away.

Her cheeks flushed hot with embarrassment.

She was about to turn around and slink back to her car when Chris ran out of the house. He stumbled to a halt in front of her and once again dropped to one knee. His face was red and he seemed out of breath, as if he'd run up and down the stairs a few times.

"Julie," he said, between deep breaths, "I need your left hand for this."

She crossed her arms. "I'm not sure I trust you now."

He gave her that irresistible half smile. "Yes, you do. You've always trusted me."

"Well, almost always," she said.

He pulled a black velvet box out from behind his back and opened the lid. A solitaire diamond ring sat in the middle of the plush velvet, sparkling in the sunlight.

She gasped and covered her mouth with her hands.

"It's not very big," he apologized. "But it's the best I could do for now on a cop's salary."

She cleared her throat and lowered her hands. "When…when did you buy that?"

"The day I got out of the hospital. But I wanted all of the loose ends tied up so nothing would stand in our way when I proposed. Then your grandma sent that letter and I thought—"

"You thought wrong."

"I know, I know. I'm trying to fix that now. Julie Elizabeth Webb—"

"Linwood. Julie Elizabeth Linwood. I changed it back to my maiden name."

"Julie Elizabeth Linwood, I love you. Will you do me the honor of becoming my wife?"

In answer, she held out her left hand and smiled so hard her face hurt.

Chris slid the ring onto her finger and stood. "I love you."

"I love you, too."

He swooped down and kissed her.

The deck erupted in applause and laughter as everyone rushed forward to congratulate them.

It was impossible to kiss Chris the way she really wanted to with everyone slapping their backs and telling them how happy they were for them. She broke the kiss, laughing and beaming up at him.

He framed her face in his hands, staring at her in wonder. "I can't believe you gave up all that money to be with me."

"I didn't have a choice," she teased.

"You didn't?"

She shook her head. "It all came down to destiny."

His answering smile filled her heart and soul with happiness. And then he kissed her again, the way a man kisses a woman when he loves her more than life itself, the way a man kisses a woman…when he's found his destiny.

* * * * *

Look for more books in Lena Diaz's series
TENNESSEE SWAT *throughout 2017.*

You'll find them wherever
Mills & Boon Intrigue books are sold!

MILLS & BOON®

INTRIGUE
Romantic Suspense

A SEDUCTIVE COMBINATION OF DANGER AND DESIRE

sneak peek at next month's titles...

In stores from 9th February 2017:

Holden – Delores Fossen *and*
Hot Target – Elle James
Fugitive Bride – Paula Graves *and*
Secret Stalker – Lena Diaz
Abduction – Cynthia Eden *and*
The Missing McCullen – Rita Herron

Romantic Suspense

Colton's Secret Son – Carla Cassidy
Nanny Bodyguard – Lisa Childs

Just can't wait?
Buy our books online before they hit the shops!
www.millsandboon.co.uk

Also available as eBooks.

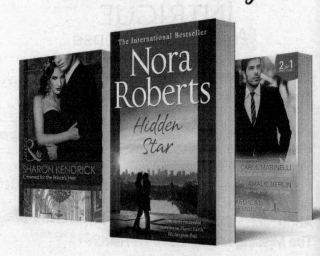